REUNION

R V BIGGS

Originally published 2012
Copyright © 2012
Revised August 2018
Author R V Biggs
All rights reserved.
ISBN-13: 9781795265584

DEDICATION

For Julie.

My partner in all things, and living
proof that destiny shapes our lives.

CONTENTS

Prologue	1
Birth	4
Growth	166
Reunion	297
Epilogue	379

ACKNOWLEDGMENTS

My deepest thanks to Dawn, my virtual sister, for proofreading a very early draft. To Craig for providing me with a comic line in chapter 32, and everyone at Birmingham Children's Hospital who read Song of the Robin and pestered me for a sequel.

For Abbie Rutherford of Bloomin' Brilliant Books and Pilcrow Proofreading; my heartfelt gratitude for her support and encouragement, and for providing a critically revealing beta read and final proofreading.

To Amanda Ní Odhráin of Let's Get Booked, I express my excitement and appreciation for taking my two dimensional cover image and giving it life, depth and drama.

Most of all, my love to Julie, for never asking any questions and leaving me to create and live inside my dream world.

'Seek not to measure the material, but consider rather the power which reason has and mere substance not.'

        Manilius (Roman astrologer)

Prologue

13th October 1710

A bramble thorn ripped across the side of the little girl's face as she ran for her life along a muddy track through the woods. The small but deep scratch on her cheek blossomed red, but she cared little for the momentary pain. Her mother had taught her how to treat scratches and she would find the right herbs later… if she survived.

Despite the loud voices and heavy thud of booted feet giving chase, she stopped and waited a moment for her young brother to catch up. Tiny scratches covered his face, and tears mingled with the blood making him appear almost grotesque in the gathering gloom.

'Come Hamish, we must hurry!' the girl hissed. 'It's not far now and then we can hide.'

Little Amber grabbed her brother's hand and ran a few more yards before veering off the path to the left among the trees. The woods were dense and to a small child seemingly endless, but she knew exactly where she was going. Her mother had shown her where to hide if trouble arrived at their door again, and even in the dead of night she would have been able to find the hidden place.

A fierce wind had picked up, and the trees swayed violently, but the roaring of the leaves helped cover the sounds of their hurried escape. The gale also brought the strong and acrid smell of wood smoke, and Amber thought she could smell something else, something sickly, but she dared not think of what it may be, not until they were safe.

As they ran together, ducking under low hanging branches and jumping over a labyrinth of roots, she recalled her mother's words to her, her last words only a short while ago.

'Amber my angel, I'm hurt and cannot run this time. I think the end is near. If they come tonight, you know where you must go, you and your brother. Take him, and keep him safe. Go to your Aunt Mary at Colmonell when it's quiet. And Amber?'

'Yes Mama?'

'Never forget who you are. We have always been persecuted but we have never given up. You must follow your path, and don't be afraid.'

'I'm not afraid Mama,' Amber replied, and indeed she spoke the truth. She had the strength of her forebears, more than anyone, in fact, for several generations, and she understood the legacy bequeathed to her.

Suddenly Hamish stumbled and fell again, but in an instant Amber pulled him to his feet and all but dragged him on.

'We're here, Hamish. Stay close now and soon we can rest.'

After a few more yards they came upon a wall of shiny green leaves, a dark and natural shrubby barrier, thick with bramble, gorse and holly, and at first glance impenetrable. Amber however knew what to do, and reaching behind the thick undergrowth placed her hand on a large wooden pole which stood upright from the ground. She lifted the pole up and pulled it outwards revealing a dark entrance. Pushing Hamish into the gloom, she followed him into a hidden cave then turned and lifted the pole back into position. She knew from the many times she'd been here with her mother, that from the outside, the entrance would be invisible.

At last she felt safe.

Outside, she could still make out the shouts and yells of their pursuers, but as she listened the sound faded into the distance. Within the darkness, she grabbed Hamish, pulling him close. She sank to the ground and wrapped her arms about him whilst his breathing slowed.

'Where's Mama?' he whispered.

'Hush now, Hamish. Wait a wee while. Be still until I say. I'll light a fire when it's safe.'

Fire.

Still she dared not think of what she had smelled out there in the woods, but steeled herself for what she needed to find out later... tomorrow.

As the last distant shout ceased, Hamish's breathing slowed even further, and Amber thanked the spirits he had at last fallen asleep.

With the patience and serenity of her mother, she sat still and in silence. Being in no rush to light a fire, she stared with unseeing eyes into the darkness, and wondered if her life would ever be her own, if she and her brother would ever live in peace.

Birth

December 2007

One

Sarah Macintyre opened her eyes and lay unmoving, staring into the darkness. She listened to the sounds of the night and wondered what had disturbed her sleep.

Her husband John lay on his back next to her, but his breathing was slow and peaceful, telling of a deep sleep. Mags, her black Labrador who lay on her blanket on the floor at the foot of the bed, let out a long yawn, stood up, turned around and lay back down again. In the distance, the remote sound of a car was too quiet to have awakened her, and apart from a few creaks as the house relaxed for the night, Sarah heard nothing else.

She wasn't aware of having been dreaming, and as she didn't need to use the toilet, gave no further thought to it. Turning onto her side, Sarah closed her eyes again and stretched an arm out under the covers toward her husband. Moments later she heard a quiet moan from Claire's room, and in an instant her senses were on full alert. She turned her head to listen with both ears.

The seconds ticked by and all was silent again, but still

Sarah rolled over and without a sound slipped out of bed, sliding her feet into cosy slippers. With a glance at the glowing fingers of her bedside clock she noted it was still early, only just past two o'clock, and she tiptoed across the room out onto the landing. Easing open the door to Claire's bedroom, she peered into the gloom. A smear of blonde glowed within the darkness as Sarah crept in. She leaned over her daughter and with care pulled the quilt up to cover her shoulders. Claire muttered something incoherent as she often did in her sleep, and Sarah froze for an instant so as not to wake her.

After a few moments of listening to the dreamy sound of breathing, Sarah turned to leave the room, but in the dim light noticed a dark shape resting against Claire's pillow and reached towards the object. Sarah retrieved a large crystal, one of her own mother's, and turned it over in her hands. It was heavy, and though the colour was lost in the darkness, she knew it to be rose quartz, a large and pinkish gem which usually sat on the window ledge of the living room. Odd, she thought, that Claire should borrow it. She'd not paid much attention to the gemstones that Graham, Sarah's father, gave to Sarah many years ago after her mother Rose died. Rose owned many crystals and always liked the multitude of sizes and shapes but never did anything with them, except to keep them free from dust. Sarah herself loved the contours, colours and shades, and a few cut crystals hung in her bedroom window. During early mornings and late afternoons in spring and autumn they often caught the low sun, and a myriad of rainbows would dance about the room.

Rather than put the crystal somewhere safe, she placed it back on the pillow close to Claire's hand. As she let go of the gem Claire spoke again, just as a faint tingling sensation caressed the tips of Sarah's fingers.

'Thanks, Mommy. Night night.'

Sarah froze once more, wondering if her daughter were playing tricks on her, but she appeared to be genuinely asleep. Sarah stood upright and reached towards the crystal again, but then stopped as she sensed a vague touch on her forehead. Within seconds the feeling became quite firm as if someone's hand rested against her. The moment came as little surprise however as Sarah had felt it every night since coming home from hospital. It was an odd sensation, as if an area of her forehead had become numb, but paradoxically whilst the sensation was upon her, touching the same place with her own fingers felt normal. She could feel her own touch with both her hand and her forehead, so in reality there was no numbness. Thinking over it during the past few days, she kept coming back to the idea that a hand lay upon her.

Odd. Must be a reason for it.

Five days had passed since Sarah's discharge from hospital, and despite suggesting she may go back to work, the notion was met with extreme resistance from everyone. Her husband, family and work colleagues all vehemently opposed any idea of her returning so soon. A dozen greeting cards stood on the mantelpiece in the living room... well-wishing cards from her colleagues at the office reminding her to take care and not to hurry back.

In quiet moments when Sarah was honest with herself she actually felt no urgency to rush back which surprised her as she was a very loyal and professional employee. Deep inside she realised she needed, or perhaps wanted, a break. The memories raked up whilst she was in a coma left her troubled and raw, and the bizarre journey her dreams had taken her on still unsettled her. With the festive season looming she was happy to take a longer break.

But now, in the depths of the night, Sarah made her way in silence out of Claire's room pulling the door close behind her. Heading back into her own bedroom she sneaked under the quilt next to her husband where the bed was still warm.

John was still deep in slumber, but Sarah lay for a while staring up at the ceiling waiting for sleep to take her. As she lay unmoving, a smile curled her lips in memory of last night's romantic escapades with her husband. Despite wanting to make love on the night she returned home, exhaustion erased any possibility, and they did little more than fall asleep early. For most of the week the pattern repeated itself. But last night they had put Claire to bed and taken a warm bath together, whilst the frost settled outside under a clear sky. They took their time soaping each other down, teasing each other with gentle caresses, slowly building their need. After drying off, and wrapped in cosy dressing gowns, John carried his wife downstairs amidst stifled giggles trying not to end up in a heap in the hallway, and they settled on the sofa with the candles lit and the lamps low.

Sarah smiled as she recalled their energy and passion. Memory may have been playing tricks on her, but she thought it a long time since they had been so vigorous and urgent in their lovemaking… their desire for each other burning and imperative. Now, as she lay next to her husband, she wanted him again, but a wide yawn pushed aside any thoughts of waking him. She turned over once more and slipped an arm around John as sleep climbed up from her feet and cocooned her within its comforting blanket. Her eyelids fluttered a few times, and before she slid back into peaceful slumber the hand lay on her forehead again and she was comforted.

Two

Several hours later, Sarah awakened to the aroma of coffee. The scent triggered a memory, one she would rather forget. For one tense moment before she became aware of her surroundings, the recollection transported her back to a moment from within the dreams she'd had while in hospital. In the dream Sarah had been sitting in her car, in darkness, parked in a secluded lay-by off the remote country lanes of Cannock Chase having a surreal conversation with a spectral John.

Her fears however were short-lived as her daughter's long blonde hair came into view, and the young girl leaned over her mom to give her a kiss on the cheek. Drawing a deep breath, taking in the scent of her daughter, Sarah heard Claire proudly pronounce, 'I made you coffee this morning mommy, and toast!'

'Oh thank you, angel. Aren't you a clever girl?'

'Daddy says I can help make dinner tonight. It'll be a surprise!' Claire said, with emphasis on her last word.

'Oooo. I can't wait. How about we have fizzy pop in a wine glass again?' asked Sarah.

'Yes please!'

Claire paused smiling at her mother as if thinking of how

to say something.

'Mommy?' she said in a pleading tone. 'Do I have to go to school today? Can't I stay here and look after you?'

Sarah laughed.

'I knew you were going to ask me that? You know you have to go. I want you to be the cleverest girl in the whole school, so you need to pay attention to your teachers. You already missed over a week.'

'Ok,' replied Claire. She was, as ever, happy with her mother's decisions. She had never been one for whining, accepting things for what they were, but nevertheless she continued.

'Well, I'll get a good job and take care of you and Daddy when you're old.'

Sarah laughed again and kissed Claire on her forehead.

'That sounds lovely, but it'll be a while yet. I only want you to be happy, sweetheart, whatever you do.'

'I wasn't happy when you were in hospital,' answered Claire. 'But I'm glad my birds helped.'

Sarah kissed Claire again before checking the time.

'Look it's half-past eight, you'd best get your shoes on and get ready for school.'

In the same moment, Sarah heard John call from downstairs.

'Claire! C'mon, angel, it's time to go!'

'Coming,' Claire shouted and jumped off the bed and made her way to the bedroom door. But before Claire left the room a thought occurred to Sarah.

'Claire. What did you mean when you said your birds helped?'

'The robins,' Claire said. 'They're mine,' and off she went, leaving Sarah somewhat mystified. She recalled the single most important trigger that brought her back to wakefulness in hospital had been the sound of robins calling to each other. John had played a recording of birdsong, knowing the sound held a powerful emotional and even spiritual significance for her. Why Claire suggested the birds were her own was puzzling.

John walked into the room.

'Aha! I see you got your coffee.'

He walked around the side of the bed and sat next to his wife. Sarah raised a hand and caressed his face.

'Last night was rather special,' she whispered.

'It was rather, wasn't it,' he answered, and leaned forward, closing his mouth around Sarah's throat.

'Oh God,' she whispered. 'Careful or you'll make Claire late for school.'

'What an excuse she'll have,' replied John. '"Miss, I was late because my mom and dad were having sex."'

'Behave yourself and get out. I need to take a bath. Anyway what are you doing today?'

John feigned disappointment but stood up and glanced at his watch. He'd been granted extra compassionate leave following Sarah's discharge from hospital, and had been using his time to make sure his wife had everything she needed.

'Spoilsport,' he said. 'Well, I need to go shopping then I'll nip into work to take another sick note. How about you? Are you still going into town?'

'Yes. I'll meet Rachel for lunch and maybe take a walk around the shops.'

Rachel was Sarah's dearest friend; indeed they behaved more like sisters.

'Ok. Will you be all right?' John asked.

'Yes, I'll be fine. I'll see you this afternoon sometime.'

'Ok, sweetheart. I love you.'

'And I love you back,' replied Sarah.

John gave his wife a quick kiss and headed downstairs to Claire's impatient calls to hurry. After a few moments Sarah heard the door close and listened as John turned his key in the lock. As if in response to the noise, Mags lifted her head and flapped her ears. She loped around to Sarah's side of the bed and stretched open her mouth in a huge yawn.

'C'mon, sleepy,' said Sarah. 'It's time we were up and

about.'

Sarah grabbed her mug of coffee and carried it into the bathroom where she turned on the bath taps and poured a little oil into the running water. As the water level rose she stirred it well and then wandered through to the airing cupboard for fresh towels. While she waited for the bath to fill, she sat on the closed toilet seat and sipped at her drink. Through the frosted window she could see a blue sky and the orange ball of the sun shining brightly. The sound of birdsong drifted in from outside. Starlings were whistling to each other... a blackbird was clucking a warning call, and a robin played solo.

For a few moments she sat and listened to the avian orchestra, then finishing the last dregs of her coffee, stood, turned off the taps and climbed in to the deep water where she spent the next twenty minutes soaking herself in oils of lavender and clary sage. She pondered the day ahead and how she may react. Not having been into Wolverhampton since coming home from hospital, she had willingly, if uncharacteristically, cocooned herself in the sanctuary of her own home despite feeling fit and healthy. But during the previous evening, she and John had discussed her plans.

'It's time I went out again,' she said. 'I can't stay indoors forever, so I'll take a wander around the shops and have lunch with Rachel.'

John expressed his concern and his reluctance to let her go on her own.

'Why don't I come with you? I can browse around while you meet up.'

'No, sweetheart. I need to do this on my own. Take my time. I'm a big girl and I can take care of myself.'

Sarah didn't admit to John she was nervous, but she was insistent. John would take Claire to school and go to the supermarket while Sarah visited Rachel. In fact, Sarah wanted to catch up on some gossip she'd heard from John. Rachel had shared her telephone number with Peter Danecourt, Sarah's consultant, and Sarah wanted to know if they'd met.

John and Sarah had known Peter for several years, and Sarah had always liked the man. He was quietly spoken and gentle but misfortune had changed his life. Cancer had taken Peter's wife at the tragically young age of thirty-three, leaving a devastated Peter to raise their daughter on his own. Sarah felt Peter had made an excellent job of being a single parent, but she thought he needed and deserved a good woman to share his life and help raise Sophie who, at the age of seven, was a year younger than Claire.

While Sarah languished in the warm silkiness of her bath, her thoughts turned to Rachel. To most outsiders Rachel would not have appeared to be the ideal match for Peter, who needed a steady and lasting relationship with a woman who was less flighty than Rachel seemed. But Sarah knew her friend well... knew she maintained a facade. In odd moments, Rachel revealed a weaker side to her nature, a vulnerability that stemmed from something she kept concealed. But then she would rebuild the wall and be her usual self. To many she was simply shallow, caring and fun-loving but shallow, and Sarah was adamant that one day Rachel would reveal her hidden secret.

Busy with these thoughts, Sarah hadn't noticed Mags appear in the bathroom. The dog sniffed at water that rippled dangerously near the rim of the bath and sneezed at Sarah.

'Huh. Thanks, Mags. Ok, ok, I'm coming out now,' and Sarah reached over to pull out the plug. She stood, grabbed a large towel and wrapped it around herself before stepping out of the bath. The water gurgled away as she wound a smaller hand towel around her hair. Wiping away the condensation from the mirror over the sink, she stared at her distorted reflection. She inspected her left temple. The dark bruise which had been there following the attack that resulted in a head injury was now indistinct with only a slight yellow discolouration remaining. As she stared at herself, the faint but very present caress touched her forehead again, and for a fleeting moment she closed her eyes. Opening them once more she sighed aloud to the mirror, misting the surface.

'What is that? What does it mean?' she asked.

With a puzzled shake of her head, she left the bathroom and headed for the bedroom to get dressed. Sarah dried herself before selecting warm clothes from her wardrobe and dropping them onto the bed. Mags lay out on the landing, head on her front paws, watching every move, waiting for a sign.

'You're so transparent, but you'll have to be patient,' Sarah said. 'I need some proper breakfast and then I'll take you out.' Mags wagged her tail and lifted her ears.

Sarah pulled on underwear and as she did so felt the light touch on her head again. She turned to the bedroom mirror and stared at her semi-naked reflection. For a moment she pictured John's hands on her, pictured his gentle movements, recalled his passion, his need for her. She stood a while longer in front of the mirror, but with her vision off in the distance, arms hanging at her sides. The sensation on her forehead was firm and real, and the world around her faded. She stayed still for several minutes until a touch on her thigh brought her back from her inner world, the cold touch of Mags's nose. Sarah glanced down at her expectant companion and pulled at the dog's ears. But as if in response to an outside influence, she peered up at her reflection and said aloud,

'Yes, it's time to have another child.'

What! she thought, with a frown.

Three

A few hours later, Sarah stood shivering outside Cafe Nero waiting for Rachel when a voice from behind shouted, 'There you are!' and arms wrapped themselves around her pulling her into a close embrace. Sarah returned the hug with affection, and for long moments the two friends stayed entwined in each other's arms.

Rachel eventually spoke. 'God, I've missed you so much. You wouldn't believe how difficult it's been not to phone you at home all the time.'

'You should have called,' said Sarah, pulling away so she could study her friend. She gazed into Rachel's eyes and felt a surge of love. After all, they were as close as sisters, but Sarah thought her friend appeared tired, perhaps worried, or tense.

'I wanted to let you and John have some space. I didn't want to pester you. You both deserved time alone after you were discharged.'

'Well,' answered Sarah, 'It was kind of you, and I've missed you too which is why I thought it was time to get out of the house and come and visit. But will you do me a favour?'

'Of course.'

'Can you keep it quiet at work I've been into town?'

'Well yes. Any particular reason?'

'Well,' she said, 'I'm a little muddled actually, and that's not normal for me.'

Rachel feigned surprise, but didn't expect her friend to be herself after having spent a week in hospital in a coma.

'Muddled?' she said. 'Unusual word for you? I'm the one who's supposed to be a bit scatty.'

Sarah laughed at her friend's comment and found the laugh brightened her mood. It had been a difficult week in some ways. John had been overcautious, treating her as if she could break at any moment, but she understood his worries. After last night's lovemaking, though, she was sure he would realise his worries were unfounded.

Claire had stayed off school for an extra couple of days, but then Sarah insisted she went back. It was time, Sarah realised, life should return to normal, but she wasn't sure she wanted it the way it used to be and found those thoughts disconcerting. The whole hospital coma experience had left her unsettled. She felt exposed and vulnerable and recognised a need to grow a new skin around herself for protection.

Aware Rachel was waiting patiently, she drew a breath and spoke.

'You know what I'm like… in control, got everything sorted and organised… everything in its place. Professional at work.'

Rachel sniffed with amusement.

'You sound like you're quoting from your CV!' she laughed.

'Sorry,' answered Sarah. 'But it proves my point. Since I saw you and the others last Saturday for the meal, I've been adrift, fidgety.'

'Fidgety?' asked Rachel.

'Yes, but there's more. Look, let's get lunch and we can talk somewhere warm.'

'Ok,' answered Rachel. 'In here? Nero's?'

'No!' Sarah replied quickly. 'Somewhere different. Let's go to Costa instead. I need... a change.'

'Ok!' said Rachel in surprise. 'I can see there's a story to tell, but come on, I'm hungry.'

It wasn't far to walk, and the two friends hurried to where Costa's welcomed them in with its irresistible aroma. Sarah offered to buy Rachel lunch and while she placed their order, Rachel found a table at the rear of the cafe away from the hustle and bustle.

Sarah carried over a tray loaded with coffees and cream and a ticket for lunch, and stripping off her coat and scarf, sat down with a satisfied sigh.

'C'mon,' said Rachel. 'What's happening? What's up? I want to know what you mean by fidgety.'

Sarah sat for a moment staring at her coffee as if gathering her thoughts. She brushed her long hair back behind both ears.

'I didn't tell you everything I dreamt while I was in a coma did I?'

'Bits and pieces. We haven't really had a chance. From our conversation when you were still asleep, I guessed something weird was happening.'

'Actually that pretty much sums it up,' replied Sarah. 'Weird or bizarre... or just plain odd. I've thought about it a lot and I think I was transported, if that's the right word, into a different life, one that could have been mine if Steve and I had married all those years ago. Everything was so real... to a point.'

'To a point?' asked Rachel. 'How'd you mean?'

'Well I knew where I was living, in the house at Huntington, y'know where Steve lives now, but it wasn't right somehow. Being married to Steve in a dreary life but not being able to remember actually getting married. My mind convinced itself of the reality of everything because I could see and hear stuff. But I had no memory of events, like marrying or going on honeymoon, so in my dream I guessed something was wrong. Which of course it was.

Sorry, I'm sure this isn't making any sense.'

'It's difficult to grasp but go on,' Rachel said, trying to encourage her.

Sarah took a moment.

'Y'know sometimes just before you wake up in the morning, you have a dream that seems real?'

'Yes of course. You're not sure if you're awake or not?' said Rachel.

'Exactly. You might dream of being late for something, or someone's stolen the car, and it seems so real you're utterly convinced it's happened... you're actually late... the car's actually gone. But in your logical mind, you know something's wrong, but the dream is so real and you go back and forth until you wake up.'

'Yes. Now I understand.'

'Well that's what it was like in my coma. And because everything felt so real, it gave me a... a... compelling sense of what my life could have been like if Steve and I hadn't split up and John and I hadn't got back together. And that's unsettling. Not that I'm not good friends with Steve, it's just we don't make a couple. But it's also more than that. It's made me realise how fragile life is, how a single moment or particular choice can change everything.'

'Huh. Yes. Quite. Particular choices... good or bad,' replied Rachel, as if to herself. Then she continued, 'But no... you weren't meant for each other because Steve is gay.'

'Possibly,' sniffed Sarah.

'Possibly? What do you mean?' Rachel asked.

'Y'know... I'm not convinced he is,' said Sarah. She lifted her coffee and took a careful sip. The aroma filled her senses and for a moment she was inside her dream again. The lively roar of a forceful gale and the creaking of tree branches replaced the murmured chatter within the coffee shop. But Rachel's voice broke in, and she was back in Costa, piped music replacing the sounds of nature.

'Sarah?' Rachel said.

'Sorry… Steve. Yes. I'm not sure he *is* gay. I mean have you ever seen him with another man?'

'Well no,' Rachel replied. 'But I've not seen him with a woman either. He confessed to being gay years ago didn't he?'

'True, but I have an odd feeling there's more to it. That it's not quite that simple.'

Rachel smiled. 'Huh. You're gonna tell me he's had a sex change now aren't you.'

'No!' Sarah chuckled. 'I'm sure that's *not* the case!' She paused a moment before continuing, speaking as much to herself as to Rachel. 'I don't know. I think I'm a little uneasy.'

'Well,' said Rachel. 'It's not surprising after what you've been through. And it's only been a week since you woke up. You're bound to be unsettled and coming back to work is the last thing you need. But why is it you want me to keep quiet about you coming into town?'

Sarah stared into Rachel's eyes, and as she did so, for a fleeting moment, she thought she saw a vague coloured hue sitting around her friend's head and shoulders, a gentle shimmer that disappeared as soon as it appeared.

More puzzled than disconcerted, she answered the question.

'I just don't want any prying questions. Don't want to face them. Questions that is. Until I've figured out some stuff, I don't need a lot of gushing concern from people I don't know well. That probably sounds horrible and unfair of me because they care. But I don't have the energy for it. As for work itself, I'm not sure I want to go back at all.'

'I'm sure I don't blame you. Most of us wish we didn't have to work, but that's a sudden change isn't it? Don't you enjoy your job?'

'Well I do… I did… I don't know. I've been thinking a lot about this over the past few days. I think I'm in need of a change, and perhaps its natural after what I've been through, but it feels more.'

Sarah began talking rapidly.

'This job I can do with my eyes shut. It doesn't challenge me any more, and it's like I can't really make a difference. I want to help people in a more direct way. Shuffling budget stuff around to support the local community is one thing, but the job always means we're robbing Peter to pay Paul. It's a never ending pointless bloody circle that's damn frustrating. In fact, it's fucking annoying sometimes. I want to meet the people I help, peer into their eyes and know I've done something useful for them.'

The abruptness with which her friend's demeanour changed shocked Rachel. While Sarah was speaking, her voice became quieter but more intense, even aggressive, if possible for someone who controlled their emotions. Rachel placed her cup on the table and leaned forward to speak in a whisper.

'What? Hello! Where the hell did that come from? Are you sure you're all right?'

With chagrin Sarah stared back at Rachel, aware of what she'd said. She never swore in normal conversation and only used profanities when under severe duress, which, for her, was very rare.

'Sorry Rachel.' She paused and struggled for a moment, not knowing how to continue. But concerned for her friend, she needed to allay Rachel's fears. 'Look, I'd better tell you everything. Firstly, I'm fine. No need to worry something bad is going to happen, or I have an incurable brain dysfunction or severe damage or whatever. Rachel, there is a before and an after going on here. There's before my accident, and there's after. Beforehand, I was happy with my job. I had a wonderful life with John and Claire. We had everything we needed and everything we wanted. Then afterwards occurred. My job isn't enough. My life with John and Claire isn't enough. Or perhaps I mean *our* life isn't enough. I love them both with my soul, but I'm sure the three of us could do more. Make a fresh start on something new.'

Sarah stopped to take a drink before continuing.

'Ever since I got back home from hospital, I've been having a strange sensation on my head. Not in it, but on it. Every night when I close my eyes it's like I can feel a hand resting on my forehead. It's gentle and very comforting, but it never used to happen. Sometimes it happens during the day if I'm quiet and relaxed. I've also started to see colours around people... like a blanket or... or... a halo. Some people anyway. I've seen one around John, I've just seen an orange glow around you and I don't know what it means. The odd thing is I'm not worried about any of it. Far from it. Sounds odd but it's exciting, because it's something new I want to understand... well more like *need* to understand. Things are different. I'm not sure how much or why, but they're... well... different.'

Rachel was troubled.

'An orange glow? Are you telling me you're seeing things? Sarah, you need to talk to the doctors again, talk to Peter. You're worrying me.'

'There's no need. I'm fine. I don't have a headache. In fact, overall I'm pretty chilled despite the restlessness, if that's possible. As I said, I'm not worried about it. You know last night was the first time John and I made love since I came home. We've been cautious around each other. But last night something was right, and we made love downstairs on the sofa and on the floor... after we started in the bath. You've heard the stories about how married couples get after years of being together? Their sex life becomes stale? Well we never seemed to have suffered with that. Less frequent of course but it's always been exciting. Last night, though, John was like someone possessed. Talk about energetic, and I was the same. It was more than a rediscovery, it was like a different level... getting deeper into each other.'

Sarah paused again, gazing off into the distance, gazing without seeing. Rachel waited in silence while the muted sounds of chatter and soft piped music washed over them.

After several moments Sarah spoke once more.

'I'm sure I'm not making any sense, but before and after seems to cover a lot of things.' She leaned back in her chair again, lifting the coffee cup to her lips.

'Well!' replied Rachel, 'and... wow! I'm not sure what to say, except have you talked to John?'

'Not yet,' said Sarah sheepishly. 'I don't want to worry him unnecessarily. Don't want to say anything until it makes more sense.'

'You'll worry him more if he finds out you've been hiding something from him. Oh, and one other thing.'

'Yes?'

'I don't want to lose you.'

'What? You're not going to lose me. What a strange thing to say. Why would you think that?'

'Sarah. You're scaring me. I'm sorry... I know it's selfish of me. It seems like you're heading somewhere different, and I'm not sure I'm part of it with all this talk of change. What would I do without you? You're my sister, if not in blood in spirit. I love you!'

'I love you too, Rachel. But you're not to worry. I'm not sure anything is going to happen, but if it does I'll make sure you are a part of it. In fact, I'm sure you're already a part of it though I'm not sure if that makes sense either. Something's going on and I'm not sure what yet. How many times have I said sure? Oh, here we go... food.'

For several minutes the two friends did not speak, as with gusto they tucked into their lunch. Eventually, through a mouthful of food, Sarah changed the subject and teased Rachel with a question.

'What's this I hear about you trying to seduce my consultant?'

Rachel put on a smile that didn't extend to her eyes.

'I'm sure I don't know what you mean.'

'There's no stopping you. There am I lying in a hospital bed, lost to the world, and all you can do is flash your eyes and wiggle your bum at the medics. But seriously, have you seen Peter out of work?'

'Yes I have, but I never wiggled my bum,' she laughed and took another mouthful.

'Well?' asked Sarah.

'Well what?' replied Rachel with raised eyebrows and wide innocent eyes.

'C'mon, you know what. How was he?'

'Well before your dirty mind runs away with itself we haven't done anything,' said Rachel, though to Sarah it seemed as if her friend was being evasive.

'Wow. Don't you fancy him? He's a bit of a catch, y'know.'

'Yes, I'm sure he is,' Rachel muttered, gazing into her coffee cup. 'He took me to dinner, but we didn't have time after. Well I don't mean time… the right moment perhaps. Well… I don't know.'

'Rachel. Is there something you're not telling me? This isn't how things usually go with you. Did you kiss him?'

'Yes we kissed. He kissed me goodnight at my front door. And, I might add, it was long, and very sensuous. But there was nothing else. He didn't want to come in… just said he needed to go. Not sure what to think.'

Sarah stared at the top of Rachel's head since her friend kept her eyes averted. It was as if Rachel's last comment was again aimed at herself. Sarah smiled and once more spotted a shimmer of orange colour that flickered around Rachel's shoulders. But as the colour faded, Sarah thought it changed into a weaker shade of red, a feeble colour and, in a moment of clarity, she thought the glow was bereft of light and energy. She spoke again.

'How much do you like him? I always thought he was a lovely man after John introduced us a few years ago. He'd make a wonderful partner for someone. Someone else anyway. How much do you know about him?'

Rachel raised her eyes.

'Well for one, I do fancy him, but that may not mean much to you because you expect me to fancy anyone as long as they can move. Don't look at me like that. You know it's true. Might not be the whole truth, but what do you mean when you say he'd make a partner for someone else. Not me? Is that it? Is he too good for me?'

'No. I don't mean that at all,' said Sarah with a frown. 'You know I don't. I only meant he's already had one partner.'

'Yes of course, he was married before. When we went out last week, we talked about trivial stuff, didn't get into anything too deep, but it was easy, relaxed, and I enjoyed myself. I hope he did too. Why do you ask how much I know?'

'Rachel, I think the two of you would be well suited, and I don't want to spoil the discovery by speaking out of turn. But it's no secret he's a widower.'

'A widower? God. How? What happened?'

'Cancer. It was quick and very aggressive. It's a few years ago now, but he's a very special man.'

'I'm sure he is,' Rachel said again.

'Yes he is. I know it and I think you do too… but I can see through you. You're being cagey. What's up?'

'Look,' said Rachel. 'You're not the only one who feels different. Your stay in hospital terrified me. I was scared to death I was going to lose you. So if it seems like I'm a bit off it's probably because I'm a little unsettled too.'

Sarah wasn't convinced that was the real reason for Rachel's guarded manner, but her friend seemed uneasy so Sarah let the subject drop. It was obvious Rachel was hiding something or at least unwilling to carry on the discussion. Sarah would have to tease it out bit by bit.

'Anyway, let's talk about something else,' Rachel said. 'What's your plan for the rest of today?'

'Well, this afternoon I'm going to wander around town. There's something I need to do.'

'Yes?'

'Probably sounds daft, but I want to walk the same route I did before the attack.'

'Is that wise? Do you really want to rake it all up?'

'Not raking it up. More like finishing it. What's the phrase… closure?'

'Well if it helps. I'll come with you if you want.'

'No, no there's no need, and I'd rather do it on my own. You'll probably think I'm mad but I want to walk it backwards… or rather in reverse.'

'Probably think you're mad? I already know you are! But whatever you think's best. Will you promise to call me if you need me?'

'Of course,' Sarah replied.

Rachel checked her watch.

'Damn, I suppose I'd better get back to it. You sure you'll be ok?'

Sarah nodded, and a smile curled her lips.

'Yes I'll be fine. And will you keep me posted about what happens with Peter?' Sarah prompted cautiously.

'Not sure anything will happen,' replied Rachel.

The two young women stood and dressed in coats and scarves, readying themselves for the shock of the winter chill. The sun was bright and cheery, but struggled to pull the temperature much above freezing. Once outside, they walked back a short way until Sarah stopped at the corner of Darlington Street and Queen Square and pulled Rachel into her arms. Her friend responded in kind, and for a few moments Rachel clung to Sarah with such urgency Sarah was perplexed and a little concerned. With what seemed like reluctance, Rachel finally let go and spoke in a husky voice.

'Sarah, take care and call me… soon… tonight even.'

Hastily she turned away but not before Sarah caught a shine in her friend's eyes. Crossing the road, Rachel headed onto North Street and before disappearing around the corner, turned and waved.

Sarah stood gazing in the direction her friend had taken, gazing without seeing. Instead, her thoughts wandered back into Costa Coffee shop and to the weak red colour she'd sensed hovering like a shroud around Rachel. She recalled the violet halo she'd seen several times around John since her return home, and puzzled once more about what the vision and strange colours may mean, and while she stood lost in thought, the light touch feathered her brow once more. For a few seconds the comforting hand stayed with her.

With a slow shake of her head, Sarah turned away and headed along Darlington Street, past the department store, past Cafe Nero, and onwards to the place where a single, selfish and violent act had changed everything.

Four

With mild trepidation, Sarah walked down the hill. She knew nothing would happen, there was no one lying in wait, ready to pounce on her or push her to the ground, but still she was tense, or was it expectant? It took less than a minute to arrive at the mouth of the alleyway where the attack took place. She stopped before entering the narrow way.

'What am I doing here?' she muttered to herself. 'What am I after?'

Sarah was suddenly unsure why she *was* here, not that she had any clearly defined goal. The whole affair was out of character for her as she was acting on a whim. Under normal situations her actions were calculated, her purpose understood. Sarah could be spontaneous when she wanted to, but her spontaneity always had purpose… never random or pointless. This retracing of steps made no sense. Closure she said to Rachel, but the event was already closed. Sarah tended to be somewhat philosophical about life… what had happened had happened… what was done was done. An event couldn't be changed so there was no point in mulling over it. The energy involved in discussing, worrying or stressing over something for years and keeping the whole thing alive could overwhelm a life or lead to depression, embitterment or, worse still, extreme loneliness. Of course the exception to Sarah's innate philosophy were things that really mattered, things intensely painful, such as the loss of a loved one. Experience, though, taught her it was even possible to manage bereavement as life continued and the pain became less acute. One could dwell repeatedly on the loss, or let it take its place, allowing it to rise as it saw fit.

As Sarah pondered these thoughts, she found she had turned into the alley and had begun walking again, unconsciously deciding that since making the decision to do this, she would follow it through, whatever happened.

The time was now approaching one thirty, and everywhere was busy with shoppers, even along the narrow way where she walked. Behind her, the squeal of brakes cut through the air from a vehicle moving along Darlington Street. She jumped and spun around, suddenly fearful. She almost bumped into a man who walked close behind her.

'Careful luv,' the man said, good naturedly.

'Oops... I'm sorry,' Sarah answered.

'It's all right. You ok?'

'Yes, yes, thank you.'

The man hurried on, and Sarah started walking again.

'This is ridiculous,' she said to herself. 'Let's just get it over with.'

The alleyway appeared as it had done on the day of her attack, which of course is what she expected. The same diagonal pavers underfoot, the same boarded up windows and doorways, and the covered delivery zone at the far end. Everything was the same, but it was she, Sarah, who was different, she who had changed. She stopped again and peered over her shoulder. A constant stream of people crossed the mouth of the narrow way, going about their hurried business. For a moment she closed her eyes and could visualise with disturbing ease the hooded youth leaning against the wall near the entrance, could clearly see his hand shoving her in the chest.

With a shudder, she opened her eyes again. For an

instant, and in sudden fear, Sarah was overwhelmed by an urgent need to break into a run and had to fight hard not to turn on her heels and escape the madness. Her breath coming in short gasps, she forced herself to continue walking… the reverse of the route she had taken two weeks ago.

Two weeks? Is that all?

After a few more yards, she made it out onto the street and continued with her plan to retrace her steps. As she crossed the road to the charity shop she had visited before, a measure of calm returned and her mild panic dissipated. With no inclination to enter the shop, she passed by, just wanting the journey to end. For a moment she thought about calling John, wanting to hear his voice, to listen to his words if only for confirmation she wasn't dreaming again, but decided against it. He would only worry.

In frustration that nothing positive seemed to have come from her trip, she hurried back up the road to the gift shop she visited on that fateful day. Stopping outside the shop, she eyed up the Christmas decorations and colourful gifts displayed in the window.

As Sarah gazed through the glass, she saw a hooded reflection, the reflection of someone behind her. Suddenly, wide-eyed and with pounding heart, she spun around in time to see a woman lifting a hand to wave at someone across the street. Sarah lifted her own hand to her mouth to stifle an urge to throw up, and turned back to the window. Her nausea was abruptly replaced with anger, a rage utterly unknown to her, at least not for many years. Sarah rarely became irritable let alone angry, and didn't know how to handle the intensity of the emotion. Her anger was directed at the bastard who had done this to her, the drugged-up little shit who stepped into her life one day and nearly destroyed it, a worthless animal who had left her irrational and fearful.

WHY? She almost shouted. WHY ME?

As the burning rage seethed inside her, her world promptly became grey and foggy, the background noises receding, the sounds faint and indistinct. For one fearful moment she thought she may pass out, collapsing in the street and ending up back in hospital. But from within the grey mist, a quiet and gentle voice spoke, a voice both calming and comforting.

'Sarah, my angel. Look for me. Look ahead and find me.'

The voice was clear and present, and broke into her raging thoughts, distracting her and dissipating her anger. The mist lifted, returning Sarah to the real world where she found she was still gazing through the little shop window. In response to the words and with little conscious thought, Sarah scanned the window display inspecting each item, each ornament, each piece of jewellery and clothing until her gaze rested on a gemstone. At first glance it appeared to be a very simple object... one of several grouped together on a small box covered with red cloth trimmed with a green ribbon. The stone that caught her eye was orange or red in colour and appeared to her eyes to glow, a bright gem amidst the others.

Again without conscious decision, and feeling somewhat detached, Sarah entered the shop and with purpose walked up to the counter where a middle-aged man stood marking up price tags with an ornate pen.

'Merry Christmas,' the man said cheerily. 'Can I help you?'

Sarah spoke with someone else's voice. 'Yes please. I'd like to buy one of the stones in the window? It's orangey in colour and about this big?' and Sarah made a small circle with her fingers, about the size of a two pence piece.

'The beryl stone?' asked the man.

'Is that what it is?' questioned Sarah.

'Well, let's take a look.'

The man led Sarah across to the window where she pointed to the stone that caught her interest.

'Yes, that's the one,' the man said. 'It's called beryl. Very common but no less attractive for it. It's quite large so it's four pounds fifty, I'm afraid.'

'Oh that's fine,' said Sarah with surprise, thinking it ought to be more expensive because of its beauty.

'Ok,' the man said. 'If you come back over to the till, I'll pop it into a box for you.'

Now more like herself, and having made the purchase, Sarah relaxed, her anger forgotten. The man presented her with a small but colourful little gift box, and Sarah reached into her purse and paid in cash.

'Thank you,' she said, 'and a Merry Christmas to you too.'

Leaving the shop, she stepped out onto the street, and for a moment sensed she was not alone, as if someone were nearby... a presence. She felt no fear, only a strange sense of belonging, of being at home... the same feeling she had when with John. It occurred to her that the trip hadn't been a waste of time after all. Her journey had indeed had a purpose, though she didn't understand what it was.

Standing for a moment outside the shop, she pulled out her phone and sent two messages. The first was to John saying 'I love you xx', and the second to Rachel saying 'Dina tmz 7. Luv u xx'.

A response from Rachel came back impossibly fast saying, 'Ys pls. C U tmz xxx'.

With a smile, Sarah dropped the phone back inside her handbag, but all she could think of now was going home and closing the front door. Tugging the collar of her coat up close around her neck to keep out the searching fingers of an icy wind, she headed off to find her car.

Five

In one swift movement Sarah entered the hallway, hung up her car keys and pushed the front door shut behind her with a foot. Yanking off her coat she dashed into the downstairs toilet.

Long moments later, she emerged in a more sedate manner and took off her shoes, replacing them with cosy slippers. With puzzlement furrowing her brow, she pondered the odd feeling she'd experienced back in Wolverhampton, the notion she was not alone. Wandering through into the kitchen, she poured herself a glass of water and carried it through to the living room. It was pleasantly warm indoors after the cold of the winter's day… the south facing patio doors soaking up what little heat the low sun offered. A pile of unopened letters lay on the table, a growing stack now ignored for over two weeks. Sarah picked them up and sat near the window where she could see into the garden.

It was around half past two and Claire would be at school for another hour, though where John was she wasn't quite sure. Probably waylaid at work, she thought.

Taking a sip of water, she flicked through the envelopes. There was a typical assortment of flyers, offers of credit, unmarked envelopes to the homeowner, bills or statements and a few early Christmas cards. Sarah discarded the junk mail immediately, and opened the official letters. These were mostly statements she could file, and one with a Christmas wish from a company offering ways of spreading the cost of Christmas. She consigned it to the rubbish pile.

Left with a couple of white envelopes and one thicker brown one, she settled back and opened the two white ones first. Smiling at the greetings, she felt joyful and mellow at the thought of the looming festive season. One was from John's grandfather from north of the border, and the other was from Claire, one of Sarah's work colleagues. The first card had a 'See you at Christmas' message and Sarah felt a warm anticipation at the thought of travelling up to see Hamish. The latter card a simple 'Merry Christmas' and a 'don't hurry back to work' message.

With only the brown envelope remaining, Sarah paused before reaching for it… hesitancy held her back. For unknown reasons, she abruptly felt a sense of expectancy, as if the envelope contained notification of a long awaited decision, some expected news. Time seemed to slow as with a sense of detachment she moved a hand toward the envelope. As her fingers approached the brown paper, the light touch was on her forehead again and, for an instant, Sarah was certain the envelope moved, the corner lifting the tiniest of fractions as if in response to the presence of her fingers. The frown on her forehead deepening, she moved her hand away, and back again. Once more she saw, or imagined she saw, the paper move, and a gentle tingling sensation caressed the tips of her finger.

She finally grabbed the envelope and turned it over to examine the rear. The only mark of any distinction was a little round sticker that sealed it, a sticker with the word 'Apothecary' printed around its edge in a semi-circle, with the image of a rose flower in the middle.

Sarah flipped the envelope back over and studied the front. In fine spidery script was written her name and address. Still feeling hesitant, she made to drop the letter back onto her lap, but as she loosened her grip on it the letter stayed stuck to her fingers. She had to flick her fingers before it fell away. Mystified, she picked it up again and turned it around and around, feeling the paper to see if it was sticky. Finding nothing of the sort, she dropped it again and the same thing happened. To release what seemed like an invisible bond, she needed to throw the letter away. In a moment of inquisitiveness she moved a single finger slowly towards the envelope, and to both her surprise and dismay it moved slightly just before she made contact. Her previous imaginings were true.

Unable to believe her eyes, and feeling threatened, Sarah jumped up, letting the letter fall to the floor. For long minutes she stayed upright, heart pounding, staring at the envelope as if she expected it to move on its own. But when she sensed the light touch on her forehead again, she began to relax. Calming herself with reason and logic – what she saw must be her imagination – she bent to retrieve the letter, but in the same instant she heard a key in the door and John came in with a, 'Hi, princess, I'm home.'

Grateful John had returned, Sarah left the letter where it lay and walked into the hall to greet him.

'If I bring these bags to the door can you carry them into the kitchen for me? I'll put the shopping away,' he said, but seeing the expression on Sarah's face paused.

'Are you ok? Is everything all right?'

'Sorry! Yes, yes and yes,' said Sarah.

'What?' asked John.

'Yes, I'll carry the shopping in. Yes, I'm ok and yes, everything is all right. Oh, I missed one. No! *I'll* put the shopping away. You'll put stuff in the wrong place and I'll never find anything.'

And with that she reached up to John and planted a sensuous opened-mouthed kiss on his lips.

'Hmmm,' he replied after a few moments. 'Yes I can see you're all right. How long have we got before Claire needs picking up?'

Sarah laughed as John snaked a hand down her back and around her bottom.

'Not long enough,' she said. 'I want it slow tonight. Less energy than last night, and anyway you're not shagging me here in the hallway with the front door wide open.'

'Why's that? Is it too cold?' John replied, all innocence.

Sarah slapped the back of his head and pulled away. 'Get the shopping and behave,' she said. 'Where have you been anyway? I thought you'd have been here when I got home.'

'Well,' replied John as he returned with more bags. He placed them in the hallway and stepped outside again. Sarah followed him into the chill air and grabbed two of the others. 'I dropped Claire at school and went to work. I needed to fill out another leave request but stayed for a chat. Everyone was asking about you.'

'That's nice,' replied Sarah. 'When were you planning on going back?'

'Huh! You trying to get rid of me?' he snorted.

'No!' laughed Sarah. 'It would be nice if you could stay off with me until the new year, but I know I'm being ridiculous.'

John closed the front door, banning the chill air, and they carried the last of the shopping bags into the kitchen. He took off his coat and hung it in the hall. Sarah was emptying the bags as John re-entered the kitchen and he clicked on the kettle. 'Tea?' he asked.

'Yes please.'

John busied himself for a few moments with cups and saucers, laying out a tray to take through to the living room for when Sarah finished organising the groceries.

'To be honest,' he continued. 'I wish I *could* stay off, but they always need everyone working in the run up to Christmas. I've got a long break over the holidays so we can get away as usual.'

He stopped and looked at Sarah. She was standing still, staring at a packet of rice. For long moments she seemed lost in thought, until John reached across and placed a hand on her arm. She turned towards him.

'Are you sure you're ok?' he asked again.

'No. I'm not sure.' She paused a moment. 'Well, yes I'm fine. It's just been an odd day.'

'Odd? Sorry I should have asked. How did your trip into town go?'

'Oh, it was fine. It was nice to have lunch with Rachel. I asked her about Peter.'

'Oh yeah. What did she say? You do know he's smitten... hook, line and sinker. I've warned him to be wary of getting his heart broken, but if he's intent on making the journey he must follow his own path.'

Sarah regarded John with an eyebrow raised.

'What?' she said with surprise. 'His own journey, his own path. What have you done with my husband... the one who doesn't believe in destiny?'

John wrapped his arms around his wife and pulled her close. She nestled her head under his chin... a sudden need for safety and comfort overwhelming her. John answered her question. 'I never told you about the dream I had of your Mom and Dad. It was they who made me remember the robins. I'd forgotten all about them, but Graham and Rose appeared in a dream and made me... well, compelled me to remember.'

Sarah nodded her head.

John continued. 'I did a lot of thinking about us, about how we met, how we re-met too. How we survived losing our parents. It's easy to believe we were always meant to be together. I can't rationalise any of this anymore by saying it's all pure coincidence because it doesn't feel that way. It's as if I was born to love you and you to love me. So, in the same vein, and though it sounds out of place in the twenty-first century, I suppose Peter must follow his own path and see where it goes.' John kissed the top of Sarah's head and took a deep breath. 'Oh... and now I've said all that hippy stuff, I think I ought to go into the garden and chop a few logs.

Should I do it with my shirt off or can you imagine my rippling muscles?'

Sarah raised her head and with eyes shining and a smile curling her lips said, 'You don't have to make a joke of it. It's lovely to hear you speak this way. There may be more before and after's.'

'Before and after's?' asked John with a quizzical expression.

'Oh nothing. Just a conversation I had with Rachel. I'd naively thought it was only *my* life affected, but it's obviously affected you too. And Claire as well, I imagine. Oh and on the subject of chopping logs in a macho way, you can wear what you like and I'd still watch you all day.' Sarah paused a moment before reaching up and kissing her husband. 'Fancy a shower together tonight?' she suggested.

John swallowed hard before speaking. 'Sounds like a great idea,' and returned the kiss. Then remembering the main reason for Sarah's journey into town, 'What else did you do today? Did you take a walk around?' he asked.

'Yes I did. I walked the same route though I walked it in reverse. Seems a bit daft now.'

'Not really,' John said. 'There's no right or wrong, remember.'

'How come you're so understanding?' asked Sarah, and she broke away from John's embrace. 'It always amazes me how you are the way you are.'

'Police training, police work. Having to deal with people under duress. Up to a point you have to let people react in their own way and in their own time, and anyway you're my wife and you'll do things in your own way and no reason's needed.'

'Police training you say? I think it's built in. It comes naturally to you. Y'know I'm so lucky,' Sarah said with a smile.

'I know you are!' replied John with a smug grin but dropped the facade and asked, 'So was it worth it? Walking the route?'

Sarah frowned as she thought about it. 'Well yes. It means I'm not afraid of being attacked at every street corner. But there weren't any enlightened moments. The only tangible thing I got was this.' Sarah reached into the pocket of her jeans and pulled out the small box with the gemstone inside it.

'What is it?' asked John.

'Take a look.' Sarah placed the box in John's hand. As she let go, a tingling sensation prickled the tips of her fingers. John opened the box and tipped the contents into his palm. His eyes settled on the Beryl stone and he rolled it around in his hand.

'Ok, so you bought a pebble.'

'It's not a pebble, you twit. It's a gemstone. A crystal. It's called beryl according to the guy who sold it to me.'

'And?' asked John.

'And what?'

'Why did you buy it?'

Sarah was abashed but had no logical explanation. 'I don't know. I was window shopping, which was what I'd done on the day I was attacked, and I spotted it.' She paused a moment and pictured herself standing outside the shop, gazing into the window, feeling a need to buy the stone, a need that seemed to come from outside of herself. 'Actually it was as if something compelled me to buy it. Does that sound weird or what?'

'Huh!' John sniffed. 'No weirder than your parents appearing to me in a dream. So, what's it for. I've heard crystals are supposed to do stuff, but what does beryl do?' He handed the stone back to Sarah who put it straight into her pocket, discarding the box.

Sarah smiled, turned and grabbed a packet of frozen peas. 'I don't have the faintest idea so I'll Google it later. Anyway,' she said briskly, 'this ain't getting the shopping put away. Oh! I've got something to show you when we've done this. A letter in the post. Something else that's weird, but in some way I get the feeling it's important.'

'A letter, what about?'

Sarah was busy in the utility room putting food into the large freezer. She called back, 'Well, I don't know since I haven't opened it yet. I wanted to wait for you to come home.'

'Hang on. You've a letter you want me to read, so it must be important. But you haven't opened it yet so how do you know it's important.'

'Smart ass,' laughed Sarah walking back into the kitchen. 'I don't know anything about it, except when I went to open it, I…' Sarah paused. 'Look, it'll be easier to show you. Let's finish in here first.'

'As you wish my darling, as you wish.'

John turned the kettle back on to bring the water to a fresh boil, filled the pot and covered it with the tea cosy. Armed with two cups, the teapot and a plate of biscuits, he wandered through into the living room. After a few moments, Sarah joined him.

'Oh, you asked about work,' John said. 'I need to go back next Monday… up to Christmas… till the twenty-first. Much as I'd not bother, they need me.'

Sarah raised her eyebrows in surprise. John had always shown irrepressible commitment to his job as she had to her own. With little hesitation he would happily volunteer to cover extra hours or someone else's shift. To hear him admit he'd rather not bother was a big change. But then, she'd said as much to Rachel about her own job. Another 'before and after' she thought.

'I think we both need a break,' she said. 'Staying with Papa over Christmas will be perfect.'

'I'll drink to that,' John said as he settled on the sofa. 'Come and have a brew and show me this mysterious letter you know nothing about!'

Sarah walked across to the chair by the patio door and bent to pick up the letter. John glanced at his wife's bottom. The sway of her hips and the tightness of her jeans aroused him. He felt an unexpected and urgent need for Sarah, quickly, before they needed to collect Claire from school.

What the hell is up with me today, he thought. *C'mon get a grip.*

When Sarah turned toward him with the letter in her hand, he spoke again. 'So it was that important you just chucked it on the floor?' he said facetiously.

Sarah sat down and placed the unopened envelope on her lap. She turned and gave John the benefit of one of her impressive glares.

'Ok, ok,' he said. 'I'll be serious. Now shall I open it? Or do you want to?'

'I'll open it.'

Sarah pointed a single finger towards the envelope as she had done earlier. Once again, the object moved a little as her finger approached. She moved her hand away.

'John. Do me a favour will you, to humour me? Can you pick the letter up and put it back down, letting go of it slowly?'

'Why?' he asked, puzzled but intrigued.

'Please. I'll explain in a moment… if I need to.'

'Ok. No problem. Gently you said?' and Sarah nodded.

John reached toward the letter. Time and motion seemed to slow down to Sarah as she watched John's hand getting closer to the envelope. The faint ticking of the clock all but ceased, and her field of vision narrowed so that only the letter and John's approaching hand remained in focus. But as John picked up the letter, the touch brushed her forehead once more and normality resumed.

'Ok. Now you want me to put it down?'

'Yes, but slowly.'

With a frown, he reached back to Sarah's lap, placed the letter and let go.

He moved his hand away from the letter but found it appeared to have stuck to his fingers. Like Sarah, he had to flick it away.

'Ok. So now what?' he asked.

'So you felt it!'

'Felt what? It's sticky, isn't it. Was something spilt on it?'

'Check it yourself. Try to find something sticky.'

John grabbed the envelope again and examined it with care, moving his fingers over the material, trying to locate anything tacky. Finding nothing, he gave up and placed it back on Sarah's lap. Once again, the envelope clung lightly to his fingertips.

'That's strange,' he said almost to himself. 'How is that possible?'

'You tell me,' replied Sarah to his undirected question. 'It happened to me too. I think it's time to open it and see what's inside.'

'Go on then,' said John. 'It's addressed to you after all.'

With a mixture of anticipation and trepidation, Sarah picked up the letter, paused a moment before breaking the unusual seal, and pulled open the flap. She reached inside and slid out a single sheet of folded paper, paper with the crisp and substantial feel of parchment.

Sarah unfolded the sheet and gazed with excitement at the spidery handwriting presented before her.

Gone are the days of your mediocre ways.
   Before you were born, your life had begun.
Inspired you will be, if you find me.
   Everlasting we are, who can see from afar.
Resist those who fight to diminish your sight.
   Rejoice in the gift, for it will come swift.
Variscite is calm and will keep you from harm.
   Your truth you will find, along with your kind.
Angelite will suit you, for it will transmute you.
   Long-time I have known that your name is Moonstone.
Now all is clear, you will suffer no fear.

Sarah handed the letter to John who read it through twice before handing it back.

'Ok,' said John, scratching the stubble on his chin. 'The rhyming is questionable, but it's weird to say the least. Seems like junk mail to me... odd, but junk.'

'Junk mail? Yes it's odd, but junk? John there's a pile of junk mail there,' said Sarah pointing to the discarded envelopes. 'Junk mail normally offers credit cards or mobile phone plans with added this and that. They come in shiny envelopes, with printed addresses, and have return addresses on the back. They're not hand written. It might seem strange, but I don't think it's junk. More likely misdirected. But...' Sarah stopped talking.

'But what?' prompted John.

'But it feels as if it's meant for me because of the touch of it and the tingling sensation I get in my hand when I'm close to it.'

John seemed unconvinced and opened his mouth to speak, but suddenly flicked a quick glance at his watch. 'Shit. Look at the time,' he said, jumping to his feet. 'I'd need to fetch Claire. How about we carry on after dinner?'

Without waiting for an answer, John hurried into the hall, dragged on his coat and left with a quick, 'won't be long', leaving Sarah alone with the letter. The excitement coursing through her as she opened the envelope dissipated, and she felt unsettled again, or maybe mystified? But almost as soon as the feeling came upon her, from out in the garden she heard a sound that brought comfort... the quick babbling melody of a robin.

Six

'Hello sweetie,' Sarah called. 'Had a good day at School?'

Claire skipped along the hallway, into the kitchen and into her mother's arms. 'Yes thank you, Mommy. What's for dinner?' Claire's eyes darted around the kitchen. 'Can I have a biscuit please?'

'Huh! Just like your dad, always thinking of your stomach.'

John called from the hallway. 'You can have mashed worms and cabbage roots!'

'Dad!' Use of the shortened version of John's parental title was always a sign Claire was not amused. Her usual term of endearment was daddy.

'That won't work. It's only Auntie Rachel who can play that game.'

'Oh. Ok angel. That's me put in my place. But yes, you can have a biscuit. Why don't you put the TV on while we get dinner ready?'

Claire gave John a hug as he walked into the kitchen, meaning she still loved him. 'Ok,' she replied and off she went.

Unlike most couples who simply got in each other's way when in a kitchen, John and Sarah weaved an invisible

ound the room, a dance of perfection where one
one item while the other washed another, one
turned on the cooker while the other reached into the fridge or retrieved saucepans. In the midst of this domestic ballet, Claire wandered back into the room, and in perfect harmony fetched cutlery from a drawer, glasses from a shelf and laid out the table before exiting stage left, back into the living room.

It was John who spoke first.

'So did you read it again while I was out? Any ideas what it may mean?'

'Yes I read it again.' Sarah was slicing onions, occasionally dabbing at her eyes. 'Several times in fact. There's more reference to crystals, because of those funny names, but what they are I don't know. Seems a bit of a coincidence after I bought one in town.'

'And you're certain it's for you, not a mistake?'

'Well if I'd received a letter like it a couple of weeks ago, I'd have probably chucked it away, but after what we've both been through and this morning's trip around town, I'm sure there's more to it.'

In fact she was convinced there was more. Unexpected events had happened since she returned home. Whatever the sensations on her forehead and the tingling in her fingers meant, and how they linked to the beryl stone, if indeed they did, she did not yet understand. She mulled over what her life was like before the attack, her life of data and charts, analysis of trends... the logical life, the ordered life. It was in her nature to have a structured existence, to have control, but there was something happening she had no control over, and it intrigued her. If she felt unsettled, wasn't it a simple reaction to the unknown? She wasn't worried... she was excited and felt a need to go along with it, whatever 'it' was.

She had raised the subject of before and after with Rachel... how it made her fidgety... that the life she led was not enough. What was it she'd said? *It's actually exciting because it's something new I want to understand… well more like need to understand. Things are different. I'm not quite sure how much or why, but they are… different.*

That summed it up to perfection, she thought. Her life was different because of a young man who'd lost his way somewhere, a young man on a road to self-destruction. *There* was a challenge… to save someone on such a path.

Saving someone? Now don't get ahead of yourself, she thought. Surprised by such an unexpected idea, Sarah dragged herself back to reality. Then she remembered saying something to Rachel about wanting to help people in a more personal way, to heal their problems.

Heal. Healing? Again the unexpected idea puzzled Sarah, and she paused a moment while washing vegetables. Raising her head, she gazed out of the window. The sun was low now, but with a cloudless sky, the dusk would linger. Faded flowers and long dead stalks shivered in rhythm to a chill breeze as if to ward off the effects of low temperatures, and a few late finches squabbled over a seed feeder hanging from a tree at the bottom of the garden.

Sarah and John's garden was short, typical of modern houses, but it suited their lifestyle at that moment in time. When Claire was still a baby they'd planted a sapling for her, and after nine years the tree was now tall enough to hang bird feeders out of the reach of predatory cats. Hopping around the ground beneath the tree, searching for a few stray seeds was a robin, most likely the one she'd heard earlier. As was usual with robins, it bobbed and hopped, twisting its head from side to side as if listening, but then it pointed its head straight towards Sarah as she stood at the kitchen sink. It stood still for several moments and the sight of the bird transported Sarah back in time to the day she had knelt at her parents' graveside, tending flowers and joining with two robins who sat atop the headstone. The sun had been warm and bright on that spring day when her spirit was lifted from bleak and lost, to joyful and enlightenment. She understood in those few moments that wherever she was, she was never alone, her family was always with her. But recalling those moments, she now believed the family she was thinking of was greater than she first thought, more extensive than her Mom and Dad and John and Claire. Sarah had never had the joy of a relationship with living grandparents and always felt she somehow missed out. This was the reason she was so drawn to John's grandfather.

As these thoughts wandered around her head, she stared out at the robin while it stood and stared back. As she watched, it opened its little beak, warbled a little tune and in a burst of rapid wing beat, left the garden. A smile curled Sarah's lips as she brought her thoughts back indoors, into her kitchen and to the dinner she needed to prepare.

She focussed her attention back to the job in hand while muted chatter from the television drifted through from the living room. Behind her, John was slicing up mushrooms by the cooker, and they both worked in silence, busy with their own thoughts.

A call from Claire broke the peace, as with raised voice she asked a question from the living room. Like children everywhere, she often called from one end of the house to the other expecting an instant reply. However, the question made both Sarah and John spin on their heels in surprise.

'Mommy?' Claire called. 'What does transmute mean, and who's this Beryl in Girvan?'

Seven

Claire sat on the sofa with the letter on her lap. Sarah snuggled on one side of her and John the other. They'd eaten dinner, cleared the table, and set the dishwasher to play its steady soapy rhythm in the kitchen.

When Claire asked her question, a moment of mild chaos followed. Sarah and John almost ran into the living room and fired questions at their daughter so fast, she quickly became overwhelmed and began to cry, thinking she had done something wrong.

John knelt in front of her and took her hands in his own. 'Sorry, sweetheart. Mommy and I didn't mean to upset you. We think it's amazing you worked something out on your own that we were puzzling about. You were always good at puzzles, you clever girl!'

Despite the excitement, Sarah insisted they wait until after dinner before studying the letter again, together this time. 'Listen,' she'd said with her practical head. 'The letter is not going anywhere, whereas if I don't feed you two soon, you'll start complaining. Claire sweetheart, put the letter back on the sofa please until after dinner.'

So now, sat together, Claire showed them what she discovered.

'I saw it lying about so I read it. I didn't know it was secret,' she said.

'It's not a secret, sweetie,' said John. 'It's a strange letter that came for Mommy, and we don't know who sent it. We only just opened it, but it's ok for you to read it.'

John sat with an arm around Claire and she cuddled against him.

'Well!' she continued with emphasis and drama. 'It didn't make any sense, so I thought it might be a secret message. I read a book at school once, about messages and things... like codes. One of them was ac... ac... acrostic. They used lots of codes in the war to hide messages. But the acrostic one was dead simple.'

Claire traced her finger a line at a time down the page, and with a pencil, wrote the first letter of each sentence on a blank sheet of paper. When she finished, she read aloud what she had written.

'G, B, I, E, R, R, V, Y, A, L, N. That doesn't spell anything,' she said. 'So I looked at every other letter and found it spells different words. So, the first one is a G, the third one is I. The fifth one is R. The seventh is V. The ninth is an A and the eleventh one is N. GIRVAN. I did the same with the other letters and it spells the name BERYL.'

Sarah and John glanced at each other and smiled. John shook his head in amazement.

'Spooky or what? The day you decide to buy a beryl stone, you get a random letter that has the name beryl coded into it. I assume then a Beryl sent it.' He stopped, and after taking a deep breath, stood up and walked to the patio doors. 'Hang on. What am I saying? Sorry but I can't get my head around this. Surely it's just random nonsense. I mean... I'm a policeman right? I protect people. I arrest people. I work in one of the busiest cities in the country with noise and crime and people living busy lives. You have a job working for the council moving numbers around for the planning and finance departments. It's all very materialistic and ordinary. Just everyday stuff. Important but normal. And suddenly we're given a puzzle to solve. We have tingling fingers and moving envelopes and semiprecious stones. It's hard to swallow... surreal! Why? Why and what for?'

'Except I didn't decide to buy a beryl stone,' replied Sarah. 'Something compelled me, like I didn't have a choice.'

'Ok... compelled, if you believe that sort of thing. But what are we supposed to do with something like this? We haven't paid much attention to the mail over the last couple of weeks, so when the letter actually arrived God knows. It may have been here for a week, but certainly no more than ten days. We can hazard a guess it's from someone called Beryl. We can also assume whoever Beryl is, she's living in Girvan.'

Sarah responded with her own thoughts. 'Ok... so if you reckon it's been lying here for over a week, that means it must have been posted while I was in hospital.' Sarah gazed outside into the garden, an idea forming in her mind, an idea, she felt sure, would send John further into disbelief. 'John, there's something I didn't tell you. Something I remember from while I was asleep... in hospital.'

'Oh God!' John frowned in consternation.

'Now don't blow a fuse. Y'know I could hear you and Claire talking to me... sometimes.'

'Yes.'

'Well I had a feeling there was someone else.'

'Someone else? Do you know who?'

'No. No idea. But they appeared as a brilliant white shape, with a white aura around them. And they spoke to me.'

John was surprisingly calm when he said, 'What did they say?'

'"Sarah my child. You are not alone",' Sarah quoted.

John walked back to the sofa and sat again. 'Are you sure? Any idea what they meant?'

'Other than face value, no, but... God this will sound

crazy.'

'Well we have crazy already so a little more won't hurt. Go on.'

'Ok. I hear someone tell me I'm not alone and afterwards a letter arrives. Did the person I dreamt of send me the letter?'

John leaned back against the sofa. 'Yes,' he said. 'It sounds crazy.'

They fell silent for a while but then Sarah spoke again. 'Listen... in a way this makes *some* sense since you're Scottish, born and bred in Ayr, which is only fifteen miles from Girvan. So because it's local to you there is a connection... but to you not me. I'd never been near the place until I met you, so why was the letter addressed to me and not you. Do you know if there is anyone named Beryl in your family? It's an old name... maybe an old aunt?'

'Not that I ever heard of. We could ask Papa. My dad was an only child, so I have no direct aunts and uncles on his side. My mom had a sister who was much older, but they weren't close and never figured in our lives much. I'm sure Papa had a sister, but I don't think her name was Beryl, though that doesn't explain why the letter came to you.'

'No it doesn't.'

Claire was still fingering the letter when she asked, 'What's the beryl stone? Is it similar to my rose quartz nanny gave me?'

'Yes it's similar, sweetie. Here.' Sarah reached into her pocket and pulled out the stone, handing it to Claire. 'It's a special type of rock, I suppose,' she explained. 'A big crystal is made up of tiny pieces stuck together in very ordered ways. Um... the tiny pieces line up into special shapes with lots of edges or faces to them, like your rose quartz. If the crystal is hard, you can polish it to make a stone similar to the beryl you're holding. Softer ones can break so are best left as they are. At least that's what nanny used to tell me.'

Sarah paused, recalling Claire's comment. 'Hang on a minute,' she said with a frown. 'Rose quartz nanny gave you? Why do you say that? You were still a baby when nanny passed on, and I'm sure she didn't give you any crystals. You'd have been too young.'

'No, nanny promised it to me while you were in hospital,' Claire said as if it were obvious.

Sarah stared wide eyed at her daughter. The tiny hairs on the back of her neck prickled, and she shuddered as if a cold breeze had played across her. She swallowed hard.

'Sweetheart?' she whispered to Claire. 'What do you mean when you say nanny gave you the crystal?'

Claire glanced up at Sarah with raised eyebrows and an open gaze that, for a moment, made Sarah feel as if her mother had returned. Sarah took her lower lip between her teeth to stop the gasp she feared might escape.

'She woke me in the middle of the night while I was at Auntie Rachel's and said I could have it as soon as you were home.'

Sarah knew the brink was rapidly approaching and struggled hard not to fall over it. Claire continued.

'The day we fetched you from hospital and got you home, I found it on the window ledge. Nanny said I could have it, so I thought you wouldn't mind. She's named after it, you know.'

Sarah was nodding her head now as if in agreement and she tried a smile on for her daughter. But as she smiled, her lips trembled, and she lost the fight and stumbled over the edge. Tears leaked from her eyes in sudden streams, and the gasp that escaped her lips in unexpected grief came as a shock. She reached for Claire and hugged her with a love so all-consuming, it felt as if she could not contain it, as if her chest may burst.

'Sarah!' John was on his knees with a comforting hand on his wife's shoulders. 'It's all right, princess. It's ok.'

He lovingly stroked the back of her neck but bewilderment sharpened his own eyes.

'Mommy?' said Claire, who sat with her arms around Sarah, her head resting against her mom's chest. 'It's ok.

Nanny's with you. Look!'

With tears on her cheeks, and the hair still prickling on her neck, Sarah slid off the sofa and onto the floor. John sat beside her.

Peering out of the patio doors, they followed the line of Claire's pointing finger. At the bottom of the garden, barely visible in the growing darkness and sitting motionless on top of a wooden garden chair, was a robin. With its head turned in their direction, it sat gazing back at the house. While John stayed immobile, an arm wrapped around Sarah's waist, Claire stood behind, her hands resting on her parents shoulders. As they gazed mesmerised at the bird, they saw its beak open and heard the muted call it made. As if in response, another robin flew in and settled next to the first, turning itself in their direction.

For many minutes they were all still, both avian and human, and simply stared at each other.

Eight

A few hours later, Sarah walked into the living room and drew the curtains across the patio doors, shutting out the chill darkness of the mid-December evening. At this time of the year she loved pulling up the symbolic drawbridge, closing the virtual shutters, and cocooning herself and her family inside their castle. Sarah's father had passed on the ritual, whose first task after returning home on winter evenings was to secure his family against the world.

John had carried a sleepy Claire up to bed and sat a while reading a story. Claire preferred her mother's company at bedtime but realising the letter had distracted her mother, her innate understanding kicked in and she asked John to take her up instead. She liked the voices John used when reading to her, amused by his attempts to produce a variety of tones while forgetting which voice belonged to whom. She also knew John would find it hard to resist when she asked… 'just one more story, Daddy!'

Sarah turned the lights low and picked up the letter again before settling into a chair, drawing her legs up underneath her.

With reverence, she lifted the note and read aloud. 'Beryl in Girvan. Who are you and what have you got to do with me?'

After re-reading the whole note, and moved by a sudden need for clarity, she reached over to the pile of discarded junk mail, grabbed a large white envelope and a pen and rewrote the verse, grouping each line starting with the leading letters Claire had discovered. After five minutes of writing, she read her adjusted note.

Gone are the days of your mediocre ways.
Inspired you will be, if you find me.
Rejoice in the gift, for it will come swift.
Variscite is calm, and will keep you from harm.
Angelite will suit you, for it will transmute you.
Now all is clear, you will suffer no fear.

Before you were born, your life had begun.
Everlasting we are, who can see from afar.
Resist those who fight to diminish your sight.
Your truth you will find, along with your kind.
Long-time I have known that your name is Moonstone.

Sarah spoke aloud to Mags who lay nearby… front legs crossed and big cow eyes keeping a close watch. '"Gone are the days of your mediocre ways". Well that doesn't sound very encouraging. Is that about me? Has my life been dull? I don't think so! Well I hope not! "Inspired you will be, if you find me"? I suppose it must mean whoever wrote this has something to tell me? But if so, what? "Rejoice in the gift, for it will come swift". Well apart from being bad English, does it mean someone has something to give me?'

A flutter across her brow halted Sarah's pondering of the spidery words crafted in front of her, and her gaze wandered off into the distance. The hand lay on her forehead once more, the comforting hand which had become a close friend. Driven by curiosity, she closed her eyes and lifted a hand to the front of her head. As Sarah moved her fingers closer, the mild pressure that lay there shifted, as if the hand were caressing her, stroking her skin with tenderness. Intrigued, she moved her hand around, even upwards towards the top of her head and felt the same sensation following it, wafting around her, as if a gentle breeze brushed her hair.

A deep inner peace overwhelmed her, and she drew a long breath, taking a few seconds to exhale before lowering her hand. Opening her eyes, she focussed once more upon the words until a movement caught her eye, and she spotted John leaning against the doorframe.

'Yes?'

'Nothing. Wondering how long you've been practising archaic rituals.'

'What do you mean? How long have you been there?'

'About five minutes. Claire's fast asleep. What were you doing?'

Sarah frowned. 'Five minutes? It wasn't that long.'

'It was, or close enough. You were silent, so I stood and watched you. I wondered if you were asleep but I saw you lift your hand up to your head and hold it there for ages.'

With surprise, Sarah furrowed her brow as she was certain she had closed her eyes for only a few seconds. Unsure of what to say, she opened her mouth to speak, but instead sighed as if reaching a decision. 'John, I need to tell you something else, but I don't want you to worry. Come and sit next to me please.'

John asked if Sarah wanted a drink.

'Yes please,' she replied and John wandered back into the kitchen returning a few moments later with two glasses and a bottle of wine.

'What is it?' he questioned. 'Are you feeling ok?'

'Yes I'm fine. In fact, I feel better than I have for ages. Not that I've been feeling bad or anything. And…' with a smile, Sarah recalled the previous evening's recreation with her husband on the sofa. 'After last night I feel even better. But since I came home from hospital I've been having odd sensations on my forehead and I've seen strange colours around people.'

John's consternation was plain to see. 'Sweetheart, it's been almost a week. Why haven't you said anything?' He stood and walked across the room and picked up his phone. 'I need to call Peter and ask his advice.'

'John. Stop it. Come and sit down. You've no need to call anybody. I'm fine. Come and sit and let me finish. I need you to stay calm and pay attention.'

Though unconvinced, John did as Sarah asked. 'Ok,' he said. 'Convince me I have nothing to worry about.'

Sarah fixed him with a piercing gaze, a gaze that spoke volumes.

'Listen,' John continued. 'You can't expect me *not* to worry can you? What else has been happening?'

Sarah leaned over to John and kissed him on the lips while moving her hand along his thigh as she spoke. 'I love the way you care about me but there is nothing to worry about. Let me work through this and maybe if you stay calm I'll let you make love to me again.'

'Y'know that's blackmail.'

'No… it's seduction, but listen and pay attention. It started after you and Claire brought me home. Remember the meal Rachel prepared? Do you remember I walked around the table and gave each of you a hug? Well, when I hugged Steve and Rachel I thought I heard voices, whispering voices.'

John fidgeted and opened his mouth to speak but Sarah placed a finger to his lips. She continued.

'It was unsettling because I wondered if I was still in a coma. But the voices were clear, and the words weren't very nice. There were different voices for each of them… Steve and Rachel.'

'What did they say?'

'You'll think I've gone mad, but the voice I heard when I hugged Rachel said "Where are you hiding you little tart. Get out here now", and the one when I hugged Steve said

"You ain't got the guts you fat little faggot." Puzzling or what?'

Sarah sat back a little embarrassed and worried. What would John say? After all, it *was* unusual and she couldn't blame John for his reaction.

'Puzzling? What an understatement. Are you sure about the words? I mean, the sentence was clear rather than whispered or garbled?' Sarah nodded. 'Anything else? Any more voices?'

'No, but the colours are intriguing. They started the night I got home too.'

'Seeing colours? What sort of colours? I mean we all see colours. What are they like?'

'More like a faint glow. Like a coloured halo around people. The first time was in bed that night. I saw a purple glow around your head. It was puzzling, but calming. It was almost comforting… well not almost, it *was* comforting. Since then I've seen it a few times when the lights are dim, and I saw it around Rachel today except the halo was orange… most of the time.'

'Sarah sweetheart,' said John, leaning forward and taking her hand. 'Headaches and visual hallucinations and you expect me to stay calm?'

Sarah regarded John with the same wide-eyed, honest and open expression he had seen a million times. The same expression she'd worn on the day they met years ago. An expression that convinced him she was in firm control and everything was going to be ok.

'Yes,' she said. 'After what I've been through, yes I expect you to stay calm. And anyway it isn't a headache. Far from it. It's such a light sensation I could miss it if I was busy or concentrating on something else.' Sarah paused for a moment, gazing at the letter on her lap, mulling over an idea. When she spoke again, her words were as much an argument for herself than for John, an attempt to rationalise. 'Let's think about it a minute. One of the other reasons I'm not worried is because of the letter. It's obvious in a strange way but let's be logical. I get some strange feelings and see strange things and I get a strange letter in the post. It's all tied together. Something unusual is happening, yes, but I'm not worried about it. If I was only getting headaches and seeing things, I'd ask Peter's advice but it seems too much of a coincidence that an odd letter arrived in the post. And what about the beryl stone? I didn't go to town to buy it. Something led me to it and all the time there's a letter from a Beryl lying on our dining table. It's *not* just me. It's external as well, or seems that way. I need...*we* need to understand what the letter means... find out who Beryl is. I like a challenge,' and she smiled.

'Sarah, what do I do as a copper? Rhetorical question. Like I was saying earlier, I protect. I serve. I help. I try to be open-minded with people. Most of my work is straightforward. I deal with people in the real world with day-to-day problems, whether crime related or tragic or joyous. None of it ever gets close to the stuff you're talking about here. What are we getting into? A mystery thriller? Lost treasure? The Holy Grail? Is da Vinci gonna come knocking at the door?'

Sarah laughed. 'You always were so dramatic, but I think you're taking it too seriously.'

'Seriously?' John exclaimed with no trace of humour. 'Of course I'm taking it seriously. You're telling me you're having visions and hearing voices... what else do you expect.'

John stood up, walked across the room and put his mobile phone back on the table. He took a deep breath and turned back to Sarah with a more relaxed expression on his face, as if he realised that whatever argument he tried to use, Sarah had a counterargument.

'But...' he continued with a frown. 'Linked with the letter and thinking about what I said to you earlier about the dream I had of Graham and Rose... maybe there *is* something in it.'

'John, it's only a puzzle we have to work through.

There's nothing to worry about. Yes, it's unusual. Yes, it's puzzling, but it's also challenging. I think it's exciting. Yes, we both live in the real world with real problems and real tragedy but unexpected things do sometimes happen. What we need is a plan but I can't do it on my own. I want to do it with you because… because you're a part of me, a part of my life and I think you're involved somehow.'

Sarah held her hands out to John, and he walked over to take them. He sat again, and for a moment they gazed at each other and Sarah nestled into John and he folded her up in a warm embrace. The letter lay on her lap and in a moment of clarity, she spoke a line from the note.

'"Resist those who fight to diminish your sight".'

'What?' John asked, kissing the top of her head.

'"Resist those who fight to diminish your sight". The line from the letter. I think it means people will try to dismiss the idea something special is happening. Like now, when you were dismissing the mystery, trying to make it ordinary, to rationalise it with normal things, except I know you're resisting it because you're only worried about me. But imagine if I told the girls at work. Some would think I'm mad, some won't care, some will say it's a load of rubbish… colours and hearing things? What the line means is I have to resist disbelief and negativity.'

'Wow!' said John. 'Is that what you call an epiphany?'

Sarah sat upright again so she could study her husband. 'Maybe. I'm only guessing. I don't really know what I'm talking about,' she replied, as if not convinced. 'Seemed appropriate.'

John leaned forward and kissed Sarah again.

'Sarah, it *would* be dead easy for me to say it's a load of rubbish… some crank or misdirected mail. Dead easy to be one of those who dismiss it, but after what Claire said earlier about Rose, and what we saw out in the garden, I'm willing to go with the flow. Let's see where this goes. What harm can it do? Suspicion and cynicism and dismissing anything out of the ordinary *is* too common. It's not like the letter is asking for anything is it, like a credit card number or investing a load of cash? Most scams are about money. And I think you're right. It's obvious something unusual is going, but I want you to promise not to keep any secrets from me again? If anything odd happens, tell me. Ok? And yes, I *am* involved because I'm your husband.' John paused a moment before continuing. 'Let's have another read.'

Sarah smiled at her husband, turned, and with care placed the letter onto a small table next to the sofa. She stood up, turned back to John and sat again, straddling his lap, lifting her knees up alongside his thighs. She placed her hands either side of his face, leaned in and kissed John with passion... teasing him with her tongue. After long moments, during which she sensed the heat of John's mounting interest, she broke the kiss and breathed into his ear.

'If that was your attempt to get inside my knickers it worked. Claire's asleep you said?'

'Yes I did... fast asleep.'

'Oh good.'

Nine

Sarah crept back downstairs after taking a pile of discarded clothes up to the linen basket, using the bathroom and putting on her dressing gown. She carried John's over her arm.

John was waiting naked on the sofa and had topped up their glasses. Sarah dropped his dressing gown onto his lap as she sat next to him.

'You'd best keep warm for later. I haven't finished yet, and we've got a lot of catching up to do.'

'God, you're so demanding, but if you insist,' John stood up and pulled on the dressing gown but not before Sarah could see he was already getting interested.

'For heaven's sake, I said later! What's happened to you?' she laughed. 'Look, I can't possibly think of sex again until we've come up with some sort of plan.'

John raised his eyes to the ceiling. 'You're so difficult to impress, y'know, but once an analyst, always an analyst. So what's your plan?'

'You just impressed me and you can impress me again later. But be serious, will you. Where's my wine?'

Sarah took a glass from John and reached for the letter. As her fingers approached the parchment, she was unsure whether the tingling sensation in her fingertips was due to proximity to the letter, or the after effects of their love making. She pondered for a moment their mutual re-heightened appetite for sex. It was as if there was a renewed energy between them, an intensified lust as when they first met. Weird. Fantastic but weird.

'Right,' said John. 'All I know, assuming Claire's guess was right, is that someone named Beryl who lives in Girvan has sent you a riddle, if that's the right word. You seem to think she's also warning you to be true to your beliefs by resisting anyone who dismisses or belittles your... what? What is it you're supposed to have that others will dismiss? She mentioned something about a gift. What gift is this?'

'Well the obvious thing are the colours? I've no idea what they mean but perhaps it's part of something else. But hang on a minute. I said we needed to have a plan before bedtime. Let's take a step back. We should find this Beryl first. She must have all the answers because she wrote the letter.'

'Ok. But where the hell do you start? Girvan's not a huge place but big enough to make searching like trying to find the proverbial needle.'

Sarah stared at the letter deep in thought. The words were becoming locked in her memory so she had no need to re-read them.

'Well, Beryl's an old-fashioned name. I don't know when it would have been popular but at least sixty years ago, I suppose... or longer. She could be older.'

'Ok, so now we're searching for an *old* needle in a haystack,' replied John, with only a hint of humour.

'You're not helping much, y'know,' Sarah said.

'Look, I know you want to figure this out, but I'm no detective. A copper maybe, but not in detection. What are we going to do? House to house? Put an ad in the paper? Think about it. Where would you start? Girvan has a population of a few thousand and I'm sure there will be a significant number of pensioners. Young people often move away for work. So, we're trying to find an elderly lady, assuming your guess is correct, amongst several thousand with no notion of street name or… well anything.'

'I hope you don't give up this easily at work. It's not going to be simple, I agree, but think about what we *do* know, instead of what we don't. We're searching for an elderly lady called Beryl. We can make a guess she's at least seventy and lives in Girvan. There won't be many people named Beryl in Girvan. Yes we have to start somewhere but let's not give up.'

'I'm not giving up, just being realistic.'

Sarah said no more and they both sat in silence. John glanced at his wife. It occurred to him that over recent months they had both been in danger of becoming stuck in a pattern of routine, settling into a life that could become monotonous if they weren't careful. Nothing out of the ordinary happened to them and though they were content, he wondered if contentment was something they should aim for in their later years, not as an early thirties couple. Something out of the ordinary *had* landed on their doormat, and it was worth taking a risk. He sighed and spoke again.

'Y'know, thinking about it, you can take this thing two ways I suppose. You can either think what is this nonsense all about, it's a joke of some sort… or it's meant for someone else or some crackpot has gone off the rails. Or… as we're doing nothing special at the moment, we can grab it and find out what it's all about, who this Beryl is. If it turns out to be a mistake, we've at least done something.' John reached over and squeezed Sarah's hand. 'Sorry if I sounded negative before. Just being a prat. What should we do next?'

'Not sure yet,' Sarah replied. 'The letter implies my life's been mediocre and this Beryl has news that will change things, inspire me. How do you inspire someone in the twenty-first century? She also says I have a gift. But what?'

John yawned and leaned back on the sofa. For a few moments they both fell quiet again.

'Don't know about you but I'm knackered,' John said

after a while. 'I'm not really in puzzle solving mode.'

Sarah smiled and slid a hand underneath his dressing gown, brushing her fingertips across his thighs, making him jump.

'Are you in lovemaking mode instead? How would you like to get on the floor and open my dressing gown, see what's under it?'

'I thought you said later. See, it's not just me.'

Forgetting how tired he was, John slid off the sofa and knelt in front of his wife. He teased apart the belt fastened around her waist, but before he folded the fleecy material of her gown aside, a voice from the hallway made him jump and he shot up, tightening his own belt.

'Mommy,' said a sleepy Claire. 'Can I have a drink please?'

'I'll get it,' said John, wandering into the kitchen, taking a few moments to let his obvious arousal subside. *Christ!* He thought. *What the hell is happening to me? Never felt so damned horny.* He grabbed a clean glass and ran the water for a few moments. When he felt calmer, and less likely to attract embarrassing questions, he walked back into the living room and found Claire sat on the sofa resting her head on Sarah's shoulder. Sarah was holding the letter.

'Mommy? What are you going to do? Are you going to Girvan at Christmas when we visit Papa?'

'Yes, darling, I think so.'

'Are you going to visit the old people's homes?' asked Claire through a huge yawn.

'Old people's homes?' asked John. 'What do you mean, sweetie?'

'Well… the handwriting's all scribbly like Papa's. Like an old person's. I thought she might live in a home.'

John smiled and shook his head as if to say 'Would you believe it!' Sarah smiled too and planted a kiss on her daughters head.

'Sweetie? How long has it been since I said how clever you are? Yes, we'll check out the old people's homes. Well

done, princess! Now I think it's time for a drink and bed.'
'Ok, Mommy,' and Claire yawned again.

Ten

Twenty-four hours later, relaxing in Sarah and John's kitchen, Rachel leaned back in her chair and sighed. It was approaching nine o'clock and Claire was in bed. John topped up Sarah and Rachel's wine glasses.

'That was delicious,' Rachel said. 'As always.'

'Well it's a pleasure to return the favour after you prepared Sarah's homecoming meal,' said John. 'Why don't you two go through to the living room while I tidy away in here?'

'Ok, sweetheart,' replied Sarah.

'Can I help?' asked Rachel, and John replied with a shake of his head. 'No, you can take it easy. Have a girlie chat with my wife.'

The two friends pushed back their chairs and headed off towards the lounge. Rachel planted a warm kiss on John's cheek as she left the room but Sarah's kiss lingered a while longer.

'Break it up you two,' called back Rachel with a laugh.

Sarah giggled and joined Rachel, pushing the living room door shut behind her. Rachel collapsed into an armchair.

'That wine has gone straight to my head.'

'Well we are on our second bottle,' said Sarah with a

smile. Rachel continued. 'Y'know, after ten years of marriage, most couples take each other for granted. Not you two though. I can almost see the electricity jumping between you. What's happened? I swear if I wasn't here you'd be at it. In fact, I'm sure as soon as I'm out the door you will be. Are you on something?'

Sarah giggled again, a teenage giggle. She whispered to her friend. 'God knows, but it's like we're possessed. John's so horny all the time… we both are. It's like it was when we first met.'

Rachel smiled, but the smile didn't reach her eyes. 'Are you trying to get pregnant again?' she asked.

On hearing Rachel's question, Sarah remembered the words she'd spoken aloud to her own reflection during the previous morning after bathing. *Yes, it's time to have another child,* she'd said, and puzzled over it afterwards.

'Um… well we've not talked about it,' Sarah replied with a frown. 'I know I was in hospital for only a week but over the last couple of days we've re-discovered each other. I said yesterday it's almost like something has given us more energy. I'm not complaining of course.'

Rachel changed the subject. 'So what about this letter? You mentioned it before dinner.'

'Yes. Here… have a read,' and she handed the note and the rearranged version to Rachel.

'Well I recognise some of the crystal names,' Rachel said, 'and moonstone is your birth stone isn't it? Are you taking this seriously?'

Sarah spoke with surprise. 'My birth stone?'

'You mean you don't know? I thought most women knew their birthstones, to match jewellery and clothing. Oh I forgot. You never wore much bling did you?' Rachel smiled again.

'No, never had much interest in it apart from my wedding ring and a necklace of my mom's, and yes… I am taking it seriously, well not too much… but I am intrigued by it. But what do you know about crystals?'

'Nothing. I only recognise the names because… because a relative of mine used to be interested.' She paused a moment and Sarah sensed a change in Rachel's mood as if she remembered something sad.

'So, what will you do with it? Seems… well… not sure what it seems. A mistake? Addressed to the wrong person, though I can't imagine it being of much use to anyone without knowing who sent it.'

Sarah told Rachel of their plans, the idea Claire suggested. 'I'll dig around when we're up in Scotland over Christmas. I might end up nowhere but I have to try.'

After settling onto a chair, Rachel yawned and had become sleepy. The soft glow of table lamps lit the room and Sarah had lit a few candles on the hearth.

Rachel read from the letter. '"Variscite is calm and will keep you from harm". "Angelite will suit you for it will transmute you". Have you done any research, on the Internet?'

'Not yet, though I told John I might Google them. Shall we take a look now?'

'Ok,' said Rachel with a yawn, 'but if we don't do it now, I'll be asleep. Where's your laptop?'

'Hold on while I fetch it.'

Sarah left the room but was back within a minute and Rachel moved over to the sofa and drew close while Sarah fired up the machine. A few moments later and after entering the word 'variscite', a page full of suggestions appeared.

'Huh,' muttered Sarah, 'as usual there's a million results. We want something about crystal meanings so this one seems encouraging.' Sarah clicked on the most promising link and after a few minutes of reading, summarised. 'Well it's rare by the looks of it, so do you fancy a trip to Nevada or Australia to dig one of our own up?'

'Ha!' exclaimed Rachel. 'Sounds great. When shall we go?'

Sarah continued. 'Seems like it's supposed to promote

serenity and courage, oh and helps break old habits. Hmmm. Courage. So does that mean it will give me the courage to keep me from harm as the letter suggests?'

Sarah was talking as much to herself as to Rachel. Without waiting for comment, she typed 'angelite' into the Google search. Once again after a short delay, a huge list of entries appeared.

'Ok. So this one talks about heightened awareness, promotes understanding but also protects.'

She paused and glanced at Rachel. An orange aura once again appeared around Rachel's head and shoulders, a livelier colour than the drab and faded red she'd seen previously. *Heightened awareness? Interesting, but why?*

Aware of Sarah's gaze Rachel asked, 'What?'

'Sorry?' asked Sarah.

'You were staring.'

'Sorry. I saw the halo surrounding you again.'

'I hate it when you mention that. It scares me. It can't be normal and I'm worried about you.'

'Angelite. Heightened awareness?' Sarah wondered, ignoring Rachel's comment. 'Is that what the letter refers to? I never used to see colours.'

'No,' answered Rachel. 'And it started after a blow to the head which is why I'm worried. But what do you mean when you say you see colours? I still don't quite grasp the idea. Am I glowing or something?'

'Well no, it's different from seeing, y'know, the way you do with your eyes. I can *see* you and everything else around you as normal, like you see me. But the halo seems more as if I sense it, like you can sense someone behind you without seeing them.'

'Isn't that just body heat?' asked Rachel.

'Only if they're very close. But listen...' Sarah tried to allay Rachel's fears. 'I know there's nothing wrong with me because all of this started and coincided with me getting an unusual letter telling me about... something. Something different. Sorry, not making any sense again am I? But don't you understand… it's all happening at the same time which means it's all connected.' Sarah reached over and grabbed Rachel's hand. 'There's nothing wrong with me Rachel. But, if it makes you any happier, I can talk to Peter. I'll say hello for you if you like.'

Rachel yawned again. 'If you want to,' she said, staring into the candle flames. 'Oh my God, if I yawn any more my heads going to fall off. I'd better go.'

John pushed open the door and strolled in. 'Spare bed's made up,' he said.

Rachel turned to John. 'What for?'

'For you. Because you're staying the night,' he replied.

'Why? Don't be silly. I'll get off home.'

'No you won't. I don't want to have to arrest my wife's best friend for drunk driving. Stay. We both want you to and you and Sarah can catch up. I'm going to watch something on the TV in the kitchen.'

'Sounds like a plan,' said Sarah with a smile. 'C'mon I'll top up your glass. You can borrow some PJ's.'

Rachel opened her mouth as if to protest but clamped it shut again. Sarah sensed another change in her friend and for a few moments Rachel said nothing.

'It's very kind of you both. I'd love to if it's not much trouble.'

'It's no trouble at all,' answered John. 'I'll see you both later,' and he left the room, closing the door behind him.

They sat in silence for a while though Sarah gazed with concern at Rachel. Something was troubling her friend, that much was obvious, but she was cautious of invading Rachel's privacy. On the surface, Rachel appeared carefree, though with inbuilt intuition Sarah had always guessed there was a story underneath, a story Rachel kept well hidden. As Sarah studied her friend, the halo appeared again, but once more it gave an impression of lifeless energy, a dreary red colour. Sarah wondered in a moment of clarity if the halos became visible in times of distress or illness, unhappiness, any negativity… and conversely if they appeared in times of joy. In which case, she thought, they had always been there, but now her heightened awareness detected them. Was it possible she detected an underlying stress coming from Rachel... but why now? What had happened that could have increased her sensitivity, her perception?

A light touch feathered Sarah's forehead as if in response to her musings.

'Rachel honey? Can I ask if everything's all right? You seem a little pre-occupied, or distant.'

'What? Oh yes, I'm ok,' she replied with little conviction. 'Tired, I suppose, and these short days are a pain... not enough daylight.'

Sarah thought she was making excuses.

'It's nice of John to set up a bed for me. You're so lucky to have a man like him.'

'Luck? Perhaps it is, perhaps it isn't. Perhaps it's fate if you believe in that sort of thing. I mean, if you believed in fate, you could argue you and Peter were meant to meet when I was in hospital. But you could go even deeper. Perhaps I was attacked so you *could* meet Peter. Or maybe, it all happened so something strange would happen to me, and I would develop a gift like it suggests in the letter.'

'I think you're the one who's had too much to drink,' Rachel yawned.

Sarah laughed. 'Well I'm being partly serious. Isn't it strange that a week after I come out of hospital a letter arrives telling me stuff and at the same time I start seeing things?'

'Oh my God. You're going all hippy and cosmic on me.'

'I'll tell you something... I don't need cosmic powers to know something's troubling you and it's got nothing to do with lack of daylight. C'mon Rachel, talk to me.'

Staring at the fireplace Rachel fell silent again. The murmur of voices filtered through from the TV where John relaxed in the kitchen.

'Sarah,' Rachel said, and from under half-closed eyes she gazed at the tiny candle flames as they danced and flickered.

'Do you know what you want out of life… where you'll be in ten years?'

'That's an odd question.'

'Well you seem to have everything you want: a lovely house, a beautiful daughter and a husband who dotes on you. Difficult to imagine you being unsettled like you told me yesterday. I envy the contentment. I seem to flit from one empty situation to another with no end in sight.' Rachel yawned and lifted her feet up and tucked them underneath her, settling against the end of the sofa. 'But to answer your earlier question, I'm fine. I'm ok. A bit down. Christmas is coming, and it's always been a struggle, even when I was little. I never had much Christmas spirit. But what do you reckon… what plans do you have for the future?'

'Does anyone plan too far ahead these days? I've never been ambitious. Just want to be happy and settled, doing something useful, though, I don't want to idle away my time. What about you?'

'Me?'

'Yeah. Where do you want to be?'

'Can't see past the end of next week is my problem. I wouldn't say I'm content. I think I'd like to have children of my own one day but it seems so remote an idea I can't imagine it ever happening.'

'You need a good man and a strong relationship.'

'There's the problem. What is it they say? The best men are either married or gay? I never seem to pick the right guy.'

'Have you checked the mirror recently?'

'Odd question. What do you mean?'

'Rachel. If you look at yourself in the mirror, you'll see what I see. If you feel the person inside, you'll find a beautiful woman. You're so pretty it's unfair. You have a lovely figure which is why young men flock around you. But you are also such a caring and gentle person it's hard to understand why any man wouldn't fall for you. And I'm sure one already has. I'm not sure why you pick young men but they're only after one thing. Yes, they are fit and energetic but they're too young to be settling down. You need someone older and more level-headed *and* more caring. Carrying on the way you are… it's a recipe for a lonely life.'

'You trying to matchmake again?' Rachel smiled at Sarah but still the smile did not touch her eyes. Sarah felt uneasy as if Rachel's melancholy were projecting on her own mood.

'Listen, let's focus on the letter,' Rachel said. 'I know you're trying to help but let's move on. I can't do this now,' and at that Rachel picked up the note and re-read it. 'What are we doing with this? Trying to solve a riddle? What does it mean by "before you were born your life had begun"? How is that possible? And, "everlasting we are who can see from afar". How are you going to make sense of it?'

Sarah was silent for a few moments.

'Well, in one sense your life *does* begin before you're born. I suppose it begins at the point of conception though it may not be an independent life. I think it refers to something else though. But everlasting we are… does it mean having a long life? And…' Sarah said with sudden enlightenment, 'it appears I *can* see from afar… these colours I sense.' Sarah was fishing for ideas.

Rachel yawned again and Sarah took the letter and put it to one side.

'You need sleep. I forgot you've been at work today. Let's leave it for now? The plan is to go searching at Christmas. To find the answers I need to find the author.'

The two friends snuggled together while they finished the wine. Rachel's head dropped back against the sofa and after a few minutes Sarah disturbed her friends slumber and led her by the hand upstairs to the spare room.

'God, I'm so tired,' whispered Rachel. 'Thanks for letting me stay. I promise I'll be quiet in the morning.'

'No need to worry. Claire's an early bird as I'm sure you know.'

Sarah kissed Rachel and gave her friend a warm embrace.

'If you need anything just ask. Sleep well.'

'Night night.'

Sarah wandered back downstairs to the kitchen and found John filling the kettle.

'Fancy a cuppa?' he asked.

'Yes please. Will you come and sit with me for a minute? I've sent Rachel to bed. She's worn out and I'm worried about her.'

'Worried?'

'Yes. Are you coming through to the living room?'

'Yes. Won't be a minute.'

Five minutes later, John was sitting on the sofa and Sarah sat relaxed on the floor with one arm resting on his knees.

'She's not right. Something's troubling her.'

John was nodding.

'Y'know the colours I told you about… the halos. Well I've sensed one around Rachel and it's unsettling. It's a dreary colour. Unhappy. I suppose it sounds odd, but it's the way it makes me feel when I see it.' Rachel's mood *had* infected Sarah. 'John, why has this happened… to me I mean? It's put me on edge.'

'Sorry sweetheart, I don't know why it's happened and I'm still worried about these visions, but it's obvious why Rachel is unsettled.'

'Why?' Sarah shot a glance at her husband who was shaking his head and smiling.

'Sweetheart. Who just spent a week in a coma? Who's best friend sat by their side almost as often as I did and who's best friend took care of our daughter? It's not surprising Rachel's unsettled. She was as worried as I was and used a lot of energy looking out for Claire and me. She was scared.'

'Yes I expect you're right. But it seems more. I'm unsure how or why. Call it intuition. I think she's troubled about something else. She's not as bright and cheerful as she used to be.'

They fell silent for a moment.

'How about this for an idea?' said John. 'It's gone past ten, why don't you come to bed and try to forget all about it. Perhaps I can think of something to help.'

'Oh yeah, and what might that be? If I know you, by the time I get into bed you'll be dozing and fit for nothing.'

'I may surprise you.'

Sarah emptied her teacup. 'Ok, but I bet you I'm right.'

John gave Mags five minutes in the garden before locking up the house. Sarah went upstairs to check on Claire who she found fast asleep. With care she opened the door to the spare bedroom. Rachel's breathing was slow and deep and Sarah stood watching her for a moment, puzzling once more over her friend's change of mood. In the darkness she could make out the faint glow surrounding Rachel, a dirty red colour. Even in slumber, something hidden disturbed Rachel. Sarah shook her head and crept out of the room, pulling the door closed behind.

Despite John's bravado, and by the time they'd finished in the bathroom and slid between the sheets, they gave in to the irresistible call of sleep and settled into a close embrace, drifting away into a peaceful forgetfulness.

It was past two o'clock when Sarah opened her eyes. The house was still and quiet. John had rolled away from her and was lying on his side. With care, she lifted the quilt, climbed out of bed and made her way to the bathroom. With half closed eyes she used the toilet and dragged herself back toward the bedroom, but a darker patch amidst the general darkness of the landing caught her eye, and she realised the door to Rachel's room was open. That in itself wasn't unusual since Rachel could have visited the bathroom earlier, but Sarah noticed Claire's bedroom door was also open. Intrigued, she crept into Claire's room and saw an empty bed, the covers cast to one side. Now wide awake, Sarah pushed the door to Rachel's room fully open and peered into the gloom. What she saw both puzzled her and warmed her heart. Rachel and Claire were lying together, warm under the quilt, Claire with her back to Rachel who had an arm wrapped around the young girl in an embrace.

Claire was holding Rachel's hand.

Once more Sarah shook her head, wondering what troubled her friend and how her daughter ended up in bed with her. Rachel was fond of Claire, loving her as much as if she were her own, and the thought comforted Sarah. But, deciding to leave her daughter with Rachel, she turned to leave the room. As she walked back on to the landing, she heard Claire whisper, 'Why is Auntie Rachel unhappy, Mommy?'

Sarah turned back and tiptoed over to the bed to check on Claire, but found her daughter was fast asleep. She reached out and laid a hand ever so lightly on Claire's forehead, but the child did not move.

For a moment she wondered if Claire had actually spoken or if she'd imagined the thought in her own head. Perhaps she picked up on Claire's innate sensitivity and voiced the thought herself? But then she felt as if she was intruding, that Claire and Rachel were having time alone, and the notion occurred to her that Claire was the adult, lending support to her 'auntie'. But the moment passed, and she yawned. *Sarah, go back to bed. They are both family… everything is as it should be. Tomorrow is another day and the next.*

After pulling the door closed behind her, she padded across the landing to her own bedroom and slid into bed next to John. It wasn't long before the warmth under the covers sent Sarah back into a deep sleep.

Eleven

Two weeks later, Sarah, John and Claire arrived at Hamish's house on the southern outskirts of Ayr. It was late, and the streets were bereft of human activity. At this time of the year, sunset came early and sunrise late, leaving the people of Scotland to retreat indoors during the long dark nights.

During the day as they travelled, and especially after dusk, Claire dozed with Mags lying next to her, but as they neared the end of the journey, she'd awoken and peered with excitement through the windows noting the landmarks and guessing how much further they had left to go.

When John finally pulled up onto the drive at his grandfather's house, Claire jumped out of the back with Mags in hot pursuit and sprinted through the front garden to the door, finger aimed at the bell push.

John heard Papa's voice coming through the door and smiled as he looked forward to a wee dram and a cosy fire.

'Who the devil is it?' But then the door opened letting out the welcoming glow from a hall lamp.

'Papa!' Claire squealed and gave the old man a hug. 'Where's Frosty?'

Frosty was Papa's old cat, so named after the old man found him curled up under a bush one freezing night fifteen years ago.

'I'll give you one guess,' said Hamish.

'Huh!' answered Claire as she entered the house. 'In front of the fire, I suppose. Lazy thing.'

Sarah hurried up the path loaded with bags.

'Hello Papa,' she said as she stepped into the hall. 'Merry Christmas. How are you?'

'Hi Papa,' said John. 'How are things?'

'Och I'm still here,' answered Hamish. 'Give me your bags. Looks like you're moving in again.'

'Are you sure?' John asked, but handed them over anyway knowing that arguing would be pointless.

While Hamish took the two bags up to the guest bedroom, John and Sarah carried their other belongings into the house and with a satisfied sigh closed the door, shutting out a chilly breeze that came straight off the sea.

An hour later and after a light supper, Claire lay curled up on the floor next to the cat watching a film her great grandfather kept in for her, while the others sat in comfy armchairs and sipped at a single malt. A well-built coal fire toasted them as they talked, though John was quiet. They'd been catching up on recent news while Hamish made a lot of fuss over his granddaughter-in-law. It was clear how happy he was to see Sarah in one piece after her ordeal.

They continued a conversation Sarah began a while back… about the letter. Hamish asked a question.

'I used to like a good mystery. But where are you going first? There aren't many homes for the elderly in Girvan. You still have to find the right one assuming your guess is right, that she's living in one. But you can't just turn up and ask questions.'

Sarah admitted to herself that even though she'd thought of little else for over two weeks, she was no closer to having a plan.

'I'll think of something when I get there,' she said. 'Actually, when you think about it, whoever it is must want me to find them, so they can't have made it too difficult…

can they? Why make it too complicated because there'd always be the chance I'd never find them or I'd give up from the start. It seems important I find this person or else why bother sending the note at all.'

'Aye,' replied Hamish, 'but why the puzzle. Why not send a letter with an address or telephone number?'

'I'll find out when I find out who they are. Maybe they like creating riddles.'

While Sarah and Hamish talked, a tired John, lost in thought, gazed into the fire, hypnotised by the dancing flames. He was thinking of a hundred Christmases in this house, long Christmas breaks filled with warmth and love. But he was struggling to remember Christmases before his mom died, struggling to recall the little rituals and traditions families kept at such special times of the year. The death of his mother transformed Christmas for John, and that first year his grandparents had leapt in and taken control of the season, realising it would be a hard time for everyone, and knowing Craig, John's father, needed help. John recalled a conversation between the grown-ups that took place over twenty years ago and during their first Christmas as a fractured family. Craig had been talking to his mother and father in the kitchen and, unbeknown to them, John was listening from halfway up the stairs.

'We don't need any fuss,' Craig was saying.

Unconvinced, John's grandmother replied. 'Look dear. We're not trying to take over. We can't replace Muireall. But we are your family, the only family you have as wee John has no aunts or uncles to speak of. You can sort out presents, let us worry about food.'

'And,' Hamish added. 'Who are you going to share a dram with? You can stay a few days here.'

Craig ran out of arguments. He realised Christmas on his own, with a ten-year-old son to take care of, would be miserable for both of them... better to stay with his parents. John had been glad his father agreed. He missed his mom but was not looking forward to the big day with only his father for company. In a moment of wisdom, he understood that neither of them needed the solitude, since solitude it would have been, each alone, lost in their own grief.

A question from Sarah brought him back to the present.

'Darling? Is that ok?' she said.

'Sorry? Is what ok?' he asked.

'Keep up, sleepy. I was saying I'd rather go into Girvan on my own.'

'Yes of course. I can catch up with Papa. What about Claire? Do you want to leave her here with me?'

'I think so. I'm not sure how long I'll be or even if I'll find her. It's all still a gamble.'

Hamish spoke again. 'Aye, well it's all a mystery.'

John regarded his grandfather. The old man had been a huge part of John's life since he was a baby and even more so after John's mother died, until John's father moved them both south hoping for a new start. John renewed the ties with his grandparents after he and Sarah began dating, and they saw each other as often as they could. John knew his grandfather well, but tonight as he watched the old man, he thought he'd lost weight, and appeared a little greyer under the eyes.

'How have you been, Papa? Have you been all right?' John asked.

'Aye. A wee bit of a chesty cough but fine. The whisky helps,' and he laughed.

Sarah shared his mirth, but for a moment as she gazed at Hamish, she thought she saw a coloured haze around him, bluish in hue with a dark banded edge. The dark edge troubled her, but she didn't know why.

The film Claire had been watching came to an end, and it was only then they realised she had fallen asleep. John yawned himself, a silent cavernous yawn brought on by an early shift at work and a long drive followed by a warm fire and a large glass of single malt.

Sarah spoke to him. 'C'mon you. I think it's late enough. If you carry our daughter upstairs, I'll put her to bed and I think you ought to go too.'

'I'm fine,' said John, and yawned again. 'Well maybe you're right. Are you coming?'

'I'll be up when I've finished my drink.'

John scooped up his daughter from where she lay on the floor. Carrying her with as much care as if he were carrying fine bone china, he climbed the stairs and settled her onto the bed. Sarah followed him in, peeled off Claire's jeans and covered her with the quilt. She flicked on the night light and closed the door.

As she crossed the landing to go back downstairs, John emerged from the bathroom.

'Are you joining me?' he said, trying to muster a saucy smile. 'I have something for you!'

'Hmmm. And what's that may I ask?' she said with one eyebrow raised and no sign of a smile. 'The sound of you snoring? From the look of you, you couldn't raise a smile let alone anything else.'

'Tuh!' he replied. 'I may surprise you.'

She reached up to him and placed a warm kiss on one cheek and her hand on the other. 'Darling. You haven't surprised me in years and I doubt if tonight will be any different. Perhaps I could fit you in tomorrow.'

'Well there's an offer I can't refuse!' and he yawned again.

'Behave,' she said. 'Get yourself into bed and I'll be up soon.'

'Ok, sweetie,' he said and turned into the bedroom. When Sarah was halfway down the stairs, she heard him say, 'See you in the morning.' With a smile creasing her face, she made her way back into the living room knowing he would be fast asleep in less than five minutes. She had dozed in the car during their journey and wasn't ready for bed even though it was nearing midnight. Pushing the living room door shut behind her, she sat near to the fire and picked up her drink. Sarah took a sip and breathed out. Partaking of a single malt whisky was a pleasant pastime when in

Scotland but it needed cautious sipping. The hot smoky flavour warmed her from the inside and she lifted her legs up underneath her.

'So how have you been?' asked Hamish. 'Are you all fixed?'

'Yes, all fixed.'

'But?'

Sarah smiled at the old man. From the day she met John's grandparents she realised they could see right through a person. They knew when to ask questions and equally when not to intrude. Sarah respected their directness, as often the direct approach helped a person say things that could otherwise fester, sometimes with dreadful results. Hamish was never one to mince words. He didn't see the point in word games. He preferred things out in the open.

'You always know when to probe.'

'You mean to be nosy!' and they both laughed. Hamish continued, 'Lassie, I can tell something's different about you just by looking at you. Something's bothering you.'

'Well,' began Sarah. 'I'm not sure if I'm being stupid or not, if I'm wasting my time. What am I chasing after? Am I being daft? Am I desperate for some mystery?'

'Only you know the answer. You're lucky you had a letter in the post. I hear people get lots of that *email* stuff these days. Bad idea this email. In my day if people needed to contact you they sent a letter. They had to write it by hand. Nowadays it all comes out of a computer or a phone. It's not so personal now as it used to be.'

'Hmm. I agree with you up to a point. But hang on… Papa, you are brilliant. You've answered my question. You're right. People *do* email too much. Most junk mail comes on email these days not through the post. If this *was* nonsense, who would go to the trouble of paying postage and sending a written letter with such strange content? And whoever sent it has gone to the bother of finding out where I live. So I'm *not* wasting my time.'

'Well there's your answer.'

Hamish fell silent and gazed at the glowing embers of the fire.

Sarah took another sip of her drink and picked up on what Hamish had said two minutes ago.

'Papa. What did you mean when you said I've changed?'

'Oh I can tell,' he replied glancing at Sarah. 'You seem pre-occupied. A little less relaxed. There's something about you.' He shifted his gaze back at the fire. 'It's just a feeling,' he added as if he was shrugging off the question, but Sarah thought he was being evasive, as if he didn't want to say any more.

'Did I ever tell you about how John was after Muireall, his mamma, died?' Hamish asked, diverting the conversation.

'Only bits and pieces.'

'He became very withdrawn for a while. Perfectly normal considering the circumstances, but he turned inwards, locked himself away. He was always a bubbly lad, always outside doing something, playing with friends or helping me in the garden. He liked being outside. But afterwards he hid in his room… only came out if he needed to. Kept himself to himself. His dad didn't know what to do with the wee boy because he'd lost himself too, as anyone would have. Me and your Nana never saw either of them shed any tears.'

Sarah sipped at her drink and hung on every word.

'It was as if they bottled it all up inside. I'm a happy soul, lassie. I like to laugh. Life's hard enough without being miserable about it. But I never understood why some people don't use all their emotions. You smile or laugh when things are going well. If something unhappy happens, you cry. It's as simple as that. It's no use locking it away, pretending to be strong. But anyway, there they both were struggling together, but separate if you know what I mean, until one day it was John himself who made the effort, broke the silence so to speak.'

Transfixed, Sarah was as much focussed on what

Hamish was saying as puzzling over why it was coming out now. 'How?' she asked.

'He disappeared one day. Craig was beside himself with worry but I knew something was coming, something brewing, that John had decided to do something. John's dad was always a keen angler. Went fishing as often as he could, as often as he could get away. He loved Muireall, though she could be a demanding woman. Had a hard childhood, strict Presbyterian upbringing. But John got up and went out before dawn, took his dad's rods and crept out of the house. We searched for him in all his old haunts. Down on the beach, out at the Loch and by the river. We were about to call the police when he wandered back in in the late afternoon, cold and tired. He comes waltzing in and we all shot up when we heard him. He stood there in front of his dad and held up one small trout he'd caught. You'd think he'd be pleased, but with a poker face he stared at his dad and said, "Dad, I can't do this on my own. I need you to help me." We were never quite sure if he meant fishing or if he was talking about losing his mam. Perhaps both, but something snapped inside Craig and he reached for John and grabbed him in a big bear hug, and it was only then the tears came, for both of them. Me and John's nana just left them to it.'

Tears had escaped Hamish's eyes and the tale moved Sarah too, but she kept her feelings to herself.

Hamish continued. 'I like to think John did it on purpose. Somehow in his wee little head he understood what they both needed, knew they had to grieve together. He was a smart lad… still is.'

'Yes,' replied Sarah. 'He still is. That's one reason I love him so much, because he can be so strong, so supportive, but also so gentle. I think I now understand where he gets it from, Papa.'

Hamish sniffed and gave a little laugh. He turned to look back at Sarah and fixed her with a rigid stare. A gentle smile touched his mouth but his eyes seemed tired.

With no emotion, he said, 'It won't be long, lassie, before John will need *your* support.'

It was a short and simple statement, and it took a moment for the words to sink in, but the meaning became unmistakable and Sarah opened her mouth with a gasp.

'Papa?' she said. 'What... what do you mean?'

'You know what I mean.'

'But. What... why?' Tears started in Sarah's eyes but she ignored them.

'Sarah. I'm getting old. I can't last forever, but this is the last Christmas I'll see. There's nothing else to say. It's just one of those things. It happens, you know, and I have no complaints. One of my greatest joys is meeting you... seeing John and you happy, but I'll be off to see my Kathryn soon, and *she* was my greatest joy.'

'Papa. No... ' Sarah's face crumpled as the tears escaped her eyes. She crossed the room, knelt in front of Hamish and lowered her head onto his chest. The old man stroked her hair, teasing it from her face.

'Now c'mon, lassie, it's not the end of the world. You of all people should appreciate that. John will need your help for a while but he'll survive... it'll be all right. You'll see. I've had a good life. Travelled a bit in my early days before I met your nana Kathryn. We did what we wanted before settling down to bring up Craig. Some people get to my age and wonder where it all went. But I know where my life went. I know what I've done and I've enjoyed almost all of it. But you can't stop the onset of old age and the ravages of time.'

Sarah spoke in a voice broken with grief. 'What's wrong Papa?'

'One too many cigarettes when I was younger maybe... who knows. The doctors have said they might help with some treatment... give me a bit more time. But why would I want to make myself ill and feel terrible? It won't change the end. You'll see me again, but I'll leave it up to you to tell John if you want to. It's no use him fretting, but it's your choice. I wanted to tell you because he'll need your strength, at the start anyway. Remember life goes on in more ways than you can imagine.'

Sarah wondered how the whole world could turn itself on its head with a few small words. How in the space of a few seconds, joyful moments could change to such devastating ones? She desperately wanted to say a million things... wanted to say how wonderful it was she'd met Hamish and Kathryn. How grateful she was they had taken her into their home and their hearts, how they had become as one family and how much she loved him. But her voice wouldn't come, only the tears. Then a light touch caressed her forehead as if a nearby presence picked up her distress, a guardian angel sensing her grief and putting forth a comforting touch. And deep within her own heart she understood that Hamish was right... there *was* nothing to say. Since they came from the soul, Hamish would understand her sentiments without the clumsy use of words, without the need to taint the feelings with adjectives.

Hamish held a hand against Sarah's head and she sensed a calming influence from his touch. The intensity of her grief diminished as he stroked her hair, but after several minutes his movements slowed and stopped. For a while Sarah stayed as she was, but then she felt an energy coming from within, but from within Hamish or herself she could not tell. The intensity of it reminded her of a day many years ago when she had knelt by her parents' graveside. The energy was the essence of peace itself... tranquil and soothing, and as it coursed through her, her tears slowed and stopped. With care she slipped from Hamish's grasp and stared at the old man. Drawing in a deep and slow breath, and exhaling, she felt the same pull on her stomach as on that sunny spring day at the cemetery... a pull that was benevolent, healing and gentle as it drew out her pain.

She leaned forward and brushed the top of his head with her lips even as the feathery touch lay on her forehead once more. At the touch, a smile spread across her face, a smile that acknowledged life and the joy it held, a joy that had, for her, run throughout her life since she first met this old man. Though she knew there were hard times to come, difficult periods ahead, she was comforted.

Placing a few coals onto the fire, knowing Hamish would make his own way to bed when he was ready, Sarah left the room and climbed the stairs to her husband. In silence she undressed and slipped between the sheets, wrapping her arms around him. John stirred enough to turn over and lifted an arm up and around Sarah. As she folded into his embrace, she tried to forget the news Hamish revealed, and wondered about the timeliness of the touch on her forehead before sleep took hold.

Twelve

It was the middle of the afternoon three days later, when Sarah headed out of Girvan town towards the last place on her list, the list she'd drawn up after an Internet search before they'd left the midlands. As much as she wanted to begin her search early on the day after they arrived at Hamish's, she realised she needed to have some time with the whole family before wandering off on her own. It wouldn't have been fair to Claire or John, to take off straight after breakfast, so they spent the weekend around the house relaxing or getting a breath of fresh air with a walk along the beach.

But on Christmas Eve after giving everyone a kiss, Sarah headed off in the afternoon in search of someone unknown, in a place only guessed at, and for nameless reasons.

Girvan wasn't a huge town, with a population of around eight thousand and she had found three care homes in the vicinity. The first place she visited turned her away, saying they couldn't give out information concerning their residents and she understood this, disappointing though it was.

The lady on reception at the second place was sympathetic but simply said no, there was no one called

Beryl on their books. She seemed almost apologetic.

The final place Sarah found during her research, situated on the southern outskirts of the town, was on the main road heading towards Stranraer. It was not far from the town centre and hence not long before she drove into the car park. Overlooking the beach, the views from the windows, Sarah thought, would be stunning. *What a lovely place to spend your retirement years.* She turned off the engine and sat back, wondering how to handle her approach. If she came up blank here, she was unsure how to continue. She reached into her handbag, pulled out the letter and removed the note from its envelope. 'Inspired you will be if you find me.'

She puzzled over the line once more and reflected on the changes in her life since early December. Apart from the physical sensations, the colours, even the increased sex drive, the most profound change was manifested last night when Hamish broke his news. He would not say exactly what his illness was, but Sarah assumed cancer was the awful truth. Only a short time ago, such news would have devastated Sarah, leaving her distraught. But once the news sank in, she accepted the fact, maybe because the end was inevitable at some point... or because she understood the need to celebrate a life and not overly mourn its loss. She would miss Hamish, but, she realised, her embryonic philosophical viewpoint would temper the loss, a viewpoint triggered by a fundamental change to her beliefs... or, as Hamish put it, 'It's just one of those things.'

Sarah kept the secret to herself for the moment, but was struggling with how to break the news to John. She wasn't sure she could keep it quiet for long, or if she should. Did she have the right to protect a loved one from a truth so devastating? That was a dilemma she'd have to puzzle out soon. Time was important.

While contemplating her predicament, Sarah gazed out across the sea toward the towering island of Ailsa Craig. Even from this distance she could still make out the birds circling its rocky crown, silhouetted against the lowering sun. With its rounded top and steep sides, the island always reminded her of a giant muffin, but she knew it to be a huge volcanic plug. Legend though was far more interesting, and the most ancient tale concerned two giants, one from Ulster and one from Scotland, battling across the waters, throwing huge rocks at each other. Sarah smiled as she remembered Hamish himself telling her the story.

As she pondered the tale, a ray of sunshine lit the top of the island and Sarah peered upwards out of her side window. The sky was clearing, the clouds drifting across the sea into the west. The water had taken on a greenish hue, a mysterious reflection of the blue sky above and the variations in light from the pale winter sun. Sarah always marvelled at how changeable the weather was in Scotland. It could be misty and calm and a few hours later a clear sky would lie above a wild ocean or gentle rippling waves. Another day, a shadowy greyness would blanket everything from the shore out to the horizon... but whatever the weather, she could lose herself for hours contemplating the view.

From within her daydream, she sensed the feathery sensation caress her brow, and the distraction brought her back to the moment and her mission. Kicked into motion, she unfastened her seatbelt and climbed out of the car, placing the note back inside her handbag. She pulled on her fleece jacket as a shield against the chilly breeze and made her way across to the main entrance.

As she approached the glass doors, Sarah saw a reception desk to one side of a large hallway with a young woman standing behind, a woman of a similar age to Sarah. She pressed a buzzer and the door unlatched. Unexpectedly anxious and struggling with what to say, she entered the building, and walked toward the woman. When the door closed behind her, an odd thought crossed her mind. She felt she had crossed a threshold... and there was no way back.

A barrage of feelings and sensations overwhelmed her.

The smell of lavender filled her nostrils, a relaxing perfume, a calming scent. Fresh flowers stood in a variety of large vases set on tables and stands, adding colour and their own fragrance into the mix. The soft touch of a thick carpet underfoot and the sight of heavy drapes, now pulled back from the windows, gave the place a safe and cosy atmosphere. Apart from the slow tick of a grandfather clock, the hallway was silent.

The young woman was smiling, and in response to her smile, Sarah thought of a word to describe the place perfectly. Home.

'Can I help you?' the receptionist asked.

With little forethought Sarah said, 'Sorry to trouble you and I'm sure this sounds odd but I'm looking for someone called Beryl? I believe she's in a home near here but I'm not sure if this is the one. I've had a letter from her and I think… I think we're related?'

The words made Sarah frown, but now she had spoken them, it was too late to take them back.

'Ah. You must be Sarah. My name's Margaret. Beryl said to expect you soon. Yes, she's here. If you follow the corridor and turn left, she's in the farthest room on the right. It's called Ailsa View so you can't miss it. Beautiful views of the Rock.'

Sarah's heart rate quickened, and butterflies fluttered in her stomach. Her idea to come here was a stab in the dark, based only on Claire's educated guess. Now it was obvious she was expected. She thanked the receptionist and turned towards the corridor but hesitated, not sure what to expect. For unknown reasons she'd received a puzzle which had occupied most of her waking thought for over two weeks. She had become obsessed with finding the author, but now she was here she questioned the sense. What was she about to find out? What was the reason? Was she being foolish? But then she thought why? Why should a stranger send her an unusual but clearly meaningful riddle? *C'mon Sarah let's see this through to the end.*

Seeing Sarah's hesitation, the young woman spoke again. 'It's ok, you go ahead. Beryl is a strange one, but she's really friendly. I often sit with her and she tells me tales.'

Sarah turned and smiled but found no words to say, so she headed across the large entrance hall towards the corridor. The care home was as quiet as a library and she heard only the faint murmur of conversation. As she made her way along the corridor, she passed a large room on the right, a room with tables and chairs she guessed to be a dining room. Two young girls were busy laying out tableware ready for a late tea or evening meal. Sarah glanced at her watch and noted the time. It was nearing half past two.

Turning left as instructed, she saw a door at the end of the corridor that stood ajar, and by the open door, squinting back at Sarah, sat a black cat. Sarah strolled forward, making no noise on the carpeted floor and as she got closer to the animal, it opened its mouth in a huge yawn and stood up arching its back upwards in a tired stretch. Sarah stopped outside the door and the cat gazed up with striking green eyes. As if compelled to do so, she reached down and the animal jumped into Sarah's arms, settling its head against her chest. From within the room, a voice called out.

'Amber! Stop making a fuss of that young woman. Bring her in. It's time for afternoon tea.'

Sarah smiled and any thought of nervousness evaporated. All she needed now was to discover who had led her here, so she pushed open the door.

As she entered the room, her eyes were drawn to a large window which revealed an awe inspiring view. Being midwinter, the sun was close to the horizon and it wouldn't be long before the shadows deepened. Small ripples of water lapped the shoreline revealing a calm sea. Further out, large sea birds circled in the air looking to catch an unsuspecting meal lying unawares under the surface. Ailsa Craig lay in line of sight between Sarah and the horizon and she could still see the birds circling the island, searching for a roost for the night.

Bringing her gaze inside the room, Sarah noticed it was sparsely furnished, as if the occupier needed little in the way of home comforts. A door stood in one corner which she guessed led to a bathroom. A single bed stood out from the wall near the door, a bed with safety bars on each side but with one lowered out of position. Bedside tables stood on each side of the bed, one holding a table lamp and the other a book which lay face down and open. Against the opposite wall was a large floor standing bookshelf, its shelves bowing under the weight of large hardbound volumes interspersed with smaller paperbacks. A dressing table stood close by but little in the way of bottles or sprays adorned its top. Instead, cups and a teapot occupied most of the space. On either side of the large window sat comfortable armchairs... Queen Anne style, each with its own footstool. Both angled outwards to take in the sea views.

At last Sarah turned to gaze at her host. With her back to Sarah, the lady sat on one of the armchairs staring out across the water. Her hair was long and of an almost pure white. She sat upright, not crouched or bent by old age. Cloaked in a white dressing gown and wearing soft white slippers on her feet, Sarah had the odd feeling she was looking at a ghost.

'I knew you'd find me,' the old lady said. 'I'm Beryl, but I'm sure you guessed already.'

Sarah sensed the strength of the voice but detected a tiredness within it. A voice that, she felt, could shatter glass if raised enough in volume, but one with a strained edge as if the owner were weary or disguising pain.

'You're here in time for sunset. I love watching the sun go down. Some people like to watch it rise as if giving thanks to the fact they have survived the night. I prefer to watch it set as I can be glad I lived another day. Would you like a cup of tea? The kettle has just boiled. I think chamomile will do. Will you be a dear and pour?'

Amber the cat jumped to the floor as Beryl turned. At

last Sarah gazed into the face of the person who had summoned her. The woman who had sent clues to her whereabouts, playing a game with her, though for what reason she could not say. But as Sarah stared at the elderly woman, noting the colour of her eyes and the shape of her face, she gasped and in surprise lifted a hand to her mouth.

The face was the spitting image of her own mother Rose, or how her mother would have appeared if she had lived another thirty years. But what shocked Sarah more was the feeling she was peering into a mirror, at her own reflection and into her own future.

Thirteen

'It looks cold outside,' said John, peering through the window. 'I wonder how Sarah's getting on?'

'Cold?' questioned Hamish. 'You know what they say.'

With smiles on their faces, Hamish and John spoke in unison.

'There's no such thing as bad weather, just the wrong clothes!' They both laughed.

While Sarah was pouring chamomile tea for an elderly woman, John and Hamish sat at home chatting and nestling their own cups of tea whilst enjoying a mince pie. Insulated with layers of warm clothing, Claire had ventured outside to feed the birds and play with Mags. Through the patio doors John could see her at the bottom of Hamish's large garden opening the shed in search of birdseed.

'What do you think about Sarah's letter?' asked John. He took a bite of his mince pie.

'Seems more important to me what you think, but she's tenacious.'

'That's a fact and no mistake,' replied John. 'She's very determined… single-minded when she has a problem to solve. This is different though. She even has me hooked.'

'Do you have a choice?' Hamish asked with a gentle

laugh and then he coughed, a harsh rattling cough.

'Papa, I asked you last night if you were ok… how you had been.'

'Yes you did, and I answered.'

'Yes you did, but I'm sure you weren't being honest with me.'

'Wasn't I?'

'Well you look tired. Have you been ill?'

'Yes. Just a cold and a cough. Nothing to worry about.'

Though concerned for his grandfather, John knew him enough not to push too hard, so he made light of it, 'Better not be or I'll get Sarah to nag you,' and they both smiled again.

Claire disappeared inside the shed, while in the warmth of the living room Hamish nibbled at half of his mince pie before speaking again, 'We were talking about the letter.'

'Yes, we were. It's not something that drops on your doormat every day. There was something else unusual about it.'

'What's that?'

'When I reached for the letter, I could have sworn it moved before I touched it. It did when Sarah reached for it too. Sounds impossible.'

'Moved?'

'Yes. A little… the envelope I mean, as my fingers got close.'

'Well… there are more things in heaven and earth…' replied Hamish, quoting Shakespeare.

'There's other weird stuff going on. I hadn't told you before, but I had a dream the night before Sarah woke from her coma, a dream about her mom and dad. They told me to remember. It was so vivid it woke me up, and I realised they were telling me to remember the robins. I told you about those years ago?'

'Aye. I remember the robins.'

'Well afterwards I wondered was it really a dream, or did they actually speak to me? Papa, you know me. I had no reason to believe in spiritual stuff after Mom died. Didn't seem possible, but recently I've begun to think in a different way… and not because of the dream and the letter. I've…' John stopped and gave an uncomfortable laugh before continuing, 'I've started to… well… feel Sarah.'

'Feel? How do you mean?'

John lowered his voice, working through his thoughts.

'We've always been close. Felt each other's mood. Second guessed each other's thoughts. Perhaps every couple's the same… because they *are* a couple. But it doesn't seem that simple.' John raised his voice again. 'Recently I've begun to pick up on her thoughts when she's not even near. Well, perhaps not her thoughts, more like sensing her emotions. Is this making any sense?'

'Maybe,' Hamish paused a moment. 'Laddie, it's three o'clock. Pour us a wee dram will you.'

'Oh… ok.'

John stood and crossed the room to where the whisky decanter stood on top of an old sideboard. He poured a small measure for both Hamish and himself and carried them over.

'Here you go,' and he handed Hamish a glass before settling back in his chair. Outside, the light was fading as the pale mid-winter sun sank towards the rim of the world. Claire was standing in the middle of the lawn now, scooping seed into one of the hanging feeders.

'What you say makes little sense,' Hamish said. 'And yet it makes perfect sense. More importantly does it *have* to make sense?'

'Helpful. You always were cryptic.'

Hamish laughed. 'Lad, you were always a thoughtful boy even before your mam died, but even more so afterwards. You were a sensitive lad too, sensitive to atmosphere and aware of people's feelings… always mindful of others and how they were. Oh you were strong and tough. I remember you coming home from school with a few scrapes after being in a fight. You never cried… you toughened up…

stood up for yourself.' Hamish sipped his whisky and rolled it around his mouth before swallowing. 'What I mean is it doesn't matter whether any of what you told me makes sense at all. If it feels right to you, it is right. It's as simple as that. You and Sarah are as close as I was with your nana. We would often say the same things. Some couples are like that and whether it's a mystery or not I don't know and I don't care. Your mam and your dad weren't that way at all.' Hamish paused long enough for another sip. 'Do you remember much about your mam, laddie?'

'Not much. Not anymore. Time's faded a lot of the memories but I'm not sad about it. It's the way it is I suppose.'

'She was a steadfast woman, needed things controlled. A place for everything and everything in its place was her motto. Difficult when she married a man who was more of a free spirit and a boy who followed suit. Used to drive her mad when either one of you turned up and walked dirt into the house. She had a religious upbringing and a hard childhood. Real God-fearing parents. But she loved the both of you. You never went short of anything, Muireall saw to it. When your dad told us he was getting married, he surprised both me and his mam. She didn't seem the kind of woman he'd have chosen. But who knows what brings people together. I wonder sometimes if there is a purpose, but that purpose isn't always obvious… if it ever is. So my answer to you is stop worrying about feelings or other odd things. It's just the way it is.'

They sat in silence for a while busy with their own thoughts. John sat pondering over his wife's search, wondering how things were going. He half expected her to turn up at any moment disappointed. He hadn't a clue how he'd handle it if it happened. Sarah had been full of enthusiasm over the past couple of weeks though she understood she could be on a wild goose chase. But John knew a part of his wife *wanted* something to happen… in fact expected it, almost with a sense of premonition.

Hamish spoke. 'It's time you came home.'

His voice, and the words he uttered, cut straight through John's reverie.

'Where did that come from?'

'Well you belong here. You were born and raised here, mostly. And Sarah would jump at the chance.'

'There is the question of work, a place to live, paying for stuff, Claire's school.'

'Oh they're only minor problems. Claire can get into school easy enough. And I'm sure you and Sarah can get work. You're bound to find something... and you'll have a place to live. Here, in this house. It has four bedrooms, two of them big ones. There's plenty of room and I'm rattling around in here on my own. This house will be yours eventually.'

'Pardon me if I don't move in too soon, Papa. You're not past it yet.'

'I'm only saying I won't live forever.'

John said nothing and gazed out of the window. 'Ha,' he exclaimed after a few moments. 'The birds must be getting hungry. Just as well Claire's filling up the feeders.'

Outside, the local avian population was lining up in readiness for a meal. Several smaller birds flew in and landed in the tree above Claire's head. A clutch of starlings sat on top of the fence and John counted at least four blackbirds lying in wait underneath shrubs dotted around the garden. Even a pair of doves sat on the topmost branches of a tree.

Bringing his attention back inside the room John turned to Hamish. 'Papa, if I could find a way I'd bring my family back home tomorrow. Sarah *would* jump at the chance but we have to be practical about it. The time has to be right. But, it's very kind of you.'

'Kind? Nonsense. I need someone to look after me in my old age,' Hamish couldn't hold the laugh and it escaped too soon.

'Aha,' said John. 'And here's me thinking you missed us,' and he joined in the laughter.

The two men sipped at their drinks and fell into a comfortable silence. Only the sound of the fire broke the peace, the faint spit and crackle of coal and the rippling of flames as they flickered and danced in the hot air. Then a new sound reached their ears, a cheerful and innocent sound and one that brought a smile to both of them. Out in the garden, something had amused Claire. She was laughing with such delight her mirth was infectious and John and Hamish grinned at each other. John stood up and walked over to the patio window to get a closer look.

'What is she up to?' John took a quick look before whispering to Hamish, 'Papa. You've got to see this.' John walked over to his grandfather and helped him up out of the chair. He led Hamish back across the room and they stood captivated by the image presented before them.

Outside, in the middle of the lawn, wrapped up with a scarf around her neck and a woollen hat covering her head, Claire knelt on the ground, her bottom resting back on her heels. She was holding her arms out to her sides with her hands low, palms upwards as if in prayer. Several birds sat nearby, pecking at the food she'd sprinkled on the ground. A pile of seed lay in each hand, and several birds were feeding directly from them. The birds hopped and walked around her in friendly harmony, picking up seed as and when they needed it, without fear of her presence. To one side, Mags lay relaxed on the path, her head resting on her front paws as she watched the spectacle unfold. While John and Hamish watched from the warm comfort of the sitting room, a dove landed on Claire's head and waited a few moments before hopping to the ground to join in the feast. More birds flew in to join the party until there were at least fifty. Sparrows, finches, tits, blackbirds and many more. For several minutes the spectators watched in amazement as the feast continued, while all the time, amidst the fading light, Claire giggled in endless joy.

Fourteen

'I've always liked a chamomile infusion,' Beryl said. 'It's my favourite. It has so many health benefits as well as having a pleasant taste.'

While Sarah stood pouring tea, she scanned over the books lining the shelves. A cursory glance told her Beryl's interests didn't extend to fiction, or at least she wasn't a collector. Among the titles were words such as, Spiritual, Crystal, Reiki, Self-Help, Pagan or Herbal and many more. Specific subjects were grouped and in alphabetical order, and she smiled at this ordering since it was as she would have done. The titles related to crystals drew her attention, though the whole book collection she found interesting. Beryl's note referred to two crystals, angelite and variscite and she still kept the beryl stone close at all times. For a moment, she pictured her bedroom at home and the crystals hanging inside the window. When the early sun caught them, she found the rainbows that danced around the room pleasing.

She carried the two tea cups across to where Beryl sat, and placed one next to the elderly lady. Not knowing whether to stand or sit, she stood and sipped at her drink while gazing out of the window.

'It's a beautiful view. You're very lucky,' she said, wondering if she should begin the conversation. Perhaps, she mused, she'd leave it to Beryl.

'It's wonderful really,' said Beryl. 'But not surprising.'

'What's wonderful?' asked Sarah and turned to see Beryl regarding her with shining eyes.

'The likeness. The family resemblance.'

'Family resemblance? What do you mean?'

'I'm sure you know what I mean. It was difficult to ignore the surprise on your face the moment you saw me. I sensed it within you too.'

Sarah's cheeks reddened under the gaze of this old lady… she felt inexplicably uncomfortable, as if Beryl could read her innermost thoughts. Being uncomfortable settled her mind however, and she took the initiative.

'I hope you don't mind me being so abrupt, but before we carry on I need to ask a few questions, beginning with the most obvious… who are you?'

Beryl smiled.

'As I expected. Direct, as I would have been and your grandmother. Your mother was less direct but the poor thing hadn't the strength. It doesn't always run true.'

'What doesn't run true? And what's this got to do with my mother.'

'Sarah, my dear, why don't you sit. We've a lot to get through.'

The lady fixed her old grey eyes on Sarah and though she wanted to stay standing, if only to show her own independence, found she had already settled into the other chair.

Sarah took a deep breath and began again. 'Look it's obvious your name is Beryl and you live here in Girvan.'

'Go on.'

'I hope you'll pardon my surprise earlier but I'd guess you're related to my mother somehow.'

'Go on.'

'But how I'm not sure. My mother told me about my

grandmother, and that she'd been an only child. As far as I'm aware I have no other relations on my mother's side. Hence my question… who are you?'

'It's puzzling isn't it, but time is short. I hope you'll bear with me and trust me. You said you had questions?'

'Questions? Oh yes. The other question is why the riddle? Why not write a normal letter? And how did you find out where to send it?'

'Well, my family solicitor tracked you down. It wasn't hard but that will become clear later on. But as for a letter, would you have come?'

'What?'

'Would you have come if I had written a letter?'

'Well…'

'Sarah, what would I have written. "Dear Mrs Macintyre, we've never met but I have news for you. I'm elderly and live in a care home in Girvan. I'd like us to meet." Would you have come or would you have thought it was sent to the wrong person?'

Sarah said nothing.

'Or I could have written a long letter telling you everything I will tell you today but the result may have been the same. I needed you to be here, to sit with me and talk and listen. I wanted you to see and feel the truth of everything. A letter would have conveyed nothing.'

'But how could you be certain I'd come, and tracking you down was a challenge.'

'Well not a big enough challenge since you're here,' Beryl said with a smile that lightened her face. 'I was never any good at poetry but the riddle holds a lot of truth you'll come to understand as time goes on. I've sensed you from afar for a while, but even more so since a few weeks before Christmas, and I know you've sensed my presence too, though you wouldn't have understood what you sensed. But I'm getting ahead of myself. The riddle was, foremost, a simple puzzle for you to solve, but in a way that would hopefully trigger your interest. If you hadn't solved it or chose not to come… well… that would have been a sad loss.'

'Loss? I'm sorry, I don't understand.'

'You will.'

Beryl lifted her cup and took a sip. With a sigh she leaned back against her chair, gazing out of the window before continuing. 'I used to be a teacher, many years ago before the second world war, but a teacher who didn't simply bark out facts and figures. I used to like working through things with my pupils, helping them see the truth behind a subject.'

While Sarah watched Beryl, she saw a frown pass across the old woman's eyes, a flash of pain perhaps. Across the miles, the sun was brushing the horizon when Beryl spoke again.

'The truth is so important,' she whispered, and then raised her voice once more. 'Sarah, have you ever wondered where the sun goes when it disappears each night?'

Sarah did not answer.

'It's a serious question,' turning back to Sarah.

'Where the sun goes?' asked Sarah. 'Nowhere. It—'

'How do you know?' interrupted Beryl.

'What?'

'How do you know?' repeated the old lady. 'Humour me… please.'

The question intrigued Sarah but Beryl's direction puzzled her. The nature of the old woman's speech was also unusual. Her manner and language was typical of someone much younger, not like the elderly folk with which Sarah was familiar. Also, the unusual nature of the letter had driven Sarah to find this lady, and solving the puzzle had become an obsession. The whole thing was a mystery, but it intrigued her and led her here. Where it took her was up to her, so she decided to let Beryl take her along on her journey.

'Ok,' she said at last. 'It's the rotation of the earth that creates sunrise and sunset. As the earth rotates, the sun disappears from view each evening and reappears each morning as the planet continues to rotate. If the sun is going anywhere, it's because it's part of a bigger movement, part of the solar system and the galaxy it belongs to.'

'Well done. I'm impressed. It's amazing what you learn at school and remember for years afterwards. Often girls forget science facts but I can tell you have an enquiring mind. However... the question remains. How do you know?'

'How do I know? It's because we've discovered it. I mean science has proved it. The earth rotates on its own axis and revolves around the sun. What other explanation is there. Why are you asking me this?'

'There *is* no other explanation and you are quite correct. All I'm trying to...' Beryl stopped talking as a violent fit of coughing took hold of her. For many moments spasm after spasm wracked her whole body and a shocked Sarah realised that despite Beryl's youngish demeanour, she was a frail old lady. *How old is she?*

Beryl lifted a handkerchief and as the coughing stopped, she dabbed at her mouth. Sarah wasn't sure, but for a moment imagined she saw red stains on the cotton material.

'Are you ok?' she asked. 'Can I get you anything, or one of the staff?'

'No thank you, dear,' Beryl replied in a faint voice, and with care cleared her throat. 'One, I'm not all right but I will be soon enough, and two, all I need is you.'

'Me?'

'Yes. Let's carry on. What I was saying was we *all* put our faith in much of what we are told.... about anything. In this case, the earth rotates on its axis, it revolves around the sun. We know this because science has proven it and we learn about it. But as all the best conspiracy theorists will say, all of these so called facts have other explanations. Like the moon landings. The cynics say they took place in an aircraft hangar somewhere in the American desert... filmed and broadcast to a hoodwinked world.'

Sarah wondered again where this was going but Beryl

had triggered her inquisitive nature. She let Beryl continue, though her next question surprised Sarah, considering the previous subject.

'Sarah, do you believe in God?'

'Strange question.'

'Maybe... maybe not. I've asked the same question of many people over the years, children and adults alike, and they often hesitate before answering. Either you do or you don't. There can be no middle ground, no hesitation. I ask again, do you believe in God?'

'No,' Sarah replied with conviction. 'I find the whole idea unlikely. For me it doesn't feel right, it doesn't work.'

'Why is that? What *do* you believe in?' asked Beryl.

'Well, I think if anything exists beyond our realm, it'll be more mysterious than the existence of a simple single deity, a deity we hand over our beliefs or regrets or destiny to. If something goes wrong, it's God's will. If something goes right, praise the Lord. It's too simple. It implies we have no control because whatever happens is in the hands of God. Like I said it doesn't work for me. I *do* believe in the inherent goodness of people, their inbuilt benevolence... a willingness to care for each other. And... I think there is more wonder and beauty and peace in the natural world... as long as we take care of it... take the time to look after it.'

'Yet the majority of the world's population believe in a God. Please understand I'm the same as you. I haven't believed in God since I lost someone dear to me during the Great War after which I developed a faith of my own.'

Beryl took a sip at her tea again.

'You see, my dear, the point of all of this comes down to the small word I used... faith. We put our faith in everyone around us. Scientists, politicians, doctors, experts, magazines, you name it, we have confidence in much of what people tell us or what we read because we put our faith in it, whether misguided or not. Science or theology, astronomy or religion... particularly religion. With science, we can prove many things beyond doubt. We can see man walking on the moon... photograph the birth of a star or see a virus dividing in a laboratory. We can see how a medicine can destroy bacteria. Sarah, science is all around us, so much so we put our trust and faith in much of what we see or hear. With religion, it's different, though the result is the same. You put your own personal faith in your religion because, unlike science, proving it by empirical means is impossible. It's whatever feels right to you, or as you say, what works for you. Faith and trust are powerful motivators and the beliefs that sit behind them are as individual as each and every one of us. I'm only trying to get you to reflect on what *you* believe in, what *you* put your faith in.'

'I understand what you're saying but you haven't answered my first question yet,' Sarah said. 'But hang on! You lost someone in the Great War? How old are you? Who did you lose? If you were born during the First World War you would be at least ninety years old.'

'Remember the point of this conversation Sarah... faith? I'm asking you to place your faith in me and everything I'll tell you. Everything. It is the truth and looking at you now and seeing you for the first time I *know* you will have faith in me even though what I am about to tell you will contradict much of what you believed to be true. I can tell by your aura your mind has opened. My sense of you has strengthened over recent weeks, but I've been aware of you since your birth.'

Aura? Aware of me?

Beryl took a drink from her tea again and breathed deeply, taking in the aroma. With her gaze fixed on Sarah she continued.

'You asked about my age. I'm one hundred and seven years old.'

'One hundred and seven?' Sarah couldn't hide her astonishment.

'Yes my dear. A long time. I've seen a lot in my lifetime. But I lost my one and only love during the First World War. He was eighteen and I was sixteen. The year was 1916 when the war took him from me... and ultimately you. His name was Joseph. I was carrying our child at the time he died. I gave birth to our daughter, in early 1917, but in those days and at my age it was seen as a disgrace to have a child out of wedlock and so I had to give her away. Before I had a chance to hold her they took her from me and gave her to my older sister Amber to raise. Amber had moved to England with her husband before the war began.'

Beryl paused long enough to sip at her tea.

'Sarah, I could sense my daughter almost daily as she grew up... aware of her only in a spiritual way, since I was forbidden to see her or communicate with her. I didn't understand why I sensed her, but if she was in pain so was I. If she was happy, I felt that too. The years went on and I never met her, but my daughter followed a long-standing family tradition of having a child herself when she was young, when she was only sixteen. She only had one child whom she named Rose, and this was in 1933. Rose married a man called Graham, and they had a son David and a daughter born in 1976. Sarah, that daughter is you.'

The surprise was obvious on Sarah's face but she said nothing. Her mind raced however as she tried to make sense of the revelation.

'You never met your grandmother, my daughter,' Beryl continued. 'She died the day you were conceived, which is also common in our family... the simultaneous occurrence of death and conception. Even necessary sometimes,' Beryl added as an afterthought.

The old lady paused and cleared her throat again while holding the handkerchief to her mouth. She regarded Sarah with eyes as bright as stars, a twinkle shining in each, but eyes surrounded with tired, grey and ageing flesh. *One hundred and seven years old. No wonder she looks tired.... but those eyes.*

'Sarah. My name, as you rightly said, is Beryl and I am your great grandmother, not Amber.'

Sarah stared at the old woman, not sure whether to

believe her. Her mother Rose told Sarah years ago that Sarah's grandmother's name was Jade, and Jade's mother, was Amber. Sarah believed Amber, and her husband Thomas, were local people, born and raised in the Midlands, descended as many people were from the mining community. Now it appeared Beryl was Sarah's great grandmother and therefore Sarah had Scottish roots and a different family history. Sarah never met her own grandmother and was saddened that something was missing from her childhood. Family was everything to Sarah, but she'd not had the pleasure of living grandparents on either side of her family. Graham's parents she knew little of, both of them having died when she was so young as to have no recollection. Her mother's parents both died before she was born. Perhaps that loss, if loss was the correct word for something she'd never had, was the reason she'd eagerly taken to John's grandparents... needing a connection, albeit with someone else's family. An idea occurred to her.

'You said my grandmother died when I was conceived,' she asked. 'How in heavens name could you possibly know? Most people only make an educated guess, so how could you know about me when you'd never even met my parents?'

'Sarah, has anything unusual happened to you recently? Strange feelings... maybe sensing things out of the ordinary?'

Sarah opened her mouth to answer though she was unsure what to say. But the light touch caressed her forehead and whatever words were forming inside her head, only a single word came out of her mouth. 'Yes.'

'I knew as much already but I wanted you to say so. Tell me what you've seen. Be honest as you can. Faith and truth, remember.'

Sarah sat staring into Beryl's eyes, though her focus was elsewhere. Except for the slow, distant ticking of the clock way back along the corridor in the main entrance, the care home was in complete silence. Outside the daylight had faded, and across the water, the flash of a lighthouse caught the corner of her eye. The soft light from the table lamps wrapped them in a warm and secure blanket, shielding them from the chill air and the deepening dusk. A slight movement on Sarah's lap alerted her to the fact that Beryl's cat had settled there, but when she couldn't say.

The sensation on Sarah's forehead had ceased, but the very fact it occurred had a sudden and profound effect. She understood that her mind and heart had opened to anything this old woman could or would tell her, and she in turn would believe it to be the truth, however strange or unexpected. But the notion struck her as odd. Why should she believe Beryl? She'd only just met the woman… knew nothing of her background. On the other hand, what ulterior motive could she conceivably have at her age? What advantage was there from deceiving Sarah? Beryl appeared sensible and alert and lucid. She wasn't scatty or forgetful and appeared rational and analytical, and with sudden shock Sarah recognised these traits within herself.

While mulling over these thoughts, a sense of belonging crept over her as if, despite the belief she had no living relatives apart from David, Beryl *was* a link to her past, a link that would reveal a whole history of which she was unaware. For a moment, she imagined an enormous gulf of time stretching behind her, a vast chasm that held a long and eventful history, a past she'd never dreamt possible. A time of peace and tranquillity, joy even, but one interwoven with violence and tragedy. Without conscious decision, Sarah felt herself drawn into Beryl's world and in a deeply intuitive way, *knew* Beryl was a relative. Sarah's need for the sanctuary of family was her greatest strength and her greatest weakness. What was family, she thought, if not a place to belong? Family was everything. It was a warm blanket… an embrace… a safe place to hide when the world threatened. A refuge where the door was always open, and a friendly face welcomed. Sarah's need for family was deep-rooted, which explained the intensity of her grief after losing both of her parents.

With thoughts of family, she recalled the feeling she'd had when entering the building over half an hour ago. But the feeling of home that touched her back then, was little to do with the carpeted entrance, the heavy curtains and fresh flowers. Instead, it was the presence that called to her... a manifestation which sent forth warm tendrils of love that spread outwards from this quiet room overlooking the sea.

Then abruptly, Sarah was back in the room, speaking to a woman who revealed herself to be Sarah's great grandmother... learning from her and with poignant realisation, needing her. With emotions in turmoil, Sarah spoke in a voice quiet and forlorn. 'I spent a week in hospital... in a coma after being attacked. John, my husband, brought me out of it by playing birdsong... the song of the robin.'

'It was his love that brought you out of it, but go on.'

Sarah nodded and continued. 'Robins have a powerful meaning in my life for reasons I don't understand. I lost my mom a while back and after my dad died, I suffered with depression, and one day by my parents' grave, two robins landed in front of me and began to sing. While I listened, a heavy weight lifted from me, and my depression evaporated. Taken away. In some way the birds helped me see my parents' life as a joy and not their death as a disaster. But ever since I came out of my coma before Christmas, I've been having strange feelings on my forehead. It feels as if someone is holding a soothing hand there. Also, I've begun to sense things with my fingers. When I picked up your letter for the first time, I couldn't put it down again. Well not straight away. It was as if the envelope was sticky, but there was nothing on it to make it so. It clung to my fingertips as if... as if I was being compelled to read it. I know it sounds strange. And I see robins everywhere, and my daughter...' Sarah's voice faltered, '... my daughter Claire... things are happening to her as well and I don't know what it all means.'

A single tear escaped each of Sarah's eyes as she shifted her gaze to look out of the window. Outside and across the long miles to the horizon, the light had all but disappeared, leaving Ailsa Craig silhouetted against the sun's last weak rays. The darkness would fall quickly, taking the temperature with it and at the thought, Sarah shivered. During her time in hospital... during the dreams she had walked through... an old grief re-awakened, a loss she thought dealt with and put in its place. And that re-awakening had weakened her defences, made her raw and vulnerable again. But listening to Beryl, an urgent need was growing within her, a need to belong... a belonging lost, in part, after the death of her parents. This growing need ensured that any reluctance to accept Beryl's revelation, or disbelief in anything Beryl told her, slid away. Seeing an image of herself in this woman's eyes... the shape of her mouth and the curve of her face, it was easy to see the truth. The family resemblance was unmistakable, undeniable. An overwhelming desire to kneel in front of Beryl and place her head on the old woman's lap arose within Sarah's heart.

'Why are you crying, my child?' asked Beryl.

'I don't know,' answered Sarah. But shifting her gaze toward the old woman she whispered a single word... a word she had never before directed at a living person, a word that carried with it the poignancy of frustrated desires, unfulfilled needs. 'Nana.'

Uttering the word, Sarah acknowledged and accepted the truth. She could see it not only in her mother's likeness but in her own future, a future written in this old lady's face. Tears leaked from Sarah's eyes in a silent flow as she gave in to her yearning and slid off the chair and onto her knees. Her great grandmother opened her arms to Sarah and the young woman shuffled forward and placed her head against Beryl's chest sensing the invisible touch on her forehead as she did so.

'Nana?'

'Yes my dear?'

'Why does the past have to be so painful? Why can't it just pass away?'

'Ah, Sarah. If not for the past, what would we know of the future? How could we remember and learn? The pain of your loss is natural and will never leave you. However, it will also bring you wisdom and knowledge... and will teach you to help others and help you to teach others. Have you not already recognised you want more for you and your family... that you want to help others?'

Sarah lifted her head with a questioning frown. As her tears dried on her cheeks, a sudden love for this old woman touched her heart, but along with it an absolute puzzlement at how Beryl appeared to know so much. Sarah's thoughts fled back to the day she sat in Costa Coffee with Rachel following her return home from hospital.

'How do you know that?'

'Remember what I told you about my daughter... I could sense her, your grandmother. I never saw her again after she was taken from me. But I was aware of her. It was a gift beginning not long after she went to live with my sister. And so there is a connection between *us* Sarah... not least a family connection. I sense your soul and the intense emotions you have.'

'Gift?' asked Sarah.

'Yes, a gift. My gift began after I lost my beloved Joseph and my daughter. Sarah, for our kind the gift often begins after tragedy or trauma, times of great shock or stress. The same has happened to you. It began after your parents passed on but strengthened after your accident.

'You see, I'd lost everything I held dear... everything. My broken heart couldn't contain my grief. I lost my Joseph to the war, a horrible death like thousands of others. We were ripped apart when our love had barely begun. And I wasn't allowed to keep my child... the only link I had with him. I wasn't even allowed to hold her. It's impossible to describe the devastation I felt. My desolation was so intense that not long after, I tried to kill myself. I took my father's razor and cut my wrists. I think using my father's razor was a way of making him pay for my loss since it was he who ruled our house… he who insisted I give up my baby. He was not one of us… my mother and I… and you. We were different. Anyway, I'd tried to end my life but my mother found me in time and sent me to a convalescent home where I was watched day and night, at least for a while. It was there my gift awoke.'

Beryl stopped to take another drink. Sarah sat at her feet both horrified and engrossed at the tale.

'It happened one afternoon while I sat by a river. The convalescent home was away up north in the highlands, so remote as to remove any unwanted contact with the outside world. A beautiful place it was with large gardens, a little burn running through, plenty of places to sit and think. Unusually for the early twentieth century, it was a warm and friendly place. In those days, many institutes were governed by people who were unsympathetic. They were evil places, and some people who were sent in never came out again. I found out many years later my mother insisted I stayed at this place. My father wanted to put me in an asylum. For him I had brought shame and disgrace on the family. But my mother held sway since she knew what it was like to be in love so young and understood how devastated I felt. She was the one who insisted my sister raise my daughter, and she was not simply placed in an orphan's home. She also insisted I could name her.'

'Is that what your father wanted… to get rid of my grandmother?'

'I'm afraid to say it was. He wasn't a bad man, Sarah, but he tried to cross the class boundary. He forgot his roots in his endeavours to make what he called a better life for his family, for my mother and me. Both my parents came from a simple background. People who worked the land for others. But my father wanted to be his own master by bettering himself. Well that desire put him under pressure to behave in a way unnatural to him. I'm convinced it took him to an early grave since he'd died by the time he was fifty. There was fifteen years between my mother and my father. He'd taken her as a young wife when she was only sixteen, which was commonplace in those days. Men often took young brides while they were young and healthy and able to make large families. My mother however only had two of us and both were daughters. I arrived when my mother was only nineteen and my grandmother was thirty-five. Because my mother hadn't given birth to boys, my father became somewhat embittered since he hadn't a son and heir. My parents drifted apart not long after I was born.'

'So it seems most births in our family were to young mothers,' Sarah mused. 'I suppose it was the second world war that interrupted the tradition… for my own parents. But what about the gift?'

'Sarah, I remember the day it all began as clear as if it were only yesterday. One sunny afternoon in late summer, I was sitting on a blanket writing a letter to my mother. I'd been there for about four months and had recovered from my injuries, the physical ones at least. I was writing about how I missed her and my Joseph and about how I hoped little Jade was happy and being cared for. As I wrote, a light touch brushed my forehead as if a gentle hand lay there. It was so calming I closed my eyes and almost fell asleep. Through my eyelids I could sense the sunlight rippling on the water of the little burn I was sitting by, and I heard the contented gurgling of a small baby. It continued for many minutes and when it faded away, I knew in my heart it was my little Jade. After that day, I sensed her often and, as I explained earlier, I could feel her when she was sad or happy. From that day onwards, I experienced other things, like sensing other people's intense emotions, or seeing colours around them, which changed depending on their well-being. I took a long time to understand any of it, or how to use it, and during my whole life I never stopped learning or experiencing something new.

'The sensing gift, as I called it, increased in strength

quickly, after just a few days, until I only had to think about Jade and I could sense her from a great distance, and a great distance it was. There was I way up north in the highlands with my little Jade over four hundred miles away. But distance didn't seem to be a problem. And I found my gift affected others. I found I could sense when other people, other patients who were staying at the home, struggled with the pain of their wounds or were disturbed by other demons. I could see it, not only in their behaviour but also as a coloured halo around them. Sometimes it would be a dirty drab colour, other times almost non-existent. You see, we had injured soldiers staying with us. Men sent to convalesce after returning from the war. Men with horrific injuries, or so deeply damaged by the horrors there was nowhere else to send them. I found if I sat with them for a while, talking or even sitting in silence, their ailments improved, both physical and emotional. I seemed to have developed a gift of healing, and that has happened to you, Sarah, after your loss and your injuries. Your gift has awakened and will develop with little effort on your part, though you will have to learn how to use it.'

Beryl fell silent, and for long seconds stared into Sarah's eyes, as if searching for a sign or considering what to say next. Finally she spoke, and what she told Sarah amazed and surprised the younger of the two women, but Sarah was convinced it was the absolute truth. Sarah's faith in Beryl was now without bounds.

'Sarah, one day when I'd been away for almost six months, something troubled me though I couldn't work out what. By this time my gift had brought me inner peace... I'd learned to accept the challenge life had laid before me... the tragedy. I'd gained salvation for myself and developed a gift I could use to help others suffering from spiritual devastation. It meant I recognised within myself when something was wrong, some dis-ease that leached wellness out of my soul. What touched me that day was so potent, so unmistakably bad I stayed away from others. Another thing

I'd learnt was I could inadvertently project my mood on people around me so I hid in my room, fearing I would pass on my unease. It wasn't until two days later, when my mother arrived to take me home that I understood I'd picked up on my father's illness... the heart attack that killed him.'

'You sensed your own father's death?'

'Yes. I think it was the intense spiritual energy because of the close family connection.' Beryl took a last sip from her teacup and dabbed at her aged lips. 'Afterwards, my grandmother Celeste spoke with me for many hours. She was a young bride too, and hence a young grandmother. It's odd to think my father was the same age as my grandmother.

'Celeste revealed many things concerning the gift... explained a lot, but not too much. No one can really explain the gift to another. It would be like trying to explain the concept of love. It's always better to self-learn but with a few warnings given. Celeste also showed me our family tree. I can trace our ancestry back through many generations and one day you will see this family tree yourself.

'Sarah, my child, I've developed my gift over many years, understanding more and more about it as I've gone along. I've travelled, I've taught and learnt, I've helped people. In some ways I've become a master but I can tell you only so much about the gift. The rest you must learn on your own. It has always been this way because we are... special. You can be taught how to play a musical instrument... where to put your fingers, how to read a musical score, but no one can teach you how to become a true artist. That achievement comes through practice and continuous use and, more importantly, from within your soul... how much of your inner self you put into it. Our gift is similar. It has awakened. I can tell you about it but only you can develop it. It has been passed on throughout the centuries and will continue to do so. Sometimes it skips a generation and is at best a shadow of what it can be. But to put it simply, we are descended from a long line of people blessed with spiritual gifts, gifts of healing, of growing, of seeing. Those who were called enchantresses, followers of paganism, shamans, wise women, and more recently in the 20th century those who worship Wicca. To use a more popular word… witches.'

Beryl let her words sink in for a moment before continuing.

'In bygone times, "witch" conjured up an image of evil. Which is why they were hunted down and persecuted, tortured, burned. Powerful religious bodies demonised the ideology or practice of witchcraft, organisations that, considering their own longevity, are much younger than the simpler and more basic beliefs and connections to the energies that course through our world and beyond. These ancient beliefs go back thousands of years, back to times when we existed as a part of this world rather than masters of it. The powers that spread their doctrine throughout the land, converting and often corrupting, sought to alienate and criminalise those who went against the new religions, making up evil stories and lies and creating fear and violence.

'But all we had were extra special abilities, gifts that lie hidden in others. We, as a people, possessed many skills that worked within the natural world. We coexisted with nature not against it. In this modern age there are many so-called gifted people. Those who possess an incredible talent for a variety of familiar tasks. Some of these gifts come easily, some have to be learned through hard work. Some are simple, like learning to ride a bike. Others are complicated like being able to play a musical instrument or paint a stunning work of art. Some are even harder to grasp. For example, the unimaginable skills of an autistic child solving the most complicated of puzzles or remembering a hundred sequences of letters or numbers. This example is closer to our skills than many others in the sense they can't be learnt. They occur naturally, whether due to a dysfunction of some sort or as an inherited skill. Usually in our case, but not always, enormous stress or great tragedy triggers its growth. In my case having my only true love and my daughter taken from me was enough to do it. In your case, being attacked and lying in a hospital for a week would also do it. That was your awakening.'

'But how does tragedy awaken it?' asked Sarah, needing clarification. With stiffening legs she lifted herself back onto the chair while hanging on Beryl's every word. The power of this woman was incredible, she thought. Her persona projected comfort and understanding... and instilled faith and trust with ease. To Sarah, the thought of being descended from ancient witches didn't seem so unusual. After all, Sarah realised, witches existed. Not the black cat, pointy hat, broomstick sort of witch. More the healer or herbalist and inevitably there would be descendants.

'There are things which can't be explained... or maybe they don't need an explanation. I like to think the gift awakens when it is most needed. When does a person need spiritual help if not in times of stress? This is when our spiritual energy is at its greatest peril. Some turn to their God for help. Others continue to struggle. For us, it appears tragedy triggers the inbuilt strength we are all born with. But as for the gift, these are the gifts of seeing... of healing... of helping. In days gone by, though, these gifts brought their own peril. Persecution was commonplace. Anyone who exhibited secular behaviour or did not conform were victimised and tortured... put to death in one evil way or another. Burning was a classic way, and this carried on until around the early 1700s when the last burnings took place.'

Beryl paused long enough to clear her throat again.

'The gifts themselves varied amongst witches. Some were healers. Knowledgeable in herbal remedies, for example. Others had special gifts as natural to them as eyesight is to most other people. That extra special gift could be of seeing without looking, hearing without listening, the ones science can't explain. Sarah, you have an inherited a strong gift, or it will be once you've learnt more of it and it has developed within you. You can't stop it now it has awoken any more than you can unlearn how to walk. It's up to you how you use it, but I think you already know that.'

Beryl's tale captivated Sarah. The awesome gulf of time she'd pictured earlier appeared to her once more... the history that held peace and tragedy, joy and suffering. As she stared at Beryl, her eyes glazed and she focussed not on her great grandmother, but on the aura she could clearly perceive... the aura of vibrant violet extending many feet around the old lady.

Sensing Sarah's spiritual touch, the old woman smiled. 'See. You are playing with it already. Your own aura is white, Sarah. Did you know? White. The highest colour of them all, though yet it does not extend far. That will change. Now talk, while you can.'

The two women sat in silence, gazing at each other in the semi-darkness. The sun had now disappeared and, with only the gentle glow from the lamps on Beryl's bedside tables, the outside world was in utter darkness. Sarah was unaware of the passage of time. She could have been sat for hours or even days. Unnoticed by either of them, a shadow appeared in the doorway. Margaret, the receptionist, peered inside and made a quiet whistling sound. Amber the cat jumped off the bed where she had settled and trotted out of the room in search of dinner. With care, Margaret pulled the door until it was almost closed and wandered away to feed the cat.

Eventually Sarah spoke. 'I don't know what to say. I came here unsure of what I was searching for. It was fine by me since we were on our way up for Christmas anyway, so coming over to Girvan was no hardship. But now I've found *you*. A relative I never knew I had. Everything you've explained fits in with some of the odd feelings I've been having since my accident. What you've told me may well help me decide what I want to do with my life. The question is will you help me?'

'I can start you on the road. I can help awaken more of your energy, open the channels... but you will learn much on your own as you experiment. There are some things in this life no one can teach you how to do. But there is one thing I must tell you and one thing you must remember. The power of healing won't work with everyone. The power is there when it is given, but when a healing energy is placed, it will have to battle against negative energies. If an individual does not believe they can be helped, or has deep-rooted negativity, no amount of positive healing energy will benefit them until they allow it. Remember also that witches commanded a variety of powers or gifts. Some would have been skilled in working with one of the different elements.... fire, water, earth and air. These are the things we all need to survive and some are expert at working with them. Others like yourself are empowered to work within all the elements because you have within you ultimate powers of healing and energy. You need to learn how to channel it.'

'But where do I start?' Sarah was feeling overwhelmed.

'There is a huge arsenal of tools you can use when you have the knowledge... herbal or crystal, heat and water... colours or just your own channelled energies. But Sarah, my dear, don't concern yourself with the enormity of what I've told you. In one way, your life is the same as it always was. You could go back to your old life and carry on with what you have been doing and in the meantime play around with the gift, test it out, see what you can see. Help those around you who may need help. I've sensed there are those close to you who are lost... sensed it from your own spirit and how it's affected by their dis-ease. Or, you can change everything as soon as you go home, give up what you know and probably get very overwhelmed. I know which path I would choose since it's the same as the one I chose ninety years ago.'

'People close to me?'

'Yes. You know who they are. You've sensed their anguish.'

Sarah cast her mind into the recent past, and with little effort remembered the dinner party… the evening she returned home from hospital. She'd circled the table to give everyone a hug and heard voices in her head. Unsure if she had imagined them, the words were so full of violence she struggled afterwards to understand why she should imagine such harsh words. When she touched Steve she'd heard, *You fat little faggot, you ain't got the guts.* And when she gave Rachel a hug she heard, *C'mon out here you little tart.*

Sarah puzzled over Beryl's words. *How the hell does she know about Steve and Rachel.*

'I know about them,' said Beryl, guessing the question in Sarah's head, 'not because I can read your mind, that's impossible. But because I'm linked to you by blood and by spirit. If you suffer or experience an assault on your spirit, I pick up the negative energy. I sense it and sometimes, if powerful enough, I experience it on an emotional plane. It's been a long time since I could do that with anyone Sarah and that's because of your recent awakening. There are strong energies within you.'

'So in the same way,' Sarah considered, 'I know two of my friends have some previous pain in their lives because I picked up their anguish… the after-effect of their powerful memories.'

Beryl smiled. 'Exactly.'

'But will I be able to do it with everyone?' Sarah asked, a little perturbed. The last thing she wanted to do was to have negative energy affecting her own mood whenever she got near someone. Imagine, she thought, walking through a town centre and sensing unimaginable pain and fear.

'No, not everyone and not always. It will depend on the individual and upon your focus. The first thing you need to learn is to close your mind so you can block whenever you need to. It's most imperative or you will suffer greatly. But no, you won't be overwhelmed.'

Beryl glanced outside, staring at the flash of the lighthouse as it signalled its rhythmic warning. 'Something else I learnt early on, which I believe is very important. If someone comes to you asking for help, it's up to you whether you offer it or not. If a person doesn't ask it's best not to offer unless you think they're in grave danger.'

Sarah sat in silence for a few moments, following Beryl's gaze. Uncertainty filled her soul, and she shook her head. *How is any of this possible? Surely it's all nonsense? I've no real idea who this woman is.* But studying Beryl, she saw once more the unmistakable similarity to Rose and herself. It wasn't hard to believe this woman was related and Sarah acknowledged the resemblance was more than coincidence. However distant, the family connection was surely very real.

Eventually she spoke again. 'I think I'll take your advice. Carry on as I was but start to explore my own abilities. You said you could start me off? What was it? Open the channels? What does that mean?'

Beryl said nothing, but smiled and stared at Sarah as if she had sensed her great granddaughter's inner struggle.

Sarah remembered her conversation with Rachel. Everything Beryl revealed to her was the essence of what she'd talked over with her friend, the need for something different, something she could use or do to help people in a personal and rewarding way. The afternoon had turned out to be an unbelievable revelation, but how was she supposed to explain it to her husband. The unusual feelings and the sightings she'd been having, starting with the voices and the purple aura around John, appeared to be a part of something bigger, and she now understood what that was and how far it spread. Another question arose in her mind. 'Nana? There's something else I have to ask.'

As Sarah gazed at her great grandmother's smiling face, a fit of painful coughing wracked the poor woman's body once more. Beryl tipped forward as each violent cough shook her to the very core. The handkerchief was against her mouth but this time Sarah stood and wrapped one arm around Beryl's shoulders, whilst her other hand found Beryl's free hand and the two ladies held onto each other.

'Can I get you anything?' Sarah asked after the spasm passed. 'Do I need to call a doctor?'

'No thank you, dear. The doctor can't help me. I'm afraid I have an incurable illness. A lifetime of healthy living cannot wholly protect a person from ill health. Some fresh tea would be nice though.' and Beryl smiled.

Shock spread across Sarah's face. 'Do you mean I'm losing you when we've only just met?'

Beryl leaned back in her chair, the stained handkerchief resting in her lap. 'I'm sorry Sarah but it can't be helped so let's make the most of our time. This will be a lot harder for you than for me, at least to begin with. But you will not lose me. Only in the physical sense will I be gone. All I'm doing is taking a different path, and one intertwined with your own. Let's have some fresh tea, and in answer to the question you were about to ask me, yes… the touch on your forehead is me, or emanates from me. Right from when you were still in a coma to a few moments ago. It's simply my thought, my energy, sometimes protecting you, sometimes guiding you, but always helping. You will be able to do it yourself one day… sense and help a person from afar.'

Finding no words to say, Sarah crossed the room to the kettle. She switched it on and walked back to collect their cups and the teapot, taking them into the bathroom to rinse them. As she dried the cups she tried not to think about losing Beryl. *It's not bloody fair* she thought. Not fair she should find a link to her past, only to have it snatched away. *Damn it!* But as she poured hot water into the tea pot to warm it, the touch was on her forehead again, and amidst the song of a robin, a voice spoke inside her head:

'Fair has little to do with it, princess. It's just the way it is.'

With eyes widening, Sarah froze, and stared into the teapot. The voice she heard came not from inside the room, but far beyond. The voice belonged to Graham, her father.

'Dad?' she whispered. 'Daddy?'

'You see Sarah,' said Beryl, hearing Sarah's softly spoken words. 'It's the nature of things, the joy of it, and the continuity. Your father is a part of you and you are a part of your father as you are a part of Rose and Jade and me. With your awakening we are now a bigger part of each other. Through the generations we are linked, and beyond, over hundreds of years.'

'My father? Do you mean my dad was part of this too? How far does all of this reach?' asked Sarah pouring hot water over fresh tea leaves.

'Yes he is. He has played his part. In your case, you are your mother's daughter. It is from the female bloodline your powers and ancestry can be traced... all the way back to those early witches I told you about. Your mother with her own sight and her own subtle needs chose her husband. It's common for the women in our family to choose their partners based on those subtleties and often from within the subconscious. But he would have had his own strength different from your mother's and as for how far it reaches... that's almost impossible to answer. Imagine one of your friends tracing their full family tree, a friend who has siblings and many aunts and uncles. Imagine how long it would take to trace back every branch of the tree... and for every member.'

Sarah poured fresh tea into their cups and the powerful scent of chamomile filled the room once more bringing a measure of calm to her uneasy mind. Through tight lips she spoke. 'Nana.... how long do we have? Can I... will I be able to see you again?'

'Not long, angel. A few days maybe. I'll open a Christmas present or two if I'm lucky. It's up to you to decide if you want to see me again.'

Sarah frowned. 'Up to me? What do you mean it's up to me?'

Beryl didn't answer. Instead, she pointed to Sarah's chair. 'Sarah, lift your chair into the middle of the room and place it facing the door.'

'Nana, what do you mean it's up to me?'

'You'll see. Some things are beyond understanding and there are many things in this world greater than we are. There are those who believe in destiny or fate and those who feel we are wandering around with no clear purpose. I believe perhaps it's both, together and at the same time. Faith, remember. Now… pull that chair out. There's one last thing I need to do before I'm too tired.'

Sarah did as asked and following Beryl's instructions, sat in the chair. Behind her and out of sight, she heard Beryl groan as she rose to her feet. Grabbing a walking stick as an aid, Beryl shuffled the few feet to Sarah and stood behind her. Sarah felt a light touch on her shoulders as Beryl laid her cool hands there.

The caress was on Sarah's forehead again and a surge of heat coursed through her body and soul. With her eyes closed she could hear the rustle of Beryl's gown. As Beryl muttered to herself, speaking words Sarah could not catch, she sensed her aged relative was conducting a ritual, but one of which she, Sarah, had no knowledge. The ritual took only minutes but during that time something let loose inside Sarah and silent tears trickled from her eyes once more. Again she was back at her parents' graveside. Over the years since that day, the day when understanding had been given to her and her pain removed, a wall had inexorably built itself around her, a protective skin against the world. But the protection was never enough without a deeper strength within, a strength and power to guard against negativity… the bad energy that threatened her peace and wellbeing. Sarah suddenly understood that with the gift and the strength and power that came with it, she would have no need for a protective skin… she would have an inbuilt strength she could use to control any malignancy.

As the tears dried on her cheeks, Sarah noticed a subtle energy coursing through her and her hair felt as if it were waving around… charged with static electricity. A welcome sense of peace crept over her, dispelling her insecurities, a peace such as had coursed through her years ago as she tended her parents' grave. Then a quiet cough behind her made her open her eyes.

'That's it, my child. That is working for you and will stay with you forever. Now will you help me back to my seat for we must ready ourselves to say goodbye.'

Sarah didn't want to say goodbye, but she understood now the nature of things. Beryl was a part of her as were her parents. She had shared an unexpected story with Sarah, and the younger woman had an exciting journey on which to embark. Sarah told Rachel she needed a change in her life. How she started it and how she continued would be of her own choice and of her own making.

'Sarah, I see by the strength of your aura you are at this moment at peace. But there is one final thing to tell you. Another mystery for you to work through which will be the start of another new path for you if you wish for it.'

Sarah helped Beryl back into her chair and settled her into it, making sure she could reach her tea. She turned her own chair around and sat again before asking a question. 'Nana? I need to ask about the aura. I've seen it around a few people now but what is it? How is it I can see it?'

'You can see it, or more accurately sense it since the eye cannot see such things, because you have the gift of sight. Many people can sense a person's mood with inbuilt intuition. You on the other hand have an inbuilt inner sight. It's known as the third eye. The third eye enables you to perceive beyond ordinary sight, or reach into higher levels of consciousness. It's what you sense on your forehead when I reach for you... my touch... your third eye sensing my spiritual energies. You'll be able to read all about it from my books and my journals but much of it you will understand from practical use. But now I need to tell you something else.' Beryl sipped her tea and cautiously cleared her throat. 'There is a place for you to find,' she began. 'A place that has belonged to our ancestors for many generations and it is now yours, or will be when I've moved on. Papers are drawn up already.'

'A place? Papers? Papers for what?' asked Sarah, amazed there were still more mysteries.

'A dwelling place, but not one that can be found by accident, at least not all of it. Part of it is a secret, kept so for hundreds of years, a sanctuary where our kind could hide when danger came too close. Without this secret place, we would not have survived and you must now find it. My last bit of fun, but if I am right, its spiritual power will draw you. The place has so much energy you could probably find it in the dark. It is ready for you.

'Now listen carefully. From a layby not far out of Straiton, on the road to Barr, there is a path. The road to Barr, of course, used to be a simple farm track when I was your age but the pathway leads across a field into a wood. The wood is dense with both pine and deciduous trees. It's a natural wood, an ancient wood and protected now. You must follow a straight path across the field from the layby, and from the edge of the wood you must measure seven hundred straight steps to where the eagle sits, then four on the right and three on the left. At the wall, turn to the left and reach behind the holly. Make good use of it. It is waiting for us.'

Us? Thought Sarah.

Beryl leaned back and closed her eyes. While listening, Sarah's eyesight had focussed beyond Beryl, as if she were imagining a time long since gone. Her inner sight was taking her along an ancient pathway, through ancient woods to a place of which she had no living memory, and yet in an intangible sense was familiar. Though on the face of it the instructions given to Sarah appeared as those from a fairy tale, they seemed very real, very present and so easy to remember it felt as if she was already aware of them. She had no need to make a note.

On the edge of hearing, Beryl whispered, bringing Sarah's attention back into the room. 'Sarah, my angel, you have been awakened. I have helped as I may and, though you won't quite understand yet, just in the nick of time. Our line will continue for certain, but the gifts will continue only if you choose to use them. If you succeed, the line will have a strength it has not possessed for a very long time, not since the last burning. Good luck, though I feel luck is not needed. If you can, you may come and see me again, but if not we shall meet in the future, come what may. I've asked you to have faith in me, now you must have faith in yourself.'

Beryl's words became fainter as she slipped towards sleep and Sarah leaned forward to catch the last of them. 'Remember this is no mystery, no fantasy. It's as real as everything around us, my dear. You are not in *The Matrix*. You aren't "The One". Yes, I watched that film. There is no link to Christ. I read that book as well. We are just ordinary people in an ordinary world but with extraordinary gifts. Use them wisely.'

And with those words Beryl fell silent. A faint creak alerted Sarah to the presence of Amber the cat. With purpose she padded across the room and with fluid ease jumped on to Beryl's lap. The old lady did not move as the cat curled itself into a sleepy ball.

In complete silence and sitting still in the cosy room, lit only by the gentle glow of the bedside lamps, Sarah stared out into the darkness of the world until she too fell asleep.

Fifteen

Sarah did not sleep for long. She awoke with thoughts of family. For the first time in her life however she dreamt of flying. It wouldn't have surprised her to have dreamt of broomsticks, black cats and cauldrons, but the sensation of flying was the closest she could get to describing her passage through the dream.

Soaring above a world that flew past at an ever-quickening pace, she felt as if she were being transported back in time through the generations, through world events, past the Second World War and onwards. Past the birth of her mother and grandmother and even further backwards into earlier centuries to when life was fraught with the perils of hunger or violence, fear and prejudice. She dreamt of a simple and peaceful life, though a hard one. A life of tradition and long held beliefs of an ancient sort... belief in the spirits of the elements, instead of beliefs brought from a different world that threatened the simple lives of generations of the native people. Then her journey reversed, and she flew forward through time. She observed the slow erosion of these indigenous beliefs, and the wholesale violent destruction of them by a corrupt and malevolent force. She witnessed the torture and murder of a simple people, a people who lived and worked within the natural order, coexisting with the natural world. The final horror that shocked Sarah out of her slumber was the vision of a cottage in a small clearing... a cottage lying in ruins with smoke rising from it, while the upturned face of a small child gazed into the heavens as silent tears coursed down her face.

Peering at her watch, Sarah saw it was close to five o'clock. *Damn, look at the time. I need to get home. John will be getting worried.*

She glanced over at Beryl who still slept soundly whilst Amber lay curled on her lap. Without making a sound, Sarah stayed as she was for a few minutes until she became aware of an object laying on her own lap, a small white stone, placed there while she dozed. Mystified she had not awakened, she took hold of the gem and turned it over in her hands. It felt cool and had a milky appearance but with strands of light and dark shades spreading across and under its surface. Just the touch of it brought a smile to Sarah and with it a deeper sense of calm.

But remembering the time, she stood and, though reluctant to leave, took a last glance at Beryl. Grabbing her coat and handbag she slipped out of the room and made her way back to reception. Margaret was still on duty and sat at her desk filling out puzzles in a book.

'Oh hi,' Margaret said. 'I'd almost forgotten you were down there. How are things?'

In light of everything, Sarah was unsure what to say, so answered with a polite, 'Oh fine thanks. Beryl's asleep, and it's time I was going. It's getting late.'

'Was it what you expected? Did you get what you came for?'

Sarah returned Margaret's smile. 'Not really sure what I expected, but I got a lot more than I imagined.'

'Well I'll check on her in a minute and see what she wants for dinner. Will you come back again?'

'Oh definitely. Probably on Boxing Day if that's ok?'

'I'm sure that'll be fine. Oh and Beryl asked me to give

you this on your way out.' Margaret handed Sarah an envelope. 'You take care now and have a Merry Christmas.'

'Oh, thank you,' replied Sarah somewhat puzzled. When did Beryl give the note to Margaret? She hadn't left the room during the afternoon unless she had done so while Sarah was asleep. But she was sure Beryl would have woken her if she'd moved. Sarah was half convinced it was written before she arrived as if Beryl had no doubt Sarah would find her. *This gets better and better.*

'And a Merry Christmas to you too,' Sarah replied, and with the utterance of those words, she settled fully back into the real world. She put the envelope into her handbag and headed outside into a dark and chilly Christmas Eve.

Halfway home, inquisitiveness got the better of Sarah and she pulled into a layby. Turning on the overhead light, she reached into her handbag, took out Beryl's note and began to read.

> *Sarah, my child. By now you will be wondering what the gem is I placed on your lap. It is a moonstone. You can read all about it from my books. They will all be yours soon along with everything else, but for now you need to know that moonstone is a stone for new beginnings. It is one of your birthstones and is suited to you. It is a stone for inner growth and strength and will soothe emotional instability, which will help calm both your old and new fears. Also it will enhance intuition though you already have great strength here.*
>
> *You are on the path my child; enjoy the journey. I will see you again one day, though we will never be apart.*

Sarah folded the note and lifting it up, held it to her lips. Staring out of the windscreen into the darkness, she smiled as she caught the scent of chamomile, but her sight misted as an image of Beryl came to mind. Starting up the engine again she continued her journey, weeping to herself as she drove home. Unsure of the reason for her tears, she simply let them flow. Overjoyed at discovering her past and finding Beryl, she realised her joy was tinged with a looming sense of loss, and that before long she would be on her own again. But with sudden guilt, she realised that wasn't the case, not with her family waiting for her. *What was family?* Sarah thought once more. Family was home, and that was where she needed to be.

John, Claire and Hamish were clearing away a game of Scrabble when Sarah came in through the front door. John jumped to his feet and made his way into the hall.

'Go and get warm by the fire. Do you want a drink?'

Sarah grabbed John in a fierce hug and lay her head against his chest.

'What's this? Are you ok? Did you have any luck?'

'Yes and yes,' Sarah whispered, 'but I need you to hold me.'

John wrapped his arms around Sarah and placed a hand upon her head.

For a minute they stayed as they were, locked together as one... rigid as a statue, until Claire came through from the living room, stared at Sarah and said, 'Is Beryl nice, Mommy?'

A mixture of emotions rippled through Sarah. There was sadness from the fact she'd known nothing of her ancestors, but also joy knowing she belonged to something bigger than she could ever have imagined. She felt cheated that the time she was likely to have with her ancient great grandmother was limited, but grateful for having followed up the innocent clues in the letter that led her to Beryl. And she felt unnerved by Claire's powerful and almost mystical intuition… unnerved, but excited that her daughter belonged to the same history as herself.

She lifted her head and turned towards Claire as the young girl wandered nonchalantly through into the kitchen. 'Yes, sweetheart,' Sarah said with tenderness. 'She's lovely.'

'I take it you found her?' John asked. 'But how did Claire know? Have I missed something?'

Sarah reached up and kissed her husband. 'You haven't missed a thing, but it's a long story and yes please.'

John raised an eyebrow. 'Yes please to what? Oh a drink. Tea? Coffee? A wee dram?'

Sarah's smile was enough answer. 'Let's celebrate and I'll tell you about it. I need to get you on your own, though, to explain everything.'

Sarah turned and kicked off her shoes in the hallway, slipping her feet into warm slippers. A sudden idea occurred to her, and she turned back to John in time to catch a grin on his face.

'What are you smirking at?'

John moved closer to her and placed his hands on her waist, his lips against her ear. 'I was just staring at your bottom.'

Claire called through from the kitchen. 'Get a room!'

'How old is she? That's your fault,' Sarah said to John, who shook his head and raised his eyes to the ceiling. 'Anyway,' she began again. 'I was about to say how do you fancy a little adventure tomorrow afternoon?'

'Tomorrow? It is Christmas Day, y'know.'

'Yes, but after dinner, before teatime. Papa will doze off and Claire will keep an eye on him.'

'Where are we going?' John asked.

'I don't know,' answered Sarah with an embarrassed laugh. 'I have directions to somewhere but what we'll find there I don't know.'

John regarded Sarah with narrowed eyes. 'You don't know? You're not making much sense. I think you'd better tell me more about it first. It'll need to be something special to drag me out on Christmas Day?'

Sarah flashed her eyes at John. 'Well how about I make it worth your while after?'

'That's unfair and if you think I'd fall for it… oh go on,' and they both laughed again.

Sarah walked into the living room and gave Hamish a kiss on the cheek. 'Hi Papa. Have you been taking care of my family for me?'

'Och aye. I've pulled up the drawbridge and manned the battlements against marauding Sassenach invaders.'

'You mean you dozed off again.'

'Well I may have done. C'mon, lassie. Tell us what you found. John!' Hamish called. 'Where's that malt?'

'Coming!' John called from the kitchen and appeared with glass tumblers and a small jug of water.

Sarah sat, took a glass of neat whisky from her husband and began her tale.

She kept much of what Beryl described to herself, partly because she felt it would be difficult to explain and partly because she needed time to find a proper place for it in her own mind. Saying nothing of the ancient history and the links to mystical traditions, she simply told them of Beryl… where she lived and the family connection through Rose and Jade.

After Sarah finished, it was John who spoke first.

'Can you be sure she's your great grandmother? It's not that I don't believe you, or her, but...'

Sarah nodded her head.

'I know… it's unusual. But when I walked into the care home, do you know what I asked the receptionist? I asked if there was someone called Beryl living there because I thought I was related to her. The question surprised me. I had no plans to ask it, and I think even up to when I entered her room I didn't expect to meet a relative. But John… as soon as I saw her I knew the truth. It was like looking at my mom, or my reflection. The resemblance was unmistakable. So yes, I believe it with all my heart. And she told me her solicitors tracked me down, so they would have checked the registers for births.'

With an inquisitive gaze Hamish stared at Sarah and sipped his whisky. 'So what happens next?' he asked.

Sarah gazed back and noted a dark purple colour hovering around his shoulders, dark and faint. Even to her inexperienced prescience, it seemed weak, lacking in energy. For a moment, as they contemplated each other, Sarah wondered if there was more to Hamish's words than was apparent within his simple question. She recalled their conversation from the previous night, a conversation she would never forget.

'Well,' she began. 'there's something I want to check out tomorrow night with John, something Beryl told me about, if it's ok to leave Claire with you for a while. And I think I'd like to pay her another visit on Boxing Day.'

'Can we go too, Mommy?' pleaded Claire. 'All of us.'

'I don't see why not? I'd like her to meet more of her family. How about it? Shall we all go?'

Hamish replied first. 'You three go along. I'll keep the dog here. You can tell me all about it when you get back.'

'Are you sure Papa?' asked Sarah. 'You can come if you want to.'

'No I'll be fine here. It's too cold to go far.'

He glanced at Sarah again and gave her the subtlest of winks.

'Ok, Papa.'

Sarah drew a deep breath to take control of a barrage of emotions. Once again she battled against joy and the thought of imminent grief, of finding and losing. Aware all eyes were on her, she rose to her feet.

'Look at the time! C'mon. Let's get tea ready and after we can pick a film to watch, or play a game… or both!'

With Hamish sat in his favourite armchair, the three others sprang into action, once more weaving a pattern as they moved between the dining room and the kitchen, carrying crockery and cutlery, cold meats, bread and fruit and Christmas delights.

The evening continued with much joy and gladness, and after tea they turned the lights low, stoked up the fire and sat cosy in the living room watching a film and waiting for a yawning Claire to fall asleep. A few minutes before ten o'clock, John carried his daughter up to bed, dimmed the bedroom light and closed the door.

Meanwhile, the outside temperature fell closer to freezing, and as a stiff easterly breeze chilled the Christmas Eve air, late night revellers headed outside as if in defiance of it. And a short distance away, sat upright in a comfortable armchair, gazing out across the dark waters toward the Isle of Arran, Beryl waited in contentment and in peace.

Sixteen

It was a few minutes before three o'clock the following day when John lifted the last cup from the drainer, dried it and placed it along with the others on the dresser. Everything in his grandfather's kitchen was as familiar to him as everything in his own house, and he smiled with fondness and a little wistfulness as he recalled the Christmases he and his father had spent under the care of his grandparents. For a moment he wandered into the past and wondered where the years had gone since he left Scotland with his father, but then pulled himself back from an edge he did not want to approach, not on Christmas Day. He turned and peered through the kitchen window into a garden lying asleep for winter and noticed the daylight already fading.

The quiet sounds of the television drifted through from the living room where his grandfather and Claire sat cuddled on the sofa waiting for the Queen's speech. Hamish always watched the monarch on Christmas Day, a ritual he continued after losing John's grandmother eight years ago, and one that John, Sarah and Claire didn't mind. For John there was comfort in the nostalgia of it.

A faint rustle disturbed his reverie, and he turned to see a smiling Sarah leaning against the doorframe. She wore a seasonal red dress glittering with subtle sequins hemmed around the neckline. A narrow white belt pulled the waist in, and across her shoulders, a thin white cardigan draped. Her long dark hair fell across one shoulder and the only item amusingly out of place was a pair of furry pink slippers Claire gave to her mother as a present.

A quizzical look lay on Sarah's face. With one eyebrow raised and head tilted and angled downwards, she teased John with a provocative gaze. He felt an immediate urge to join with his wife, but the need to hold Sarah overrode his desires and he moved across the kitchen and wrapped his arms around her.

Sarah whispered in his ear. 'How are you?'

'How am I?' he responded, then sighed. 'I'm not sure. Ok I suppose, but still a little unsettled. Coming here for Christmas with all its little rituals and time to sit and chill is… perfect. But it's too easy with all this peace and quiet to remember when you were in hospital. Scared me to death. But it's no use dwelling on it. It all turned out well though it's made me wonder about our future and what's best for us and Claire… and maybe another little one.'

Sarah pulled back a little and stood on tiptoe to kiss him on the mouth. John responded in kind and feeling his wife's lips part, a more basic desire returned. But it wasn't long before Sarah's kiss broke into a smile.

'Hmm,' she pulled away again. 'I see a belly full of dinner hasn't dampened your desires! Feels like you're ready to try for another baby right now!'

'I can't help it,' he said feigning embarrassment.

'Well I'm afraid you'll have to wait because it's time to have our adventure.'

'Oh yes. Your little mystery. I haven't forgotten your offer you know.'

Sarah laughed. 'God, I don't know what's got into you recently, not that I'm complaining but be serious a minute. I need to use the toilet and then we can go. Can you grab a couple of torches?'

John raised his eyebrows.

'Torches! Ok. I'll tell the others we're going out. How long do you reckon we'll be?' he asked.

Sarah was already halfway up the stairs and called back. 'I think a few hours but we should be back for around seven.'

As John entered the living room, Claire spoke before he had a chance himself.

'Is Mommy taking you out?'

'Yes, angel she is. How did you know?'

'I remembered from yesterday.'

'Cool,' he replied. 'We'll be back before seven. Papa?'

Hamish was listening to the Queen's Christmas wishes.

'Aye?' he said in reply.

'Sarah's got something to show me so we're away out for a few hours. Will you be all right with Claire?'

'Och aye. I'll be fine with her,' was his reply, knowing it would be his great granddaughter taking care of him. 'Keep safe,' he said and turned back to the TV.

While Sarah was upstairs, John found two torches, checked their batteries and pulled on his boots. He grabbed warm coats and picked up the car keys as Sarah appeared back in the kitchen. John noticed she hadn't changed her dress for warmer clothes but wore a thicker cardigan. She pulled on her walking shoes and coat and dipped into the living room to kiss Claire and Hamish.

'C'mon then,' she said to John and took the keys off him. 'It's a way to go and I know you've had a couple of glasses so I'm driving.'

As usual Sarah left no room for argument, so John followed her through the door and into the gathering gloom.

Seventeen

Sarah headed out of Ayr and joined the main road running from Glasgow to Stranraer. After a few miles she turned onto the quieter road leading through Kirkmichael towards Straiton, and the hills beyond the village. As they drove along, the sky cleared from the north east revealing a huge bright moon. A day past full and sailing above the hills, it climbed towards the zenith. Ragged clouds were being pushed southwest across the sea towards the Isles and the coast of Ireland by a stiff wind in the upper atmosphere. Only the brightest stars appeared above as the light from the sun, now beyond the horizon, had almost faded. John knew the wind would bring chilly air from the mountains in the north, and the evening would become bitter. He glanced across at Sarah and wondered again why she hadn't changed into jeans and a warm top.

'You'll freeze if we're out for long,' he remarked.

'I'm sure I'll be fine where we're going. We have a short walk but I've got my cardigan and coat and you to keep me warm.'

John reached over and slid a hand along his wife's thigh, earning himself a sharp smack.

'You sod. You can keep those cold hands to yourself

until they've warmed up.'

In anticipation John rubbed his hands together and laughed.

For a while they continued the journey in silence until they passed through the small village of Straiton. Apart from a few parked cars, the main street was silent and empty and only the faint orange glow of warm fires and cosy lights behind drawn curtains revealed any human presence. The distance from Hamish's house to Straiton was only around fifteen miles, but with winding roads the journey took them over forty minutes. Sarah headed south out of the village driving slowly as she peered ahead. They hadn't travelled far before she found what she was after and pulled the car into a layby not far past a collection of farm buildings. She switched off the engine, turned off the lights and a silence engulfed them.

As their eyes became accustomed to the darkness, an eerie landscape appeared before them… a landscape bathed in light from the argent moon with everything taking on a silver hue. Impenetrable shadows stretched out from underneath trees, shrubs and fences.

'C'mon,' said Sarah. 'There's a path leading into those trees across there. I think we have to go that way.'

'You think?' asked a perplexed John, but Sarah was already climbing out of the car. She buttoned up her coat and walked around to John. With woollen hats and gloves they insulated themselves against the chill air.

Sarah smiled up at her husband and taking his hand led the way with confidence to a narrow opening at the back of the layby. A small well maintained gate barred the way, and it opened with ease. They shuffled through and headed in a straight line across the field towards a dark stand of trees a hundred yards ahead. In the moonlight the trees appeared inky black, a gloomy menacing wall stretching several hundred yards to left and right. At first, neither Sarah nor John could see a path leading into the wood, but as they approached a more obvious opening came into view. It was as if, Sarah thought, the entrance was meant to be invisible, except from close by, to keep it hidden from the road.

It was now approaching half past four and they took only a few minutes to cross the distance from the layby to the far edge of the field. Without hesitation, Sarah plunged straight in amongst the trees as if she were as familiar with the woodland as with her own garden.

'Do you know where we're going?' asked John.

'Not really,' Sarah muttered. 'I was only given cryptic directions.'

She stopped and turned to John, shining her torch at his chest.

'John, I don't know what we'll find. Beryl explained how to get here, but when I heard her instructions, it seemed as if I already knew about them... the directions to where we're going that is. I know it makes no sense, but after everything that's happened over the past month, nothing seems strange any more.'

She paused long enough to draw breath before turning and continuing through the trees. She spoke once more before falling silent. 'I think I'm just having faith in what Beryl told me.'

Underneath the dense canopy of pine and fir, little of the moonlight reached them as they walked now in single file. While John followed, he felt aroused again at the thought of his wife clothed in her red dress but pushed the thought away when, after five minutes of winding from left to right amongst the trees, Sarah slowed and muttered to herself.

'Sorry?' he asked. 'What did you say?'

'Seven hundred steps to where the eagle sits,' she said. 'Then four on the right and three on the left.'

'What?'

Sarah ignored the question and fell silent for a moment before shining her torch upwards and around the canopy. With little effort she spotted an unusual contortion of branches and pine needles that did indeed look, in the dim light of her torch, as if an eagle sat immobile in the tree tops.

Pointing the torch back to ground level, she took a few more steps, counting trees along the way before turning left off the narrow path and in amongst the dark trunks. Once more with confidence, and puzzling familiarity, she speeded up again, despite the trackless way.

'Where the devil are you taking me?' John asked, but Sarah did not answer. He struggled to keep up with her but then noticed, despite the random positioning of the trees, they were following a path. The ground before his feet was level and clear of undergrowth and root. Stones lay either side of the path at irregular intervals but placed in such a manner to mark the way, though they were moss covered and difficult to see.

John was familiar with the countryside out here and knew the only thing lying before them was the steep side of a hill... the outlier of a range of hills sloping upwards to a more barren landscape haunted by pine forest, birds of prey and wind turbines. John was expecting a dead end.

'I think we're almost there,' Sarah said.

They continued for a few more minutes until Sarah stopped and shone her torch onto a dark mass that blocked their way. She glanced sideways at him. John switched on his own torch and played the strong beam around them, across the ground to left and right, and even upwards. Several feet above, he could see the bare back of a huge rock face. They had come, as he guessed, to a solid barrier with gorse and holly covering the rock.

'Well!' he said. 'Much as I love being out in the countryside, I wish you'd tell me what we're doing here. There's nowhere else to go!'

With her eyes on John, Sarah recalled Beryl's instructions: *At the wall turn to the left and reach behind the holly*. She stepped to the left and, taking care to avoid the spiky leaves, stretched her arm behind the holly. To John's surprise, Sarah lifted a heavy wooden pole and pulled it outwards and to his amazement, a dark opening appeared.

'What in God's name?'

'After you,' Sarah invited.

John stepped forward into the darkness, holding his torch before him. As he crossed the threshold, a tingling brushed his fingertips... a sensation which reminded him of pins and needles. And despite the woollen hat, the same prickling brushed the top of his head as if someone were caressing him with gentle fingers. Shaking his head to dispel the sensation, he shone the torch around the enclosed space. Even by the dim light he could see the cave was large, maybe thirty feet by fifteen he guessed, with a ceiling high enough for his six foot frame to stand upright.

Sarah followed and pulled the pole back into place, shutting out the night and enclosing them inside the hidden space. While John stood still and somewhat at a loss, Sarah stepped in front and scanned the cave with her own torch. Still with unexpected familiarity, she walked across to the rear of the cave and found a lantern sitting on a rough wooden table, an old-fashioned oil storm lantern with a glass bowl. A metal tin sat next to the lamp and inside she found piles of long matches. With little expectation she struck one but was heartened when it sputtered and burst into flame. Opening the lamp she placed the match against the wick and as soon as it was alight she adjusted the flame before closing the glass bowl around it. The cave lit up with a warm glow that dispelled the shadows, revealing more and more detail.

In the right-hand corner they spotted a small well – more of a shallow bowl hewn out of the rock – with a wooden jug sitting nearby. Water trickled in from a narrow crack in the wall and filled the well before overflowing through a fissure in the floor. John thought it must form part of a natural underground spring fed from waters on the hillside. Close to the well sat pots and pans, and on the opposite side of the cave, next to the rough table, were four mismatched wooden chairs. The table stood against a wall and in a wooden beam above it, hooks of various sizes were fixed. It seemed they had found a hidden dwelling place.

They stood in silence as they moved their torches around the cave, and once more John sensed the prickling on his head and in his fingertips. Without a word Sarah wandered towards the back of the cave and disappeared out of sight, leaving John standing alone, puzzling over the unusual sensations. After a few moments, the dim flicker of another match lit up the cave so John followed in Sarah's footsteps and entered a smaller grotto… one about twelve feet square. As he crossed the threshold the tingling sensation became stronger, but in trying to make sense of it the only explanation he could come up with was the warming of his hands… recovering from the cold air.

Towards the left-hand corner, Sarah squatted in front of a fireplace striking another match. Touching it to a firelighter half covered with a log… flames immediately took hold adding to those that flickered and crackled around a few sticks of dry kindling. Above and angled back from the fireplace, a narrow opening in the rock acted as a chimney and the smoke from the fire disappeared up and out of sight. The logs caught the flames and the comforting crackle of burning wood soon filled the small space. John gazed around and saw two more chairs, but low and comfortable, meant for relaxing. They stood either side of the fire to catch the warmth. On the other side of the grotto, a medium sized cot lay against the wall. Thick woollen blankets covered it, and what appeared to be white sheets were visible underneath the heavy covering. John thought it looked fresh made and shook his head in disbelief.

'What is this place?'

Sarah unzipped her coat.

'Beryl called it a hiding place. She said it had been secret for hundreds of years.'

'What is this, Indiana Jones and the Caves of Ayrshire?'

'Now be serious. I need to talk to you. Let's sit by the fire.'

John didn't appear to be paying attention but stood still, flicking his fingers as if trying to remove something from them.

'What are you doing?' Sarah asked.

'It's weird,' he answered. 'But I keep getting pins and needles in my hands.'

'Oh that!' said Sarah with no hint of surprise. 'You feel it too?'

'What?' replied a puzzled John. 'Can *you* feel this? If so, what is it?'

'Sweetheart, I need to tell you everything about Beryl, everything she told me, but you need to be quiet and listen. Some of it… well a lot of it will sound weird, and two days ago I would have said the same, but now… I'm convinced it's the truth… I've no reason to disbelieve any of it.'

Sarah waited for John to respond but he said nothing.

'It's getting warm,' she continued.

She took off her coat and draped it over a chair before sitting. John followed her lead and threw more logs into the growing fire.

He prompted Sarah. 'Ok I'm all ears… what *didn't* you tell me last night?'

Sarah gazed past her husband with furrowed brow as an idea occurred to her.

'Can I try something first?' she asked, but didn't wait for an answer. She stood and walked around to the back of John's chair. 'This is what I feel on my head, y'know, when I get that strange sensation.'

Sarah laid a hand, now warmed by the fire, across John's forehead. With a suddenness he found surprising, an unexpected heat spread from where Sarah touched him throughout his whole body.

'Wow!' he said. 'You're hot!'

'Hot?' asked Sarah.

'Yes. Your hand… well it started with your hand, but I feel like I'm blushing.'

Sarah stepped away and returned to her chair. As she passed in front of the fire, John saw straight through the material of her dress, and at the sight of his wife's thighs silhouetted against the orange flames, his desire to make love to her increased. He cast a quick glance at the cot, wondering if the blankets were clean. *God. What's the matter with me today?* He fidgeted in his chair.

When she spoke, Sarah sounded puzzled. 'Well no I don't feel hot when it happens... only the touch... the physical sensation. Strange you feel heat. For me it's like having a comforting hand touching my head. It's reassuring.'

'Ok, but you were about to tell me the rest... what you found out yesterday?'

'Yes... of course.'

Sarah repeated the tale, explaining everything she had learnt of Beryl's past and the tragedy that befell her. Why Amber had raised Jade, Beryl's daughter... how Beryl's own gift awakened. She told John everything she had learnt of her own family history... the gifts... the links with a past that almost came to an end. The pagan beliefs and practices her distant ancestors followed, worshipping, nurturing and living within the natural world. She told him what she knew of the cave and what it meant, how important it had been.

'If it wasn't for this place, I doubt I'd be here.' She paused a moment and stared into the fire before continuing. 'Beryl told me a lot... stuff I didn't quite grasp... things I don't yet understand. I need to find out what it all means. She said she'd put me on the path, whatever path it may be, but I would need to learn more about it on my own. It seems I've inherited a family gift... a gift of seeing and healing. It all sounds crazy in the cold light of day but now I can't forget about it.'

John sat in silence while he listened to the whole story, and when Sarah's tale ended he struggled to find the right response, if one existed. The nature of his work shaped much of his own belief patterns... police work which all too often brought him into contact with the simple struggle for survival and exercise of power existing in a city landscape with its dense and multicultural population. Not the day-today lives of ordinary people… people who worked hard to raise their families and live in peace, but the darker side, that shuffled and crawled out of the sinister hollows during the dark hours. *The witching hour? That* existence held no deep meaning… it was about power and the greed of empty or damaged lives. Sarah's tale of paganism and gifts, spiritual meaning and destiny had no place in that murky and dangerous underworld.

But with a sudden shift in thinking, perhaps brought on by the tingling sensation coursing through his entire body once more, he thought how slim the chances were that he and Sarah would begin dating on the last day of school. How by seconds he may never have been in the right place to recover her handbag from a thief three years later and rekindle their relationship. And more recently, and with poignancy, the dream in which Sarah's parents appeared to him, and by indirect means reminded him of the robins.

'I'm not sure what to say. In the cold light of day, it does seem weird.'

'John, you remember the robins… of course you do, but what meaning they have I don't know. It's easy to put everything down to simple coincidence. Robins are inquisitive, so appearing before me on a gravestone is more than possible, but two together? I'm certain it was more than coincidence. And many years later, you dream of my parents while you're at the hospital and play bird song to me. Again, it could have been your memory kicking in… about what happened to me at the churchyard, but you said yourself the dream seemed more than that. You admitted afterwards it felt as if my mom and dad were in front of you, prompting you… rather than odd images, or incoherent random ramblings from a typical dream. I'm convinced there's more to it, and the first thing Beryl asked me was to have faith in her. I feel different. I sense things I couldn't sense before. Something has happened I need to explore.'

With bright excited eyes and a smile curling her mouth, Sarah leaned back in her chair and stared into the flames.

The wood John had thrown onto the fire was now ablaze and the cave had become warm and cosy. For several minutes they sat in silence… Sarah lost in her own thoughts while John tried to make sense of everything.

'So what do you think you'll do next?' he asked.

He glanced at his watch and with surprise noted it was half past five. Conscious of their daughter waiting at home on Christmas Day, he was about to suggest they should head off, but as he lowered his arm, the strange tingling crawled once more under his skin and he shuddered. Glancing across at Sarah, he saw her shiver too, and she tilted her head and gazed upwards as if listening. The smile lighting up her face had now gone, replaced by a wide-eyed look of surprise and urgency. Her lips had parted and, despite the heat warming them, John could see that through the thin fabric of her dress, her nipples stood out, stretching the material.

Sarah lowered her head and stared across at her husband, her strong man as she'd called him many times, though he was much more. He was her rock, her home, her companion and her lover. Despite the demanding nature of his job, the horrors he sometimes faced, he carried a gentle and sensitive nature that stirred her soul. She loved him without restraint and several times during the day sensed his need for her, more so since they'd left Hamish and Claire by the television two hours ago. But with a suddenness that caught her by surprise, responding as much to his obvious arousal as to an outside influence, she needed him… wanted him… and it had to be now.

Sarah stood up and stepped across to John. She took his head in her hands pulling him to her tummy before speaking with a husky voice, eyes focussed off in the distance.

'John. I want you to make love to me… here… now… before it's too late.'

John's hands were already underneath her dress, lifting it up, holding her bottom, pulling her even closer.

He glanced up at Sarah and stood up, pulling her dress

upwards still further as he did so.

'Late?' he whispered, and closed his mouth around her neck. 'Why late?'

Sarah tilted her head backwards and to one side, her breath hissing through clenched teeth.

'Oh God I want you inside me,' she replied, and tugged at his shirt, pulling it out of his trousers. She unbuckled his belt with quick, nimble movements, undid the button underneath and unzipped him in one swift motion. She moved her hands around and tugged at the waistband of his trousers, playing her fingers over John's back as he continued to tease her throat with his tongue.

John let Sarah's dress drop and reaching up behind her, found the zipper to her dress and eased it downwards. Sliding his hands onto her shoulders, he pulled the material until her dress fell off, gathering around her waist. Sarah moved away from John, slid her dress past her hips and let it drop to the floor. She reached behind, undid the hooks from her bra and shrugged it off, before stepping out of her dress.

John moved towards Sarah, his arousal obvious, and Sarah reached over and eased down his shorts, releasing him from his discomfort. He sat on his chair to remove his boots and yanked off the rest of his clothes while all the time his eyes were on his wife as she stood naked in front of him… naked but for her red laced knickers, part of the set he'd brought her for Christmas.

John knelt on the stone floor and kissed Sarah's navel, teasing her with the gentle brush of his lips while slipping the tips of his fingers under the elastic waist of her knickers. He eased the soft material over Sarah's bottom and held onto her while his eager kisses moved downwards. But Sarah shuddered again, a tremble that shook her to the core.

Unseen to John, who mistook his wife's shiver as a result of his tenderness, Sarah lifted her head once more, and tilted it to one side as if listening. Her eyelids fluttered as John's kisses moved ever lower, but she grabbed his hands and pulled, urging him to rise to his feet.

'No John,' she said with a gasp. 'Quick… take me to bed, take me now, make me pregnant.'

Sarah stood still for a moment, listening to a voice in her head, a voice she thought she recognised.

Now Sarah, before it's too late! Hurry my child!

'Now!' she whispered.

John stood and with ease took his wife in has arms and carried her to the cot. He sat on the edge and tossed back the blanket. The pleasant smell of lavender reached his nostrils as he lowered Sarah onto the bed. Wasting no time, Sarah yanked her knickers off and lay back, lifting her legs, offering herself to her husband.

Sensing that Sarah was ready, and responding both to her unusual urgency and his own aching need, John moved in, holding himself upright on his hands while Sarah tugged at his waist, pulling him closer.

Quickly, child!

Sarah tipped her head back and gasped as John pushed forward, bringing them together, making their joining tender, sensual and irresistible. He pulled away and moved forward again, wanting and trying his hardest to make the moments last. But with Sarah's sudden and urgent arousal, and her demands to be quick, he knew he wouldn't last long.

Sarah lifted her legs high and crossed her feet over her husband, keeping him close. Secured within his wife's embrace, John's passion mounted and his movements became more rapid. As he moved, he was aware of the tingling once more, the sensation that caressed his whole body as if tiny soft bristles brushed his flesh. But from somewhere deep inside his thoughts, he realised the tingling was coming from within.

Lying underneath her husband and with her own release closing in, Sarah felt her whole body burning. Her gasps became more frequent, and a moan escaped her lips. With her head pressed back into the soft yielding pillow, she stared up at the roof of the grotto with unseeing eyes, while her inner sight focussed elsewhere. A tiny pinprick of white light appeared which expanded and bloomed until it filled her vision before fading. The fire burning inside her began to shrink, growing smaller but more intense. It centred below her tummy, near to where she joined with her husband.

John's movements became tighter and faster whilst Sarah moaned louder, driving him on more and more. But his rhythm faltered, and moments later he lifted his head and through clenched teeth let out a deep groan of passionate agony. Sarah cried out herself… a loud stuttering cry, whilst her tummy burned with a heat almost painful. With her arms and legs wrapped around John, she held him in a tight embrace whilst he pushed hard against her.

In wave after wave, the intensity of their passion lasted for many moments whilst their hearts beat thunderously, shaking them to the core. After several minutes their breathing slowed and John lowered his head to the pillow. With exhausted tenderness he kissed Sarah, and they lay still, cocooned in their embrace.

With shining eyes and aching heart, Sarah whispered, 'I don't ever want to let go. Hold me.'

'I will,' John breathed. 'I promise.'

Eighteen

Beryl sat in darkness by the window, staring with unseeing eyes across the water... seeing into the future. A full moon lay out of sight to the east, behind the place she had called home for ten years, and it cast a silvery luminescence across the sea, lighting up the mountains of the Isles to the west.

It was approaching five thirty and nearing the time.

She had enjoyed the day, her last Christmas, spending much of it in the company of other residents. The staff did an excellent job of creating a welcome and nostalgic Christmas atmosphere. A few relatives arrived bringing presents and gossip and spent the afternoon chatting with their aged family members. With no relatives of her own, the staff kept Beryl entertained, and she did likewise with her stories and tales from years long since gone. In the middle of the afternoon she sat with the others, wearing a paper hat, pulling crackers and eating as much of her last meal as she could manage. But as soon as the sun approached the horizon, she yawned and said she would take a nap.

Margaret, the young woman who greeted Sarah twenty-four hours earlier, helped her back to her room and settled her into a chair, making a cup of tea and leaving her to enjoy the last of the sunset.

With a smile curling her mouth, Beryl sat and gazed across the sea as the sun sank below the horizon. The evening deepened while she waited. She had no need of visitors since meeting Sarah was all the confirmation she needed that she could go to her rest knowing the story would continue.

Sarah's recent tragedies had awakened the slumbering gift lying hidden within her, and Beryl had aided its growth. Now, Beryl thought, her young relative would have to manage on her own, but she knew Sarah would succeed as Beryl herself had done many years ago. There would be trials along the way, but that was the way of life.

There was now one thing left to do.

Beryl blinked a few times and focussed her thoughts on Sarah. Raising her bony hands up in front of her chest and with palms facing each other, she cupped them a few inches apart, sensing a light pressure tingling her fingers. It was very subtle and anyone without the gift could miss it. After several deep breaths she angled them down to her lap where she had placed a crystal. A large amethyst geode sat on her apron, sending forth its energy into her hands and into her soul. Opening her dry and aged lips, she whispered into the darkness of her room.

'Sarah. Now, my angel. Quickly while there is time.'

Fourteen miles away, hidden in a small cave warmed by a roaring log fire, Sarah received the call and responded to it without understanding the reason. The message reached John too, but in a more base way, and he felt only the need to join with his wife.

Beryl listened and within moments sensed the acknowledgment of her message.

As the minutes ticked by, she felt the intensity of her great granddaughter's arousal. Not in a physical sense, but in a spiritual way, with a deep sense of belonging, of joining, of need and joy. With a smile upon her face she spoke again, knowing her time was close.

'Now, Sarah, before it's too late! Quickly child!'

In the stillness of her room Beryl sat listening, preparing herself, and despite the distance, sensed the strength of John and Sarah's shared release… felt their love and let it flood her own soul.

As the moment passed, Beryl sighed and with an immense struggle pushed herself to her feet. On ancient legs, she shuffled across the room to a small writing table and opened the middle drawer. Inside sat a wooden box carved on all sides with ornate symbols. With care she lifted the box out and unlocked it with a tiny key that hung on a chain around her neck. From inside she drew out a large handmade envelope. Sitting by the desk, she opened the envelope and pulled out several sheets of paper covered with her own spidery writing. Finding the last page, she signed it and placed the papers back inside the envelope. With a small sticky label, decorated with the picture of a rose and the word 'Apothecary' printed around the edge, she sealed it. Placing the envelope on top of the desk in plain view, she knew her solicitors would receive it as soon as she had gone… that family of legal representatives who had been in her life from the day of her birth, and indeed long before.

With extreme effort, Beryl eased herself up and away from the desk and returned to her comfy chair. As the moon climbed overhead, the silvery shadows on the garden and along the shoreline shortened, while she watched in peace and contentment, and waited for her final transmutation.

Nineteen

The cave was in semi-darkness when John stirred. After the intensity of their passion dissipated, Sarah snuggled into John's embrace but hadn't fallen asleep. John however appeared to have drifted off into a deep and satisfied slumber, but Sarah lay in his arms staring into the fire. She realised something odd had happened, something she found both puzzling and intriguing. On planning the journey to the cave, she had left her Christmas dress on, instead of changing into more sensible jeans and jumper, knowing John liked her in it and wanted her, needed her. She wanted him in return, but hadn't planned on making love out here in the dark, not when they had the comfort of a cosy room. Had the decision not to change her clothes been made for her?

And why the increased desire for each other... since coming home from hospital? Without a doubt they were both enjoying it, but recent events led Sarah to wonder if something else was driving their lust, especially an hour ago when she sensed an external influence and heard urgent words in her mind commanding her to hurry.

Lying still with John's arms wrapped around her, she thought of Beryl's admission she was the one who had been extending her thoughts to Sarah, the one whose touch Sarah sensed many times. Was it Beryl who sent her command across the miles? Was it Beryl who told her to hurry? If so how? Was that even possible? But Sarah had accepted the fact of Beryl's presence manifesting itself as a physical caress. It wasn't much of a leap of faith to accept Beryl could also reach into her soul… into her spirit in some intangible way. *Oh my, what have I got mixed up in?*

Sarah shifted her position and John spoke. 'I don't know where that came from but… oh my God.'

With a smile Sarah moved against him, teasing him.

'Careful,' he said and brushed his lips across the back of Sarah's neck, making her shudder.

The covers had slid off Sarah's shoulder and the cooling air within the chamber chilled her. Tossing the blankets off and over John, she stood upright.

'Brr!' she exclaimed. 'It's getting cold in here and I think once you're out of bed, the cold air might dampen your enthusiasm.' She tiptoed across the stone floor and retrieved her clothes. 'But it's time we were going.' She picked up John's shorts and threw them at him. 'You'll need these, and the rest of your things.'

'Huh!' John said. 'Typical, you've had your way with me and now I'm cast aside.'

Sarah laughed at him. 'Yes… and your problem is? Anyway, I don't remember hearing you complain. Moan perhaps but not complain. Actually I'm sure you shouted. It was rather special though wasn't it?'

'Yes… it certainly was,' replied John as he clambered off the cot and pulled on his shorts. 'But I'm confused about why you said something about before it's too late.'

'Yes… and me. But c'mon we need to go. Will the fire be all right?'

John was pulling on his jeans and boots. 'Yes, it's almost burnt out. It'll be fine. And I think you're right… it's time we left.' He paused a moment before speaking. 'Sweetheart?'

'Yes?' she said turning toward him.

'Have you any idea how important you are to me?'

Sarah crossed the room and took his hands.

'Yes. I do,' she replied. 'As much as you are to me. I know all of this is confusing and maybe you're worrying, but I'm glad you're on my side, believing in me.'

'I don't understand any of it,' John said. 'But I can see it's important.'

For a moment they stood holding hands, smiling at each other until something passed through them, making them shudder.

'Did you feel that?' asked John with a sudden frown.

Sarah's smile broadened, and she raised her eyebrows and nodded, as if it were perfectly normal.

Twenty

Twenty minutes later, after sealing up the cave and taking a slow trek through the woods, they were heading back along quiet roads, following the twisting lanes with care.

After sharing their thoughts concerning the cave and pondering who could have kept it clean, Sarah fell silent. Glancing at his wife, John noticed tears on her cheeks.

'Sweetheart,' he asked with concern. 'What is it?'

Sarah wiped away the tears.

'Beryl's dying.'

'What? Why? How do you know?'

'She told me she wouldn't be around for much longer. I think it's cancer of some sort. She coughed a few times, a terrible cough, and I saw blood on her handkerchief. It's not fair, John. It's just not fair. I've only just found her. I never met any of my grandparents and this was the most unexpected and important Christmas present I could ever get. And now I'm going to lose her.'

Sarah turned to John. 'That's why I want us to visit her tomorrow. I don't know how long she has left but not long.'

John reached over and took his wife's hand.

'I'm sorry sweetheart. I really am. When you got the letter, I never expected it would lead you to a relative and

I'm so happy for you. But… well, damn. I'm sorry. And yes, we'll go tomorrow… or tonight. We could drop in now?'

Sarah thought for a moment and squeezed John's hand.

'You'd do that for me? But no. Time's running on and it's not fair to be away from Claire and Papa any longer. They are the family we've known for years.'

'I'm sure they'd think of it differently if we called them?'

'No, I'm sure.'

Sarah paused and gazed off into the distance. For long moments she was quiet. With ease she could picture Beryl's room… could see her face and the shocking resemblance to Sarah's mother and Sarah herself. At the memory, any urgency she felt evaporated, and a wry smile creased her lips though it did not touch her eyes.

'Sweetie?' John prompted.

'No… it's ok,' Sarah replied with a sigh. 'I want to get home and celebrate the rest of Christmas. Meeting Beryl was an unexpected Christmas present and one that'll stay with me forever. It's ok. I want to go home.'

'Ok, if you're sure.'

'Yes… I'm sure.'

Half an hour later, John opened Hamish's front door, and he and Sarah stepped into the warm and cosy sanctuary of their Scottish retreat. It was past seven o'clock.

'We're home!' called Sarah and heard an answering call from the living room.

'I'm glad you're back,' called Hamish. 'The wee one is getting impatient and wants to play Monopoly.'

John walked into the living room.

'It's only because she always wipes the floor with us. Ruthless my daughter.'

'Too true,' agreed Sarah. 'I think she's spent too much time with Rachel!'

'Where did you get to?' asked Hamish.

John and Sarah glanced at each other and John nodded at his wife.

'It's your story,' he said. 'You can tell it.'

'*Our* story,' she argued. 'It's a part of us all,' and nodded at Claire and Hamish.

'Look,' she continued, 'let's get comfortable, get the game out and I'll tell you what happened.'

They gathered around Hamish's dining table and laid out the game while Sarah told them everything she knew of the cave. Claire appeared nonchalant as if none of it surprised her. Hamish seemed tired.

Later during the evening, they ate a light supper before putting on another of Claire's Christmas movies. It was ten thirty when they bid each other a goodnight and headed upstairs.

A few minutes past midnight Sarah became restless and awoke. Wide eyed and alert, she lifted the covers and swung her legs out of bed. She sat still and listened… waiting long enough to make sure she hadn't woken her husband.

After standing up, she pulled on her dressing gown, and without a sound wandered downstairs into the living room. Needing to look outside, Sarah drew open the curtains and gazed southwest across Hamish's back garden… southwest, toward Girvan.

There was no sea view, but the shoreline lay only a few hundred yards away. Outside, the chill air frosted nearby shrubs but Sarah was unaware of it. She felt disconnected from the world, her mind not registering the fox padding without a sound across the lawn, nor the silver glow from the moon that cast dark shadows of mystery within the garden.

Sarah's senses were blind to her immediate surroundings while her inner eye focussed on an elderly relative sitting alone in her room some distance away. Abruptly, she sensed once more the heat in her tummy, the same heat she had felt hours ago when in a hidden cave, her husband moved inside her as they lay locked in a passionate moment not wholly of their own making. The heat increased, and in her mind she pictured a brilliant and tiny spot of white light spinning rapidly. The spot of light increased in size, getting larger and brighter. Sarah's lips parted, and a gasp escaped her mouth. Her breathing became more rapid and her heart thudded in her chest.

Unseen and behind, after waking to find Sarah missing from their bed, John stepped into the room and crossed the floor. He placed a gentle hand on her shoulder and spoke.

'Sweetheart? What are you doing down here?'

When no answer came, John turned Sarah with his hands and noticed the vacant expression in her eyes, eyes focussed in the distance.

With increasing concern, John opened his mouth to speak again, but in the same instant the clock chimed twelve thirty and Sarah gasped once more. Her eyes shifted, and her gaze settled on her husband.

'Beryl!' she managed to whisper as her legs gave way, and she slumped into John's arms, unable to stand.

John picked her up, carried her over to the sofa, and laid her down with care. Sarah appeared to have fallen asleep.

'Sarah!' he whispered, figuring she'd sleep walked. 'Sweetheart? Wake up.'

Sarah's eyes fluttered a few times before opening.

'Where have you been?' John asked.

Sarah's chest hitched and John was convinced she was going to cry, but she reached up and placed a warm hand on his cheek.

'John… my strong man,' and she smiled at him. 'I think we are pregnant again.'

Twenty-one

Deep inside Sarah Macintyre, a miracle was taking place... a miracle of nature as old as time itself. A race was underway... a race composed of a hundred million competitors that would see most of the entrants fall by the wayside and perish. Some would contain a fundamental flaw and barely begin. Others would exhaust themselves along the way, weakening the further they went until they ran out of the energy needed to reach their goal. Many would see the race through to the end only to fail at the last hurdle. But one would, and indeed must, fulfil its destiny.

The outcome of John and Sarah's passion, triggered by an outside influence but ultimately a result of their deepest love, was deposited within Sarah... this miracle of nature that contained the promise of a new life, another story.

The race continued and could take from several hours to a few days to produce a winner. But within minutes many of the strongest took the lead, heading upwards, surging forward around the strong and thick walls of the cocoon which had once before carried and protected a new life, a life that also held a promise for the future and had links with an unexpected past.

As the battle continued and many hundreds of

thousands fell behind or gave up the chase... one of the tiny players escaped the leaders, heading away from them, one goal in mind. Fate drove it... need drove it. Time was short and time was of the essence.

For several hours, and with inherent strength, it swam against tremendous odds until ahead of it lay an opening, a passageway to the future. Two such paths were available to it, offering a choice to increase the chances of success, of fulfilling its purpose, and having made the choice it entered the last leg of the race.

Still it led the pack, striving to reach the end of a journey monumental in relation to its tiny size. But now blocking its path lay an enormous obstacle... the final goal it must reach before any of the others.

At last, and with one final tiny flick of urgency, it touched the surface of the obstacle and entered in, causing an almost instantaneous reaction that closed the door, preventing any further invasion. Moments later and with utter futility, a thousand others who had reached this far tried to enter and found the way shut. They were too late. But as one chapter in the story began, another came to an end.

In the same moment that Sarah Macintyre collapsed into the supporting arms of her husband... twenty long miles away, through the cold and bitter darkness of a winter's night, an elderly lady smiled one last time before her inner sight moved on, and her vision on this world ceased.

Growth

14th October 1710

Amber knew from the muted bird song and the faint glow of daylight from the chimney at the back of the cave that dawn had arrived, and tossed off the rough woollen tartan she had draped over Hamish and herself during the night. With an innate sense of preservation, she knew it was safe now to light a fire and make a meal, so she re-covered Hamish and busied herself setting fire to the kindling in the hearth.

To the rear of the main cave was a smaller hollow. Still large enough to suffice as a dwelling, it provided the perfect sanctuary. Both the larger outer cave and the grotto contained everything Amber needed to survive for several days if circumstance required. There was fresh drinking water from a small stream running from the hillside above, entering the cave through a fissure in the rock. A large pile of logs stood on one side of the outer cave and several shelves held a store of dried and preserved food. The inner cave provided extra shelter from whatever the wild Scottish weather could throw at them, and the whole refuge was invisible to the outside world. The cave was the safest of refuges, and one Amber's mother had shown her from the moment she could walk… in case they ever needed to hide.

Within minutes the young girl had a fire going, and she mixed rough oats with water in a pot and hung it over the fire to heat. Porridge was an ideal meal to satisfy their hunger for several hours, until she figured out the safest way to get to Colmonell and her Aunt Mary as her mother instructed. First though she needed to find out what had happened to her mother… needed to sneak back to the cottage.

She stirred the oats as they heated and threw in a small pinch of salt for flavour. When the porridge was ready, she awakened Hamish.

'Wake up Hamish. It's time to eat.'

'Where's Mama?' Hamish asked through a big yawn. Blood and dirt still streaked his face but Amber could clean his wounds after breakfast. He needed something warm to eat first.

'I'll find out after we've eaten. I'll fetch her here and then we can go on together. Eat up now.'

Hamish did as Amber instructed but needed little encouragement, spooning the porridge into his mouth as if he'd not eaten for days. After breakfast, Amber washed and tidied up and made Hamish promise to stay in the inner cave until she returned.

'Don't touch the fire now. It'll burn for a while to keep you warm but just let it burn out and I'll be back with Mama soon. Hush now. I won't be long.'

Amber gave Hamish a hug and let him go. At the mouth of the outer cave, she tuned in her senses to the outside world before opening the entrance. With one last look behind, she squeezed outside and pulled the pole back into place.

With caution… making little noise and senses alert, she hurried back through the woods, taking a different way from the previous night's escape route. As she crept up the last hill and approached the clearing where her home lay, the acrid smell of charred wood reached her nostrils and her heart filled with dread. She peered out from among the trees to a sight of utter devastation.

Her home was a stone Crofting cottage, a solid building meant to last for hundreds of years, but now it was little more than a shell, destroyed by fire. Constructed of thatch, the roof had disappeared, gone in moments once the flames took hold. Black gaping holes took the place of the door and windows. Soot marks streaked the inner walls and the hen house lying to one side was also in ruins. A single chicken roamed around the glade pecking at the dirt.

Without fear, but with her heart frozen and a face showing no emotion, Amber stood up and walked upright towards the ruins of her home, needing to know the truth. But as she advanced, a rapid movement caught her eye and stopped her dead in her tracks. With a glance to the right, she spotted the bright red breast of a tiny robin as it came to rest on one blackened stump that once supported the hen house roof. The bird opened its beak and a burst of melancholic song filled the clearing. Amber's expression softened for a moment and tears moistened her eyes, but steadying her heart she took another step forward. A sudden rush of wings flashed in front of her face as the bird flew toward her, only veering to one side within the last few inches. Amber stopped again, sensing a warning in the birds behaviour, but continued on steady legs and walked past the blackened remains of the door frame into the cottage. She gazed around the open space.

The raised sleeping platform and the furniture were no more… gone in a few hours of searing heat. One or two iron pots remained, but they were bent and useless.

As she continued to scan the now roofless space, her eyes alighted on two blackened feet that protruded from under the twisted and scorched timbers where the bed had lain. The horror revealed the truth and she needed to see no more.

Amber lifted her head and stared with haunted eyes at the sky while silent tears leaked in a river of grief. And as she wept, her heart turned to ice. This was too much. The shouts and jeers, the throwing of stones, the killing of chickens… these things were bad enough. But this was unforgiveable. This was pure evil.

With curses forming on her lips, she made a silent promise. Those responsible would be held accountable. They would be brought to justice if it took her entire life… justice of one sort or another.

Caring little for the streaks of dirt on her face, she wandered back outside and gathered what wood she could find. As if to mark the tragedy, the world had fallen silent, and the only sound she could hear was the sad and quiet chirruping of the robin. But she spent no time trying to find it since there was work to do. Carrying the wood back inside, Amber laid it around the remains of her mother. She retrieved one of the remaining pots and went outside to the store where they kept a container of oil. Filling the pot, she carried it in and shook it around where her mother lay and over the wood she had collected. Back outside she made a small fire, and as soon as the kindling was ablaze she carried burning sticks back inside and set the flames to the oil. In an instant the wood caught fire and spread, roaring and surging its way through the remains of the cottage. With infinite patience Amber waited as the fire carried her mother into the air and onward into the heavens.

From the store she had carried a box of saltpetre along with the oil and tossed some into the flames. Satisfied with the result, she began throwing handfuls of the stuff onto the inferno, unafraid of the coloured smoke rising into the still air, visible for miles. She wanted everyone to notice… notice and take heed. It was meant as a message, a message telling everyone they were unsuccessful. Her mother remained… remained in both Amber and Hamish. They had survived.

Satisfied she had delivered the message and having stayed long enough, she hurried back to the cave. She knew an escape route for herself and Hamish. One that would take them away without having to use the front entrance and allow them to travel by a roundabout way to Colmonell ten miles away. That was her plan... to leave as soon as possible.

In silence, Amber entered the cave ensuring the entrance was hidden once more.

'Hamish? It's time to go.'

There was no answer. The inner cave was in semi-darkness, the fire having long since died. She reached for a lamp, set a match to it and crept forward, fearful of what she may find. But it was empty. Hamish had gone. With her heart racing she searched every nook and cranny, including the space under the cot but with no success.

Hamish had gone.

Feeling rising panic for Hamish's safety, she turned full circle expecting him to appear, having played a joke on her, but then her eyes settled on a note lying on the rough-hewn table near the fireplace, a note held in place by a pot. In an instant she crossed the space and snatched up the note. The words written there brought little comfort.

> *'Hamish is safe. He has been taken, but to where you will never know. He will be safe.'*

The words conveyed no sentimentality, no emotion... only simple statements of fact. For a moment, tears threatened to return, and the strength in Amber's legs failed as she realised with a sudden ache in her chest she was alone. She sank to her knees and hid her eyes from the world.

'Mama,' she whispered, but her words were lost in the still air of her refuge... a sanctuary that seemed now like a prison. How would she ever find the courage to leave? But as she knelt on the hard stone, her soul fearful and anguished, a tiny electric thrill entered her aura, a spiritual invasion she recognised in an instant. In one fluid motion she rose to her feet and opened her auric shield, extending her percipience outwards beyond the cave and into the wide world.

Hamish was reaching out.

Drawing a deep breath to calm her spirit as her mother had taught her, she searched for her brother and within moments felt a connection. She sensed his fear and countered it with encouragement and love, aiming at his soul. Knowing he was close dispelled much of her own anguish, but as she shared her strength with him, warning him to take care, the connection sputtered like a candle and failed. Amber felt one final caress and then there was no more.

In a moment of clarity, she wasted little time in wondering whether to search for Hamish. It was obvious now whoever had taken him meant him no harm, otherwise she would have found him dead in the cave. And… she'd been away for an hour… Hamish's captor could have taken him as soon as Amber left. To start a search now could be suicide after sending her message. So she drank her fill of water, took one last look around the cave to make sure it was ready for use again if needed, and left by the rear entrance, an entrance as well hidden as the front.

One step at a time, Amber thought as she climbed out of the cave and into the daylight, the stink of charred wood still in her nostrils. One step, and the first was Colmonell.

Twenty-two

'Well, you two... the results show nothing out of the ordinary. Which I imagine is what you expected, Sarah.'

Peter Danecourt relaxed into his consulting room chair. Sarah smiled at him.

'You understand me so well,' she said.

'Yes I do but I still think it was right of John to insist you consult me.'

'Quite,' agreed John, but stopped short of saying 'I told you so'.

Peter continued. 'I'm glad I squeezed you into a cancelled appointment for a scan. The waiting list just gets longer and longer. But it's sensible to get checked out.'

'All right, all right. There's no need to gang up on me,' laughed Sarah. 'Are you two happy now?'

'Well an invitation to dinner would make me happier still,' suggested Peter with a hopeful expression.

'Huh!' replied Sarah. 'And I thought you did this out of concern for my health.'

'Being mercenary never entered my head and anyhow, I like your cooking.'

'Compliments will get you pudding too,' said Sarah. 'But that sounds like a super idea. We haven't had a gathering since before Christmas. Why don't you bring Sophie? She and Claire get on well. Is Friday night all right? You're not working a late shift are you John?'

'No, not this week. Friday will be great.'

'Good for me too,' agreed a smiling Peter. 'What time do you want us?'

'How about half five? Means the kids won't have to wait long for their tea. I'll feed them first and we can eat afterwards.'

'OK, it's a date,' said Peter as he stood upright. 'But… though it's always a pleasure, I have to get on. John? Do you have a minute before you go?'

'Oh I get it,' Sarah laughed again. 'Now you're done with me you want to talk boys stuff. I know when I'm in the way,' she said, rising from her chair. 'I'll meet you at the car,' she said to John. 'And I'll see you on Friday,' giving Peter a kiss.

They left the consulting room and while Sarah headed off along the corridor, Peter and John walked at a more leisurely pace.

'What is it?' asked John. 'There's nothing you've missed out is there?'

'What? Oh, God no. No everything's fine. I can't find anything wrong at all. No it's not Sarah. I was wondering….'

Peter appeared hesitant.

'Wondering what?'

'Rachel… if you'd seen much of her.'

'Ah. No, I haven't seen her for a while but Sarah has. In fact they're meeting for lunch. Why do you ask?'

'Well, we met for dinner twice before Christmas but I can't seem to get hold of her. She doesn't answer my calls or texts. It's almost like she's avoiding me. I thought we were getting on ok. Christ, it's like being a bloody teenager again.'

'And you want me to put the feelers out?'

'Well, if you can without making it seem like I'm chasing after her… on the sly.'

'Which of course you aren't.'

Peter flicked eyes full of humiliation at John and they both laughed.

'Do I look like a fool?' Peter asked.

'God, you're such an old-fashioned guy, Pete, and yes, you look foolish. But I'll have a word with Sarah. I'm sure she'll think of something. I like Rachel too. She's been as much a part of our family as you have and I understand your feelings. But between you and me, Sarah's worried about her. Thinks she's been acting strange recently. God only knows why.'

'Thanks, John. And remember. Sarah is one hundred per cent. There's nothing neurologically wrong with her at all, so you can relax and figure out what's behind the visions. Remember, there are more things in heaven and earth…'

'Cheers, Pete, and thanks for today. I'd better let you get back to work. See you Friday.'

Three hours later, just before one o'clock, Sarah sat alone waiting for Rachel. She had been sitting for over half an hour people watching when a familiar voice broke into her reverie.

'And why are we meeting here?'

Sarah turned and glanced up at Rachel. Her friend was wearing a quizzical expression which quickly turned into a smile but Sarah noticed something missing from Rachel's eyes. The natural vivacity that was an inherent part of Rachel's face was lost. The smile she wore didn't touch her eyes.

Sarah stayed where she was and patted the wooden seat, inviting Rachel to sit. She had called Rachel and asked her to meet her in the shopping mall in Wolverhampton.

'You'll find me sat in the middle of the ground floor,' she'd said. 'Come and meet me. I'm experimenting,' which of course intrigued Rachel.

Rachel sat and slid her arm through Sarah's, huddling close. They were under cover, protected from the elements but no one could describe it as warm.

The mall was busy with the lunchtime crowd and Sarah had been sitting observing people as they hurried about their business. At times she had her eyes closed, at others they were open, but either way she focussed on using her other senses.

'Ok. So what's this all about?' asked Rachel.

'I'm checking for something... something that started after I came out of hospital... well round about then.'

'What something? Aren't you cold? Can we go for lunch please?'

Sarah laughed and squeezed Rachel's arm.

'You wuss! Yes, c'mon we can go eat. I'm getting a bit chilly. Let's grab a bite and I'll explain.'

'Nero's or Costa's?' asked Rachel.

'Costa... it's closer. I've made you walk all the way here already. I'm not having you moan at me even more for making you walk all the way back again.'

They dodged and weaved their way back through the crowds and pushed through the doors into the scented warmth of Costa Coffee shop.

'I'm buying,' said Sarah. 'Chicken and pesto?'

'Mmm, yes please. Can I have a piece of cake as well? I need carbs today.'

Sarah smiled and wandered off to place their order.

Five minutes later they were settled into comfy chairs while Sarah explained. It was late January and only the second time they'd met since New Year. John and Sarah had spent the whole of the festive season in Scotland, but as soon as possible after returning home, Sarah telephoned Rachel and asked her around to dinner. Sarah had brought her friend up to date with events that took place during the Christmas break.

'It was strange,' she had said. 'We all went over to visit Beryl on Boxing Day but as soon as we got into Girvan I sensed something was wrong, something unsettling. I found out she'd died at half past midnight. A receptionist found her. A lovely woman called Margaret. Margaret said Beryl's cat came trotting up to reception, which was apparently unusual late at night. So Margaret went down to investigate and found Beryl sat upright in her chair as if she was asleep.'

'Weren't you upset?' Rachel asked, and Sarah had seen unexpected tears in her friend's eyes. 'I would have been. I don't remember my mom's parents at all and only have a few vague memories of my dad's, though I don't remember having much of a relationship with them. Seems so unfair to meet an old relative only to have them snatched away before you get to know them.'

'Well I was shocked to start with. I'd taken John and Claire all the way over there only to find she'd gone and it was... well, embarrassing. Does that sound ridiculous? It wasn't until after we got back home I fell apart. I was so disappointed they hadn't been able to meet her, and cheated up to a point.'

Sarah had fallen silent for a while before continuing.

'Beryl said a lot about living and dying... about the cycle of life I suppose, though not in so many words. In the time we had together she told me who she was and who I was... our history. She communicated a lot... but not always in words. She said I would understand more by myself... she put me on the path and whether I followed it or not was my choice.'

'But what path is this? It all sounds very mysterious and... well unrealistic these days. This stuff just doesn't happen. People find lost relations, long lost family members but I don't think many of them are anything out of the ordinary. The stuff you're talking about seems far-fetched. What will happen to you... to us?'

Sarah had frowned.

'I can't answer except the *us* bit. Nothing's going to happen to *us*. But Beryl only told me I was part of an ancient history, an ancestry blessed with a gift. The gift of seeing and of healing. I think I need to let it grow... see what I can see... find out what I can do... if anything. When I heard she'd died, I understood it was the natural order of things.

But I didn't come to that realisation from any conscious thought, it occurred in a natural way... a... a deeper or spiritual way. Later on I did feel a more earthly sense of loss... not having been able to get to know her properly. After all, she was the only grandparent I ever met. But then I remembered what happened at half past midnight in the living room at John's grandfathers.'

At this point Sarah told Rachel she'd sleep walked and had wandered downstairs... where John found her and how in a moment of clarity she understood she was pregnant. Sarah hadn't shared her belief with Rachel there was a link between Beryl's death and the conception. She thought her friend would have her sectioned if she presented that idea... apart from the fact there was and never could be any evidence, just faith. *Faith.*

Sarah took a slurp of coffee as their lunch arrived and Rachel prompted her.

'You didn't answer my first question. The one I asked when I met you.'

Sarah puzzled for a moment.

'Oh yes,' she said, remembering. 'What was I doing out in the shopping centre? When we met after New Year, I mentioned a lot about "seeing"? Well I wanted to sit on my own for a while amongst all those people, work out if I could see anything.'

'Sorry. Need more information. You can see perfectly well.'

'Yes. But I don't mean with my eyes. Remember weeks ago before Christmas, I told you I'd noticed an orange glow around you. We were sitting here.'

'Yes a warm glow. Must have been the porridge I had for breakfast,' Rachel said, and they both laughed.

'Be serious!' replied Sarah. 'What I'm saying is I've seen a lot more since, a lot of colours and shapes sitting around people. They're called auras. Every living thing has an aura surrounding it. You can Google it but there's a lot of information *and* a lot of scepticism about it. With the right equipment you can take a photograph of your own aura, but most of the scientific evidence points to electrical energy fields as the reason for different colours or sizes, electric fields that may be changed by humidity or sweat for example.'

'Oh my, you've been busy since New Year and you're getting analytical on me again… either that or you've been smoking weed.' Rachel drained her coffee before speaking again. 'But you can't really see these things can you?'

'Not the way I see the colour of your blouse or the shade of blue in your handbag or even the dark patches under your eyes.' Sarah grimaced. 'Sorry. Didn't mean to say that, but you seem tired. Are you sleeping?'

'I'm fine.' Rachel dismissed the question with a wave of her hand. 'But forget about me I want to know what you mean.'

'Ok, how do I explain? As a woman you have what people call female intuition. You can sense things without seeing them or feeling them. You know when someone is not quite himself or herself, for example. On the outside they may behave as normal but you can tell something's off.'

'Well yes, but isn't that just picking up on behaviour, mannerisms or mood… tone of voice?'

'Yes, but what if the behaviour is normal?' Sarah paused and took a bite of food. 'I don't know if that's a good example but what I'm trying to say is this. No, I can't see these colours with my eyes, but I feel them with my… sixth sense, if you like. I know they are there because I… well… detect them, even with my eyes closed, if I concentrate on an individual.'

'With your eyes closed? Ok, what did you "see" before I met you today?'

Rachel noticed her friend's eyes drifting out of focus.
'Sarah?'

In a voice distant with self-musing, Sarah spoke. 'A lot, and much of it was troubling. A little depressing, y'know like on a dreary day when the sky is grey.'

'How'd you mean? What troubled you?'

Sarah focussed back onto Rachel.

'Lots of people had bright enough colours. Perhaps orange or blue... purple sometimes. But always strong and clear. Others had weak colours around them. Pale or dirty. I got the impression in these cases the individuals weren't happy, and when I looked at their faces they appeared that way on the surface too.'

Rachel seemed troubled herself.

'Sarah I'm worried about you. Are you sure you're ok? You haven't got something wrong after that bang on the head. Don't you think you should talk to Peter?'

'Already seen him and everything is fine. I made a promise to John and they ran some tests this morning. But c'mon, Rache. You know me better than that. If I thought something *was* wrong, I'd be the first to go to the nearest hospital and get myself checked out. And anyway, that bang was more like a bump. I've hit my head harder on a kitchen cupboard. And... this is all tied in with Beryl. Everything fits together somehow so stop worrying.'

'You will never know how much I worry about you,' said Rachel.

'About me. Why?'

Rachel became evasive and Sarah needed no extraordinary gift to sense it.

'Sorry, I meant worried... past tense. Y'know... when you were in hospital?'

'Rachel. Are you sure everything's ok? You *do* look weary.'

'I'm fine,' Rachel replied, and though Sarah wasn't convinced, she steered away from the subject.

'Ok. But how would you like to try an experiment? Do you have to get back straight to work yet?' she asked.

'An experiment? I'm up for it. Work can wait a while longer. What do you want to do?'

'Come back with me to the middle of the shopping centre and be my observer. If we find somewhere to sit, I'll close my eyes and try to convince you this is all real or at least has some reality to it.'

'Wow. I haven't got to do an essay on it have I?'

'No, and no homework either,' and they both smiled.

Twenty minutes later, after finishing lunch, the two friends made their way back to where they'd met earlier. The bench was still unoccupied and so they sat and cuddled up close for extra warmth.

They sat in silence for a few minutes taking in the atmosphere before Sarah closed her eyes.

'If I see anything I'll let you know where from… the direction. Perhaps you can tell me what you see with your eyes… if our impressions match there's something to it. Agreed?'

'Agreed Mistress Macintyre, but I can't believe I'm freezing my ass off for this. Perhaps I should call you "The Wise Woman" or something.'

Sarah responded with a squeeze of Rachel's arm and after a few slow deep breaths, fell silent. Rachel sat waiting for a prompt. After only a short delay, maybe half a minute, Sarah spoke.

'A bright colour over to the right, coming towards us, well I imagine coming towards us as I sense the colour's getting brighter or perhaps more present. It's green, vivid.'

Rachel scanned the faces in the direction Sarah mentioned unsure of what she may find. Sarah spoke again.

'Close now.'

Rachel peered over her right shoulder at a young man carrying a bouquet and a small shopping bag. The shopping bag was labelled with the name of a local jeweller.

'There's a fella here with flowers and a bag from Frost and Son. He's also carrying a smile. But…'

'He's behind us now isn't he?'

'Yes, but what's it got to do with green?'

'Green? It's to do with the heart. Loving and caring. You've heard the expression green with jealousy. Same thing only from the opposite end, perhaps. I read a lot about this on the Internet. Let's try again.'

'Ok.'

After a short time Sarah spoke again. 'Same side… someone with a dark or dirty yellow. Stressed.'

Once more Rachel scanned the faces.

'Not very scientific is it,' she muttered.

'What's science go to do with it? That just means you can't explain it with numbers. They're getting close… passing in front, maybe.'

Rachel spotted a young woman hurrying along, closing in on them.

'There's a teenager, carrying a bag with books in it. Looks like she's at University from her clothes and worried expression. In a rush. Ok, clever clogs, how does yellow fit?'

'Life energy. Might be hers is wearing thin from studying too much. Just a guess. Oh damn!'

'What?' asked Rachel.

'Damn, damn… damn it,' she repeated. 'This is horrible.'

'What is?'

Rachel felt Sarah twitch and tighten the hold she had on her arm. Air hissed through her teeth as if she were in pain.

'Behind us… dark grey or black. So much pain and fear. So much distress. Rachel c'mon let's go. It's making me nauseous.'

Sarah opened her eyes and rose out of the seat but kept her gaze to the floor. An air of malignancy threatened her, a sickness invading her very soul. Now she sensed it she couldn't stop it.

'Sarah, wait!' Rachel was on her feet too and reached for Sarah's hand, gripping it to stop her from walking away. Rachel turned around to scan the faces behind them. It soon became obvious what had upset her friend.

'Sarah. There's an elderly couple. A woman in a wheelchair with a man pushing. He looks miserable and the old woman looks ashen. Shit. She's so thin… she doesn't look well at all.'

'Please, Rachel. Let's go. It… it hurts. Oh God, I think I'm going to throw up!'

'Hurts? Ok, Sarah. It's ok. Come on. Try to think of something positive. Let's get out of here.'

And with that Sarah moved again. Rachel linked arms with her friend and taking the lead hurried off in the opposite direction, heading for an exit and an escape into fresh air.

Twenty-three

John poured hot water over a teabag and handed the mug to Sarah. The aroma of chamomile permeated the kitchen and John breathed in the strong herbal scent.

'It smells pleasant enough,' he said with surprise. 'What does it taste like?'

'Give it five minutes to steep and have a sip. Perhaps you could try growing it in the garden.'

'Maybe. You always wanted a kitchen garden. I'll dig out the plant guide and check it out.'

John poured himself a glass of water and they both sat at the dining table. Muted sounds emanated from the living room where Claire was watching television with Mags.

'So c'mon. What happened today? You mentioned something about feeling sick. Was it morning sickness?' John prompted.

Sarah regarded John through the cloud of steam rising from her mug and wondered from his remark on gardening how such a strong man, a tough man who chose a career as a policeman, found solace in the art of growing things. John's colleague Dave chose a variety of competitive sports to let off steam, which Sarah knew was typical for people in that particular career. John however was different in that respect, and Sarah took it for granted. But it did make sense. Taking time out as John did, to potter around in the greenhouse or the garden, was so much a contrast to the stresses of his working life, it was small wonder he gained peace from doing so. Similar to his love of angling.

'No it wasn't morning sickness,' Sarah replied, sounding a little flat. 'It was sickness but not mine.'

'Ok. You said you were trying to prove to Rachel you could see... with the gift Beryl told you about, by experimenting? Did the experiment work? Does she believe you?'

The experience at lunchtime left Sarah unsettled, and she needed support from her husband and affirmation she wasn't following a pipe dream. She asked him a question.

'John, can I ask if *you* believe me? I'm not going mad am I? I'm not still living in a dream of my own making?'

John reached over and lifted Sarah's mug. He inhaled deeply and took a careful sip. Sarah guessed he was buying time.

'It's strong but yes, I could get used to it. I'd need to drink a whole mug first though, to be sure.'

Sarah stared at him, waiting for an answer. John took a deep breath and sighed.

'Sweetheart... you know you've no need to ask. Whatever's happened is very unusual. I'm sure it doesn't happen every day. Somehow, there's something switched on inside you. I've seen what you've been able to do since Christmas... how you can read people. Me and Claire. Peter and your brother. Rachel too. You seem to recognise their moods or feelings just by being with them, even though they seem their usual self. Unless it's obvious. The difficulty *I* have is... is... well, the same as if I were trying to experience someone else's dream. If you dream something powerful and try to explain it afterwards, whoever you explain it to has no way of grasping the feelings that went with the dream. It's impossible. No amount of description can make the dream clear because the experience was personal. What *you* are feeling or seeing is very real to *you*, but all I can do is accept what you say and understand it *is* real. So in answer to your question, yes I believe you.'

Sarah half smiled at John, but he could see there was no mirth in her eyes.

'A simple yes would have done,' she teased and John raised his eyes and shook his head.

'C'mon,' he said. 'Tell me what happened today?'

Sarah shuddered and her smile faded. 'Ok. Well, after I sensed that elderly couple I became nauseous, as if I'd eaten something bad. Rachel led me away but the feelings kept getting worse. Even after we were out in the fresh air, the image stayed with me and I couldn't switch it off. Everywhere we went I sensed negativity and sickness, almost as if everyone was ill or angry or… or frightened or depressed. It was horrible. I couldn't switch it off, John. It wouldn't stop.'

John needed no gift of his own to see the anguish in Sarah's eyes as she retold the events, her voice tones becoming stressed. He reached across the table for her hand and she grabbed at his as a drowning person may grasp in desperation onto a lifeline.

'It's ok, sweetheart. You're ok,' he soothed. 'You're home now. Take a few breaths and tell me the rest.'

Sarah obeyed, drawing in deep lungfuls of air, overloading her senses with essential oils of chamomile. As the vapours filled her lungs, Beryl's face appeared in her mind's eye and a measure of calm returned.

'It wasn't until we were back at the car park the nausea stopped. As we got close to the car, Rachel pulled me into a hug. She kissed me and said she loved me. It was like a slap in the face. Her words pulled my attention away from myself onto her, and the nausea disappeared… in an instant.'

'So it seems you need something as a distraction if it happens again. A diversion? Something to focus on? A charm or something? What do they call it… a talisman?'

'Hang on,' said Sarah, and she peered at him with narrowed eyes. 'I thought I was the one who's supposed to be witchy. What have I done to you? You want to drink herby tea instead of a pint and you're talking about charms.'

'Ah… I never said I'd swap beer for tea. But it's basic psychology isn't it. People who dwell on something bad need something to distract them, to take their mind off it. It's the same as me burying myself in the greenhouse after a shit day at work. A diversion.'

Sarah raised her eyebrows as John spoke. *Is he reading my mind now? I was thinking about gardening.*

'John, I'm… scared. I'm supposed to be the one in control. Everything I ever did, I did because I wanted to, because I balanced all the possibilities and came up with a decision… a plan. My choice. But this stuff is way beyond me. It's happened without my say so, without a choice. Beryl said I could choose to go back to my old life and ignore all of this, or accept it and see where it leads. But I never had a choice. You can't suddenly decide *not* to feel something as big as this. It's like… like falling in love. When you get the first pangs of love, you can't decide *not* to be in love. I never had a choice. This has happened, and it's robbed me of it. And now Beryl has gone, I have no one to help… no one to turn to.' Sarah flicked her eyes at John. 'Well no one who fully understands… you know what I mean. When these visions or feelings come on me, I can't stop them. I realised when I was with Rachel that what I first thought was exciting or a bit of fun may be dangerous.'

'Dangerous?'

'Well… yes. Dangerous because of how it affects me, my moods. It's all well and good picking up a happy person's mood. It fills you with warmth, with… peace. But sitting on a bench in town, most of what I sensed was pain or anger or fear and it left me feeling… tainted… poisoned.'

Sarah stopped again and drank from her mug, savoured the soothing intensity of the herbal tea.

John spoke again. 'Didn't you say Beryl called it a gift, a

gift of healing?'

'Yes. Now I'm not so sure I want it.'

John frowned. 'Sarah. This isn't like you at all, getting despondent. Give you a challenge or a problem to solve and you're unstoppable, obsessed even, until you come up with an answer. I guess it's easy for me to lecture but don't fall at the first hurdle, sweetheart.' John gulped at the water in his glass and continued, 'Y'know, I'm hearing what you have to say… have done for weeks now, and still it's hard for me to accept it all, which is why I nagged you to see Peter. But you did what I asked, passed all the tests and proved you were right. There's nothing wrong with you, though we still don't have all the answers, the explanation. Seems the only way to get them is to follow the road Beryl put you on, however hard it is. Remember I'm right here with you, so why not give what I suggested a try? If you can't stop these things coming at you, these… visions, then you need to protect yourself from them.'

John paused and shook his head. 'God. Don't let them hear me talking like this at work, will you?'

Sarah smiled and took John's hand again.

'I promise I won't say a word. But I guess you're right, though what am I supposed to use? What did you call it? A charm? A talisman? I wouldn't know where to start. C'mon clever clogs. You seem to be the problem-solver.'

'Sorry. Can't help you with that one. The psychologists would say it has to be personal… something *you* identify with, that comes to mind without effort.' John stood and walked over to the fridge. 'All this mystical talk is making me thirsty. I need something to bring me down to earth. Can I get you a drink?'

'Hmmm?' Sarah replied, absently. John pottered in the fridge for a minute and returned to the table with a can of beer and a glass of wine for his wife.

'It's early isn't it and I am pregnant, remember.'

'Well you've earned it today. A trip to the hospital. A trip into town. I doubt if even Peter would begrudge you one glass.'

'What would I do without you?' Sarah asked. 'I'll just have half of it.'

John settled back down and poured his beer into a glass.

'By the way,' Sarah said, changing the subject. 'What was it you and Peter were talking about?'

John laughed to himself. 'I'll give you one guess!'

'My closest friend by any chance? What's he got to say?'

'Hook, line and sinker. He's head over heels with Rachel but she's not playing ball. It seems she's not answering his calls or texts and he's acting like a teenager… mooning around.'

'Well, I get the impression Rachel's a bit off colour at the moment.' Sarah smiled at the irony of her use of the word colour. 'But… Mistress Sarah has a plan.'

'Huh. You'll be calling yourself the "Wise Woman" next. What plan is this then?'

'Ha. Rachel wants to call me that too. Anyway, we've invited Peter and Sophie over for dinner on Saturday. How about I ask Rachel over here too?'

'Oooo. Playing with fire. Dangerous. You will warn her… please,' John asked with little hope.

'I might. I'll give it some thought. But she loves me so I'm sure she'll forgive me.'

'God help us,' groaned John. 'Witches and love spells. What am I going to do with you?'

Sarah lowered her head and fluttered her eyelids.

'Anything you like, my husband. Anything you like.'

Twenty-four

Sarah thought of a plan while shopping the following morning. Despite John's warning about tempting fate, she decided a tiny white lie wouldn't hurt.

'Well she's your friend so I hope you know what you're doing,' he'd said. 'I hope there won't be any pieces to pick up afterwards.'

'You worry too much. It'll be fine.'

John sent a text to Peter suggesting he arrive around six o'clock, later than planned. Claire and Sophie could have dinner early and the adults could sit down to eat at half past seven. Sarah called Rachel a few minutes after John's text and invited her to come at seven.

The two young girls were halfway through bowls of ice cream when Rachel rang the doorbell at five to seven. Sarah opened the door.

'Hi, hon,' she greeted with a smile, but in a quiet voice, and trying to feign embarrassment said, 'bit of a mix up but Peter and Sophie are here. I hope it's ok.'

'Peter?' Rachel sounded startled. 'How come?'

'I'm sorry… it's our fault. I hadn't realised John had invited him to dinner, and he hadn't told me before I invited you. We didn't want to call either of you to put you off. It's not a problem is it?'

Rachel recovered her composure and said, 'No. Why would it?'

'Good,' replied Sarah. 'Let's have your coat. You go through to the living room while the girls finish their pudding. I'll bring you a drink through.'

As Rachel made her way along the hallway, Sarah hung back, driven by sudden intuition and the need to observe. She saw Rachel hesitate before walking into the living room, pause and draw breath, as if seeking courage to face a difficult task. Sarah shook her head while hanging up Rachel's coat, pondering Rachel's apparent reluctance, her restraint. Around men, Rachel was full of confidence and control. She preferred to be the game setter, setting things out according to her own rules. Men often made assumptions about Rachel, expecting her exceptional good looks to put her at a disadvantage, be easy prey, or she would be diminutive in her behaviour. They were always mistaken, often to their own humiliation. The only reason Sarah could imagine that may explain her friend's unusual behaviour was she thought more of Peter than she was prepared to admit. Rachel appeared, for once, unsure of herself. For a moment, Sarah wondered if tonight was a mistake but it was too late. She'd set this up and had to manage it. She sighed and made her way into the kitchen to check on Claire and Sophie.

Despite Sarah's momentary reservation, the evening went well. The conversation was relaxed, though Rachel was quieter than usual, and the food and wine perfect. Rachel drank little, saying she needed to be up early. Claire and Sophie played together in Claire's bedroom while the grown-ups ate, and afterwards asked to come back downstairs.

Sarah stood and gathered the empty plates but before John could get up, Rachel was on her feet too.

'I'll give you a hand,' she said, but John stood and laid a

hand on her shoulder.

'No you won't. It's not allowed. Why don't you and Pete go through to the living room? We won't be long.'

There was no escape for Rachel so she glanced at Peter as he rose out of his chair.

'After you,' he said, and Rachel led the way.

Rachel whispered to Peter as they sat on separate chairs. Sophie and Claire were sifting through a pile of films.

'I think…' Rachel said, 'we've been set up. I think they engineered this little gathering.'

'You may be right.' Peter responded. 'I'm sorry. I guess it's my fault.'

'Your fault?'

Peter paused as if measuring his response.

'Yes. I asked how you were and I think they must have misinterpreted my meaning or jumped to conclusions.'

'Oh. Well… that was silly of them,' Rachel replied, avoiding eye contact. 'Still, you're not to blame. It was nice.'

'Yes. Sarah is an excellent cook.'

They both fell into an awkward silence for a few moments as they watched the two girls deliberating over the choice of an animated comedy or a children's musical.

A few minutes later, Sarah and John joined them.

'So,' John said to Claire. 'What's it going to be? Nothing too long please. It's almost nine o'clock already.'

'Well actually I ought to be going. I have to visit a relative tomorrow,' Rachel said.

'So soon?' Sarah asked.

'Yes I'm sorry to say. I hate to break things up.'

'Yes, I ought to get Sophie home too,' Peter added. 'I need to make a few calls… arrange a sitter for Monday and Tuesday.'

'Sitter?' asked Sarah.

'Yes. I've a medical conference to attend and I've still yet to find someone to look after Sophie. My sister in Stoke would have her but she's away and I can't send her to my father's. He's getting too frail.'

Sarah answered. 'Well why don't we—'

In an eager voice Sophie interrupted. 'Can't I stay with Rachel please, Daddy? We had a really cool time at Christmas.'

Sarah was taken aback. She'd no idea Rachel had seen Sophie at Christmas.

'Christmas?' she said. 'Is there something I don't know about?'

Rachel gave a quick glance at Peter before answering.

'Sorry, Sarah. Peter asked if I wanted to spend Christmas day at his house and I said yes.'

In surprise, because she and Rachel shared everything... had no secrets, Sarah opened her mouth without knowing what to say. But before she could speak, Sophie jumped up and launched herself onto Rachel's lap and wrapped her arms around her neck.

'Oh please. Can I Rachel... stay with you, pleeeease?'

Sarah saw an involuntary smile flash across Rachel's face, and when Claire jumped onto Rachel too, she gave in and laughed. In an instant, Rachel's mood transformed and for moment Sarah saw a flash of bright orange engulf her friend... an energetic colour... full of zest... the colour of Rachel's aura. But Rachel took her lower lip between her teeth and the colour faded. She lowered her head and surprised Sarah even more by kissing Sophie's forehead.

'If your dad says it's ok, it's fine with me,' she said. 'But only overnight because I have to go to work.'

Sarah cut in, desperate to keep moving whatever just happened. 'I can help with the school run if you like.'

Peter looked pleased. 'Are you sure? It would be a big help if you can and it's obvious what Sophie wants.'

Rachel nodded again and cleared her throat. 'Yes. It's fine and it would be nice.' Then with an effort she said to Sophie, 'I can do you bat wings and mashed pigs liver for dinner!'

'Yuch!!' said Sophie, and everyone laughed.

'Well, that's settled,' said Peter. 'You must let me show

my gratitude somehow and soon.'

'No need. I'm happy to help,' and Rachel shot a quick smile at Peter.

'But I'd better go,' she said and Sophie planted a kiss on Rachel's cheek before sliding off her lap.

Rachel made arrangements to pick up Sophie from school and then said her goodbyes. At the front door, Sarah stood with her friend for a few moments.

'Rachel. There's something wrong with you I know, but I can't tell what it is. You're not your usual self. I'm surprised you never told me about Christmas with Peter.'

Rachel said nothing but wrapped her arms around Sarah.

'I'm fine,' she whispered. 'A bit moody maybe. Thanks for this evening. It wasn't as bad as I thought it would be, not that I thought it would be… bad I mean. I'm sorry I'm not making any sense am I? Got stuff on my mind that's all.' She pulled away from Sarah and spoke again, 'I know what you were trying to do, Sarah. You set this up, but I don't need help.'

'Rachel, I'm worried.'

'Don't be silly,' Rachel replied, trying to be indignant. 'I'm a big girl, I can take care of myself. Look, I'll see you on Monday. I'll drop by with Sophie after I pick her up from school.'

'Ok, sweetie. I love you.'

'And I love you too,' and with that Rachel turned and headed off into the night. In the orange glow of the streetlights, Rachel appeared to slouch as she made her way to her car, as if the world spread its weight across her shoulders. The aura misting around her head seemed weak and faint, worrying Sarah even more. With a wave at her friend as she drove away she stood a while longer before muttering into the gloom, 'We all need help sometimes Rachel… all of us.'

Then with a shiver, Sarah remembered how more comfortable it was indoors.

Twenty-five

'Hi, sis. How are you? How is everyone?'

It was ten o'clock the following morning and Sarah had telephoned her brother for a catch up.

'Perfect thank you and so is everyone else. What are you up to? How are things?'

They spoke on the phone at least twice a week, and always at the weekend when David was at home.

'Oh same as ever. They're keeping me busy. I have to go to Newcastle this afternoon to be ready early tomorrow morning. Big systems upgrade and it has to start around half four. I'll be there a couple of days to make sure it all works but back home on Wednesday. What about you? Any more strange visions? I'm not going to get them as well, am I?'

Sarah met with David earlier in January after her stay in Scotland. She'd told him everything concerning Beryl and the family history but David was sceptical. At the time, he wanted evidence of the family connection. Sarah gave no proof but asked him to have faith in her ability to perceive the truth. It was difficult for him but he respected his sister enough not to be scathing in his response. David, who was well rooted in the modern world, never felt the need for spiritual beliefs or 'archaic faith' as he called it.

'Strange visions?' asked Sarah, responding to his question. 'Well if you want to call them that then yes. Plenty in fact.'

Sarah relayed what happened in town when she'd met with Rachel, the ill feelings she'd experienced.

'And before you start to nag,' she continued, 'I've seen Peter and had a load of tests and there's nothing wrong with me. So I believe whatever Beryl told me is the truth. Something has awakened. It seems to get stronger every time I ponder it.'

'How do you mean stronger?'

'Well, let's see. Imagine a body builder or athlete. They exercise to become stronger or fitter, faster even. I suppose it's like that. If I take time to explore my ability, my… my gift, I find I can sense more, understand more.'

There was a silence at the end of the phone line and Sarah laughed.

'Look,' she sniggered, 'This is like you trying to explain your computers and your networky stuff. It goes straight over my head. Obviously this stuff goes straight over your head. In fact in one way the two examples are the same. I don't have to understand how the Internet works, I only *need* it to work. My gift is the same. How it works doesn't matter. I need to practice using it though.'

David laughed back. 'You're right, as always. Yes it goes over my head. The whole thing seems ridiculous but each to their own.'

'Exactly. I was reading something last week about faith healing, energy lines and alternate medicines. The article mentioned reiki. I believe Beryl did something to open my energy channels as a part of reiki introduction.'

'Sorry, what was that? Rake something?'

'Reiki. R. E. I. K. I. It's an energy healing but roughly translates to universal life energy. We all have energy lines running through us. Every living thing does. It's what acupuncture keys into, to name one form of accepted healing, and I *know* you trust in that since you had treatment for your back once. Remember all the pain you were in a few years ago from sitting in front of your computer for hours?'

'Hmm. Yes, ok, I remember.'

'Well, you said the whole thing seemed ridiculous? One thing about reiki is it requires no belief structure, no faith. Like acupuncture it works because it operates at a different level than your conscious, structured mind with all its prejudices, selfish motivations or disbeliefs.'

'Well ok. I give you the acupuncture,' said David. 'But it's hard to accept this stuff from someone you never met before. Come on, Sarah. You've got to admit it all sounds crazy. Colours, sensations, invisible stuff. This is the twenty-first century, y'know. What does John say?'

Sarah laughed again. She was in a light-hearted mood and wasn't going to let David's scepticism dampen her spirit.

'You're nothing but an old cynic, and I don't see what the century has to do with it. But as for John, he worried at first but seems to be on my side.'

'You mean he does as he's told! But, yeah, perhaps you're right... about me being a cynic, I mean. Anyway, what are your plans for the week? Are you going back to work sometime soon?'

There was no hesitation in Sarah's response. Before she had time to consider the question, she replied.

'No. I've hinted to both John and Rachel I'm not sure I want to go back at all. It's time for a complete change and I'm close to deciding to hand in my notice. In fact I *have* decided... I just need to do it.'

'Wow! So what will you do instead?'

'I'm sure you can guess. I could take a training course in healing, or several courses so I could become a qualified practitioner. You know I always wanted to help people. Well this is a chance for me to do it on a different level, helping people on a personal basis.'

'You'll never get rich, y'know.'

'Typical. Just like you to think of money. You *know* that's not what it's about.'

'Yes, sis, just winding you up.'

There was a moment's silence before David spoke again.

'Look. I know I'm sceptical, but I hope it all works out for you, whatever you decide. And I must admit, I'm not convinced you were ever *that* happy in your job. Something you did at the time I suppose.'

'Yes… maybe you're right. All part of the journey. But to answer your other question.'

'Which question?'

'You asked if you were going to start seeing things too? Well if you do, I'm sure you'll rationalise it by saying you've had too much exposure to something or not enough sleep, so I wouldn't worry if I were you.'

'Hmm. Not sure if that's helpful or if you're being sarcastic,' David laughed.

'Aha. Got you thinking though.'

'I tell you what,' David continued, 'how about I drop in on Wednesday evening before I go home… on my way past? Say around sevenish? We can catch up properly.'

'Yes… it'll be nice to see you for a change instead of just a quick phone call.'

'Ok. It's a date. You can bring me up to speed with everyone else. Like Rachel and Steve. I've not seen him since before Christmas.'

Sarah puzzled for a moment.

'Funny you should say so but neither have I. How long has it been? Over a month now? In fact, I don't remember having a Christmas card from him either and he always sends one. Hmm. I'll try to get hold of him, later perhaps.'

'Aha, a bit of a mystery.'

'Yes,' mused Sarah. 'Well, breakfast is ready by the looks of it, courtesy of my lovely husband, so I'd best get to the table. I'll see you Wednesday.'

'No problem. See you.'

An hour later, Sarah called Steve's house phone but with no response. She left a message on his answer machine and followed up with a call to his mobile phone. After the same result, she left a further message saying she wanted to meet. After an hour, she'd had no reply to any of her messages.

'Odd,' she said to John. 'I know we don't meet as often as we used to, but we always swapped text messages.'

'Mmm. So what are you going to do?' John asked absentmindedly, his attention elsewhere. He was browsing through a Sunday paper while Claire was drawing pictures. Sarah borrowed a piece of paper from Claire and with singular purpose folded it into the shape of an aeroplane. With perfect precision she floated it across the room and straight into John's ear.

'Ow!' John's response was more than rewarding and Claire giggled into her hands.

'Are you listening?' Sarah asked, all innocence.

'Do I have a choice?'

'No... you never did my darling,' replied Sarah, sweetly. 'But since I now have your full attention, I'll pop round tomorrow to see if he's in.'

'Okay darling... whatever you feel is best. Can I go back to my paper now?'

Sarah lifted herself up from where she sat at the kitchen table and wandered over to John who stood leaning over the work surface. She draped herself around her husband.

'Yes, my lover, you may. I'm going to surf the web and think about life.'

Sarah planted a kiss on John's cheek, taking the trouble to flick her tongue over his ear.

John shook his head in despair.

'Dangerous... very dangerous,' he groaned. 'Men might have most of the top jobs, but woman rule the world.'

'And your problem is?' replied Sarah as she left the kitchen.

Half an hour later John entered the living room with a

mug of tea for Sarah.

'You've been quiet,' he said. 'Have you thought about life?'

Sarah sat upright on the sofa gazing at her laptop with fierce concentration. 'Thanks for the tea. Yes, and I've come to a decision too. Plus I have two things to tell you.'

'Ok,' John sat next to his wife. 'So what decision is this?'

'I'm handing in my notice at work. I can't go back. I've just typed up a letter of resignation. I'll get it printed and posted off tomorrow.'

'Well, I guessed that from comments you'd made after Christmas. Besides, with your innate sense of loyalty and commitment, if you wanted to go back you would've done so weeks ago. So tell me something I don't know.'

'Ok, smart ass.' Sarah elbowed John in the ribs. 'I found a place, well several in fact, but one that looks better than the rest where I can train to be a reiki healer. It's not straightforward because I have to have a session first to see if it would be worth it. But I don't think I'll have a problem because of the family history.'

'Ok, if that's what you want. Will this be a substitute for your job?'

'Not sure about a substitute. It's a complete change. A change into something I really want to do. It seems right to start here. I remember saying to Beryl I didn't know where to begin or what to do. She told me not to get overwhelmed, but to explore the gift a little at a time. Doing this feels right John, feels like I'm finding out more. Whether it *is* the right thing to do or not... well, time will tell.'

'Go for it, sweetheart, but can you learn massage as well. I could be your guinea pig.'

'I can do that already,' she smiled. 'No need for training.'

Claire called through from the kitchen. 'Are you two being rude again?'

'Your daughter,' laughed Sarah.

John shook his head in resignation before continuing. 'You said there were two things?'

'What? Oh yes. A minor point. I've had an email from Beryl's solicitor. It appears I own a cottage and some land!'

Twenty-six

'Hang on, hang on. Let's not get ahead of ourselves. We've no idea what's involved yet.' Sarah raised her voice to calm her husband and daughter.

'But—' began Claire.

'But nothing,' interrupted Sarah.

Since revealing her news about owning land, John and Sarah migrated to the kitchen to share the news with Claire. The young girl jumped up with excitement.

'Can I have a pony?' she pleaded, hopping up and down.

'Perhaps I could finally grow some veg,' John chipped in. 'Maybe start a garden shop, sell to the locals.'

'And chickens! I like pigs too,' Claire added.

'Claire…' Sarah warned.

John joined in the excitement. 'Yes, chickens… perhaps a pig or two. This sounds like a way out of here… to go back north.'

At this point Sarah called a halt to her family's runaway enthusiasm. Once she had John and Claire's attention, she spoke calmly.

'Listen, the email doesn't go into much detail. It simply says an area of land and a cottage. For all we know the cottage may be derelict and the land no bigger than a postage stamp.'

'Yes, but if it was a postage stamp,' John countered, 'I'm sure they wouldn't say land. Surely they'd say cottage and garden. Anyway, you seem a bit unimpressed.'

'Can I have a pony?' Claire asked again.

'They may,' said Sarah, answering John's point, 'but it still gives no clue to the size. It may be nothing more than a large garden or a paddock. But it's not that I'm unimpressed, I'm just being cautious. I love the idea of owning a Scottish Croft, but in some way it feels wrong to say I own it when not long ago I hadn't even met Beryl, let alone be in her will. I feel like I have no right to it. But let's be practical for a moment. How big is an acre?'

'Well if I recall, an acre is 4,480 square yards, so Papa told me. We'd know it as a bit over 4,000 square metres.'

'Is it enough room for a pony?' asked Claire.

'Not really, sweetie,' replied John.

'I need something to visualise,' said Sarah. 'Claire's school is a mile away. How does that relate to acres?'

'Are you trying to test my maths?' quizzed John. 'Where's my phone and I'll work it out.'

John fired up the calculator on his phone, using the Internet as a source of unit conversion. After a few minutes he spoke once more.

'Ok, so an acre is sixty-three metres by sixty-three. That's less than a hundred metre sprint either direction. A mile is roughly 1,600 metres, the distance to school. So with a strip of land sixty-three metres wide and 1,600 metres long, it would cover an area of around twenty-five acres. Our back garden is about ten metres wide, so to get twenty-five acres you're talking a length of six times the distance to the school.'

'So one acre is quite a size really, for a garden,' mused Sarah.

'Yes, enough for some decent veg growing.' John grinned.

'Ok... enough,' Sarah laughed. 'We don't know what we

don't know so let's leave it for now. Talking of veg, it's time we chopped some ready for dinner.'

'Can I have a pony?' said Claire without much hope.

Twenty-seven

Sarah shook her head with sadness as she stared at Steve's front door a few minutes before lunchtime of the following day. Convinced Steve hadn't repainted it since they'd chosen the colour years ago, when they lived together for a while, Sarah wondered why that was. Though she visited often, today was the first time a faded and peeling front door had a profound effect on her. It made her ponder Steve's life, how happy he was… or wasn't. How much he took care of himself, his overall wellbeing. Steve had always been self-reliant, but when they tried to set up home as a couple, it hadn't been long before he'd become slovenly and idle, and that was due to his realisation Sarah still loved John. Struggling with the reality of it, Steve fell into a mild depression.

But that was years ago. Sarah slid into her new life with John after she and Steve split up, but Steve had stood still. On the outside and to others who knew him little, he appeared happy enough, but Sarah knew otherwise. She was able to read his mood… a legacy of living with him, but of late, and leading up to Christmas, she'd sensed a sadness in Steve. It worried her she'd had no contact from him since she came out of hospital and felt a sudden pang of guilt for not keeping in touch herself.

Still, she thought, *there's been a lot on my mind,* and now there was even more to occupy her thoughts. Events were occurring with the potential to change her life and that of her family forever.

The email she'd received from Beryl's solicitor hadn't gone into great lengths, but stated that documented proof confirmed everything Beryl had said... Sarah *was* her great granddaughter. Driven by the need to hide away what he saw as shameful deeds... giving little Jade to Beryl's sister to raise, Beryl's father had, it seemed, drawn up legal documents relating to the birth, but kept them hidden. Though she may never know for certain, Sarah convinced herself Beryl's mother had played her part. Besides the confirmation, the email noted that a full report and survey of the estate was to be undertaken as part of Beryl's last wishes before making available the final detailed notification of title deeds. There was no mention of property location.

Sarah couldn't understand why Beryl would specify such a delay. Surely she had known the condition of her own estate. Still, she could only wait, but the notion grew in her mind that Beryl still had a game to play, or at least a hidden purpose that would show itself, a reason for the delay. *Is she testing me?*

After Claire had gone to bed the previous evening, John opened up to Sarah.

'Y'know, I understand how you feel and, if I'm honest, I'm feeling the same way myself.'

'How do you mean?'

'Well, life has changed because of an incident that may have been much worse. What was it you'd said to Rachel? Before and after? Well it's true. With you being at home so much, seeing how different you are, how Claire is behaving too, and also how frail Papa is becoming, the before seems less satisfying. The after seems more challenging, something to relish, to look forward to. I guess part of what I'm trying to say is I want to move back north... go home. Papa hinted at it at Christmas while you were out searching for Beryl. I never told you at the time because I couldn't see how to make it work, how to make the break and move on. There's a lot to consider. And you had a lot on your mind at the time. Perhaps your news about Beryl gives us all the possibility to move, to make the change. If you want me to live in a cottage with you.'

Sarah hugged her husband.

'Well I might meet a hunky Scots landowner instead, someone who wears a kilt all day.'

'Ha! Are you after a bigger sporran or something?' and they both laughed.

'But to be serious,' John continued. 'Police work was always my goal, my life plan, but I'm thinking it's not enough anymore. It doesn't drive me the way it used to. Perhaps I've become... poisoned by some aspects of it.'

Sarah remembered saying something about having a plan so they could move north and start a fresh life, and John shared her vision. Where there was a will there was a way, they said, and the irony of the comment didn't escape them.

But now Sarah turned her thoughts back to the sight of faded and peeling paintwork on an old warped wooden front door. Drawing a breath she knocked and waited, feeling uneasy. Her day had started well and in a light mood. She had risen early and driven to Rachel's apartment to pick up Sophie and take her to school, while John took Claire in on his way to work. Rachel appeared more cheerful than on Saturday night and Sarah thought Sophie brought out a hidden side to Rachel, a motherly instinct. But on the drive to Steve's, Sarah's mood sank into something bordering on bleak. The reason was unclear. Maybe the vivid dreams during her stay in hospital had presented the possibility of how her life may have turned out. Or was it the memory of the voice she'd heard in her head as she hugged Steve before Christmas? The sight of a depressing and ill maintained front door may not have helped, or maybe it was these things combined. Either way she couldn't escape now since she'd knocked on the door. *C'mon Sarah it's only Steve.*

After a few moments, someone fumbled with the lock and the door swung open, accompanied by the grating sound of swollen wood as it screeched against the door frame. The doorknocker and letter box cover clattered, echoing across the street, but this troubled Sarah little compared to Steve's appearance.

'Oh!' said Steve, and Sarah thought his exclamation sounded more of disappointment than surprise. 'What can I do for you?' He made little effort in standing aside but swayed as he held onto the door.

Steve's frosty manner surprised Sarah as he was usually more welcoming. But more worrying were his looks. He was unshaven… for many days judging from the beard on his chin… his hair was unkempt and unwashed, and he wore only pyjamas with a dressing gown hanging from his shoulders. When Steve spoke, his voice sounded tired and slurred as if he'd been drinking and his eyes were dull… tired with dark grey patches. It horrified her to think he'd sunk to this in only a few weeks. She took a few seconds to respond.

'I thought I'd visit to see how you are. I haven't seen you since before Christmas. Are you going to invite me in? It's chilly out here.'

Steve shuffled to one side, turned and walked back along the hall. Sarah was a little annoyed. This was not normal, not for Steve. He was always hospitable to visitors though he didn't have many as he worked away from home most of the time, but she followed Steve into the hallway and closed the door behind her. He wandered into the living room and all but fell into an armchair, pulling his dressing gown around him as if folding himself into the fabric. It was only then Sarah realised how cold it was. Her breath misted as she entered the living room and she could smell the dry heat from the gas fire. With a quick scan around the room she saw a bottle of scotch on the coffee table and an empty dinner plate, the remnants of an evening meal or breakfast drying on the surface.

'Steve, it's freezing in here,' she said. 'You trying to save on the bills or something?'

'It's fine,' was Steve's curt reply.

'You look terrible,' Sarah said trying to be light-hearted. 'Are you ill? Is there anything I can get you?'

'Not ill,' he muttered.

Steve's attitude was unaccountably rude, but Sarah recalled the reasons for her visit. He'd returned none of her calls. His mobile phone was on because it rang out when she telephoned, but, after a delay, switched to voicemail. It seemed he was ignoring her calls.

'Are you sure?' she asked. 'You don't look well and I'm sure this cold won't help. It smells damp and musty.'

Steve didn't respond.

'Well how about offering me a drink?' she said, hoping to get a response.

'Kitchen cupboard's empty,' he slurred. 'Got something warmer here that'll do the trick,' and he lifted the whisky bottle and gave it a pat.

'No thank you. Not at this time of the day. Haven't you got any tea or coffee?'

'No. Cupboards bare,' he repeated.

Sarah sat in the armchair next to Steve. He lounged back, nursed the bottle of whisky and stared at the gas fire. Sarah recalled a day ten years ago when they had sat in this very house and on these same chairs. Steve was wearing the same dejected expression now as back then, the day they agreed to go their separate ways, but this time a missed morning shave could not explain his demeanour. It was clear he'd been neglecting himself for days, weeks even. She worried he'd not been eating enough and the bottle he held caused her concern. With caution she reached out and placed a hand on his knee.

'Steve. What's happened? You've always been tidy and pretty well organised. You're not yourself. Are you drunk?'

Steve lifted his gaze away from the fire and Sarah noticed

his focus floated around before settling. His eyelids were slack and half closed. From somewhere deep within her growing spiritual awareness, she perceived there was little life left in Steve's eyes... no energy.

'Yes I'm drunk, but nowhere near enough.'

'When was the last time you ate a decent meal?' Sarah asked.

Steve turned away, and a frown creased his brow as he thought for a while.

'Ate? Who knows? What's a decent meal?'

'C'mon, Steve. I think you've had enough of this,' Sarah pointed at the bottle. 'How about I go to the shop and get something to make us a meal?'

'Shop? No, don't bother. Got food being delivered later. Groceries. Online. Don't bother.'

'Well, ok, if you're sure.'

'Sure? What's sure?'

'Steve, you're worrying me. Why is the house so cold and why isn't there any food? Why didn't you answer any of my calls yesterday if you've been here?'

'Why... why... why not!' Steve raised his voice. 'Why don't you stop mothering? I have a mother already. I don't need you to nag!'

'I'm not nagging, I'm just worried.'

Steve's eyes drifted into focus again and he locked them on Sarah.

'What do you want?' he asked in a louder voice. 'Why did you come here?'

Sarah was feeling unsettled, even frightened. Something was going on that Steve wouldn't share, and his manner appeared threatening, if possible from someone with such a gentle nature. Sarah leaned away from him.

'I'm sorry,' she said in an apologetic voice and changed the subject. 'I came for two reasons. One, to find out how you are, and two, to share some news with you. I wanted to tell you I'm pregnant again. I'm expecting in late summer.'

'Well good for you,' Steve spat back, but as soon as the

words passed his lips he seemed to realise what he'd said. He spoke again, but this time with sensitivity.

'Good for you… good news. Yes… good news. Good news. What's good news?'

For long moments there was silence between them. Then Steve spoke once more but in a whisper Sarah could only just catch.

'I don't want to see or speak to anyone, especially not you… not you… not now.'

'Why not? And why not me? Steve, you're frightening me. What's happened?'

Steve pushed himself upright and stood still for a moment, before shuffling over to the patio doors. He bumped into the glass and steadied himself with one hand against the frame. Sarah rose from her chair, worried he would fall. Outside a pale winter sun shone that comforted the soul but brought little warmth to wherever its rays landed. A cool breeze rattled the remains of dead leaves clinging to a beech tree at the far end of the garden, while a few sparrows pecked with unerring optimism at the ground beneath. Tall blades of grass shook in the breeze, as if shivering, trying to generate their own warmth, but Sarah paid little attention. Her focus was on the man who had once been her lover, if only for a brief while. A man who would always claim a place in her heart. She spoke again.

'C'mon, Steve. What do you mean not me? I thought we were friends?'

Steve said nothing.

'Steve,' Sarah began again. 'I came here to share some news with you. I wanted to tell you in person I'm pregnant. But now I'm worried. What's going on? Is everyone ok? How are the family? How's your mom?'

Sarah saw Steve's shoulders slump, and he shuffled back toward her before collapsing into his chair, still clutching the whisky bottle.

Sarah's patience was wearing thin, and she was in danger of becoming annoyed. At the least, she thought, he could show her the courtesy of talking to her. She stood over Steve and stared down at him. For a moment she argued with herself whether to ask him a question. A question that had been on her mind since before Christmas, and more so since meeting Beryl. Backwards and forwards the argument went, but then, rightly or wrongly, and with increasing irritation overriding caution, she asked him.

'Steve, if you won't talk it's your choice but I have to ask you something... something that makes no sense but something that's been bothering me since last year, since the dinner party. I wasn't going to say anything but... well, I need to know.'

Sarah paused for a moment realising she needed to explain the changes that had happened, the things she could now sense.

'Since my accident I hear things I couldn't before and see unusual things. It's like I can sense them more than see them... y'know, like sixth sense.'

Steve gazed at her with eyes moist and old, as if tired... tired of a great effort that haunted and drained him. Sarah would have expected his expression to belong to someone who had been in pain for many years, and the weak aura which became visible to her inner sight and floated around was a dark and dirty brown. For a moment, and in her mind's eye, she perceived an image of Steve struggling to wade through a huge lake, a lake with no visible shoreline, a lake filled with a thick sludge of dark grey matter. The sudden image disappeared, but the effect on her wellbeing was profound. With a suddenness which made her shudder, Sarah felt tense and alert, as if her senses detected a threat and her body readied itself for fight or flight. Despite the nausea flooding her stomach and soul, she continued, needing an answer to her question.

'Steve, I know it sounds crazy but I can see things... sense them... but not all the time. I can only sense them occasionally. I've also heard voices in my head. It's disturbing because the first time it happened I thought I was still in hospital in a coma. It was at my house when you all came for dinner the day I came home.'

Sarah paused for a moment, cautious once more, but she had gone this far and Steve's manner frustrated her, and her experience with Rachel in Wolverhampton town centre had left her unsettled.

'Steve, when I hugged you at our house, I heard voices. Well, a voice. I thought at first you'd whispered something, except the voice was aggressive... nasty.'

Steve's eyes widened, and he seemed suddenly on edge. 'What? Voices? What are you on about?' he stammered, slurring his words.

'I don't know, which is why I'm asking. The voice I heard spoke the words, "*You fat little faggot. You ain't got the guts!*" What it means I don't know, but... well, that's it.'

At Sarah's words, Steve jumped up, eyes widening, full of shock and panic. When he spoke his voice rose in anger.

'Why are you saying this? Who told you? Who have you been talking to?' Steve took a lurching step toward Sarah and his fists clenched and shook. 'Who told you?' he asked again, swaying on the edge of balance.

Sudden fear paralysed Sarah. Steve's face was full of rage and anguish and his aura was now a shocking red, moving and wafting around his head. Sarah spoke with a tremor in her voice.

'Steve? Stop it! What's going on? What does it mean?'

'You know full well don't you, you nosy BITCH! You've been nosing around trying to get hold of me, trying to get to the truth. Well someone must have TOLD! SOME BASTARD TOLD YOU. YOU'D BETTER NOT TELL! YOU'D BETTER KEEP YOUR FUCKING MOUTH SHUT YOU BITCH!'

Tears started in Sarah's eyes. All she wanted now was to escape. She feared for her safety, but at last that fear released her from inaction. Shocked and crying she backed up and stumbled through into the hallway, turning as she went. She grabbed at the lock on the front door and tried to yank it open. But strong hands gripped her arms, spun her around and slammed her against the woodwork. Steve's face was so close she could smell the whisky on his breath, see the madness in his eyes.

'I know what you deserve you fucking bitch. What if I did to you what you did all those years ago? What if I ruined your life too, YOU FUCKING SLUT!'

Sarah tried to shrink into herself... to make herself smaller... become invisible. She moaned at Steve as his fingers dug into her arms.

'Steve! Stop it. Please. You're hurting me.'

'How would you like it! Me forcing myself on you like YOU DID TO ME?'

Steve leaned in closer and he pushed her arms up and back against the door, but sudden anger overrode Sarah's fear. With restricted movement she did the only thing she could. Lifting her knee sharply upward she struck Steve hard between the legs. But even in anger she acted with compassion, and adjusting her aim jabbed Steve's thigh. Blinded by irrationality and alcohol, Steve did not expect the retaliation and his leg collapsed sideways. Knocked off balance he let go of Sarah and dropped to the floor at her feet. He looked up with such intense pain and guilt Sarah gasped aloud. Tears poured from her eyes as she fumbled for the door handle.

'Sarah! I'm... sorry... I'm so sorry,' Steve whispered. But in a voice filled with torture and anguish he cried, 'Please just go... just get out... LEAVE ME... LEAVE ME AND DON'T COME BACK!'

The stiffness of the door gave way to Sarah's frantic efforts and swung wide open, slamming against the wall. She shot out onto the pavement and sprinted to her car, pressing the key fob as she ran. Yanking open the door she threw herself into the front seat, rammed the key into the ignition and the instant the engine roared into life, floored the accelerator. In horror she ignored the squeal of tyres and the blaring horn of a passing vehicle, and sped up the road, blinking through the tears streaming from her eyes, desperate to put as much distance as possible between herself and Steve.

Twenty-eight

'Hi, I'm back!'

It was nearing six o'clock when John arrived home. His shift over, he'd picked up Claire from one of her friends on the way home.

'Hi, Mom,' Claire shouted.

Without a sound Sarah wandered through from the kitchen into the hall.

'Oh hi, sweetie,' John said as he hung up his coat. 'What've you been up to today? Did you visit Steve?' John turned to his wife and only then noticed the look on her face. 'Sarah? What is it? What's happened?' In three quick steps he crossed the hallway and grabbed Sarah's hands. 'Are you ok?'

Sarah leaned into John and mumbled into his chest. 'Yes… yes. Everything's all right, just need a hug.'

Claire stood to one side and tugged at Sarah's sleeve. 'Mommy. Does it hurt?'

John shot a glance at his daughter.

'Does what hurt? What's going on here,' he demanded.

'Come into the kitchen. Have a drink and I'll tell you.'

Fifteen minutes later, Sarah was trying to manage John's fury.

'John, listen. I understand you're angry. I'm angry too but I'm also afraid. For heaven's sake… you know Steve like I do. Is this normal behaviour for him? No, it isn't. Something's wrong but what it is isn't clear. Anyway…' she took off her cardigan to show the bruises on her arms. 'These will heal a lot quicker than Steve will. I'm more annoyed with myself because I pushed him too far.'

'Pushed him too far? I'll do more than push him.'

'Daddy. Don't be too angry. I don't like it when you're angry. I think Uncle Steve is ill. He wouldn't hurt a fly.'

John took a deep breath. Caught between the two most important people in his life urging him to calm himself was far too much of a challenge, and he collapsed onto a stool.

'Ok, so I'm not going to beat the shit out of him but I'll have a few words to say… tomorrow, and I'll not change my mind.'

'Yes, ok. I think it's a good idea but only if you stay calm. Perhaps with you there I might find out what's going on. You should have seen the state he was in. It's not like him.' A thought occurred to Sarah. 'I wonder if he's lost his job or something. He'd work from home occasionally but still dressed for work.'

'Whatever the reason, he's no right to take it out on you. You of all people.'

'Like I said, I think I pushed him. I asked him about the words I heard, words I heard weeks ago.' Sarah stopped and regarded John with sudden fear. 'John. I'm scared.'

Claire sidled up to her mother and Sarah gave her a hug. 'Don't be scared, Mommy. It'll be ok.'

'I know, sweetie. I'm only worried about Steve.'

But Sarah spoke only half the truth. It was the gift that scared her… what it may do, or what it may reveal. How was she meant to control it, this thing she'd inherited, though in reality it appeared she'd always had it, lying dormant, awaiting the moment to awaken. And what worried her the most was how it may affect her family. Claire appeared to have it as well. Sarah guessed it began at the same time as for Sarah herself, at a time of severe stress. How else did Claire know of the bruising on her mother's arms? Claire must have felt it with her own awakened senses.

'I see no reason for you to be worried,' John said with little sympathy. 'Steve's a big man. I'm sure he can take care of himself.'

'John… that's the point,' Sarah said with growing impatience. 'You're not listening. I'm fearful because he's not his normal self. This isn't the Steve I know and I'm not so sure he *can* take care of himself. If you can't be understanding I'll go on my own. I don't want you making matters worse.'

'Ok. Ok… I'm sorry. But when someone threatens my wife, I think I have the right to behave this way.' John took a deep breath. 'Look. It's clear I'm angry but we'll see him together tomorrow after I come home. If you're as worried as you seem, I'll come with you and see what's going on. Can we ask Rachel to babysit?'

'I'm not a baby any more,' said Claire.

John apologised. 'Ok. Child mind. How does that sound?'

'Better,' came the reply.

Several hours later, a weary Sarah laid her head on John's shoulder as they settled into bed. She'd spoken little during the evening, only staring at a drama repeat they found on the television.

'Sweetheart,' John whispered as he wrapped an arm around her shoulders. 'Sorry if I went off on one earlier. I guess you're right about Steve. The way you described it must mean something's happened to him. He was never the happiest of people. Perhaps it *is* about his job.'

'Y'know, I love that you want to protect me, especially now I'm pregnant again, but I need you to help me too. When I talked about being scared earlier, it wasn't just because I'm scared for Steve.'

'Yes I know. I'm not a complete idiot. This... thing you've got, this gift must be daunting. Change is always difficult, but remember it's not only you who's going through this challenge. Claire and I are going through it too, so, sweetie, you're not on your own. If you get scared, tell me. We'll work through it together as a family.'

Sarah made no sound and only nodded her head, so John reached over and turned off his light. It wasn't long before he felt Sarah twitching as she succumbed to sleep.

Sarah awoke in the early hours needing to use the bathroom. At the foot of the bed Mags sighed and lifted her head as Sarah stood. Claire was just heading back to her room as Sarah crossed the landing and Sarah planted a kiss on her head.

'I'll come and tuck you in sweetheart,' she whispered.

A few minutes later Sarah pushed open Claire's bedroom door. Her daughter appeared to have fallen asleep again, but as Sarah pulled the quilt up the young girl turned and spoke.

'What made Uncle Steve unhappy?'

'I don't know, angel, but I want to find out,' Sarah replied. 'Daddy and I think he may have lost his job. It's hard when that happens. Sweetie, you know he's not your real uncle don't you?'

'Yes of course, but I call him that like I call Auntie Rachel my auntie. I don't have many real ones do I?'

'I'm sorry, angel, but no, only Uncle David. So it's ok to call them auntie and uncle.'

Claire yawned as she slid towards sleep and then muttered a few final words. 'I wish we could have helped him.'

'I'll help him... I promise.' Kissing Claire on the forehead, she crept back to her own bed.

For half an hour Sarah lay wide-awake, turning from one side to the other, but sleep failed to return. As the minutes crawled by she felt very alone, an isolation that comes from having a problem to solve with no one able to understand or help. Something was taking place she couldn't fix on her own, and there was no one to offer advice or give her aid.

With increasing unease, and in danger of lying awake for the rest of the night, she slid once more out of bed and made her way downstairs.

One of Sarah's age-old cures for sleeplessness was to pour herself a small glass of milk and have a biscuit. It often did the trick. So she made her drink and wandered through into the living room where she settled onto the sofa. As she sipped at the milk, her thoughts settled on Rachel, on how her closest friend seemed to have problems as well. Why was she cautious around Peter? Had she fallen for him? And if so why was it a problem? Rachel deserved happiness, deserved love.

While staring at the fireplace Sarah focussed her inner thoughts on her friend until her sight dimmed and the fireplace disappeared from view. She found she could see every feature of Rachel's face, her flawless grey eyes and long dark hair. And as she concentrated, she detected a quietness to Rachel, which made sense since she suspected her friend was asleep, but as she stretched her thoughts still further and pondered Rachel's recent behaviour, she picked up a disturbance, an uneasiness which made Sarah herself become even more restless... edgy, and she shuddered. The physical motion broke into her thoughts and the fireplace fell back into focus.

What was that? She thought. *What was I doing then?*

Sarah ate the biscuit and emptied the glass of milk and stood up to make her way back to bed. But as she turned to the door sudden nausea settled in her stomach, and for a moment she feared she might vomit. An image entered her sight but not of Rachel. Once more, but this time unbidden, the room faded from her physical senses. With her inner sight she could see Steve... saw once again the sight of him slumped in his armchair, the bottle of whisky nestling in his arms... replayed the angry outburst from the previous day. With an overwhelming sense of dread and despair she struggled to stay upright, but the nausea became urgent and running to the downstairs toilet she lifted the seat just in time to empty the contents of her stomach.

'Oh God... Steve,' she gasped. 'What is it? What's wrong?'

After waiting a few minutes to make sure she wouldn't be sick again, Sarah stood and rinsed her mouth. Sleep was now impossible to resist and with barely the strength to climb the stairs, she made her way back to bed, trying hard to push the image of Steve from her mind. With utter desperation she wanted to wake John, but realising whatever she told him would not make sense, she curled into a tight ball under the covers and waited for sleep to bring forgetfulness. She did not have to wait long.

Twenty-nine

For the second time in as many days, Sarah stood at Steve's front door and tapped the door knocker. The sound it made was thin and metallic and seemed lost as if it lacked the capacity to raise attention. It was after four o'clock, and Sarah stood with John waiting for an answer. They'd left Claire with Rachel and Sophie, who was staying with Rachel for a second night. Rachel was only too happy to leave work early and help out, but the promise of dinner was a big motivation.

'C'mon, Steve,' muttered Sarah through teeth that rattled in sympathy to a gust of chill wind... or was it nervousness? She'd been on edge since her episode during the previous night, but said nothing to John. The event only deepened her sense of isolation. There was no one to help, except Beryl and that was no longer possible. But at odd times during the day, while she was puzzling over it, a comforting hand touched her forehead, the same touch she'd felt before she'd met Beryl. Her puzzlement only increased because she now understood, as Beryl explained, that the touch had been Beryl herself, or a non-physical part of Beryl. But Beryl was gone... so who? While she'd been musing over these thoughts, she questioned the whole thing once more, the

Reunion

ancient connections, the growing gift, the seeing. She began to doubt the reality of it and even her own sanity. Was it only a dream? Was she still lying unconscious in a hospital bed? Did Beryl even exist? But refusing to succumb to those fears, those irrationalities, she remembered amazing things *did* happen in this world. Miracles occurred every day. People possessed uncommon gifts. So she had taken several deep breaths, begun the washing and cleaned the house from top to bottom. These simple tasks eased her worries, and she'd readied herself for the trip to see Steve, hoping to understand and ease his pain.

When the biting wind ruffled her hair, she reached out and rattled the door knocker again.

'Do you think he's out?' asked John hunching his shoulders, hands thrust into deep pockets.

'Always possible I suppose, but I doubt it. If you'd seen him yesterday, you'd think he'd not left the house for days or longer. Let's give him a few minutes. I'll try the house phone again.'

Sarah pulled out her mobile and tried the number. Though she heard a ring tone, there was no sound of the phone inside the house ringing. It was possible Steve had disconnected it.

In a moment of inspiration, or perhaps desperation, Sarah recalled last night, how she'd focussed her mind on Rachel and afterwards, albeit without intention, on Steve. Deciding to extend the reach of her senses again, she took a few slow deep breaths to calm her nerves. With unblinking and unseeing eyes she stared at the front door, placed a hand against the faded paintwork, and emptied her mind of extraneous thought. She pictured Steve's face… saw again his unshaven looks, the dark patches under his eyes and the sallow nature of his skin… his drunken behaviour. On a non-physical level she sensed the chill air of the living room and shivered. Though it made her nauseous again, she recalled the vision she'd had of him as she sat in her own living room sipping milk in the middle of last night. A vision of Steve slumped in his armchair.

With this image in her mind the seconds ticked slowly by, but then with the unexpected force of a physical blow she lurched away from the door and fell against John. In the same dreadful instant she recalled Claire's words, words spoken during the early hours as she tucked her young daughter back into bed, words that, with horrific realisation, Claire had uttered in the past tense.

'What made Uncle Steve unhappy? I wish we could have helped him.'

'Oh, God?' she breathed, and the hairs on the back of her neck stood up in response to sudden fear. 'John we need to get inside. You need to break in. Oh, God?'

'What?'

'Please, John. I'm frightened. Break the door.'

'Sarah. Calm down. I can't just break in.'

Sarah turned back to the door and began pounding on it as if she could force her way in with her fists.

'You must! We have to get in! Please, John, help me!'

John stepped forward and grabbed at Sarah hands. 'Sarah! Stop it. What the hell are you doing?'

With unexpected ferocity, Sarah spun around, eyes blazing, rage burning in them.

'JOHN… JUST BREAK DOWN THE FUCKING DOOR WILL YOU!'

With shock as sudden as his wife's outburst, John let go of her and stepped away. He held up his own hands in a placating gesture, but the surprise on his face hadn't gone unnoticed. Sarah calmed herself but tears filled her wide and fearful eyes.

'Oh, John, I'm sorry, really I am, but I'm scared to death. Please. We have to get in!'

Sarah's fear and obvious desperation became infectious and nudged John into action.

'Ok. Ok. Wait here. Don't try to get in… do you hear? Don't. Stay here.'

John waited a moment until Sarah nodded her head, and

then made his way to the gate that opened onto an alleyway leading between Steve's house and the adjoining property. He disappeared into the darkness and hurried to the rear of the house. At the end another gate led into Steve's back garden and John opened the gate and banged on the back door. Not waiting for an answer, he moved to the patio doors and peered through into the living room. What he saw only increased his fear.

Without hesitation he turned back to the door, and testing it with his shoulder found it loose in its frame. Despite his earlier words to Sarah, he stepped away from it and using the weight of his tall frame kicked his foot against the old wood by the handle. With a loud crack the wood around the lock splintered, and the door slammed open against the wall. John ran into the kitchen and through into the living room where he found Steve collapsed in his armchair, head to one side, eyes open and unseeing. Beside him on the floor lay an empty bottle of whisky and an empty plastic bottle. John leaned forward and placed his fingers onto the side of Steve's throat in a gesture well practised, but from the pallid colour of Steve's face he knew the test was a formality.

'Damn it,' he whispered to himself. 'God damn it. Steve you damned fool. Why?'

Standing upright once more, a sudden lurching horror hit John as the full weight of what he found hit him. Full of compassion for Steve, his heart went out to him for why he'd taken such a way out… why so desperate he thought he had no choice. Sarah's voice came echoing along the hallway.

'John! John! Where are you?'

Now with no urgency, John made his way towards the main entrance and with a calm solemnity that surprised him, opened the door.

'Have you found him?' asked Sarah, and she tried to enter the house.

'Sweetheart,' John said and blocked the way, holding the

door half closed.

'John. Have you found him?'

'Sarah... sweetheart... I'm sorry.'

Sarah's voice softened to a whisper.

'John... please tell me.' But scanning her husband's face, she guessed the truth. 'NO!' she cried, and with a surprising burst of energy, tried to push past John.

'Sarah!' John stood firm, blocking her attempts to gain entry.

'No! It can't be. Let me in. We can do something. John... let me in!'

'Sarah... no! You can't go in... it's too late. I'm sorry but there's nothing you can do.'

John grabbed his wife and held her with a strong but caring grip until she ceased. She searched his eyes... could see his pain even through his strength and gave up the fight, lowering her head against his chest. John was talking again, trying to calm her.

'Sarah... princess. We must stay out. The police need to be here. We can't contaminate anything. I'm sorry. I know I'm being an uncaring bastard but it's too late and we can't help. We must call the locals.'

Sarah spoke in an anguished whisper, tears coursing down her cheeks.

'Oh, God. Steve. I'm sorry. John, it was my fault... my fault.'

'No. Not possible. You aren't to blame. You're not. Come on. Let's go to the car. Let's stay out while I make the call.'

Sarah allowed John to lead her away after shutting the front door. The local police could gain access through the rear entrance but he needed to make sure his wife wouldn't try to get inside again. He stood with his arm around her while he called the emergency services. Sarah fell quiet and every few seconds shivered. John guessed it was due to more than just the chill air. Despite the falling temperature, he kept her outside and wrapped his arms around her while they waited for the police and emergency services to arrive. After a few minutes, when the crying of sirens sounded in the distance, she spoke, 'John. I'm sorry I swore at you. You didn't deserve it. I don't know if you realise it, but you are my life. You and Claire are everything. I don't think I could survive this world without you.'

Despite knowing whatever he said would bring little comfort, John spoke anyway, 'It's ok, princess. It'll be ok. I'm here… it's all going to be ok. Everything is. I promise.'

But despite his words, John realised a part of his own spirit had died along with Steve.

Thirty

It took a month for the coroner to decide a verdict of suicide was appropriate and agree to release the body. Sarah took a phone call from Margaret, Steve's eldest sister. Margaret gave her details for the funeral and asked if they would come. Born and raised in Nottingham, the family hadn't moved far from home, apart from Steve who left in his early twenties and had lived in or around Wolverhampton for over ten years. Margaret told Sarah they'd made arrangements to take Steve home and lay him to rest in his local parish. Without hesitation but with sorrow, Sarah accepted the invitation.

John voiced his concerns. 'This'll be very awkward.'

'Isn't every funeral?'

'Yes, but I mean with us being the ones who found him.'

'Maybe... but perhaps they're thankful we did. I mean... imagine if we hadn't. He may have been there for weeks otherwise. I'm not sure how often he spoke to his family, perhaps seldom.'

'I suppose you're right. But are you going to be ok? I mean do you still feel guilty, because you're not. Not at all.'

'I know.'

John was unconvinced with Sarah's reply. She'd

understandably not been herself over the past month. John understood his wife, that somewhere deep inside she was struggling to find her own answers and maybe she would always feel a measure of responsibility, but until she found a place for it, he could only stand by... close by, and wait, lending a hand when needed. After all, he pondered, it wasn't the first time.

A long week later, they joined everyone in bidding farewell to Steve. Margaret welcomed them and insisted Sarah and John sat at the front with the family.

'Sarah, you were a big part of his life,' she said. 'If only for a little while. Part of his family. It's only right you should be with us.'

Sarah bit her lip and managed a nod, allowing Margaret to take her hand and lead her to the front. Only a handful of people sat in the congregation which saddened Sarah, but what puzzled her more was why Steve's mother wasn't among them. Steve had told her she suffered long-term illness, but Sarah still expected her to be there to say farewell to her only son.

Later, back at Margaret's house, the immediate family and a few friends gathered for simple refreshments and a chance to share old stories. John was restless and felt he was intruding, but worrying for his wife's state of mind he stayed near, keeping a close watch.

When most people had made their promises to keep in touch and said their goodbyes, Sarah and John stayed in the kitchen chatting to the remaining family and a few friends. Margaret spoke to John asking if she could borrow Sarah for a while.

'I've seen you watching over her but she's in safe hands. I want to talk to her if it's ok?'

John smiled and nodded, 'Of course. Take as long as you need.'

Margaret took Sarah upstairs into a small bedroom. A

made up single bed lay on one side of the room, along with a bedside table and lamp, and against the opposite wall stood a wardrobe. The room was bright, but she sensed it was little used.

Margaret patted the bed in a gesture that encouraged Sarah to sit.

'Make yourself comfortable,' she said. 'I have something to show you.'

Sarah watched Margaret as she crossed the room. Resembling Steve in both looks and build, she carried Steve's smile, easy but with a tiredness, as if life had been a struggle, leaving the owner with an air of acceptance that real joy would come only on rare occasions. Margaret too had broadened with the years, but she *was* the older sister and closer to fifty than forty.

Margaret walked over to an old freestanding wardrobe that stood alone in a corner. It appeared to have been in the family for years, or picked up from a house clearance, but it was solid and ornate with inlaid marquetry in the single door. Margaret opened the door and stood to one side revealing a variety of shirts and trousers. Sarah recognised them as belonging to Steve. She assumed Margaret had brought them back. She sighed.

'Have you emptied Steve's house?' she asked. 'What will you do with those?'

'Oh I didn't get these from his house. These have been here for a while.'

'Sorry I don't understand. Why would they be here?'

'Sarah. Steve's been staying here on and off for a while. He's not been well.'

'Not been well?' Sarah asked in a plaintive voice.

'Look. There are things I need to explain. Steve wanted me to tell you so you would understand, so you wouldn't blame yourself for anything.'

Tears stung Sarah's eyes. 'Blame myself?' she whispered.

'Yes. He put his wishes in his last letter. Steve used to write often. Did you know?'

'I remember he used to write to you years ago when we were together. He often wrote little… little love notes and leave them all around the house where I'd find them. Such a gentle soul.'

'Yes, Sarah. He was the gentlest. Of late though his notes all but stopped coming… not so frequent. We'd agreed between ourselves years ago a good therapy for him was letter writing, a way of staving off bad thoughts.'

'Bad thoughts? Was Steve ill?'

'In a sense. He suffered from depression. Undiagnosed because he never saw a doctor about it. Flatly refused since his last attempt at suicide.'

Sarah's eyes widened in horror.

'Last attempt! Oh God! When was this?'

'Oh it was before you met. A long time ago when he was in his late teens. He moved away not long afterwards. But we dreamt up the idea of exchanging letters and phoning often. Somehow writing helped him rationalise his thoughts.'

Margaret gazed at Sarah for long seconds before pulling an envelope out of her pocket. She moved to the bed and sat, placing a hand onto Sarah's.

'My dearest, Sarah. These are Steve's last notes. He never posted them, just kept adding to them. The police found them in the house. You need to read them. It will help. I promise I'll explain more afterwards.'

A few tears escaped Sarah's eyes, as with care she unfolded the papers. Written there lay Steve's neat and flowing handwriting, with an extra-large capital letter at the beginning of each sentence, as was his habit. Shuffling through the sheets, she noted the few lines on the last page, scrawled in a rush or as an afterthought.

As if her very spirit was under attack, Sarah sensed a stream of negativity emanating from the papers in wave after wave, and she gasped with sudden nausea, 'I can't read this!' and offered the papers back to Margaret.

'No, Sarah. It's best you do. I can explain afterwards. It's all right. Remember he's at peace now.'

With a shuddering sigh, Sarah did as asked and started reading the few short sentences, the last words of a desperate soul.

Dearest sis.

It's early November now and I've decided to put pen to paper like I used to do and write a few notes as a warning to myself to stop and think when times get bad. I can use it as a safety net if ever I think about ending it all, a way to help me take stock and think about what is worth living for.

I came close today. If you are reading this, then I lost the battle. I ran out of strength. I know you will understand the reasons.

I've been so grateful to you these last few weeks for putting me up. I'm sure that Simon was never too happy about it and I'm sorry for causing him any discomfort. If I can ever find my way again, I'll try to pay you back somehow. For now though, I'm trying to ready myself for a Christmas that will bring me no cheer and I think it's best if I stay at home so you can have a good time, just with your family.

All in all I can never hope to express my thanks and my love to you for how you have helped me over

*the years, but I will try.
God bless.*

There was a gap before the writing continued.

I need to write this down though I can barely hold the pen. I got a call to say Sarah had been hurt, and she was in hospital in a coma. Some youth attacked her, and she fell over and banged her head. I've been over to see her and John was there. It didn't seem right to stay too long. She needs her family around her but it was hard to leave. I wanted to stay by her side until she woke up but that just wouldn't have been right. It was horrible. She was always a light to me, a beacon that shone in my darkness even though I couldn't be with her. But today when I saw her, the light had gone out. It was as if someone had extinguished it. I'm rambling and it sounds silly but if Sarah wasn't here I don't think I could be either. Just the thought of her keeps me going even though her love is given to another.

Another gap.

Sarah is ok again and out of hospital. They asked me around to dinner and I couldn't say no. Felt like I was invading somehow but John insisted so I went. It was ok, but I felt like an outsider. Dave was there too though I know he never had much time for me. I suppose he was always just protective of Sarah so I never blamed him.

Something odd happened. Sarah gave me a hug. Gave everyone a hug, but when she hugged me she jumped, like she'd been stung. Said she was ok but there was a look on her face, just for a moment. It was odd, but I had a feeling she wanted to ask something. Doesn't make much sense I know.

I left as early as I could, just made an excuse. But thinking back at the evening, it was like I was watching in at a window. Seeing another family having fun.

We had fun didn't we after He was gone? Sis? Didn't we?

Christmas day. The house is cold today. Thanks for sending a card. And thanks for buying a present for me. I'll come and see you soon and we can swap.

Do you remember Christmases after He was dead? Mom did her best to make them fun, and we did enjoy them with what little she could give us. She always made a special effort with dinner. I remember one year when she miscalculated the turkey. It hardly went in the oven and we were eating it for over a week. Think we were all sick of it by New Year.

I hate New Year. It's a lonely time, an exhausting time, how many people don't have the strength to carry on?

Sis what am I doing. What's the point? What is today all about without family? Feeling the old way again. Sorry. Trying to think positive, but about what?

Not sure if I can get through New Year's Eve, but will have a drink or two to see out the old and bring in the new. No good me being anywhere else but here. Would only make a mess of anybody's celebration. Promise not to drink too much.

Sarah noticed Steve's writing had become more fragmented, less well structured.

15th Jan. Can't think what to write. Nothing to say. I know you tried call cos I got message on machine. Part of me wanted to call but couldn't do it. It's getting close to the day He died.

Here a rough line had been drawn followed by a large gap. In a shaky hand, the remaining sentences continued with random punctuation and poor spelling, as if the author were fighting to write the words.

Sis sorry but cant keep it up feeling Very sleepy now but need right some word. Sarah came see me and I hurt her badly and I cant face her any mor

Need you to tell her Im sso sorry an tell her everything thats happened, evrythin. I think she guessed somehow. Tell her I allways lovd her....stilll do. Plese dont tell mom what I done   tell her I got job

somewere
> *I think ive had enough   nothing*
> *makes sens nothng left to do*
> > *Sis, I remember hush a bye baby*
> > *with mom. Do you remember?*
> > > *Hush a bye baby on the tree top*
> > > *Wen the bough brakes*
> > > *so tired of everything sis so tired*

Love you
Nite nite sis nite nit Sarah
sleep tite.

Sarah turned the last sheet over, hoping there were more words to hold on to, however irrational the hope. But the sheet was blank apart from a rough, uneven crease. She folded the message again and handed it back to Margaret. To her exposed and vulnerable spirit, the note seemed to be screaming with anguish and pain, and nausea flooded her soul.

Margaret reached across the bed and grabbed Sarah's hand. In desperation Sarah hung on, wretched and ridden with guilt.

'I'm so sorry, Margaret,' she whispered. 'It was my fault. I was careless, and I drove him to it. I know I did.'

A fresh flow of tears escaped Sarah's eyes but with surprising firmness Margaret spoke.

'Sarah. Stop this. You aren't to blame at all whatever you think you may have done. Steve became the way he was a long time ago, way before he moved from here.'

Margaret drew a deep breath as if preparing for a tale that would need every ounce of energy to tell. She gave Sarah's hand a gentle squeeze and let go. She stood and walked to the window and gazed out into the garden. A handful of small birds were squabbling over the seed feeders while a blackbird pecked at the remains of an apple lying on the lawn. The sky was heavy with low cloud and a few spots of rain streaked the glass.

Margaret began her tale.

'You heard about our father didn't you? Steve would have told you a little of the truth, some of the horrible stories. We were lucky, us two and our sisters. Mom used to deflect his violence. She could predict his moods and if any of us didn't toe the line, she stood in his way so she took the brunt of his temper. I lost count of how many times she covered up bruises or black eyes. He even put her in hospital once. Knocked her out and gave her concussion. Thank God our grandmother took us while she was away. But it could have got worse if it hadn't been for Steve. He was the youngest, but he'd got it into his head he had to be the man of the house. Steve tried to look after us in what small way he could. Fetching and carrying, keeping the place tidy, running errands. He was a lovely boy and cheerful in his way because he felt he was being useful, which he was. Whatever he did though was never good enough for our father on the odd occasion he was at home. He belittled Steve whenever he could.'

With the telling of the story Margaret's composure failed.

'Fucking evil bastard. I hope he's burning in hell!'

Sarah stood and joined Margaret who turned towards her.

'I'm sorry, Sarah.'

'Don't apologise,' Sarah said, somewhat calmer. 'Life must have been horrible. Here's me worrying and wailing but I can't imagine what you must have gone through.'

'I can see why Steve loved you so much. I wish we could have been closer, you and I.' Margaret turned back to the window and continued. 'Our father died, thank the Lord, when Steve was ten. I'll not say God rest his soul. He was just evil. Peace took over after he'd gone, though Steve was the only one who never quite enjoyed it… being wracked with guilt.'

'Guilt?' asked Sarah. 'Why guilt?'

Margaret peered at Sarah and sighed once more.

'Sarah you need to prepare yourself. This was what Steve wanted me to tell you, what he was referring to in his note. But it will be hard for you to hear. He wanted me to tell you everything. When Steve was ten, I was seventeen with our two other sisters thirteen and coming sixteen. Steve wasn't a child. With sisters all around him he understood what life was about and one day he'd noticed his father was watching Tracy, our youngest sister, catching her in her bedroom or peeking into the bathroom. Steve came and told me about it. We shared everything, which was our way of keeping from going crazy. The eldest and the youngest. When he told me, neither of us could figure out what to do, but one day, a few days before our father died, Steve said he'd got an idea. He seemed a little… different… troubled, but he didn't tell me what his plan was until the morning after our father's birthday, the morning after he died.'

Margaret paused long enough to swallow hard.

'Sarah, I've not told anyone about this before but Steve killed our father.'

Sarah's eyes widened once more in disbelief and horror.

'What? But how… how can that be? He was only ten?'

'It might sound horrible, but I believe anyone can kill, Sarah, even the smallest of us, given the right motivation and circumstance. You see, Steve knew his dad would get pissed on his birthday. Huh. Most nights he was, but he would go on a real bender because it was his fortieth. So Steve took one of the garden spades, a small one, and left the house late. He waited for his dad around the back lane from the pub. It was a shortcut through some trees between the main road and the estate where we lived. When his dad appeared, it was late, after midnight. Our father could just about stand upright but Steve told me his dad saw him with the spade, may have guessed what Steve planned and insulted him again with his preferred names.'

You fat little faggot. You ain't got the guts!

Sarah recalled the words and their intensity. Sick to her stomach, she covered her mouth to prevent the gasp threatening to escape.

'That was the final straw for Steve. He hated his father. Hated what he did to our mother, and the thought he might do something worse to either one of his sisters was intolerable, so he hit his dad with the spade. Hit him right on the forehead. He told me afterwards what he did next. Somehow, he became calm, perhaps he shut down, y'know traumatised or something. But he dragged his dad onto a kerb so it looked as if he fell over and banged his head. Our father was known to the police, and they never questioned accidental death at all. Whether Steve killed him outright or not we'll never be sure, but the verdict was hypothermia so either way the result was what Steve wanted. Well life brightened up afterwards. None of us cared what happened because everyone felt safer. But Steve never got to grips with it… torn between the right thing to do for the sake of us all and the intense guilt he'd gone ahead with it. Events scarred his life, Sarah, from the beginning. When he was old enough, he moved away hoping to make a new life and put the episode in its place, but he never managed to. It was only when he met you he changed, moved on, and his life seemed to take on more meaning.'

Sarah's heart ached with sadness and an overwhelming sense of loss.

'I can't believe it. It doesn't seem possible. A boy so young. But how did you bottle it up? How could you keep quiet?'

'I used to ask myself that too, and for a long time I argued back and forth between telling mom and keeping quiet. But keeping quiet seemed the best idea. Sometimes it's easier to do nothing. You must remember, Sarah, our dad was violent, drunk or sober, though those latter occasions were few. No one missed him, not even those he drank with. The police didn't care. His father didn't care. His mom had died years before. To all intents it was clear cut and when it came down to it I asked myself what use was it to anyone to tell the truth. It would only destroy our family. We all became closer afterwards so life was better. But Steve continued to struggle. He managed through his teenage years keeping himself to himself. But he tried to end it all just before his twentieth birthday. Took a mix of tablets washed down with whisky, but I found him in time because I was keeping a close eye on him. I understood how difficult his life was.

'When he moved away from home he seemed to do well, though I worried about him. He got a job in sales which kept him busy. He had a flair for it. And then he met you and fell in love.'

Sarah collapsed back onto the bed and hung her head. How awful to have someone in love with you, a love you can't return. *Oh Steve. I'm so sorry.*

As if reading her mind Margaret settled on the bed once more.

'Sarah, don't blame yourself for how Steve was or how he felt. Sounds a bit poetic, but he was as a moth to flame. He got burnt but found it hard staying away. There is one last thing, though, one last thing to tell.'

With haunted eyes Sarah lifted her gaze to Margaret.

'More? Oh God, Margaret.'

'I'm sure you guessed it but Steve was no more gay than you or I. He wrote often about the two of you. He told me how you started out. How he asked you to move in and how he proposed to you. Everything seemed to be going well, and I was so glad he'd at last found peace. But one day another letter arrived, and it was obvious something had changed. It was after New Year. I forget which one. His letter was… different. There was little joy in his words. You see, he wrote saying it was obvious you missed John. He'd seen it in your face over Christmas and New Year and realised your heart lay elsewhere, and he didn't have a chance. Took a while to accept it, but he couldn't bear the idea of you being unhappy. That was why he let you believe he was gay. He'd heard the rumours, unfounded as they were, and played on it. He figured it was the easiest way for him to let you go without too much hurt for you.'

Tears started in Sarah's eyes again and spilled over, carrying her pain and anguish.

'Oh, Steve,' she cried and covered her face with her hands. Her shoulders hitched as the intensity of her grief and loss took hold. Margaret reached over and pulled Sarah towards her.

'It's ok,' Margaret said. 'It's ok. He was a gentle soul throughout his life, always gentle, except for one extreme act of violence, but one of utter selflessness to save the lives of others. He'll be at peace now… at last. Let's remember his smile.'

Through her tears Sarah whispered as much to herself as to Margaret.

'Yes,' she said, 'Let's remember his smile.'

John wandered upstairs to find them a while later. He'd been chatting to a few friends of Steve, leaving Sarah and Margaret alone. There weren't many people to reminisce, but those who remembered him in his early years came to pay their respects. When people ran out of stories and condolences, they drifted away one by one, leaving John and immediate family to tidy the kitchen.

John could hear Sarah and Margaret laughing and tapped on the bedroom door.

'Come in, sweetheart,' Sarah called and Margaret smiled at her.

'I can see you two *are* close, unless you can see through doors.'

'It's a gift she has,' John said as he entered. 'Still surprises me sometimes. What were you two laughing at?'

'Old photos,' Sarah said. 'Margaret's been sharing family memories with me.' She turned to Margaret. 'It's nice you have these to look back at. Some happy memories to prove it wasn't all bad.'

'No it wasn't all bad. We had a few holidays on the cheap. What more do you need than a splash in the sea and fish and chips. That doesn't cost much at all. But now I've an idea your husband is here to take you home.'

'Only when you're ready,' John replied. 'There's no rush.'

'Well I suppose we ought to be going. We need to pick up Claire anyway. And it'll be dark by the time we get back.'

Margaret stood and led the way back downstairs.

A thought struck Sarah.

'Margaret. What are you going to do about your mom? Will you say anything to her?'

'I can't,' came the reply. 'She's too old and too frail. I feel terrible I've robbed her of saying farewell and I'll have to live with that. But the truth would destroy her. Isn't it better she believes her son alive and working away somewhere than dying alone in a cold house? She's not got much time left. Her chest is always giving her trouble now. One more bad infection might be her last and then we'll have another funeral.'

Margaret waited in the hallway while John and Sarah said their goodbyes to those left. When they emerged and tugged on their coats, she spoke again.

'Sarah, I'd like us to keep in touch. But you know how it is. People make promises at these occasions with the best of intentions. We both have separate lives, but we have each other's addresses and phone numbers so just drop me a note to say how your new addition is when it arrives, and send me a Christmas card.'

Sarah smiled at Margaret and wrapped her arms around her in one last embrace.

'I'll do more than that I promise. Christmas *and* birthdays!' and they both laughed.

'But,' Sarah said. 'I'd like to keep in touch too. I'll send you some pictures of the little one but I'll call you… soon.'

'That would be nice. Oh, and I have one last thing. A small gift.'

Margaret held up a picture frame and handed it over. Framed in the picture was a photograph of Steve and Sarah. They had straws in their mouths and were sucking with eagerness from the same glass. With a wistful smile Sarah recalled the event. It was the night of her parent's wedding anniversary, their twenty-sixth and the night Steve proposed to her. They'd been drinking cocktails and shared a large mojito. Smiles lit up their faces and Sarah remembered the evening with fondness.

'It was one of the happiest nights for Steve, and I thought you'd like this photo to help you remember the way he was.'

'This is so precious. Are you sure?' Sarah asked, but as she gazed at Margaret, she perceived a strong violet glow around her head, the colour of serenity, and was comforted her new friend appeared to have found tranquillity in knowing her young brother was himself at peace.

'Yes... I'm sure,' Margaret smiled, and they hugged once more.

Thirty-one

'Rachel. I wish it was last November,' Sarah hissed, 'and none of this had ever happened.'

'Calm down. Calm down. I feel the same for different reasons, but you can't turn the clock back.'

It was eight o'clock in the evening and Sarah stood in Rachel's apartment peering out of the living room window across the city landscape with its orange streetlights and flash of car lamps. She'd called Rachel earlier and agreed to visit for a late tea, leaving John and Claire at home.

'It doesn't seem possible, about Steve I mean?' Rachel said after hearing the news from Sarah.

'It's all true and on some level I guessed something was up. I sensed it the night of my homecoming... when I hugged him.'

Sarah turned to Rachel with an air of tortured despondency.

'How can that happen, Rachel, why does it happen... that I can sense things? I even guessed Steve was dead. Why me? It's not a gift. What kind of gift brings such pain and anguish.'

'What's happened to you?' Rachel asked, a frown deepening the lines on her forehead. 'You were so enthusiastic about your new gift.'

'Yes, before horrible things happened.'

'It can't all be horrible. And I hate to say this but what can you do about it?'

Sarah sighed and leaving the window sat next to Rachel. Despite her words and her desire to reject the gift, she probed Rachel with her inner senses, sensing her friend's mood and noting again an inner struggle. Then she realised she'd done so without conscious effort. *Oh God… I'm doing it without thinking.* Sarah turned away and tried to focus on something else… anything to break her subconscious probing.

'What can I do about it?' said Sarah, repeating the question. 'Nothing I guess. Try to find my way forward… make sense of it… control it.'

'That's what's getting to you more than anything isn't it. You're not yet in control of it. I know you… I understand how you like to manage everything and keep it in order. It's easy for me to say but you have to find a way. It's like everything else we learn, from walking to windsurfing or playing the violin. Practice… familiarity.'

'Huh… you've turned the tables,' answered Sarah. 'You being big sister for a change?'

Sarah leaned back on the sofa and closed her eyes. They sat in silence for a few minutes while only the faint and rhythmic ticking of a clock disturbed the stillness. Sarah opened her eyes and sat upright.

'Rachel, there's something I've been keeping from John… since Christmas.'

'Oh God, Sarah. What now?'

Still with a haunted expression, Sarah replied in a whisper, as if ashamed of her secret.

'It's about Hamish, his granddad. Hamish told me…' Sarah paused a moment to draw in a controlling breath. 'He told me he would leave us soon… that he'd not long to live. He said he would let me decide to tell John or not tell him.'

'And you've not told him?' Sarah's shake of the head was

the only answer Rachel needed. 'But Sarah, don't you think he has the right to know? Why haven't you said something?'

'Rachel, so much happened afterwards, so much happiness at Christmas and meeting Beryl and everything else and I kept putting it to one side. But how could I spoil John's last Christmas with Hamish after everything he's been through? How could I worry him even more?'

'But isn't Hamish his last living relative?'

'Almost. There may be an aunt somewhere.'

Sarah stood again and shuffled back to the window. Rain smeared the glass, creating distorted reflections of the streetlights.

'The problem is,' Sarah continued. 'As time went on and I left it and left it, it became harder to say anything. But I figured if I told John, the knowing would taint their relationship. They'd be circling around each other trying to make normal conversation, trying not to talk about the end and I'm certain Hamish wouldn't want that. He wouldn't want any fuss. I'm not sure why he told me but perhaps it was to prepare me to help John when the end came. I do hope we are there with him. Oh God, Rachel. Am I right or wrong.'

'Sarah... you can only decide what seems right at the time. I understand why you've made this decision and who knows, I might have done the same. You can never know until you're faced with the same dilemma.

'Will you tell John at some point... before or afterwards... that Hamish told you?'

'Not thought that far ahead yet.' Sarah sighed again and changed the subject. 'Sorry. Here's me prattling on about my problems. What about you? How's your love life going?'

'Me?' Sarah sensed a rising barrier and Rachel's aura dimmed, not that it extended very far. 'If you're asking if I shagged anyone new the answers no. I'm off men at the moment. I need a break from complications.'

'Well I wouldn't be so crude but complications? Why complications? I thought the whole point was you didn't want complications, or are you referring to Peter?'

'No,' replied Rachel. 'I'm referring to men in general. Need a break that's all.'

'What, from sex? You're not going off it are you? C'mon, Rachel. What's going on?'

The change in Rachel's manner was sudden, and she became quite indignant.

'Y'know it's not always about sex. Some of these men I've quite liked. I do have some morals. I wouldn't just shag anyone for fuck's sake.'

Rachel sat up and gathered the mugs and plates together. Sarah was shocked at Rachel's anger, but guilty at having upset her.

'Sorry, Rachel. I'm being unfair. I guess I'm wound up. Didn't mean to take it out on you.'

Rachel stood up and dropped a mug, spilling the last dregs of coffee onto the carpet.

'Fuck it,' Rachel muttered under her breath, but lifted her gaze and spoke directly to Sarah. 'Look. Lots of people think I'm an easy lay. A tart. I don't need you to join them. I've simply not found the right man. They're either married and users, or boys and users. I doubt if the right man even fucking exists!'

'Rachel, hang on,' Sarah stepped away from the window. 'Where did that come from? I don't believe you're a tart at all. You're my closest friend. My only real friend in fact. If I could, I'd make you my sister… today… now. I'm sorry I've been jabbering on about my troubles but Rachel, something's bothering you so please tell me.'

Rachel retrieved the fallen mug and gazed at her friend with softening eyes as if her outburst had drained her strength. She continued in a plaintive voice.

'Nothing's up. Guess your troubles are putting me on edge too. I believe you're drifting away from me, Sarah… a day at a time, moving away and I'm… well I'm scared. I wish it was before Christmas too, and you were still at work… before any of this happened. But it isn't. Things change.

Things happen. We can't go back. We must go on. Both of us.'

Sarah reached for Rachel and they hugged each other in an embrace lasting many moments. Sarah thought Rachel's lingering embrace held an air of desperation, but realised she didn't want to let go either. After a while she asked a question.

'I meant to ask, how did you get on babysitting Sophie? Remember when Peter had to be away.'

Rachel unwound herself and wandered through to the kitchen, returning with a handful of paper towels for the spilt coffee.

'When was that?' she pondered. 'Over a month ago? Yes it was fun. She's a lovely girl but I haven't seen them since. Peter wants to take me out to say thanks but I've not been.'

'How come?' and Sarah sat once more. She was trying for casual because she didn't want to probe too deep. Rachel was being guarded and pushing her too hard was a bad idea. Sarah realised pushing Steve had been a mistake. Not a mistake big enough to make his last actions the result of Sarah's questioning, but still a mistake. She needed to tread with care and let Rachel's story unfold in its own time.

'He's nice, though it's complicated. But c'mon, have you and John chosen names for the new baby yet, male or female?'

'Not yet,' was Sarah's reply. 'Things have been hectic and we've not had time to…' Sarah fell quiet, stopping in mid-sentence.

'Time?' asked Rachel as she stood up with a pile of damp paper in her hands. Sarah did not answer. 'Sarah? Sarah… what is it? You've gone very pale.'

Sarah shifted her gaze over to Rachel but her focus was elsewhere and she spoke as if to herself.

'I need to get back home. I'm worried about John.'

'Worried about John? Why? Why are you worried? You can call him, y'know.'

'Something's wrong…'

They both fell silent and stared at each other. Rachel waited for Sarah to speak again, but it was obvious her attention was elsewhere... not in the room. The silence spooked Rachel and an involuntary shiver ran along her spine. But in the same moment Rachel opened her mouth to say something else, the strident ring tone of a mobile phone cut through the air, shrill and piercing, making them both jump. Sarah lunged for her handbag and snatched out her phone.

'John!' she shouted. A shocked voice answered.

'Wow! Yes. That's me. God, you're loud. You all right?' asked John.

'Sorry. Yes. What is it?' Sarah asked.

'What is it? Do I need a reason to call you?'

Sarah took a breath to calm her voice and collapsed onto the sofa.

'Sorry. It was quiet here, and the phone made us jump. I was about to leave. Is everything ok?'

'Yes,' replied John. 'All is well. Claire's just gone to bed but I've had a call from work and they want me to change my shift tomorrow. They want me to do a late instead, so we can eat breakfast together. I'll leave at lunchtime. We haven't made plans have we?'

'No, sweetie. No plans... except...' Sarah smiled at Rachel, though the smile didn't reach her eyes. 'Except we could discuss baby names in the morning.'

'Huh, you and Rachel been talking by any chance?'

'Might have,' Sarah replied but added, 'John, you will be careful tomorrow won't you?'

'Careful?' John sounded puzzled. 'Strange question but I'm always careful. You know me.'

'Yes. I *do* know you. Listen, I'll be home soon. I'll see you in about half an hour.'

'Ok, princess. Drive safe,' and John cleared the call.

Rachel sat next to Sarah. 'You don't look well. Do you want me to drive you back?'

'No... no its ok,' replied Sarah. 'Just suddenly sensed

something, something strange. I feel edgy and that worries me. Oh God, Rachel. This damn gift is taking over my life. Is this the way it'll be from now on… getting random feelings and visions? I wish I didn't have it. It's ruining my life.'

'I wish I could help but…' Rachel grabbed Sarah's hand.

Ten minutes later, they kissed each other a farewell and a slightly more relaxed Sarah headed home. She was keen to see her husband, eager to hold onto him, needing to tell him again to take care. The need was impossible to resist.

Thirty-two

'I'm sure you won't mind me gloating about the Blues kicking the shit out of Wolves last night?' Big Dave was an avid football fan, supporting Birmingham city, his local team.

'Dave?' said John. 'Check my face. Do I look like someone who gives a shit?'

'Huh! No I guess not. That's the problem with you. I spend so much time with you and I can't even take the piss out of your local team.'

'Well you understand Wolverhampton isn't my team. If you want to be accurate about it you'd have to go a lot further north. Ayr town would be who I'd support if I was interested and they wouldn't figure in your league anyway.'

'Ha! An opportunity arises. Scottish football. Not in the big game are they? Not real contenders on the world stage?'

Dave's face lit up with a chance to rib John but John wasn't interested.

The two friends were both in uniform strolling along the streets through one of Birmingham city's local wards. Asian, European and Caribbean communities populated much of the inner city, each with their own unique blend of culture. In the past, John had enjoyed getting back to street level as a policeman, since it meant being in touch with the people he served. Over the years, he'd built something of a reputation, getting to know many of the shop owners and residents. A mutual respect existed which was as important to him as it was to the people he met. There was an underlying inner city problem, involving gang culture, drugs and elements of organised crime, but John tried to keep an open and fair mind. He understood that inner city issues knew no boundaries of race, culture or age. It meant everyone was at risk and anyone could be a victim.

Of late however John had become restless. Ever since Sarah's assault he'd developed a growing belief he was fighting a losing battle and his efforts could never go far enough. Beforehand, he appreciated the little he could achieve was still important… could change lives, but now he was feeling unfulfilled, that he could do more elsewhere. Perhaps even change his career. And Sarah's behaviour last night troubled him. When she'd returned home from visiting Rachel, she ran through the house to find him, giving him an embrace he could only describe as desperate. It was as if she'd not seen him for weeks and there was insistence in her embrace, an urgency. He asked her what was wrong.

'I don't want you to go to work tomorrow!' she'd blurted out. 'Not tomorrow. Please John. Tell them you can't do it. Tell them you won't!'

John frowned in puzzlement.

'Well I've already said yes, but I can't refuse, sweetie. What's happened?'

But she became evasive, vague and even irrational.

'Nothing's happened. I… I want you to stay with me. John… I'm scared.'

'Scared of what?'

'I don't know.'

'Much as I hate to say it but I've an idea you're being a bit hormonal, and you know I wouldn't use that as an excuse for fear of physical abuse. But you're not making any sense.

I'm just shifting my day ahead to cover an absence. It'll be fine. I'm not doing anything out of the ordinary. Just out on the streets with Dave.'

Sarah realised her behaviour appeared ridiculous… but she couldn't make any rational argument or produce a tangible reason for John to stay at home, only a worrying notion she'd had, and one that would not go away. It disturbed her on a spiritual level, but she had to concede… there was no logical argument she could use.

'Not biting today?' Dave prompted.

Dave was John's closest friend and on the face of it had everything he wanted in life. He was a good copper. Motivated, strong-willed and fair, and, like John, well respected. They made a good team and complemented each other, though on a personal level David could be superficial. Having a deep or sincere conversation with him was like trying to explain the theory of relativity to a three year old. Pointless. Dave liked the 'good' things in life. He was a 'gadget' man. Always with the latest phone or television, but Dave's calming influence was his fiancé Kelly.

John had known Kelly since childhood, attending the same school in Ayr. She and John had not seen each other for years until John and Sarah visited Scotland in the early days of their relationship. They bumped into each other one day in Ayr town centre and had become close friends. After John and Sarah married, Kelly was visiting in the midlands and stayed at John and Sarah's. It was during this stay she and Dave met. Kelly moved in with Dave not long afterwards and they'd been together for five years.

On the face of it Kelly was perfect for Dave. She was the classic blonde bombshell with long hair, long legs and striking good looks, and hence fitted Dave's vision of the perfect woman. But she was no dumb blonde. She held a degree in physical science and nutrition and had no problem in getting work with a sports fitness centre treating injuries and advising on healthy diets. The two couples met up often and when Claire came along John and Sarah asked Dave and

Kelly to be godparents, to which they had agreed.

'So how is the missus?' Dave asked, changing subjects. 'I haven't seen her since just after new year.'

John didn't answer for a few minutes, just strolled along deep in thought until Dave continued:

'I put it to you that since you haven't answered my question, all is not well in the Macintyre household and you are reluctant to say so because you are hiding the truth.'

'Guilty as charged, m'lud.'

'Case for the prosecution rests.'

'Guilty... except,' John continued, 'I haven't presented the case for the defence yet.'

'C'mon then. Out with it. How is Sarah... the truth... don't perjure yourself.'

'Well, all *is* well in the Macintyre household. Sarah is fine.'

'Yeah but you know what FINE stands for don't you, Fucked up, Insecure, Neurotic and Emotional.'

They both finished the sentence with a laugh.

'Yes quite,' John agreed. 'But to be honest everything is ok, though Sarah isn't quite the same. Things have changed.'

'How'd you mean?'

'Well you remember when you and Kelly came to dinner after New Year?'

'Yeah, after you came home from Scotland. I remember the damn hangover.'

'Sarah showed Kelly the letter from her great grandmother. Did you see it?'

'No, but Kelly told me about it afterwards. She was quite, how'd she put it?... not excited... intrigued, I think.'

'Well it was intriguing, but to cut a long story short, whatever Sarah's great grandmother said to her or did to her has changed her in some fundamental ways.'

'Did to her? Like what?'

John was cautious, not wanting to reveal too much to his friend, certain that talk of sightings or sensing would elicit disbelief or even disdain. But he needed to tell Dave something.

'I don't know. Something's changed. I told you about Steve, how we found him? Well you should have seen Sarah when we went to his house. She was like someone possessed... hammering at the door. She even swore at me and you know my wife rarely swears.'

'Yeah but after what he did to her it would be a natural reaction, y'know, wanting to get inside the house to make sure he'd not done anything stupid.'

'Possibly, but it's not like she made me drive there in a rush. She even waited all day for me to come home. No, Dave. It was out of the blue, so sudden, like she sensed something was wrong.'

'Hang on... sensed something. Like sixth sense?'

'Might be... sounds strange I know but...'

'But what. You're not going all hippie on me are you? You been smoking weed or something?'

'Course not, you prat. Tell me this... what did Kelly tell you about the letter from Sarah's great grandmother?'

'That it contained a rhyme... and Claire cracked it and it led you to an old woman who turned out to be a long lost relation.'

'That's about it... but she told you nothing else?'

'No. These discoveries *do* happen I suppose, but more often it's someone separated from their parents at birth, trying to locate the rest of their family or their parents through social services, not through some cryptic rhyme. Is there something else to tell?'

'This is gonna sound crazy but bear with me.'

John paused again. The afternoon was running away with them and the heavy cloud that threatened rain lived up to its promise. A thin drizzle drifted downwards, dampening everything around them and dripping off their helmets. The road glistened with reflected shop front lighting and the traffic sounds became muted. John continued.

'When the letter arrived, Sarah asked me to pick it up. She hadn't even opened it. This is the weird part. When I reached for it, I swear the envelope moved... did the same for Sarah too.'

'Moved? How'd you mean moved?'

'Just that. It moved. The tiniest amount as my hand got closer. I thought I'd imagined it but I tried it again and sure enough it moved again. The only thing I can liken it to is holding a magnet and moving it towards a metal object. The metal object moves.'

'Must be a sensible explanation.'

'Dave, believe me, we ran through every possibility we could dream of and came up blank. The rest as they say is history. We followed Claire's lead and found Beryl and since then Sarah has changed. In fact so has Claire.'

Dave reached up, wiped rain from the brim of his helmet and flicked the water away.

'Ok,' he said. 'So in what way has she changed? She's physically ok isn't she?'

'Yes one hundred per cent. But she's changed her beliefs, her motivations, even how she rationalises.'

'Beliefs? What... like a born-again Christian. Is she going to knock on doors and preach the word of God?'

John laughed. 'No chance. She's not that way inclined. Sarah's always been very logical, very ordered and analytical... works things out and then takes a practical approach. Whatever Beryl said left these things in place but added to them, gave her some new stuff to consider. She's become interested in, driven to distraction almost, by healing therapies, faith, alternate medicine.'

'What you mean these expensive therapies we hear about.'

'Huh, trust you to bring up the money side of it but yes, except that she *does* feel or sense things, hidden things. She picks up when someone is ill or unhappy or... well anything.'

'What, like she sensed that Steve had killed himself?'

'Well in a way. More like she sensed something wrong rather than knowing he was dead.'

'Sorry... not convinced. Most of this therapy stuff's a rip off isn't it and there's never any proven evidence any of it works.'

'Well that's where you're wrong.'

'C'mon, John. You don't believe in faith healing or laying on of hands, all that kind of stuff do you?'

'Doesn't Kelly's therapy centre have healers? You've seen the brochures... reiki, reflexology, crystals, acupuncture?'

'Yes they do...'

'And the classes are busy and appointments fully booked?'

'Well yes they are, but...'

'But what. There's no proof any of it works?'

'No there isn't.'

'Dave, let me ask you a question. You're Catholic?'

'Yes... well raised by Catholic parents though I'm beyond salvation.'

'Well there is no evidence God exists is there, no empirical evidence. Yet the majority of the world's population believe in one form of God or another without ever having a hope of seeing the person. In simple terms, they have faith. And if you examine the theory and evidence, there's more likelihood crystal therapy works, for example, than God existing. I mean, as an atheist, if I argued believers in God are deluded, then by right I should use the same argument for believers in reiki or crystal therapy, because there is no measured scientific evidence. I prefer though to believe in God as a collective idea or ideal than as a single entity we worship. You know, a belief in goodness and rightness... treating our fellow humans with courtesy or fairness and so on. If the world's population adopted that approach there may be more peace. But anyway, if people put their faith in the unprovable idea God exists and in any form, surely they can also put their faith in crystal therapy as a healing treatment and believe it works.'

'Ok, makes sense, but crystal therapy? What have you

been reading?'

'Well it's amazing what you find out on the Internet when you have a quiet moment. And I've been trying to understand what's happened to Sarah. But my jury's out. All I'm doing is playing devil's advocate because I'm not convinced about it either. It's just that Sarah is and I'm being sucked into it.'

'Ok, so what's the argument for crystal therapy? Aren't they only different coloured pebbles?'

'Pebbles? You're such a cynical bastard,' John said with exasperation. 'Maybe, but the treatment involves placing them close to your skin where they have an effect.'

Dave rolled his eyes and shook his head. 'Christ… are we having this conversation? I only asked how the missus was.'

John laughed, 'So you've only yourself to blame. Ok. The argument. I suggest you can examine it in three ways. In fact, you could apply these arguments to lots of different therapies. First, you can accept it's all true and placing a crystal on your body will have its effect and heal you or help you. You don't *need* to know how or why, you accept it… you have faith in it. Second, you can accept the placebo effect… some people convince themselves they'll get better, and they experience the benefits when there are none. This happens all the time in standard medicine or clinical trials. A group of people will get a real pill, others will get a sugar pill or placebo. There's always a percentage of people who were given the placebo who show an improvement, and they compare this to the percentage who improve after having the *real* medicine to work out its efficacy.'

'Yes I know all about this. And the third?'

'Well this gets technical. Crystals produce minute electrical currents. The atoms within them, like all objects, are moving around, vibrating at different rates. You remember this from school?'

'Yes, I remember my physics. Atoms consist of protons and neutrons that circle the core. They are always on the move, expanding or shrinking the space between each atom depending on heat, bit like water turning to steam if you heat it enough.'

'Exactly, and crystals are vibrating at such a high rate they can produce electrical currents. For example, that radio you have on your belt has a crystal in it to keep it in tune. Your watch has one in it to keep its time spot on. Your computer and games machine has one. Loads of electrical stuff these days have crystals in them to keep them running. Now, how does your body work?'

'I see where you're going. Ok. My body works on electrical impulses. Tiny electrical charges within the brain pass along nerve fibres to muscles causing them to contract or release producing a physical movement.'

'Well done. You paid attention at school.'

'Right, so what you're telling me is that a small electrical field caused by vibrating atoms from a pebble can interfere or affect the tiny electrical currents in my body. I'm having difficulty here because I could accept the electricity bit, but how is it supposed to cure an illness?'

'I don't know, but there's plenty of evidence about the negative effects of overhead power cables on people who live under them. And it's only an idea and I may be way off the mark. Just an indication these things may actually work so they're not as farfetched as you may imagine, especially when you use the *believing in God* idea as another example of something that has no proof and works on faith.'

They both fell quiet for a moment as they strolled along until a voice spoke to them from behind a pavement fruit stall.

'Sergeant Macintyre. How are you today, sir?' Mr Joji was always very polite. 'Will you take a few bananas today? Or some grapes?'

'Hello, Mr Joji. I'm well thank you. Bananas are perfect. Four please. How's business?' John reached into his pocket.

'Business is very good but no, no. Please. A gift for you and your beautiful wife!' said Mr Joji and handed John the bananas and a bunch of grapes.

'As always, Mr Joji, I couldn't. Here let me pay you,' and John handed over some money.

'Ah. Sergeant, as always you are too honest. Here, let me get you the change.'

Mister Joji disappeared into the shop for a moment and then coming back outside handed John a few coins. John pocketed the money knowing full well he'd have the same value in coins he'd offered.

'Rain's begun?' said John.

'Yes,' said Mr Joji. 'But we are used to it are we not?'

'We are indeed. Well, thank you and you have a fruitful day,' and John and Dave carried on their way.

Dave spoke, 'How long have you been playing that game?'

'Forever, I reckon,' replied John.

'Ok. So where's all this leading… this healing stuff?'

'Well I'm not sure. Whatever Sarah decides, I'm sure she'll let me know straight away. Sod's law as soon as she meets the old woman, she pops her clogs. Sarah had mixed feelings about it.'

'How'd you mean?'

'Well she never had time to get to know her so I think she feels as if she missed out… cheated, I suppose. On the other hand she's not missed what she never had. Shame she didn't have more time with her if only to answer some of her questions.'

'Questions about what?'

John said nothing concerning Sarah's visions. Dave's feet were planted firmly on the ground, in the world he could see. He had no sense of the extra ordinary, or the spiritual, or at least none he'd ever admitted to John.

'About the family history and all that stuff. Anyway, her consultant gave her a clean bill of health, but she's got a lot on her plate. She's not going back to her old job but she doesn't want to give up work altogether. Wants to do something. She's not sure what yet.'

John opened and closed his mouth as if unsure of what to say next but then reached a decision.

'Y'know, I'm not sure if *I* want to do this work anymore either.'

'What?' said Dave with surprise. 'Where's that come from? I thought they'd drag you out of the station in thirty years' time kicking and screaming, or more likely wheeled out in a chair drooling and farting.'

John smiled without humour. 'Thanks for the image. You paint a wonderful picture. To be serious, I'm tired of the violence, the noise of the city. Facing innocent victims. Remember that young woman and her son a month ago? The hit and run? Thank God they survived, but we never found who the driver was. Some bastard who was drunk or stoned or on his phone and didn't give a shit. Then there was the young family getting verbal abuse from the woman's ex until it escalated. He almost killed the husband. And we're battling a legal system that sometimes seems as if it's working against the victim while we know who the guilty are. And there's the bastard who attacked Sarah? I've had enough crap, Dave, I'm fucking fed up of getting home at night feeling like I've not made a goddamn fucking difference!'

'Whoa. Hang on. Not heard you talk like this before. How long has this been going on?'

'How long? Since the mugging.'

'So, it's a reaction. Understandable but you'll get through it. We all feel like it sometimes, even me. If I have a bad day I feel like kicking the shit out of some young bastard who knows what he can get away with, but it's all part of the game. You can't let it get to you. Just have to do what we can.'

'Yes,' replied John, 'except doing what we can isn't enough. You're right, it is a reaction to Sarah's attack. What else? But it doesn't mean I'm not serious, doesn't mean I have to stay in this line of work, doesn't mean the reaction isn't right. It takes something like this to make you realise you can do something different. We don't have to do the same thing forever. Perhaps I'm done with this line of work, need something different, quieter perhaps.'

'Like what. What's on your mind?'

'Well what is it a person needs to survive... y'know, the basic essentials? It's got to be food, warmth and shelter. Nothing more.'

'And I thought it was a few beers, a curry and a good shag!'

John burst out laughing and felt more relaxed. 'Y'know, I've always enjoyed having a deep and meaningful conversation with you, you ass wipe! But listen. My dad was a teacher all his life. Killed him in the end, and a bad diet I suppose. My grandfather however worked on the land, out in the fresh air and he's reached a grand old age. He never owned a farm, but he worked on them. He worked with livestock, agriculture, gardens, woodland. Even after he retired, he got an allotment and grew his own stuff. Always figured the land was in his blood, and of late I've been wondering if I'm the same.'

Dave laughed, 'What... you as a farmer? Can't picture it somehow.'

'Well that's because the closest you get to the land is when your whacking a ball around a fairway or screaming your bloody car around the lanes.'

'And? Your point is?'

'My point is if you lift your eyes and look beyond the end of your nose there's a big world out there, a world of opportunity. All you need is the courage to make a change and the faith to trust in yourself.'

A few spots of heavier rain spattered on their helmets but it did nothing to dampen the spirits of the people around them. Shopping continued while businesses offered a service.

Dave raised his eyebrows and regarded his friend. 'You getting all religious on me again... faith and trust? But could you see yourself leaving this behind after over ten years? It's a big change, leaving the security behind… for what it's worth?'

'Faith and trust,' replied John.

They fell into a comfortable silence once more until Dave gave John a playful nudge in the ribs.

'You're not the only one planning big changes you know, and I have beliefs too.'

'Oh yeah. What're you planning? A new phone again? And what beliefs are these?'

'No… not yet. But I believe in the miracle of life, and it may come as a surprise to you but Kelly is pregnant. Confirmed. Big Dave is gonna be a daddy!'

A huge smile wreathed John face, and he turned to his friend, grabbed his hand and shook it with a firm and friendly grip.

'Fair play to you mate! Well done and congratulations. Kelly must be really made up. We having a pint after work?'

'Any excuse you piss artist!' said Dave shaking his head. 'But not tonight. Got to be at home. It's an anniversary for us so we're off out for a meal. Could do the weekend though if you want to come over. Bring my goddaughter with you.'

'Ok. I'll ask Sarah but I'm sure it'll be fine. It's about time, y'know. You're not getting any younger and having kids when you're over forty will kill you when they're teenagers. When's it due?'

'In July, round about Sarah's birthday. We—'

A sudden anguished scream cut into their conversation. As they spun around to locate the source, a voice from back along the way they had walked yelled 'STOP HIM!'

Thirty-three

Sarah sat in the living room gazing into the garden. She'd spent the afternoon adrift with no notion of what to do with herself. Today she felt listless and idle... expectant, as if waiting for something to happen to give her direction.

A few birds squabbled over the seeds she'd put out earlier and as she watched them peck and lunge at each other, a few light raindrops dotted the glass of the patio doors. Outside the daylight faded as the clouds darkened.

As she sat, she wondered how to tell Rachel she had resigned from her job. Too much had changed, too many things happened for her to want to return. In a few short weeks she'd been mugged, found and lost a relative she never knew existed and inherited land. What that amounted to she did not know yet, but she'd inherited more than material goods. There was the gift, a gift which awakened more as each day passed, though she was still unsure whether it would be a help or a hindrance. But the good news was she was pregnant again, which helped ease the pain of losing a relative. The end of one life and the beginning of another? A constant renewal. The whole cycle of life had become more meaningful to Sarah. It conveyed a very earthly meaning, one which lay in the heart of everything around her. Indeed it lay in all four elements, she mused, and surprised herself at the thought.

But the death of Steve hung over everything like a dark cloud.

She'd forgotten one of the golden rules Beryl told her about. Don't force her intentions onto others. If a person needs help, wait… and if a request is made, then offer to help. The horror of Steve's guilt and his final inability to come to terms with it created an unspeakable pain for Sarah. Margaret's explanation of Steve's life helped her understand, but she still carried her own guilt. She should have listened to Steve, got him to talk. Discovered what had been at the heart of his troubles and helped him. Instead, she'd let her emotions take control and trampled in with huge feet, stomping her way across Steve's pain, leading him to take his terrible last steps.

How will I ever be able to forgive myself?

For long minutes she gazed unseeing out of the window but memory of the irrational fear she'd expressed to both Rachel and John during the previous evening pulled her back into the room. She'd been on edge during the night and woke often, but kept her anxiety to herself throughout the morning until John kissed her goodbye. Then she'd almost broken down but had again hidden her worry for fear of scaring John.

Sarah sat still for a while longer making every effort to empty her head. But an urgent need to do something forced her up and out of her chair. Her breath came in shallow gasps and she no longer wanted to sit and think, she needed to occupy her mind.

'This is silly. C'mon Sarah, get a grip,' she muttered to herself. After taking a deep slow breath, she made her way into the kitchen.

She loaded up the dishwasher and filling the washing bowl with hot water, hand washed the more delicate objects including two wine glasses they'd used after Claire was in bed. Sarah had drunk a tonic in her own glass since abstinence was now necessary, while John drank a couple of glasses of wine before they'd called it a night.

With care she washed the crystal wineglasses she'd inherited from her parents, and placed them onto the drainer before reaching for a tea towel to dry them and put them away.

Halfway through drying the second glass, Sarah felt nauseous and stopped what she was doing. Lifting her head as if in response to a call, she gazed through the kitchen window. As she peered through the rain streaked glass, a dark hole appeared in front of her... an inky blackness which grew larger, pushing her view of the garden to the edge of sight. Within the darkness and at its very core, a tiny spot of light appeared, a pinpoint of brilliant white that began to revolve. The light grew closer, filling the black hole and in its midst she saw John. He was standing motionless and Sarah could see that the purple aura often surrounding his head and shoulders had shrunk, becoming weak and indistinct. John's mouth moved and inside her head she heard his voice.

'Oh, God no. Sarah... I love you!'

The glass Sarah was drying slipped unnoticed from her hands and fell to the floor where it shattered into tiny fragments. With wide-eyes and shallow breath, gripped with a sudden terror she feared would stop her heart, Sarah whispered back:

'John. Please stay with me. I love you too!'

In the same instant and from somewhere deep inside her subconscious mind, Sarah sensed Claire screaming from afar, from her school classroom a mile away.

'DADDY!'

A sudden blow to her chest sent Sarah reeling backwards and then silence fell. Within the hush, the only sound she could hear was her own heart beating.

Thirty-four

At the sound of the scream, John and Dave spun on their heels and saw Mr Joji, many yards back, stagger out onto the pavement. Even from a distance they could see blood running from a gash on his face.

A hooded figure hurtled towards John and Dave, a young man. In one hand he held a rucksack, and as he ran, he pushed something underneath his hoody. He appeared to catch sight of the two policemen and veered into the road and into the path of a car. Stumbling around the front as the driver hit the brakes, he sprinted away.

In scant moments both John and Dave assessed the situation and John broke into a run while Dave grabbed his radio and barked into it, relaying the message they were giving chase following an assault. Dave began to move and followed John, but John being the shorter and lighter of the two increased his lead and was soon almost a hundred yards ahead of his friend.

'John... wait for God's sake,' muttered Dave. *You don't know what this is.*

John shot across the road in pursuit, and increased his pace to close the distance between himself and his target. For several hundred yards the chase continued, past shops and side streets until John noticed the young man losing energy and the gap between them closed. Ahead, a wide alley loomed closer and the young man shot sideways into it. The alley ran between two rows of buildings and John skidded into it only seconds afterwards. He knew the young man had run into a dead end and so stopped short inside the mouth of the passage.

'C'mon, my friend,' John said, gasping for breath. 'There's nowhere to go. Let's stop and take a moment to think about this.'

The youth ran from side to side clutching his bag while searching for a way over the wooden fence that blocked his escape. Realising his search was futile, he stopped and spun around to look back at the entrance. John stood still and firm, blocking the exit. The youth's arms lay loose by his sides but balled fists gave away the tension he carried. John moved one step towards the youth and despite the hood could see the face of a young man, a face he recognised. In the same instant, the youth reached under his jacket and snatched out a small handgun from inside the waistband of his trousers.

John froze, keeping his distance. He spoke, barely above a whisper:

'Raoul? Is that you? It is isn't it?'

Raoul was silent... nervous energy making him sway from side to side as if trying to spot an escape route.

'Come on, son. What's up? You don't want this.'

Despite the danger, John spoke in calm and soothing tones, trying to defuse the tension, but the gun came up and John could see the unsteady shake in the young man's grip. John raised his hands, palms out in a placating gesture and moved a half step backwards.

'Raoul, my friend. Listen. You know me. Officer Macintyre? John? Remember when I brought you home to your mom that time? All the way from the hospital? I sat with you while they fixed you up. C'mon. Let's be careful, just lower the gun and we'll have a talk.'

Raoul was silent except for the sound of rapid breathing. John peered into Raoul's face. He could see straight into the young man's eyes. They were wide and staring with huge dilated pupils. Despite John's words of encouragement, no sense of recognition lay on Raoul's face, only the mad stare of someone high on drugs.

The gun continued to shake in an unsteady hand.

Behind John, back in the busy street, everything appeared to have quietened as if a sense of expectation hushed every sound. Within the stillness John heard his own slow breath being drawn in and forced out. His heart pounded a heavy rhythm in his chest as, with foreboding, he saw the barrel of the gun move upwards until it was pointing at his head. John stared straight into the end of it, and saw an enormous black hole into which he pictured himself falling forever. But within the cavernous opening, a tiny pinprick of brilliant and pure light appeared in its very midst, a dazzling white spot that revolved on its axis.

As John stared ahead towards his destiny, the spinning light became brighter and closer and within its centre he saw Sarah standing in her kitchen. Saw her drying the two crystal wine glasses they'd used the previous evening… sensed that she raised her head to look towards him… lift a hand to cover her mouth and gasp in horror. With utter clarity he saw the glass she was holding fall onto the floor and shatter into a thousand pieces.

With sudden overwhelming dread, he opened his mouth and whispered: 'Oh, God no. Sarah… I love you!'

Nothing else mattered to John but the image of his wife, and though the vision filled his heart and soul, he still registered the brilliant flash of light as the gun exploded, heard the deafening roar that shattered the silence. Simultaneously he heard a warning yell from Dave, while a darkness obscured his vision. A heavy object punched him in the chest throwing him backwards, and as he tumbled, his head collided with an unyielding surface and then silence fell.

Thirty-five

Sarah pushed herself away from the kitchen cupboard, the solid object that had stopped her from falling to the floor. She stood immobile with none of her five earthly senses outwardly active. Instead, her innate sixth sense was flooded with a myriad of tiny perceptions, as if her spirit were trying to reach out beyond the room in which she now stood. But a gentle touch to her hand roused her from her self-induced catatonic state... the touch of Mags's nose as the dog wandered into the kitchen to investigate.

'No. Mags, out you go girl... out!' Sarah commanded, concerned the dog could cut her paws on the fragments of broken glass littering the floor.

Mags slipped back out of the room with a single backward glance that hinted at displeasure for being disturbed. Sarah kicked into practicalities, stepping over to the sink unit in search of a dustpan and brush. With deliberate care, focussing on the job at hand, she swept up the shards of glass and deposited them into a carrier bag, but as she worked, her mind was a turmoil of emotions. On one hand, she worried for Claire and why she had screamed, but in utter confusion she wondered how she'd heard her daughter at all since the child was over a mile away.

But the image of John horrified her, and she was creeping closer to the edge of panic. She'd been restless since the previous day, for reasons she didn't understand. All she had known was she feared for John's safety. Now it appeared those fears had been realised. She'd had a vision of John, sensed his fear and fought the sudden urge to run out of the house, get in the car and drive to Birmingham.

But an idea occurred to her, an idea that brought an even higher level of bewilderment. If she, Sarah, had seen John in trouble, why had Claire screamed for her daddy? Had Claire experienced the vision too? Much as Sarah worried for her husband, Claire's well-being surpassed those fears, and she rushed to the living room, snatched up the telephone and keyed in the number for the school.

With mounting impatience she listened to the ring tone while wondering what to say. She couldn't say 'Oh I heard my daughter scream, is she ok?' but then someone picked up the call.

'Oh hi. I'm Claire Macintyre's mother. My daughter is in year four. Can I ask, how she has been today? She wasn't too well this morning when she woke up.'

Whoever answered sounded surprised.

'Oh, hello Mrs Macintyre. I was going to call you. She's sat here in the office at the moment. Her teacher said she suddenly screamed in class and began to cry. She's quite upset, so we thought it best if you came along and picked her up if possible?'

'Yes. Yes of course. I'll come straight away,' and she hung up the phone without waiting for an answer.

Within a minute Sarah was in her car driving the short journey to Claire's school. She held her mobile phone in her hand and as she pulled up into a space on the school car park, hit the speed dial for John's personal mobile. The call went unanswered. She cleared the call and rang the number again, but still it rang out a few times before switching to voicemail.

'Oh God. John please answer me.'

Sarah tried again as she climbed out of her car but a voice behind interrupted her.

'Claire wait! Wait for mommy… watch the cars.'

Sarah turned in time to see Claire running across the car park and she too broke into a run. As they piled into each other, Sarah scooped Claire up in one swift movement and hugged her to her chest.

'Sweetheart? What is it? What's wrong.' *Stupid question.*

'Mommy. Where's Daddy? Where is he? I can't feel him.'

Tiny pinpricks of fear crawled across Sarah's neck.

'Feel him? Darling. What do you mean?'

'You *know* what I mean,' replied Claire, pulling away and staring into her mother's eyes. 'You know because you can't feel him either.'

'I'm sorry, Mrs Macintyre.' Sarah turned as the school secretary approached. 'Claire spotted your car and let herself out. I tried to stop her.'

'Don't worry about it,' answered Sarah. 'There are other things to think about. Look, I'll take Claire straight home. I'm sure she'll be fine tomorrow. A bad dream last night perhaps, or something she ate.'

Sarah turned and without another word carried her daughter back to the car, leaving a puzzled secretary standing in the middle of the car park.

Before she drove away, Sarah tried John's phone again but still had no reply. Once they were out on the road, she spoke to Claire.

'Sweetie, what did you mean when you said you couldn't feel Daddy?'

'You *know* what I mean. I've felt him ever since you were in hospital but I can't feel him now. I feel you too.'

Sarah shuddered as the hairs tingled on the back of her neck again.

'Sweetie, I've been trying to call your dad, but he's not answering. He might be just busy.'

Claire had been peering through the window but now turned and stared wide-eyed at her mother.

'You know that's not true because you can't see him.'

'Darling, I don't understand. What do you mean I can't see him?'

'Mommy, you *know* what I mean,' Claire insisted. 'Have you tried?'

The short journey from school was soon over and Sarah took a moment to ponder Claire's words as she pulled onto the drive.

'C'mon, let's go inside,' she said and led the way.

'Mommy?' Claire was pleading now and unrelenting as she followed her mother into the house. 'Have you tried? Have you?'

Walking into the kitchen, Sarah dropped the keys onto the work surface and turned to her daughter. Claire was crying again.

'Mommy... please. I can't feel him. I can't see him. Please try.'

'Claire,' Sarah whispered, close to tears herself, but after a few seconds gave in, seeing the panic in Claire's eyes. Sensing the aura shimmering and wafting around her daughter as if it were under duress, Sarah acknowledged her child's simple and unconditional understanding. Her own voice broke as she continued.

'Sweetheart, I don't know how. This... thing just happens. I don't know how it works or what to do.'

Claire's cheeks glistened as fresh tears spilled from her eyes. 'Just think about him Mommy, just think and look for him.'

Staring into Claire's bright blue eyes, seeing the fear that surely reflected her own, Sarah furrowed her brow as she struggled to do as her daughter asked. But as she peered into her daughter's soul, the image of an elderly lady appeared to her inner sight, an old lady who had told her of an ancient gift, a gift that needed no learning to use, only a willingness and a belief. As if watching a picture show controlled by someone else, her inner sight shifted from Beryl onto John and her heart beat faster. Once again the image of him standing frozen in fear appeared and she saw his lips move and heard his voice. She used this image of him to stretch her focus still further, search for him, try to sense him, but her efforts were fruitless.

Sarah and Claire stood immobile in the kitchen, staring at each other, mother and daughter, sending out their thoughts, searching in vain for the spiritual touch of the man who stood tall and strong in both their lives. Without conscious effort and in some essential way they joined, their efforts becoming one, increasing the reach of their spiritual strength as they tried in desperation to find John. Within the silence of the kitchen the struggle continued, but as they began to lose thread, a warmth coursed through their hearts and souls, a warmth that carried with it a song, the song of a love so intense they both gasped. But within moments the song faded and Sarah spoke with urgency, both with her voice and with her thought.

'I love you, sweetheart. Please stay. John? John? I can't see you. Please John.'

There was no reply.

'John... please... come back.'

Sarah and Claire stood frozen, listening and searching, using senses which for most people were weak or non-existent. They had perceived, with senses not of this physical world, the touch of the man who was Husband and Father. But then the touch disappeared and the intense fear that rose in their hearts filled them with dread. The sudden touch and the nothingness which followed could only mean one thing. Sarah almost collapsed, but cutting into their shared panic, the strident ringing of the telephone shocked them both. Letting go of her daughter, Sarah ran into the living room and grabbed the phone.

'YES!' she shouted.

'Mrs Macintyre? Sarah?'

'Yes.'

'It's Mike Jacobs. John's Governor. A car is on its way to pick you up. It'll be about twenty minutes. There's been

an incident.'
'An incident? Mike? Is he ok? Mike?'

Thirty-six

'I love you, sweetheart. Please stay. John? John? I can't see you. Please John.'

The words, soft and on the edge of hearing, whispered from inside a dream. Or were they real? John couldn't quite tell. The voice was familiar, but he perceived it in an odd way as if sensing it rather than hearing it.

He felt nothing... just floated in a vacuum with no physical contact, nothing to make him feel real. But the sound of the voice triggered memories, comforting memories, memories that were everything.

But as he floated alone with nothing but the memory of the voice, a delicate and light fluttering caressed his face and vague shadows started in front of his eyes. The voice spoke again and a vague discomfort within his head disturbed the dream.

'John... please... I can't see you... please John. Come back.'

The voice, pleading and full of desperation broke into his thoughts, pulling him out of the dream until the discomfort surged from vague to agonising and a moan reached his ears. He thought it must have been his own voice, and he tried to move but found movement impossible. His eyes registered little, only elusive blossoming lights which expanded and faded, expanded and faded and again he tried to move.

'Lie still.' Another voice, deeper, a man, but accented. 'Don't move. Help is on its way.'

Despite the command, John made the attempt and found he could raise an arm, or so he thought. Everything was still obscure, and the movement seemed remote as if pins and needles dulled his sense of touch. Despite the numbness, he raised his arm to the source of the pain, and pressed hard, trying to diminish the hurt. He wanted to say something and after an immense struggle found he was able to form words.

'Why can't I see? Why can't I move?'

'Sergeant Macintyre. I must insist you stay still. You're hurt. Please do as I say.'

John recognised the voice and memory flooded back.

'Mr Joji? Is that you? What are you saying? Why shouldn't I move? Why…'

John stopped talking as grey light filtered through, dispelling the darkness. The brightness increased until he found he was staring up at a sky that appeared so far away as to be unreachable… unreal. Raindrops fell on his face, a gentle rain, at the same time chill and refreshing. Tall brick walls towered above and surrounded his view of the sky, while a dark circle floated nearby. He moved his focus towards the circle until his eyes settled on a face full of concern. Mr Joji. Blood still streaked his forehead and at the sight of his injury full memory returned to John. With sudden lurching horror, he remembered the deafening sound as Raoul fired the gun and realised Raoul had shot him. He must have. But where was Dave? In the distance, the haunting sound of sirens reached his ears, and he hoped to God they'd get here soon.

'What happened to Raoul? He's dangerous. No one tries to stop him. No one. Do you understand?'

John let out another moan as a fresh wave of pain surged

through his head.

'Yes I understand. Please, Mr Macintyre. Try to be still.'

'No! I need to call my wife, and where is Dave? Where is he?'

John tried to get up despite the throbbing in his head, but found he couldn't move his body or his legs. With extreme effort he shifted his hands and pushed at the floor until he was able to lift himself into a reclined position. Though the darkness within his eyes had lifted, tears still smeared his vision.

'Mr Macintyre, sir. Please, don't.'

'What is it for God's sake? Raoul shot me didn't he, but I feel ok apart from my head. Did he shoot me in the head?'

'Mr Macintyre. You haven't been shot, but you have sustained a blow to your head. Please stay still.'

'Not shot? Not shot? But I heard the gun go off.'

Pushing himself upright still further, John wiped at his eyes and only then did the awful truth reveal itself… the reason he found it difficult to move. Across his legs and lower body Dave lay face up and unmoving, his heavy 17 stone muscular frame pinning John against the pavement. Only with sheer determination had he been able to roll Dave over enough to lift himself.

'Dave! Christ… Dave! For God's sake man, talk to me!'

Amidst his exhaustion and with little strength left, John shook his friend's shoulder and Dave gasped. Still trying to clear his sight John stared at Dave, searching, hoping for more signs. Then with mounting horror he caught sight of the awful red stain seeping from David's neck.

'Dave. Talk to me you bastard, talk to me.'

Heedless of the consequences, John pushed at Dave's shoulder once more and again heard a gasp.

David moved his lips, trying to speak. 'John?' he rasped. 'John. Did we get him?'

John ground his teeth and spoke through his pain, 'Yes mate. We got him. We'll bang him away forever.'

'Good.'

Dave fell quiet, but with one final effort spoke once more. The last words he would ever speak: 'John... did I tell you... I'm gonna be a daddy. If it's a girl... we'll call it Sarah... Jo... John if... if it's a boy.'

'Yes, Dave, you told me. Well done, mate. You're gonna make great parents. C'mon man, let's get you up and sorted.'

John held a hand against Dave's face, but his friend's eyes had focussed off into the distance and after a few seconds John could see there was no life left in them. A few heavier drops of rain found their way onto where the two friends lay, to where an act of insane madness had torn away another young life. Closer now the sirens came, but for David they would be too late. *Oh Kelly.*

'Dave,' John whispered once before bowing his head, closing his eyes and closing his heart.

Thirty-seven

Sarah and Claire followed the policeman into the emergency department of the Queen Elizabeth Hospital, the largest near to Birmingham city centre. Claire held onto her mother's hand and the further through the maze of corridors they went, the tighter her grip became. Police officers were familiar with A&E departments since many were regular visitors. The police officer who now led them hurried along, knowing two of his colleagues were now more than just visitors. The officer's instructions were simple though. Get the family and blue light them to the hospital.

Sarah and Claire were silent during the endless journey from Penkridge into Birmingham, silent but only in voice. Terrified of what she may find, Sarah's greater concern was for her child. Fear emanated in rolling waves from the young child who sat wrapped in her arms, but in a moment of detachment she realised she wasn't nauseated by the intensity of Claire's emotional state, unlike the elderly lady she had sensed weeks ago when she had sat in Wolverhampton with Rachel, experimenting with her ability to 'see'. Why is that, she wondered? Is it because Claire's my daughter? Is it because Claire isn't ill? *Oh Beryl. I wish you were here to help.* As the traffic built in front, the muted crying of the siren dragged her back into the reality of shared fears.

Now as they raced through the hospital, she probed once more for any impression of John, and sensed Claire join with her. Still they failed to detect anything.

'It's just along here,' said the officer who led them, understanding their worries. 'Just here.'

As they rounded the last corner, Sarah and Claire halted at the sight confronting them, but within seconds Claire freed herself from the chains of emotion that rooted her to the spot. She hurtled along the corridor into John's arms as he opened them wide to take possession of his daughter and the sanctuary she promised. Sarah however found she couldn't move. The fear she'd held inside her soul for over an hour evaporated. Here was positive proof John was still alive, slouched on a chair seemingly unhurt, but the sight of him caused her pain of a different kind. To begin with, blood stained his shirt, huge angry stains that spoke of a serious injury. His face was a mask of loss and anguish with eyes of utter torment. The haunted expression he wore pierced her very soul. These things filled her with horror and pity, but the one thing that caused more pain than anything was John's total lack of aura… that vibrant and comforting blanket she had seen around him ever since before Christmas. Now it had disappeared. To her eyes and her soul, it made him appear empty and lifeless, as if her husband had lost an essential part of his being. Now she understood why she couldn't sense him from afar. Despite her lack of understanding of this element of her gift, her ability to perceive a person's spiritual energy and her inability to switch it on or off or use it at will, she realised her own spirit always sensed her husband in a subconscious or elemental way. She was attuned to it, joined with it and maybe within her soul always had been. Now, Sarah felt as if she herself had lost something essential as if part of her own being had gone.

'John,' she whispered, and the sound of her voice

loosened her immobility. In desperation and fear she made her way toward him.

'Sarah. I… I'm sorry. I should have stayed with you today, like you asked me to. Perhaps if I had…'

'John? Sweetheart.' Sarah knelt in front of her husband and laid her hands on his knees. He appeared to cling to Claire in desperation, afraid to let go. His eyes were staring and manic, unblinking and Sarah was sure his sight focussed elsewhere.

'What is it?' she asked in a quiet voice. 'John, what's happened?'

As she waited for John to answer, a door opened at the furthest end of the long corridor and a young woman emerged from one of the emergency treatment rooms, led by Mike, the officer who'd called Sarah at home. Sarah recognised Kelly, Dave's fiancée. Kelly lifted her gaze and saw Sarah with John, and even from a distance Sarah registered the pale colour of her skin and the redness of eyes that had shed many tears. Sarah thought she had never seen an expression of such desolation and with a sudden lurch understood the truth.

'John, please. What's happened? Tell me.'

'Sarah. It's Dave. He's dead. Shot… and it's my fault.'

With an anguished shout, Kelly ran along the corridor towards them. John stood to meet her and Kelly grabbed the front of his shirt, grabbed it with both hands despite the blood stains, and shook him with surprising ferocity.

'John!' she cried. 'What happened? How did this happen… he was so careful? John! Please tell me!'

Mike was only a step behind her.

'C'mon Kelly. Careful now. Leave it to us to do our job. C'mon, love. Dave's parents are on their way. We need to meet them when they arrive.'

'Kelly,' John whispered. 'I'm sorry. I…' but words failed him.

'How!' she cried. 'How!' but then as if her burst of emotion drained her of energy, she collapsed against John and dropped her head against his chest. With chagrin and an urgent need for forgiveness, John grabbed her and hugged her while her breath came in ragged gasps.

'C'mon, love,' said Mike again, and laid an awkward hand on her shoulder. 'You can see John later.'

Kelly allowed Mike to lead her away, back along the corridor and out of sight. A few moments later Mike returned.

'John? Get yourself off home. We've got your initial statement, we'll send someone to see you tomorrow. Get something to eat, have a drink, be with your family.'

'What about Kelly and Dave's parents?'

'We'll take care of them. Do what I say,' Mike ordered. 'Look after your own. There'll be time for you to meet another day. Go on, leave us to do what we have to do.'

Mike stared at John until he saw acceptance on his colleague's face, then he turned and left.

Sarah took John by the hand and tugged him back the way she had come towards the policeman who drove them from home.

'Yes,' she said. 'Let's go home. I need to get you out of here.'

Sarah spoke with compassion but she felt torn between the intense relief John was unhurt, at least in the physical sense, and utter horror his closest friend was dead. She wanted to get her family back within their own sanctuary, that place called home where she could work out what to do to bring them peace, to make them safe and whole. But in a moment of guilt she wondered if Kelly could ever have peace again, or David's parents.

Oh Dave.

Thirty-eight

'John?' Sarah called from the kitchen. 'Do you want tea… or would you prefer a whisky?'

When John didn't answer she walked through into the living room and found him prostrate on the sofa, fast asleep. It was early evening and after the day they'd had, she was glad he'd relaxed enough to switch off, if only for a short while.

It had been draining for everyone concerned, but for John and Sarah, attending a second funeral so soon after the last one was exhausting. A police officer's funeral was always hard to bear, a man taken under tragic circumstances in the line of duty, but the coroner's report left no doubt about the verdict. Internal investigations would continue for a while to explore any lessons to be learnt.

After John and Dave arrived at the hospital, the news came through that Raoul had died in a road accident. As soon as he'd fired the gun, the young man panicked and ran straight out of the alleyway and into the street. He'd charged into the path of a car which collided with him. Raoul died at the scene.

Several of John's colleagues commented on the young man's death with satisfaction but it only added to John's grief, yet another young life ruined before it had a chance to begin.

John was on extended leave and during the first few days he spoke to Hamish who once again suggested he, Sarah and Claire move to Scotland. Hamish explained to John that he was sole beneficiary in the will and hence Hamish's house and estate was his whenever he wanted.

John listened to Hamish's news with mixed feelings. On the one hand his growing desire to do something different with his life increased after David's death. He worried ever more there was an unstoppable descent into madness in and around such a dense populated inner city... a slow deterioration of decency and communal spirit he was powerless to stop, or even affect in any way. His efforts therefore were pointless. Sarah tried to temper his mood by suggesting it was only recent events that had tainted John's view, but he was not ready to accept her suggestion yet. He needed time to work through such bleak thoughts.

But after listening to his grandfather's comments concerning a will and bequest and estate, John felt an increasing sense of dread at the possibility of losing someone else. His life revolved around Sarah and Claire and the new addition set to arrive in the early autumn, but Hamish was a link to John's roots and one he feared may end all too soon and leave him floundering. An urgent need was growing inside him, one that involved moving back to Scotland to be with Hamish and building a new life for himself and his family.

While John dozed on the sofa, Sarah busied herself with tidying up the kitchen and checking on Claire who was taking a bath. Claire voiced Sarah's concern for John.

'Mommy? I thought everyone cried at funerals. I thought that's what people did.'

'Well they're very sad occasions and most people cry, even those unrelated. There are others who try to be strong and hide their feelings. But why do you ask?'

'Because Daddy didn't cry. I thought he was best friends

with David. Kelly cried a lot. Is Daddy all right?'

Sarah had noticed this herself. But knowing her husband, she understood John had turned inwards, closed his heart, but she was unsure of the reason, or reasons… though she suspected one of them was guilt. Survivor's guilt was commonplace under the right circumstances and maybe, she thought, that was it… John figured he'd no right to grieve. Sarah knew only too well that a moment earlier, the bullet could have ripped through her husband instead of David as he ran around the corner. Sarah herself would always have conflicting emotions… happy to have her husband still alive, but horrified another person had lost their life. How she would reconcile herself to that emotional dilemma, she did not know, and it was clear John's struggle would last even longer.

Sarah answered Claire's question. 'No sweetheart. Daddy isn't all right. Not at the moment, but if we love him a lot and make sure he knows it, I think he'll survive.'

Claire nodded. She appeared deep in thought, but after a few moments spoke again, 'He's awake.'

Sarah stared into Claire's eyes and focussed her intent on her husband. She sensed a faint presence… detected with her inner sight a weak image of John and found the sensation encouraging.

'Yes. I think you're right. How about you get dried now and I'll see what he's up to?'

While Claire finished bathing, Sarah crept downstairs and into the hall. Driven by Claire's words and her own need to stretch her skill, she stopped a moment and closed her eyes. She tried to build a mental image of John and found she could do so with ease. But the image in her mind's eye shifted with no conscious effort into something raw, something more essential, as if she detected the essence of his being, rather than just his physical presence. She saw a bright purple haze that conveyed to her the quintessence of John's soul… that which made his spirit what it was, that which shaped him. But within the haze lay a disturbed emotional state, the pain and grief locked inside troubling his well-being. She breathed a sigh of relief in knowing, despite what had happened, John wasn't lost to her, but suffered from an emotional injury which, with intuition, she knew she could heal.

Sarah opened her eyes but still stayed where she was. Through the half closed door to the living room, she could hear John moving around and knew he was awake. Then in a sudden moment of clarity, she understood the magnitude of what she had done. From the hallway, she had projected an element of her gift in an effort to see how John was… beyond her physical sight and into the living room. With subconscious ease Sarah had achieved this, and the knowledge brought her a sense of accomplishment, despite the sadness of the day.

But this won't do. I need to find out how he is.

'How are you doing?' Sarah asked as she walked into the room.

With a cavernous yawn John stretched his arms up to the ceiling. He gave her a wan smile but Sarah saw the ache in his eyes.

'What's the phrase? As well as can be expected?'

'Are you hungry?' she asked.

'Not really,' John replied. 'I must have slept because I seem to remember dreaming.'

'Do you remember what about?'

John stared at Sarah for a long second as he struggled to remember.

'Colours… bright ones… dull ones.' Deep furrows creased his brow. 'Dirty ones. Y'know how you've described them… your visions? And I saw Kelly, and she had no colour. Does that sound odd? I'm sure your ideas are rubbing off on me or am I going mad?'

'You're not going mad,' Sarah smiled. 'But I suspect you've dreamt of stuff I've told you about.'

John nodded and was silent while they stood still and stared at each other. As Sarah probed her husband's soul once more, a hand lay across her brow, the light touch which had become familiar to her since before Christmas but had all but ceased. John was speaking again.

'I need to visit Kelly, find out how she's doing. Do you mind? I'll only be a couple of hours. It worries me she left the funeral and went home alone, rather than staying with friends or at the hotel with her parents.'

Sarah moved across the room and lifted a hand to her husband's face.

'You know you don't have to ask. If you're concerned you should go. Will you be ok? I know how you feel about... about what happened.'

'You understand far too much... but I'm glad you do. What a shit time it's been. How much more can we take?'

'It's not what happens, John, it's how we handle it. But if we have each other, we'll survive. Now, off you go. Text me when you're on your way home.'

Half an hour later, after going upstairs to freshen up, John left the house and drove with reluctance but with necessity to where Kelly lived. After a moment's hesitation, he tapped on the front door and waited. A voice, muffled and cautious called, 'Who... who is it?'

'Kelly it's me, John. Can I come in?'

The sound of a key turning was answer enough. Kelly stepped aside as John walked in and closed the door. She brushed past him and headed off to the living room at the back of the house.

'C... come in,' she said, slurring her words.

John had driven here with concern but now his anxiety rose as he watched Kelly bounce off the wooden staircase and veer to one side. She'd removed the black suit she'd worn for the funeral and replaced it with a short lightweight satin dressing gown. When she'd opened the front door, John noticed she still wore make-up but now it appeared smudged, worse for wear after her ordeal. Following her into the living room, he only then noticed the bottle in one hand, a half-empty bottle of wine. An empty glass dangled in the other.

'Have a drink,' she said, and turned to face him.

'Best not. I'm driving home after.'

'Oh come on… Mr Policeman. You can have one can't you?'

Kelly stepped toward John and waved her glass in front of his face. John realised he'd stepped into an awkward situation. But perhaps that's why he had come, what he expected to find… that Kelly needed help this night.

'Well… just the one,' he muttered.

Kelly spun on the spot, placed her glass on a table and emptied the bottle into it before swaying into the kitchen. Within moments she returned with a second glass and another opened bottle. She handed the glass to John, held his hand to steady herself, and poured out the wine. With exaggerated care she placed the bottle on the table and retrieved her own glass before stepping back up in front of John. As if preparing to make a toast, she clinked her glass against his own and lifted it to her lips.

Kelly was so close to John her perfume filled his senses. He swallowed hard.

'Here's to you my big, strong man,' she slurred. 'My brave boy,' and she took a long gulp.

John took a sip from his own glass.

'Kelly. How much have drunk?'

'Not enough John,' she said. 'Not nearly enough.'

John stared into Kelly's bright blue eyes, eyes that were a perfect combination for her natural blonde hair. Blessed with facial proportions universally classed as attractive, Kelly was taller than Sarah, longer limbed, agile and slim, but of course her chosen profession kept her that way. However, her pre-occupation with fitness and health was now of no consequence since she was drunk and heading towards an unhealthy hangover. John felt concern for the baby she was carrying.

'I thought you'd spend the night with your parents at the

hotel?' He tried to make light conversation.

'There was no room. And I wanted to be at home, close to… everything.'

A weak smile crossed Kelly's face, though it didn't reach her eyes.

'Do you remember much about school?' Kelly continued. 'All those years ago? Remember we used to play by the shore in the summer… getting wet in the puddles. You used… you used to throw seaweed at me. Huh! And in the winter, sometimes we had snow… and you'd use snowballs instead.'

Kelly slurped at her wine and continued.

'I remember the fishing you did. You sometimes let me come along and dip in the Loch while you sat with your dad's rods… as long as I didn't make a noise… didn't talk or make a splash. I liked just being there.' Kelly sniffed in reminiscence. 'Y'know, I once had a fight with Mary Stewart. You remember Mary? I had a fight with her because she said she was gonna marry you. Told her it wasn't true… you were gonna marry me. Yes I had a fight over you…'

Kelly fell silent and John could see tears in her eyes. While she gazed at him, John noticed her focus shifted in random fashion as she struggled to keep awake. She closed and reopened her eyes and as her smile faded, she turned away and stood still, talking over her shoulder.

'We were only ten, John… but I'm sure I was in love with you.'

Kelly shook her head and moved again.

'Let's have some music,' she said. 'I want to dance.'

'Kelly.'

'I like dancing… don't you? Don't the Irish dance when they bury their dead?'

On the point of imbalance, she turned towards him again and moved closer. John noticed her dressing gown belt was now hanging loose and underneath her gown she wore only knickers.

'Kelly. Listen... I came around to check how you were.'

'Me? I'm ok. What about you, John? How are you getting on?'

She lifted a hand to his cheek and caressed it with delicate fingers before turning away again. She stooped over an iPod dock sitting in a corner and jabbed at the buttons until quiet soul music drifted into the awkward silence. Turning back to John she attempted to sway in time to the music but her efforts appeared childlike. With the effects of alcohol slowing her reactions, her attempt at seductive motion only made John's heart ache.

'C'mon, John. Dance with me.'

Kelly emptied her glass and dropped it onto the sofa. She stumbled over to John and wrapped her arms around his neck drawing him close, pressing her body against his. John swallowed again and felt the heat of her body even through his clothes. Kelly continued to sway against him.

'Do you ever wonder what would have happened to us if you hadn't moved away?' she whispered, hot breath against his ear. 'Do you think we'd have been married?'

Her lips were against John's ear and he couldn't help the shiver that ran along his spine.

'Kelly. You shouldn't do this.'

'C'mon, John. I always wondered how we'd have been together, what we would have done...'

'Kelly don't...'

'... where we would be now.'

Kelly brushed her tongue against his ear... stroked the back of his neck with her long fingers.

John lifted his arms up and grasped Kelly by the wrists, pulling her hands away from him.

With sudden wide-eyed excitement spreading across her face she gasped. 'Oh my. You're so strong. I bet you want me, John... I bet you want to force me, be inside me. C'mon, John. You can have me.'

Kelly twisted her arms so that John loosened his grip and she dropped onto the sofa. In a movement that mortified

John, Kelly lifted her knees up and splayed her thighs wide revealing the full extent of her eagerness to give everything to him.

'Kelly... stop this now. This isn't you. Please... stop it.'

John raised his voice a little in both pity and fear, pity for Kelly and fear that he may become angry, angry at himself. But then Kelly spoke words which broke the moment, wrenching it apart and exposing her madness. Lifting one foot onto the sofa and splaying her thighs even wider, she said, 'C'mon Dave... it's time to make me happy.'

The words stabbed at John as a physical blow might, the mention of his friends name, but despite his pain, the sudden change in Kelly was unmistakable, the realisation of what she was doing. The shifting focus of her glazed eyes stopped as they widened in horror. A gasp escaped her mouth and in one swift but clumsy motion she brought her knees together and in desperation yanked at her dressing gown, trying to cover her body. She tried to get up but instead rolled onto the floor.

'Dave! Oh God I'm sorry. Dave!'

'Kelly? It's ok. Kelly, it's me... it's John.'

'What... John. What am I doing?' Kelly let out an agonised wail of pain and grief. 'No!' she cried. 'No! Please God no!'

John knelt beside her and tried to help her onto her feet.

'I'm sorry,' she wailed. 'John... what am I doing. What have I done?'

'Kelly... it's ok,' he repeated, but his soul was screaming. 'You've not done anything. It's all right. I'm here as a friend. Let me help you.'

Still on hands and knees, Kelly twisted to look up at him, blinking through tears that blurred her vision.

'John. I'm sorry. Please help... I'm sorry... really I am. Oh God... I'm going to be sick. John... the baby!'

Without a moment's hesitation, John lifted her up and carried her into the downstairs cloakroom where she collapsed in front of the toilet just in time.

Thank God, thought John. *It's better this way.*

'Ok, sweetheart. It's best to get rid of the drink. I'm here… don't worry. I'll take care of you.'

'John. Don't leave me. Please. Not…' another violent heave followed another, until she emptied her stomach, '… not on my own.'

'Ok, sweetheart… ok.'

With a hand towel soaked in cool water, John cleaned Kelly's face and made her sit upright while he gave her a glass of water to sip.

'C'mon… you need to be in bed. You need to sleep.'

'Stay with me. Please,' she moaned, as her chest shuddered once more in anguish. 'I promise I won't be stupid again.'

Out in the hallway Kelly's strength failed, so John picked her up and carried her upstairs. In the bedroom he sat her on the bed while he pulled back the covers.

'Kelly,' he said, kneeling in front of her. 'I need to take off your gown. You were a little sick on it. You can't sleep in it. Is that ok?'

Kelly swayed from side to side and in slow motion her eyes opened and closed several times, but despite the alcohol, she answered.

'Yes… of course… I don't care. There's not much left to see… just… just don't leave me.'

Kelly lifted her arms up and stood long enough for John to remove the stained garment. With the gentlest of care he laid her on the bed and pulled the quilt up to her chin.

With one last effort before sleep took her, she dragged one arm out and grabbed John's hand.

'I'm sorry John. I'm so sorry you lost your friend.'

Kelly said no more but John sat beside her holding her hand until she fell asleep. His heart ached knowing that amidst her own pain she still sympathised for his loss. Feeling the sharp anguish of his compassion for Kelly, he tried to push his grief deep inside and felt a sudden need for Sarah, wanted her nearby. But as he extended his thought towards her, he frowned in wearied puzzlement. For a split second, an image of his wife came to him… stark and present… an image of her sitting at home cuddling up to Claire on the sofa as they watched television. With utter clarity he could see her as if he were in the room beside her and sensed she lifted her head as if in response to his thoughts. But then the image vanished, leaving him troubled and confused and very alone.

Reunion

21st June 1716

As sure-footed as a roe deer and as silent as an owl, Amber shot out from under the trees and onto the bare back of the hills that climbed above the settlement of Kirkmichael. For half an hour she ran like the wind, tireless and driven, intent on putting as much distance as she could between herself and the cooling body of her first victim.

In the half-light of dawn she felt safe, sure she would not be seen as she headed towards Rodgerston Burn and clean water. She needed to wash, aware her clothes were soaked in blood... some of the life force of Jimmy MacDonald seeping through her garments and onto her skin.

Ahead now she could see the stream glinting as the early sun broached the hilltop, and she sped up, needing only to drench her body within its cleansing promise. Without hesitation she plunged into the stream and lay down, letting the rush of water cover her body. But then she rose up and began tearing at her clothes, ripping them off in haste, caring little for the damage caused. Moments later she knelt, naked but for her boots, and began scrubbing the blood from her face and body with handfuls of mud and grit. Only when her skin was free of stains did she cease, and she fell forward onto her hands, kneeling on all fours waiting for her pounding heart to slow.

Within moments she began to feel calm, but shock replaced the urgency of her escape and nausea flooded her soul. With a violent lurch she threw up, emptying her stomach and cleansing her spirit of the horror of what she had done. And then the tears came and she wept, but not for the man, her first victim. The tears were for her mother, Rose, and her brother, Hamish.

Six long years had passed since she made her promise to her mother, standing amidst the ruins of her home, and during those six years she had not been idle. Four men were responsible for her mother's murder, four men who gave chase to her and Hamish as they fled through the woods. She had seen their faces as she and her brother escaped, and the evil of their actions was etched in her memory. But there was a fifth. He was not among those who committed their cowardly act upon that day, but he was no less responsible through his failure to control others. He was the local magistrate… a man who'd had the power to prevent the tearing apart of her family and who had power enough to have brought those men to justice. But he had failed. So during the long years, Amber plotted with stealth and inner strength, and made her plans to meter out justice.

She would destroy them all, and last night was the first.

Blessed with her mother's bewitching beauty, her dark eyes and dark hair, long legs and fullness of figure, she understood, despite her young years, that men were weak and easily led. It was easy to lead her prey to his death… tease him to a quiet place, and there she cut him where it would hurt the most… destroying his weak manhood. With her victim writhing on the floor in horror and agony, she finished him with a slash to the throat. But the blood sprayed everywhere… a shocking and vivid bright red that covered her clothes, splashing across her face. And so she had run across the fields and through the woods carrying her dirk with her, fleeing to a safe distance.

Still kneeling in the cool water her tears slowed and

finally ceased. Within her inner sight she sensed her mother's touch upon her soul, she perceived anguish and took it for fear from her mother, fear for Amber's own safety, both physical and spiritual. Rose had been a woman of peace and tried to live her life that way, forgiving and forgetting. But Amber harboured anger that spread to her very core, and it would hold firm until her promise was complete. There were evil men in this world, and these five always had been and always would be so. Therefore she would rid the world of them.

But as she knelt, a new perception reached into her thoughts. Before a movement caught her eye she sensed a presence and knew someone was watching. Probing with her gift, she felt no threat… indeed she detected concern and compassion. Rising out of the water, caring nothing for her naked body, she turned and peered upstream. Further up the burn towards the hilltop stood a young man… taller than she, blonde hair and blue eyes. A brace of rabbits hung from one hand while a shepherd's crook sat comfortably in the other.

Amber stared at the man, and though she said nothing her inner sight was alive and probed into his heart and soul searching for motivation… of any sort. She discerned nothing but a tranquillity that belonged on these hills, and closing her eyes for a moment detected a purple aura shrouding his head and shoulders, a halo that spread even to his heart.

'I see you,' Amber said. 'Why are you here?'

The young man said nothing but raised the results of his hunting as if the reason were obvious. He glanced downwards, scanning her body. Aware of the quick shift of his eyes, Amber raised her knife and took a step toward him.

'Mind your thoughts. Take a step toward me and it may be your last. I am unafraid.'

At last the young man spoke and as he did so the deep and gentle tone of his words halted Amber's threatening behaviour.

'I don't doubt what you say, and I also am unafraid. But you have no need to mistrust me. I have no thought in my head but concern for your safety. Your state is not wise in these parts, even at dawn.'

At that the young man stepped closer, and as he did so he took off the tartan plaid draped across his shoulder. Aware of the risk, he stopped a few feet from Amber and offered the cloak. With the hint of a comforting smile but without humour, he spoke, 'I see your own clothes are far downstream by now though I'm certain they are of no use to you. It would calm my concern if you received my gift. And… your blade is stained and dull I fear.'

For a moment Amber stood firm, her dirk held out and her chin raised in defiance. But as the young man stared into her eyes a calming hand lay across her brow bringing with it the voice of comfort, and her heart told her to trust this tall man and accept his gift. She lowered her blade, turned and once more knelt in the water where, with grit and dirt, she scrubbed away the blood stains. Standing swiftly she snatched the tartan and threw it across one shoulder.

'I will not show my gratitude in the way most men wish it,' she spat. 'But I am in your debt.'

'It is of no consequence. I am honoured to give aid where it is needed. But…' Now a smile did reach his eyes. 'Though I have skill in catching meat, I have poor skills in cooking. If I may… I would gladly accept a hearty meal.'

His humour and honest suggestion caught Amber off guard and chagrin raised a colour in her cheeks. She wrapped the plaid about her, at last covering her body. This man had shown kindness and respect and for a moment she cast her thought back into the past trying to recall the last time she knew such compassion. With a sudden weakening of her strength tears blurred her vision once more as she realised she had no memory, not since fleeing her Aunt's house at the age of thirteen. She turned away and waited for the wind to dry her eyes. As she did so a vision forced away her view of the hilltop and the forest below. The vision caught her by surprise and as it faded she stared back at the man to where he still stood waiting for an answer.

With sudden conviction she had seen a future, a future beyond her current need for vengeance and justice, she spoke once more before turning away and climbing to the hilltop.

'I see you and hear you, and I will repay your gift as you suggested. My name is Amber, and you will find me here at midnight each new moon. Bring food and I will make you a meal. If I do not come it is because I am dead. But one day you will be my husband. I have seen it.'

Thirty-nine

While Kelly lay deep in forgetful slumber John crept downstairs and called Sarah. He explained everything and that he'd put her to bed though he mentioned nothing of Kelly's drunken attempt to seduce him.

'What am I supposed to do? She asked me to stay but I'm not comfortable with it, much as I'd like to help. But she says she can't be on her own. What should I do? You tell me because I can't think straight any more.'

'It's a good idea to have someone there when she wakes up, John. She'll need help for a while.'

'But are you ok with me staying?'

'John, you've known Kelly for years, since you were both kids. It's ok with me. It's clearly not ok with you though.'

Sarah waited for John to answer but he had fallen silent. After he'd left the house earlier, she and Claire ate a light supper and settled down to watch television. Sarah wanted to experiment with her 'gift' once more after her success in the hallway earlier when she sensed John's aura. She'd extended her percipience in John's direction while cuddling up to Claire. With mixed feelings she'd found it easy to do so, but as soon as she'd sensed him she detected an overwhelming hurt emanating from his spirit, a sense of desperation as if an outside influence were bringing him into danger... a danger to his wellbeing. The sudden emotional attack on her own well-being forced her to draw back and concentrate on the television. The energies arising from her spiritual connection to John disturbed her soul causing a pain for which she had no name... yet. But the idea of probing into another's heart and soul made her feel guilty, as if she were invading personal space even though, in this case, that person was her husband. This gift, she mused, needed careful consideration. She needed to learn not only how to use it, but when.

But later, while she sat trying with little success to pay attention to the television, she sensed a presence nearby, a caress as tenuous as someone's breath... delicate as the touch of a feather on her skin. It spoke of her husband, carried with it the very essence of his soul and she realised it was a sudden cry for help from John. She sensed an urgent need for her support and... guidance? She'd puzzled over this for only a few seconds until she did just that... reached out towards him. Then his presence disappeared and around half an hour later he'd called using more traditional methods. She said nothing of what happened.

But now listening to him on the telephone, hearing his struggle, she understood he needed a way out so suggested an alternative plan.

'Look, why don't I drive over and sit with her. You can come home and get into bed.'

'Yeah but what about Claire?'

'What about her? She'll be fine for a while on her own. What do you say, sweetie? Will you be ok for an hour?'

Claire gave her mother a withering expression.

'I think she says yes, John.'

'Ok. Kelly will sleep for ages so I'll see you in... what, half an hour?'

'Yes. I'm on my way,' Sarah said, and cleared the call.

It took an extra five minutes because Sarah had to get dressed again, but not long later John opened the front door to his wife. Eager not to leave Claire on her own for a minute longer than necessary, he began pulling on his jacket.

'Nothing's changed,' he said to Sarah. 'She's out cold.'

Sarah hugged her husband.

'Thanks for this,' John said. 'It didn't seem right staying on my own. And I'm sure she'll be happy to see you in the morning.'

Sarah regarded John but needed no special gift to recognise his discomfort.

'John, what's up sweetheart? I can tell something's wrong.'

'Nothing... everything. Anyway, I'd best get going.'

John kissed his wife and hurried to the car leaving Sarah to whisper a quiet, 'It's ok, John. It's ok.'

Sarah locked up and made her way upstairs to check on Kelly and found she was snoring in alcohol fuelled slumber. The quilt had slid from Kelly's shoulders uncovering her breasts and Sarah remembered from John's description of events he'd put her to bed. A wry smile touched her lips as she understood why he didn't want to stay the night. Sarah trusted John. She knew well enough how pretty Kelly was, but she also knew them both too well to suspect any risk of infidelity. Nothing and everything John had said when Sarah asked what was wrong. Yes she mused. Nothing had happened, but everything was wrong and the alcohol was enough to make some people step over the line in a desperate need for reconciliation or comfort. Grief could do that but she detected nothing from John's behaviour to suggest anything had happened. Simple embarrassment was what she perceived and, as she suspected before, survivor's guilt.

Sarah turned off Kelly's bedside lamp and went back out to the bathroom where she turned on the bathroom light so she could find her way in the dark if needed. Pulling the door close behind, enough to allow a little light, she kicked off her shoes and slid off her jeans and climbed onto the bed next to Kelly. She draped the quilt over her legs and lay still, expecting to lie awake. But the day's events caught up with her and sleep soon took its hold.

It was still dark outside when a gentle touch awakened Sarah. She checked her watch and found it was close to four o'clock. Kelly stood over her, still semi-naked.

'Sarah?' she sounded puzzled. 'What are you doing here?'

'Oh hi. John's tired and asked me to stay with you. How are you doing?'

Sarah sat up. Kelly lifted a hand to her head and, even in the semi-darkness, Sarah could see her frowning.

'I feel like shit,' she said.

'C'mon, get back to bed. You'll freeze. Where have you been?'

'I needed the toilet and a drink,' Kelly answered and still puzzling allowed Sarah to help her to her side of the bed. She laid her head back onto her pillow.

'Why didn't John stay? How come you… ' Kelly stopped in mid-sentence and sat back up holding a hand to her mouth. 'Oh God!' she gasped and stared at Sarah. 'Oh Sarah I'm sorry!'

Sarah knelt in front of Kelly and took her hands in her own. Her discomfort would have been plain to anyone, but Sarah could see deep inside, see the emptiness, the weak energy and the dirty red colour which made Sarah feel nauseous again. For a brief moment she pictured Kelly drowning in lifeless waters and in dismay tried to shift her inner sight elsewhere. The struggle was immense because she feared she might pass out. But Beryl's face came to the rescue, followed by the face of a small child… a child with blonde hair… Claire. The image of Kelly's struggle weakened and ceased and Sarah drew in a deep breath. She spoke with a voice full of sympathy and understanding.

'Kelly. Look at me. What do you have to be sorry about? I understand… I'm not blind. I know John put you to bed.'

Speaking with a voice broken with despair and guilt, and with fresh tears leaking from her eyes, Kelly confessed.

'Sarah. I wanted John. I wanted him to come to bed with me. But we didn't… we didn't do anything I promise. But I wanted him… tried to get him to… to…'

'It's ok, sweetie. I guessed what happened but I trust you both. It's not your fault. Not after what you've been through.'

Kelly grabbed at Sarah's hands in urgent need for forgiveness.

'C'mon, sweetheart,' Sarah said. 'You need more sleep. Let's get you laid down. I'll stay with you. I'll be here.'

Sarah eased Kelly back onto the pillow and walked around to the other side of the bed. As she lay down Kelly rolled over to face her. Sarah wrapped her arm around her friend and laid a hand upon her head. As she did so Sarah sensed a coldness creeping into her hand, and as she opened her heart to the young woman in desperate need of help sensed a sudden release, almost like an exhalation, though of what she could not tell. Maybe, she wondered, it was just a relaxing of tension as a person might relax when given good news of a loved one, or told a worry or concern was unfounded. But inside Sarah's inner sight a vision appeared, an image of Kelly swimming under water and struggling to gain the surface. But as she watched she saw amidst the murky waters a hand appear before Kelly, a hand that grasped at Kelly's own and pulled, lifting the young woman upwards to freedom and light.

Long after Kelly fell asleep once more, Sarah puzzled over the image before realising it had come from within both Kelly and herself, triggered by Kelly's unspoken and obvious need and Sarah's own gift. It happened without Kelly asking for help, and without Sarah's conscious effort. Sarah understood the healing needed for the bereaved was as different and as varied as the number of people who suffered, but for Kelly she felt she were playing her part in that healing.

Beryl. It's happening… the gift… it's working.
Oh my.

Forty

'I'll be fine now,' Kelly was saying, though Sarah was unconvinced. 'Thanks for staying. I don't know how I'll repay you.'

Sarah hugged her friend and then held her at arm's length. The effects of excessive alcohol showed in Kelly's eyes and on the waxy pallor of her skin.

'You don't have to,' Sarah said. 'But thanks for breakfast. A good fry up is often a cure for many things... not least a hangover.'

'Yes... it is. Sorry about that and I'm sorry about John. Will he forgive me?'

'There's nothing to forgive. I suspect he was just embarrassed, but remember this: John came here because he guessed you needed help. He would have worried about you being on your own. He came to check on how you were and I bet you're glad he did.'

Kelly nodded. 'Yes I am.' She paused for a moment, giving Sarah a chance to peer into her soul. What Sarah sensed was comforting. Difficulties lay ahead for Kelly, but she suspected her friend would find her way.

'Y'know,' Kelly said. 'It's strange but I feel a bit better this morning. Everyone always says once the funeral is over it's the start of moving on. I always imagined it was what people say when there's not a lot else to say. But this morning I guess it may be true. When I think of Dave…' Kelly's eyes filled up, and she blew out a ragged breath. 'When I think of Dave my chest hurts so much it feels like I'm suffocating. But today I'm certain I'll get through. Before the funeral it was hard to go on, as if I wanted to fall asleep and not wake up. The hurting has been unbearable. But going on doesn't seem impossible somehow whereas yesterday it did. Am I making any sense?'

Sarah nodded. 'It doesn't have to make sense but I understand.'

'And…' Kelly continued. 'I have a reason for going on.' She patted her tummy. 'I have a wee one growing inside, a miniature Dave and Kelly.'

Sarah smiled and gave Kelly another hug. 'Yes, John told me your news. I'm so thrilled.'

For a few moments they stood in silence until Sarah spoke once more.

'Kelly, this'll seem strange to hear, but when I look at you I see a very strong person hidden underneath. You may not believe me, but I see someone who can handle anything life throws at them without fear and with passion, with a commitment to carry on. Perhaps it sounds odd in this day and age, but… well that's how it seems.'

Kelly's face crumpled again, but through her tears she smiled.

'When the baby's born, if it's a girl can I name it Sarah? If it's a boy… John? If it's ok.'

Sarah's own eyes moistened and with tight lips she nodded agreement. 'John and I would love that.'

Kelly walked Sarah to the front door. 'I think I'm going back to my Mother's in Ayr,' she said.

Sarah raised her eyebrows. 'Wow. That seems sudden. What about work and Dave's parents?'

'Work won't be an issue in a few months, and I can get work back home when I'm ready. Part-time teaching or instructing. As for Dave's parents, it'll be hard for them and it's a conversation I need to have. But I made my mind up last week. I want to go home.'

'I'm sure you're right, and we'll bump in to you soon because I have an idea we won't be far behind you. Things are changing.'

They bade each other farewell and Sarah made Kelly promise to call if she needed, to talk or for company, day or night.

Sarah drove straight home, but as she pulled up onto the driveway next to John's car sudden grief took hold and she sat on her own with tears running down her cheeks. It was so unfair, so damn cruel. Yes, Kelly would survive, but she shouldn't have to face the struggle. Neither should John… losing such a close friend. But with a sudden surge of relief she stared at the front door knowing John was somewhere behind it waiting for her to come home.

A gentle rain was falling, and condensation misted the windows. Sarah glanced sideways and through the moisture noticed a few early daffodils getting ready to flower. They promised to join the pure white crocus that had been on show for a few weeks. It was early spring, and the snowdrops had finished and the realisation came as a sudden shock to her. Since late January when Steve took his own life Sarah had been so wrapped up in recent events she'd almost forgotten the year moved on regardless. During the weeks John had been off work she'd handed in her notice on her own job. And though the year began with the wonderful news of her pregnancy, it descended with horrific speed into the depths of tragedy. Also, the late winter period saw her gift and her awareness growing, but at a pace that outgrew her ability to control and understand.

With an effort she recalled the occasions when she had first *seen* or *felt* someone's spiritual energy, what she now thought of as essential being. She had seen it with John soon after being discharged from hospital, and sensed Claire's energies a few days later. There was also Beryl, vague and puzzling, from three hundred miles away, though she only perceived a manifestation of her soul without knowing what it was. Rachel and Steve were others. But the first time she'd felt intense dis-ease, as she had come to call it, was the woman in the wheelchair in Wolverhampton. She had since detected the same dis-ease or 'non-wellness' with several people, Kelly being the latest whose pain and despair was obvious, and one which she, Sarah, could not block.

In a moment of enlightenment she realised what she needed was the ability to shield herself from the unwanted attacks on her own well-being, otherwise she too would suffer pain and anguish if she were forced to share everyone's illness or anger. Either that or become immune and uncaring which, she mused, would be worse. What was it Beryl said? Sarah asked if everyone's pain would affect her and Beryl had replied:

'No, not everyone and not always. It will depend on the individual and upon your focus. The first thing you need to learn is to close your mind so you can block whenever you need to. That is most imperative or you will suffer greatly. But no, you won't be overwhelmed.'

A wry smile touched Sarah's lips. *Overwhelmed... huh... too late.*

However, Beryl's advice was crucial. She needed to develop this blocking skill. How though was a different question.

A gentle tap on the window broke her reverie, and she jumped. The car door opened and John spoke to her.

'Coffee? Would you like me to bring it out here for you?' A smile curled his lips, but the emotion didn't extend into his eyes.

Sarah laughed. 'No thank you. I'm coming now.'

'Good because I have something to tell you.'

Ten minutes later they stood leaning against the work surface in the kitchen sipping at fresh coffee. Sarah's heart was beating faster at the news John had shared, in part because it was something she'd dreamed of for ages.

'Are you sure about this? I mean, it's a big step.'

'Yes,' John replied without a smile. His only emotion was of decisive commitment.

'I've spoken to the gaffer,' he continued, 'and typed up my formal letter of resignation. I know I should have discussed it with you first but it's in my head, it's what I want to do. He wants to see me which is what I expected. He'll try to talk me out of it. "I don't want to lose two excellent coppers" he said when I called him, but he won't sway my decision, Sarah. It's time to go back home. I want to be with Papa, away from this madness. Yes I know what you're thinking… I'm overreacting, that it all started with you being attacked and ended with Dave being killed, that I'm seeing the worst of everything. But of late I've noticed things getting worse anyway. There seems to be more and more evil around, some really sick people. Yes, I can do my best to get them locked away, but it's a constant battle I'm losing. For every one I arrest there's two more to take their place. Yes, it's a distorted view because there is a lot of good in the world… more perhaps than bad, but I don't want to expose myself to the bad any more. I've had enough. We're going home.'

Sarah set her mug on the counter and stood in front of John. While he was speaking his voice rose in volume and he'd become more animated. Sarah noticed the purple aura around him was still tenuous but what she detected wafted back and forth around his head and shoulders, one moment becoming invisible, the next in plain view. But its hue changed all the time, reflecting John's chaotic spiritual state.

'John. My husband. I wasn't thinking that at all… you're not overreacting. I'd go tomorrow if it was possible. But now we have a plan for the future. And I agree it's the best decision for you. If your job is affecting you in this way perhaps it is time to let others take over. You've done your bit. I sure you can do other things just as well, or even better. Any ideas?'

'Something to do with fungi and flora,' he said without a moment's pause.

Sarah smiled in surprise but on reflection John had always been green fingered, always enjoyed pottering in the garden or growing a few vegetables.

'That's a big change but can you make a career out of it?' Sarah recognised John's conflict.

'Look,' he said. 'Sounds dramatic but if I want to get my family away from this sprawling metropolis, I'd sell my soul. Papa has asked us to come and stay with him. The house is plenty big enough. He gets a family around him again, we get a place to live. He's already told me the house is mine, or rather ours... one day. We can sell up here and bank the cash. It'll give us a nest egg to help us through while we decide what to do, get ourselves set up. I can take formal training at agricultural college and we can either start a small business or... or something. It'll be a challenge but I've always got my police career to fall back on. And well... that's it. Not the smartest of plans but to be honest I don't care.'

Sarah wrapped her arms around John and laid her head against his chest.

'Sweetie. I don't care either. Have you told Claire yet? She needs to be told.'

'Not yet. We can tell her after school.'

Later in the morning Sarah called Rachel and suggested they meet for lunch while John headed off to Birmingham to speak with his boss. They were both eager to set things in motion so between them they made a few calls to local estate agents asking for valuations on their house. Midmorning, John called Hamish and gave him the news. The old man was delighted and asked when he would see them again.

'How about this weekend?' John had suggested. 'After this week we could all do with a break.'

'Och. That'll be fine. I'll see you on Friday.'

Just after midday Sarah entered Costa and found Rachel

sitting by the window.

'Hi sweetie.'

Sarah leaned over and gave Rachel a hug. 'How are you?' Rachel look tired. 'Oh fine,' she answered with a yawn.

'What about work?'

'Well, not so fine.'

'Oh. How's that?'

'Same old same old,' Rachel sighed. 'Sorry. Not being sociable am I? No… it's just boring. I'm getting fed up with it and I'm tired a lot recently, and it's not much fun without my best friend.'

'I'm sorry, Rachel. Really I am. My last official day is the end of the month. I know how much it hurts you.'

Sarah said nothing of her recent news, the decision to move away. That would require careful handling when they were alone.

'Yes it does,' said Rachel, 'and I know it's selfish of me. I'm sorry to lay it on you. It's not fair and like I said before, I think I'm losing you. Who am I going to talk to? Who am I going to have lunch with?'

'You're not losing me,' answered Sarah, but she could see Rachel was struggling, clearly in torment judging from the waves of unhappiness rising and falling around her. Rachel's sorrow was plain to see, it was on the surface, but the intensity lying underneath was visible only to Sarah. Yet at the same time she realised the effect of Rachel's discomfort upon her own well-being appeared to be less, as if Sarah herself had developed a little strength to ward off the ill effects. Sarah asked a question.

'Have you not been sleeping well, if you're tired?'

'No. Lots on my mind I suppose.'

'Like what? Has something happened?' Sarah paused a moment, pondering an idea before adding, 'Have you been in touch with Peter or Sophie?'

'No, nothing has happened, but funny how you always ask me about Peter. I told you before he's a nice guy.'

'And Sophie?'

A gentle smile touched Rachel's mouth.

'Sophie's so sweet, isn't she?' Rachel sighed. 'Yes, to answer your question, I've seen them both. Peter insisted on asking me round to dinner to repay me for babysitting a few weeks ago.'

'And?'

'I had a nice time. He's an excellent cook, and I took a decent bottle of wine and homemade pudding.'

'And will you see him again? Sorry, I'm being nosy aren't I?'

Rachel gazed through the window.

'Yes… maybe… maybe not. I told you he's nice but they all can be.'

Puzzlement furrowed Sarah's brow. Rachel appeared to be confused… uncertain.

They sat and ate lunch but soon after they finished Rachel checked the time and made her excuses, saying she had work to finish. Sarah promised to call her later and with a hug they parted.

Driven by sudden compulsion, Sarah decided to take a quick turn around the town. She needed nothing, had no wish to spend money, but wanted to wander around and use her senses to see what she could detect. She felt nervous, since the last thing she wanted was to become overwhelmed with negative energy, but she had a desire, or perhaps a need to extend her reach and figure out a way to protect herself.

Once out of Costa Coffee, she turned left and strolled through the indoor shopping centre. Hundreds of people were milling around and within moments she sensed a variety of spiritual attacks. She sat on the same seat she and Rachel had sat at many weeks ago and tried to pinpoint those in need. She spotted several straight away. People with weak or dirty auric colours. Some who with plain sight were not well… but others who appeared to harbour fear, anger or anxiety not visible on the surface. A touch of nausea troubled her again, so she tried to block the energies by concentrating on something specific. She pictured Claire in her mind's eye and wondered what the young girl was doing at school. The image of her daughter came with ease, almost as if Sarah were standing next to her. At the same time she perceived the faint touch of something less defined, a comforting touch which calmed her nerves and the scent of Claire's shampooed hair filled her senses. She smiled, wondering if Claire's own percipience detected her mother and the young girl had tried to reach out.

Oh my.

Feeling more settled Sarah stood, but as soon as the image of Claire drifted from her mind the psychic attacks returned. She wasn't able to resist them for long and she couldn't concentrate on Claire forever. Her mood slipped downhill once more, and she wandered back the way she'd come.

As Sarah exited the shopping centre, she turned left and walked along the street as far as the gift shop where she found and bought the beryl stone. Stopping outside the shop and gazing into the window her eyes fell upon an ornament, a commonplace decoration adorning many a household these days. The object was large, though they were available in many sizes. This one was a dark brown and was around twelve inches in diameter. It depicted a group of people carved as effigies forming a circle, their arms entwined and their formless heads peering with sightless eyes across at their companions on the other side. Within their midst was a shallow dish, large enough to hold a tea light candle or something a little taller. The object, known as a 'Circle of Friends', had an immediate and profound effect on Sarah. With single purpose of mind, without deviation or pause, she walked into the shop and purchased it.

Perfect, she mused. *Just perfect.*

Forty-one

John found a quiet spot along the promenade and pulled the car into a parking space facing the sea. There was plenty of choice. It was early evening and most people were indoors getting dinner ready or stoking up fires. Even though the daytime weather had been mild, it was still early in the year and the temperature would fall as the evening wore on bringing only hardened dog walkers out to take an evening stroll along the shore.

John turned off the engine and apart from a few gulls crying at the late sunshine, silence engulfed them. It was Sunday evening and John, Sarah and Claire had been with Hamish for over a week. Claire had missed three days at school but it was now Easter weekend and she would be on holiday for another week. During their stay they'd discussed at length their plans to move to Scotland. Hamish insisted they do as they wish in the house. 'It'll be yours soon enough, you may as well make it your own.' He said this several times until John told him to be quiet.

John chatted to Hamish, laying out his plans to turn his green fingers to something more sustainable instead of only a weekend hobby.

'Well I can sign over the allotment and you can make a

start in the greenhouse,' Hamish said. 'I won't be needing them again. Too much like hard work these days apart from a few salad leaves in the summer.'

Hamish's enthusiasm gave Sarah renewed hope, but she still recalled the old man's words before Christmas, his words of mortality, and she feared for John. John however seemed to have developed a business-like approach to their plans. He'd stated his need to make changes but his lack of emotion concerned Sarah. There was little joy or mirth in anything he did and though his humour was there, it was a dry humour, laconic, and she worried she'd not seen or heard his laughter for far too long. Perhaps it was early days yet. It hadn't been long since David's funeral and John needed time to come to terms with it and understand his guilt was unfounded.

They had, as planned, travelled up to stay with Hamish the day after John handed in his resignation. The interview had gone as John expected… his boss trying every trick to convince him to stay, but John was adamant. He realised, as Sarah did after her attack, that something fundamental had changed, things were different and this change was driving him to move on to an alternate future. Kelly called him that same evening full of apologies and gratitude.

'I'm so sorry for embarrassing you,' she said, and John heard her voice break.

'Try to forget it,' John replied. 'I understand why it happened and I'm sorry for everything… for Dave.'

Kelly was crying as she spoke with vehemence.

'Don't John! Don't apologise. It's not your fault. It couldn't be. I know how close the two of you were.' Kelly sniffed and sighed. 'Y'know what my Nana would say.'

John could guess because he suspected Hamish would say the same.

'She would say "it was his time" and perhaps it'll help to think of it the same way.'

'Kelly?'

'Yes?'

'They're good words y'know, but don't try too hard to be strong. Promise me you'll let loose as much as you want… as much as you can. Time doesn't heal, but it helps.'

'I promise. Are you all right?'

'Yes, I'll be ok. We're off up north tomorrow for a break. What will you do?'

'Already called my parents. I'm getting a few things together and going to stay with them. Leaving on Sunday. I'm moving back home, John. I'll stay a while then come back to empty the house and sell it.'

'I'm happy to hear you say that. It means we'll be able to keep in touch.'

'That would be nice.' Kelly was quiet for a moment. 'John, can I ask you something?'

'Yes?'

'How is Sarah? I think…' Kelly paused again.

'Yes?'

'I'm not sure. I think she did something. Sorry. Sounds crazy.'

John smiled to himself. 'No it doesn't, because she probably did.'

'But what?'

'Who knows? A lot has happened to Sarah since before Christmas but where it's leading her is unclear. What I *do* know is she has a desire to change her life, change it in a way that'll enable her to help others. She always wanted to be of service to people, help those in need. I think she's decided how to do it. Did you feel better after she did… whatever it was?'

'Well yes I did. I was… less distraught… at the time.'

'Good. That's what matters. Anyway, will you call me next week when you're settled at your mom's and we'll all meet up.'

'Ok. I promise. Thanks, John. I love you.'

'And I love you too. Take care.'

And John cleared the call.

He, Sarah, Claire and Mags left for Scotland the day

afterwards and John had the idea he was leaving something behind, something he no longer needed, and the notion puzzled him. He said nothing about it to Sarah though.

But now they sat in the car gazing out across the sands to where a low tide rippled and glittered in the last rays of the sun.

'Do you still want to take a walk, Papa? It'll be chilly outside by now,' John asked.

Hamish cleared his throat with a gentle cough as if he had not the strength for too much effort.

'Och aye. It's a balmy evening. I want to sit and watch the sun go down. A wee stroll will be enough. I'll sit with the lassie while you two take the dog away along the sand.'

'C'mon then,' John said, and climbing out of the car he opened the rear door to give his ageing grandfather a hand.

Dressed up to guard against the chill air, they strolled along the sea front for ten minutes listening to the distant piping of small sea birds and watching the sun lowering closer to the horizon. John figured it would hit the water south of Arran in fifteen minutes. Hamish spoke again and there was tiredness in his voice, a sleepy quality as if he were drifting into slumber.

'Go on you two. I'll sit here with the wee one for a while and catch the last rays.'

Before John had a chance to speak Sarah replied. She wanted to take her husband onto the beach to give Hamish space.

'Ok Papa,' she said. 'We'll take Mags for a sniff of the sand. We won't be long,' and with that she leaned over and gave Hamish a kiss. He grabbed her hand and for long seconds held it with surprising firmness. She held on to him in return but with a tight smile and a dull ache in her chest, finally let go.

'C'mon, sweetie,' she said to John. 'Our dog needs to run.'

'Sure you'll be all right?' John asked of Hamish.

'Aye. Claire will sit with me. Go on son and don't fuss.'

John and Sarah descended the nearest steps onto the sand and then linking arms headed in a direct line to the sea. Mags roamed ahead with her nose brushing the sand, tail wagging as she vacuumed up a multitude of scents undetectable to her mere human companions. The sun dipped for a moment behind a thin curtain of grey cloud but its glory was still visible. It lit the edges of the veil with a sharp red outline and blushed a handful of fluffy clouds riding high above their heads. A gentle sea rippled in muted serenity a hundred yards away, and still the piping of birds echoed across the sand.

'I've lost count of how many times we've walked this beach, and each time it's as wonderful as the last,' said Sarah. 'How are you feeling?'

John was quiet for a moment as he tried to gather and voice his thoughts.

'Troubled,' he mused. 'Raw… lost…' Sarah squeezed his arm, tugging them closer together.

'Go on,' she encouraged.

'I feel terrible about what happened to Dave and responsible for Kelly. How am I ever going to face her again?'

'Kelly knows it wasn't your fault. She doesn't blame you. You must have been close when you were kids. I'm sure she cares for you as much as you do for her.'

'We were. Like the sister I never had.'

They walked on in silence for many minutes, comfortable in each other's company but then John stopped and turned to face Sarah. She could see his eyes moving as his vision roamed about her face. The sun dropped below the thin cloud and the last deep red rays lit them both, giving them a warm and comforting glow. For a moment, John thought the glow lit Sarah's face on both sides, not just the side facing the sunset. His voice was soft and gentle when he spoke.

'Angel. You're so beautiful, so good to me. I'm happy you want to move back here too, y'know, to be with Papa.

It's the best plan we've had for ages, next to having another baby… though I'm not sure we planned that.' John recalled their passion in the cave. 'And,' he added as his gaze took in the scenery, 'I want us to raise our family here. It's my home. Perhaps all my life I've yearned to come back. Perhaps I was waiting for you to come along before I could make the choice. Does that make any sense? Huh… am I talking destiny here?'

Sarah took John's hands in her own, remembering an evening somewhat warmer and many years earlier when he proposed to her along this shoreline, a life-changing proposal but one no less overwhelming as the one they had just made.

'I guess so… and why not?' she replied. 'I've wanted to live here for years, ever since my first visit. But as for destiny, every decision we make in life comes when it's the right time to make that decision, but what makes it the right time I don't know. All I know is I'd follow you to the ends of the earth if you wanted to go there.'

John replied with dry humour and a tired voice. 'Perhaps next year.'

Sarah smiled and opened her mouth to speak again, but a faint gasp escaped her lips. A sudden rush of air ruffled the tips of her hair, or so she thought. In puzzlement she noticed John's hair hadn't moved and realised the breeze seemed to come from the east and not from across the water to the west. The imagined draught carried with it a musical tone, but one she could not hear with her ears. The ethereal music spoke of tranquillity, and she had to suppress the urge to smile in response to its serene quality. She wondered if John sensed it too since a frown creased his forehead as he glanced towards the promenade.

'Papa's up again. He's standing by the wall waving. We'd best head back. It's getting colder.'

Sarah followed John's gaze, but what she saw was different. She indeed saw Claire standing against the concrete wall, but Hamish wasn't on his feet. He still sat as they had left him and as Sarah peered through the dusk she saw a white glow that dimmed even as she perceived it. As it faded she understood its meaning and her heart went out to John. She turned her head towards him.

'Sweetheart, I'm sorry.'

John turned back to his wife and as he did so, his smile faded.

'What do you mean?'

'John, you've no need to worry about Hamish getting cold.'

The sun had now gone, leaving a red glow fading on the horizon and everything on the shore a dimming grey. The frown deepened on John's forehead but within moments sudden realisation appeared in his eyes. He turned back, but could see only his daughter standing by the wall… the only sign that Hamish was near was the top of his hat from where he had settled on the bench.

'Papa,' John whispered. 'No… not yet.'

John broke into a run but Sarah stayed where she stood. With strength given to her that came from both within and from what she thought of as her spiritual family, she calmed herself, putting aside her own grief.

'John,' she called.

Her husband was now twenty yards away stumbling on the dry sand.

'John! Wait!'

As if John realised there was now no need to rush, he came to an abrupt halt facing toward Hamish. Sarah stepped up behind him.

'Darling, it's too late. Papa is with your nana now. He's where he wanted to be. He was very old and very tired.'

John stayed where he was as if unable to move. Ahead of them Claire still stood by the sea wall, waiting for her parents.

Sarah stopped in front of John and took his hands.

'C'mon. We need to be with our daughter. She needs us now.'

John spoke distantly, with a voice that struggled to raise itself above a whisper.

'But... I never said goodbye. It's too soon... too soon.'

Sarah sensed John's grief and his distress tore at her soul, but she drew a deep breath and calmed her spirit.

'John. You said goodbye in so many ways, both of you. Think of all the times you spent alone, even this last week chatting and sharing stories. Sweetheart, every conversation between you has been a hello and a goodbye. Hellos to begin with, bringing each other up to date with recent events or plans for the future. Goodbyes with all the nostalgia, the laughs and the wee drams on cold winter nights. All those stories about fishing and the big one that got away. Papa's prize vegetables and those tales about your nana's excessive Christmas dinners.' Sarah paused long enough to stare deep into her husband's soul. 'Darling, why do you think Hamish wanted us to come home? It wasn't to look after him in his old age. He wouldn't have wanted that. It was to bequeath to you his home and I don't mean just the house and garden. I'm talking about *your* home, your roots, Scotland. He knew you wanted to be here. Just like me, he's seen it in your face more and more each time we've visited since losing your nana. It was his way of getting you back. And it's never a final goodbye. Our parents and grandparents live on inside us, in our hearts and souls, and in our children. John... you said goodbye, sweetheart... a million times and in a million ways.'

John found no words to say but squeezed Sarah's hands and lowered his head. A moment later he lifted his gaze into the west. In the gloom, Sarah could just make out his furrowed brow.

'I think I sensed him you know... the breeze. I think... I think I smelled him pass through me. Sarah... does that sound crazy?'

'No, but how did it make you feel?'

John stared unblinking into Sarah's eyes for long seconds, but could not speak.

'I'm sorry,' she whispered, while the tears on her cheeks reflected the silver glow from lamps on the nearby promenade. 'That was a silly question… but I sensed him too. I felt his… his song.' And without understanding where the words came from or what they meant Sarah frowned too.

'Claire,' John said, and turning they walked side by side back to where their daughter still waited.

When Sarah and John stepped up onto the promenade, they found Claire sitting next to her great grandfather. On the surface she appeared unperturbed.

'He squeezed my hand and said to look after my daddy,' she said. 'He's asleep now.'

Claire stood and wrapped her arms around John.

'I'm sorry, Daddy. I don't think he wanted a fuss.'

'Are you ok, sweetie?' John asked her. He felt Claire nod her head and guessed gentle tears leaked from her eyes. She was a strong child but she was still young.

'We'd better call for an ambulance,' Sarah suggested.

'I'll do it,' replied John, and Sarah knew he wanted to be busy. As an afterthought, he spoke with a voice bereft of emotion, but one full of fatigue. 'I'm so exhausted. I wish we could all sit here till morning.'

He peered at Hamish who sat comfortably, as if he had dozed off. John sighed and turned to gaze upon the last glow from the sun, a narrowing crescent along the horizon. He walked away a few yards and used his mobile phone to call the emergency services though the situation was hardly an emergency.

A few minutes later, he returned to Sarah and Claire who had settled next to Hamish. With an ache in his chest, an ache that threatened to choke him such was its poignancy, he regarded them with love and with confusion. He said nothing to Sarah while they waited for the ambulance to arrive, but just for an instant, he was sure he'd seen a white halo encircling his loved ones, a halo that spoke of utter calm and the deepest serenity.

Forty-two

For the fourth time in as many months, Sarah, John and Claire attended a funeral, the second in Scotland. Such was the popularity of Hamish amongst his neighbours and people he'd worked with that there was little seating room left in the church. With her heart in tatters but emotions kept under control for John's sake, Sarah stayed close to her husband as those friends and colleagues dearest to Hamish sought to retell many a tale to the old man's nearest relative.

In the days after the funeral, Sarah agreed John should stay for a while to sort through immediate formalities. Hamish's will was precise and bequeathed his estate to John as immediate next of kin, but there were documents to read and paperwork to sign. Since Claire needed to be back at school Sarah took the car and drove back home while John would travel by train a few days later.

The parting was hard for them since they'd rarely been separated. Concern for John's well-being nagged at Sarah all the way home as he'd still not shown any emotional release. He'd become withdrawn… internalising his grief, retreating into his cave while he tried to work through everything in his own way.

When Sarah and Claire arrived home they telephoned

John to say goodnight, but he sounded remote as if he were further away than the three hundred mile distance. Sarah figured it was just her own tiredness and reaction to being away from him.

'I had a call,' he said, trying to make conversation. 'A call from Peter… sending his condolences… asking if we're doing ok.'

'That was nice of him. How is he?'

'Not sure how to put it. He didn't want to bother me but I could tell by his voice he had something to ask. He's smitten with Rachel but he's still not making any headway. Seems she's blocked him.' John fell quiet and Sarah guessed he was sipping from a whisky tumbler. 'Sweetheart,' he continued. 'Men don't share their feelings with each other. It's simply the way it is, but Peter said he'd not met anyone who'd got under his skin like Rachel since his wife died. He was thinking about her day and night and he thinks she feels the same. You couldn't help could you? See what she's up to?'

'You mean you're asking me to poke my nose into my best friend's love life?'

'Yup, that's about it.'

'Ok,' and she gave a little laugh for his benefit. 'I'll visit her tomorrow. I've sensed something troubling her for a while but I didn't want to push.' Sarah changed the subject. 'I've had a letter about Beryl's estate. Some legal stuff I have to sign that'll hand ownership over into my name. The letter also says where the land is at last. It lies off the road out of Straiton, which is interesting as it must be near the cave. I need to view the estate so we need to think about how we can arrange a visit. I don't suppose there's any rush so we could wait until half-term when Claire is off school.'

'Sounds like a plan.' John sounded more animated, bordering on enthusiastic. 'Does it say what kind of land it is?'

'They sent me a copy of the deeds but you know what legal jargon is like. It mentions rods and poles which I had to Google to understand. The deeds are about eight pages long and all one sentence so you lose the thread, but I haven't looked too close yet. I imagine whatever is there is pretty run down.'

'Well I expect you're right judging from how old Beryl was. We can have a look over the details when I get back if you like, but half-term sounds fine.'

'Ok. I'll give the solicitor a call and set a date with them. I'll explain the delay. I'm sure they're in no rush.'

Sarah let out a huge yawn, and so after handing the phone over to Claire they each said goodnight and ended the call promising to speak the following day.

That evening after dinner, Sarah sat for a while trying to find John, searching for his touch, the touch of his soul, but she could sense nothing. Perhaps the distance was too great or his energy levels were so low, touching him from afar was impossible. She sighed and wondered once more at the speed in which her gift had grown, though she understood there was still much to learn. What was it Beryl wrote in her rhyme? *Rejoice in the gift, for it will come swift.* It seemed an age since she first read what were once meaningless words but now she understood their significance. Change had happened at a pace she struggled to keep up with, too fast in many ways since she'd had little time to accept the simple fact of it. But then if she'd understood and learnt more several weeks ago, maybe she wouldn't have gone stomping around in Steve's head. This was the reason she was so cautious around Rachel whom she loved as a sister, but the very essence of that love was how she knew she needed to help Rachel. Her friend was so unhappy.

Later on she ran a bath for Claire, and after a short story tucked her up in bed. Downstairs, Sarah called Peter, suggesting a plan she hoped would answer his question concerning Rachel, and with gratitude he agreed to it.

'Thanks for doing this Sarah,' he said. 'I feel embarrassed about asking but I thought we were getting along ok. She won't answer my calls.'

'Peter, I'd do anything for Rachel, or you, because you've done so much for me and John.' Sarah finished the conversation by saying something that sounded strange, even to her, because she was unsure what triggered the thought. 'I think a change is coming. I'm not sure why or what but I feel as if something is about to happen. Either an ending or a beginning... or perhaps both. Remember the plan and I'll see you tomorrow.'

Sarah hung up and called Rachel to say she was back home and asked to see her the following teatime. Rachel agreed.

Leaving Claire with a neighbour, it was around five thirty when Sarah pressed the buzzer for Rachel's apartment. After a short delay an inharmonious electronic squeal assaulted her ears, and she pushed open the security door. Once inside the relative warmth of the vestibule Sarah headed for the staircase. Every floor had three dwellings and Rachel's was on the highest. Sarah climbed the six flights of stairs and headed off along the corridor to number ten. When she arrived at the door she found it ajar and entered, calling Rachel as she did so.

'Hiya!'

There was no answer but Sarah could hear the sound of a kettle boiling and headed for the kitchen. She found Rachel putting teabags into two china mugs and plating up a small selection of biscuits.

'Hi, sweetheart. How are you?' Sarah asked.

'Fine,' Rachel replied with little enthusiasm.

Sarah tried to be light hearted. 'Ah. You know what FINE stands for don't you?' she asked.

Rachel glanced up with a half-smile that didn't touch her eyes and both woman spoke the words in unison.

Sarah laughed but Rachel just sniffed.

'Here,' she said. 'I'll hang your coat up. Go and make yourself comfortable. I'll bring the tea through.'

Sarah handed over her coat and wandered through into

Rachel's living room. She stood for a few moments gazing out of the large window, surveying the scene. It was hardly picturesque as it showed only a sprawling panorama of the suburbs of Wolverhampton but it was elevated and there was plenty of daylight. *Well*, she thought, *some people enjoyed a cityscape.*

She turned away from the window and scanned around Rachel's living room. As a regular visitor Sarah knew its appearance was typical of someone who cared about their personal looks and demeanour, so Rachel kept her apartment with the same attention to order and neatness. However, something was different. Although the room wasn't messy there was an element of untidiness. Discarded magazines were piled on the floor by the sofa. A coffee mug perched on the table without a coaster underneath it and over the back of the sofa lay a coat Rachel must have draped there instead of using the coat stand. To a casual glance these minor things would have gone unnoticed, but Sarah spotted them straight away. She knew her friend almost as well as if they lived together and recognised, as she expected, that something had changed, something was amiss. She'd known ever since before Christmas Rachel was troubled.

A voice from behind made her turn. Rachel entered the room carrying a tray. She kicked the door shut behind her.

'It's nice to see you,' Rachel said. 'How do you feel? How's the bump?'

'Not showing much yet,' replied Sarah giving her tummy a gentle pat. 'But I'm good. How about you?'

'Me?' Rachel paused while she lowered the mugs onto the table and offered the plate to Sarah.

'Mmm. Thanks,' said Sarah and reached for a shortbread finger.

'Well y'know me,' muttered Rachel. 'I just get on with it. What else can you do?'

'Get on with it? And what *it* are you getting on with.'

Sarah settled into an armchair while Rachel collapsed full

length on the sofa.

'Life I suppose,' replied Rachel. 'The things it throws at you.'

'Huh. I know what you mean but what *things* has life been throwing at you?'

'Oh nothing in particular.'

They sat in silence for a while, Rachel staring off into space, Sarah watching her friend. With a heavy sigh, Rachel spoke again.

'How's John doing? What's he up to in Scotland? Is there much to sort out?'

'He's getting there bit by bit,' Sarah replied. 'In his own time and his own way. He's very withdrawn and I suppose that's expected. He blames himself for Dave's death. Thinks he shouldn't have given chase… he should have waited. But only he can resolve that one.'

'And what about Kelly?'

'She's back in Scotland with her parents. Says she's gonna stay there and start over.' Sarah paused and stared at Rachel before speaking again, treading with care. 'Seems like there's a lot of change going on… things out of our control.'

'Hmm. You might be right,' Rachel mumbled, but then livened up a little. 'I'm thinking it's time for a change too. Perhaps a change of job. I mean, look. We've been in the same place for years you and me. You said yourself before Christmas you were all done with it and look what's happened to you since. The changes you've been through. It's made me wonder about my life. And I know it sounds silly but I'm not sure I want to go on working there without you. It's all suddenly changed. Life has changed. I'm tired of the same old same old.' Sarah sat munching her biscuit, letting Rachel do the talking. 'I guess you understand what I mean but apart from the baby, how are things? How is your… gift… your sight? Is it more manageable? How do you feel about Steve? It's been a few weeks since he died.'

'Steve? I know it's not my fault. Steve was damaged a long time ago, but I still feel responsible for giving him a final push. I should have been more careful. But as for my gift I've learnt a new trick. I've discovered how to block out the visions and the voices, at least unless I get a strong message. Y'know, if someone is sending out distress signals?' *Gently, Sarah, gently.*

'How have you managed to do that?'

'By imagining a circle.'

'A circle?' asked Rachel, as she reached for a biscuit.

'You can use anything as a defence as long as it works. The idea is to build a shield of some sort around yourself as protection. It's only a symbol for the mind to use… or maybe it isn't… maybe it's more. Who knows? But you could wrap yourself in a sleeping bag or imagine a pyramid made of pure crystal or a brilliant white light that drowns out any other energy. It's whatever works for you and that one does it for me, most of the time. Like I said, it blocks out random crap… only lets through real distress, powerful feelings and I can't stop those… yet.'

For a moment, Rachel regarded Sarah with weary eyes before swinging her legs off the sofa and rising to her feet. She walked over to the window and lifted her mug to her lips.

'So,' Rachel said changing the subject, forgetting she'd already asked about John. 'You were saying about John?'

'He's not well, Rachel. He's closed himself off, trying to keep a grip on his guilt and grief. But something will let loose soon.'

Sarah finished her biscuit and sipped at her tea. *It's now or never* she thought.

'But I have some other news Rachel. Another reason I came here.'

Rachel would take Sarah's news hard, and it worried her. More than worried because of how close they were. And because she'd sensed a growing anxiety in Rachel, but what reason there was for it she didn't yet know. Rachel sighed again and lowered her head.

Since buying the Circle of Friends Sarah had developed

and enhanced her skill at blocking psychic attacks, she could open or close her spiritual shield at will… for the most part. At this precise moment though it was easy to see with more earthly senses the struggle Rachel was trying to manage, but driven by concern she lowered her shield anyway. What she perceived, what she felt streaming from Rachel in rolling waves of distress was an assault on her own well-being, and she had to use all her strength to calm her own spirit.

'Other news?' Rachel's voice was a whisper, as if speaking as much to herself than to her friend. She placed her mug on the window ledge.

'Rachel. I'm sorry but John and I are setting things in motion to move to Scotland. John wanted to be with his grandfather as much as possible while he was still with us. But now he's gone he wants to get away from here, we both do. We both have a new life to start. He has a backup plan for work and we can get Claire into school before she gets nearer to secondary education. I can get work too and I have ideas about what that may be. He has Hamish's house and I have land left by Beryl.' Sarah paused a moment. 'Rachel? You know I want to move on… how much I've bored you over the years with stories of Scotland. Sweetie… there are thousands of reasons for me to move but only one to keep me here and that's the one breaking my heart.'

'What's that?' Sarah could hear the break in Rachel's voice.

'It's you, Rachel.'

For several seconds silence hung in the room, a silence broken only by the hum of traffic from the nearby ring road and the soughing of the wind as it caressed the fabric of the building with searching fingers.

Rachel spoke with an effort, and as she did so it was obvious to Sarah her suspicions were correct. Rachel was broken-hearted.

'Sarah, I've missed you since the accident. It's almost like you've moved away from me a little each day. Lunch times aren't the same. The evenings seem empty even though I didn't see you often at night. You always go away at Christmas, but even after this Christmas I haven't seen as much of you as usual. I'm missing you Sarah… so much it hurts.'

Rachel turned around and Sarah's throat tightened at the anguish she saw in her friends eyes.

'Oh Rachel. What will you do?' Though wretched herself, Sarah contained her own sorrow for the sake of her friend.

'What will I do? I don't know. Without you I don't know.'

Despite an aching need to walk over and hug Rachel, Sarah kept her distance for the moment. The weak and dirty aura shimmering around Rachel's body had become all too familiar since her sight awakened. This time though there was something new. A bright but tiny pinpoint of white light centred on Rachel's tummy. It took only a moment for Sarah to realise the truth, and though her eyes widened in surprise she kept her emotions under control.

'Rachel? You're right and I'm sorry. I've not seen you much since Christmas with everything that's gone on, but what happened with you and Peter, y'know, on Christmas day? It was a surprise to find out you'd seen him but I feel bad I never asked about it.'

Rachel turned back towards the window before speaking, as if to hide her face. Once again, her words were quiet and forlorn.

'Y'know I go over to see my aunt in Stafford at Christmas. Well this time Peter asked me around for dinner. Half of me wanted to see my aunt as usual because it was Christmas but the other half wanted something different.'

Wanted or needed, Sarah wondered.

'How did it go?'

'Oh it was lovely. His daughter Sophie is so cute and friendly. We got on well and had a whale of a time.'

Rachel stopped and Sarah thought she saw her friends shoulders hitch. Rachel cleared her throat to stop her voice from breaking.

'How did you get on with Peter? Was it just the three of you?' Sarah was searching, trying to tease her friend to let out more.

'Yes it was the three of us.' Rachel sighed before speaking again. 'Sarah, I know what you're trying to get me to say, so yes, I had a nice time. I took a present for Sophie and Peter bought me something too. A pretty necklace in fact. It was awkward because all I took him was a bottle of wine for dinner. It was embarrassing, but he said it wasn't important because he was happy to have me there. We ate dinner, played games with Sophie and watched television. And yes, before you ask, we had sex downstairs after Sophie was in bed.'

Rachel turned around to face Sarah. Tears glistened on her cheeks and to Sarah's confusion there was a look of fear in her friend's eyes. A trapped expression maybe as if she were being forced to decide on something but didn't know how to make the choice.

'Sex?' asked Sarah, convinced it was more.

Rachel's lips quivered and her words were a struggle when she spoke them.

'Yes... well, no. We actually made love, Sarah. I didn't just fuck the guy. He was so tender and gentle. He took his time, thought about what I wanted and I lost control.'

'Control?' A mystified frown furrowed Sarah's brow.

The tears were coming thick and heavy now, coursing down Rachel's cheeks as she whispered, afraid of being overheard, or perhaps of hearing her own voice. 'Sarah. He made me cry... when I came... I lost it and fell apart... I cried like a baby. I couldn't stop and he just held me. He didn't care... I mean he *did* care... he just held me for ages and ages until I stopped. And then he *kept* holding me.

'Sarah, I'm terrified I'm in love with him but I don't know what love is. I've never known what love is. And he's bound to let me down like they all do... men... they turn into shadows and let you down. Sarah... he'll let me down,

I know it. Oh God, Sarah!'

In utter torture at the sight of Rachel's anguish, Sarah's chest ached as she watched her friend's shoulders slump, her hands lifting to cover her eyes. Rachel had always been alive and vibrant, but now she appeared as helpless as a small child, vulnerable, lost. In an instant Sarah stood and crossed the room. She pulled Rachel close and wrapped her arms around her. As the two became one, a picture formed in Sarah's inner eye, a picture of Rachel drowning in a sea of black treacle. Treacle that was not sweet, but sickening, cloying, dragging.

'Rachel. Why should Peter let you down? It's obvious he adores you. And what do you mean men turn into shadows? What men?'

But as the last question passed her lips, Rachel's auric image formed a sudden and complete picture of dis-ease in Sarah's mind. And unbidden and with a rising sense of dread, she recalled the words she'd heard as she hugged Rachel at the dining table several months ago on the day she, Sarah, returned home from hospital:

Where are you hiding you little tart! Get out here now!

Even as the words returned to her, a terrible coldness crept into her chest, an appalling realisation. Steadying her own voice Sarah now repeated those words aloud, readying herself for the reaction, but with percipience knowing she needed to utter them.

'Where are you hiding you little tart?' she whispered. 'Get out here now!'

Locked in Sarah's embrace, Rachel tensed, became rigid, but Sarah spoke again, 'Rachel, you are my sister, if not in blood in every other way. I love you with all my heart, with my soul. What do those words mean, Rachel? What do they mean?'

As Sarah uttered the words Rachel curled tighter into her embrace as if she wanted to disappear.

'No?' Her voice muffled and thick with emotion, Rachel wept against Sarah's chest, tears soaking into Sarah's jumper.

'Rachel. It's not your fault. You aren't to blame, Rachel, you aren't to blame.'

'No, Sarah. Don't... please don't!'

'Rachel, tell me...'

'Sarah... no, please!'

'Sweetheart... say the words... I'm here for you. You'll never understand how much I love you.'

'Sarah... oh God.'

Rachel's knees buckled under the weight of her grief and Sarah lowered her friend to the floor where they folded into each other, staying close as one while Sarah placed a hand onto Rachel's head. To Sarah, her friend's very soul screamed in anguish and pain, burning in a fire of guilt and anger, but Sarah held on and refused to let go as waves of energy streamed from the top of Rachel's head, energy that threatened to numb her own hand. Rachel huddled ever closer and began talking, choking through words she had never before dared utter.

'Sarah... my stepfather raped me... three times... when I was fourteen... and my mother knew. She knew! I couldn't stop him, Sarah... he was drunk every time and... he was too strong. My mother saw him but she was drunk too. Sarah... she knew, and she did nothing... oh God, Sarah... she knew and she didn't stop him... oh please, Sarah... don't leave me... please... don't ever let go.'

Rachel buried her face in Sarah's jumper while her chest hitched and shuddered under the burden of the awful truth she'd revealed. With shock and intense grief of her own, tears ran down Sarah's cheeks but she kept silent, holding one hand against Rachel's head, while with the other she held her friend close for safekeeping. Without conscious thought, and with the hairs prickling on her neck, Sarah sensed the opening of a spiritual pathway... an ethereal channel providing a way for her friend's pain to escape, leaching out the years of anguish and guilt. For long minutes, the two young women sat on the floor sharing the agony and the misery until giving way to exhaustion, Rachel's paroxysm eased. She turned her head to one side but still kept a tight hold on Sarah. After several quiet minutes in which Sarah wondered if Rachel had fallen asleep, her friend summoned the strength to speak again.

'I'm sorry,' she whispered. 'I'm sorry you had to hear. How did you guess? How could you?'

'Rachel. I heard the words when I hugged you a few weeks ago. Whispered but clear. I thought I was still in a coma and it freaked me out.'

'You heard them?'

'Yes somehow… in my head.'

'I suppose being a witch you hear all sorts of stuff.'

Rachel sighed, a long shuddering sigh.

'Not much. Only twice… and only from people I'm close to it seems.'

Sarah kissed the top of Rachel's head and felt her lips tingle. Rachel spoke again. 'It was when I was fourteen. My mother's second husband had been with her for almost two years. He was a piss artist just as she was. God knows how they'd met. My real dad left when I was only two and I don't know why. I don't remember him at all. Nothing at all… except… a hat of some sort.'

Rachel shook in Sarah's arms again while a fresh flow of tears escaped.

'I never liked my stepfather or the way he stared at me,' she continued. 'He always seemed to be around when I got out of the bath or was getting ready for bed. I tried to say something to my mother about it but she told me to shut up. And he'd tried to hug me a few times, but it was horrible… dirty. Then one night they came back home from some pub somewhere and I think they must have been arguing. I was in bed and I buried my head under the pillow so I didn't have to listen to them. But my bedroom door opened. He wasn't even quiet about it. That was when he said… he said those awful words. Oh God, Sarah!'

'Rachel, you're safe, sweetheart. It'll be ok. I'm with you.'

Sarah tried to be soothing but knew her words were useless.

'He yanked the bedclothes off me and pulled me by the ankles. I couldn't stop him. He just… did it… he raped me. He put a hand over my mouth so I couldn't scream. It only took him a few minutes and when he climbed off me I could see my mother out on the landing. I couldn't work out what she was thinking until she turned away. Then I understood that she blamed me. The useless fucking bitch blamed me for being raped! I wanted to get away and tried to talk to her but she wouldn't listen. Three times it happened.

'One day he came for me again but I was ready. I'd packed a small bag with a few things and stole money from his wallet. When he came into my room I hit him hard over the head with a heavy book and ran away. There was an aunt living in Walsall, the one I see at Christmas? I caught a bus over there and never left. She never questioned me. She had one grown-up daughter of her own who'd got married. My aunt never asked, and I never said. Thank God I never got pregnant. Perhaps she guessed, or understood my mother was useless.'

Rachel sat up and with haunted eyes stared at Sarah.

'Sarah. My mother never came to find me. Not once. My dad left me. That bastard of a stepfather only wanted me for one reason. I lived with my aunt from then on. She took care of me but now she's old and she…' Rachel's voice broke again, 'she doesn't remember me any more… doesn't remember anything. I've even lost my aunt. Sarah, the only person I have in this whole world is you and… and I'm terrified of being on my own.'

With desperation Sarah watched her friend's face crumple into a mask of deepest misery. She leaned forward and kissed Rachel on the forehead before pulling her against her chest again, holding her in a protective embrace. It was clear now why Rachel had such a low opinion of men, or a low opinion of herself… why she felt the need to take what she wanted and push them away. She'd been let down her entire life, so why trust anyone? Sarah suspected her mother had been through a succession of boyfriends or husbands who cared little for the daughter. Rachel would have been treated as baggage instead as part of the package. She didn't know why Rachel's father left, but her mother ensured by simple inaction Rachel grew up with little self-worth, carrying a deep sense of blame and guilt. With such violent and violating acts it was no wonder she never entered into a caring relationship since she either expected failure to commit, or thought herself unworthy. *Oh Rachel, you poor, poor girl. To carry this around with you.*

For a long time they stayed as they were, locked in an embrace that held the very essence of everything they meant to each other. The love, the sharing, the sisterhood… family. The slow minutes ticked by while Rachel's outburst of grief and fear diminished and came to an end. But still she held on as if fearing to let go. After an age Sarah heard Rachel sniff before speaking in a husky voice.

'I never had anyone to talk to, y'know, not that it's something you drop into a conversation. I suppose I just wanted it to go away, and perhaps never speaking about it was a way of pretending it never happened. Staying with my aunt helped because she looked after me and cared for me, and over time it all became a blur. I suppose I buried it until I was older and my life started as an adult. God, sometimes it's easier to do nothing.'

'Rachel, you poor baby. How you kept this inside all these years. I'd have gone mad. I can't imagine how you coped. The very thought is horrible.'

'I think I just did,' replied Rachel. 'Go mad that is. I had it all bottled up until you were hurt. And the thought of losing you terrified me and it all came to the surface. It's always the same with bad things, bad memories. You deal with them, put them away but something happens, the demons return and you can't stop them. Not until they've had their way with you again. Why can't the past disappear, why can't it just die?'

Rachel's words reminded Sarah of her conversation with

Beryl and the old lady's reply came into her thoughts:

'Ah Sarah. If not for the past, what would we know of the future? How could we remember and learn? The pain of your loss is natural and will never leave you. However, that pain will also bring you wisdom and knowledge... and will teach you to help others and help you to teach others. Have you not already recognised that you want more for you and your family... that you want to help others?'

'Sweetheart? Some things should never happen. It's only evil people that makes them so. But the past makes the future, shapes it, and a strong person can take the past and shape it as they wish. I like to think fate has a way of helping us on our way, opening the best courses to us if only we can see them. There's no way of making this all go away. But perhaps your life has been on hold waiting for a new path to appear.'

'What's happened to you? This doesn't sound like the Sarah I remember.'

Sarah kissed the top of Rachel's head again. 'Perhaps not,' she said. 'But I'm still here. Just changed a bit. But there's no need to be terrified any more. I won't leave you on your own. Neither will others. There are people who love you, one in particular, but you have to trust him or perhaps trust yourself. You must give yourself the chance of a life... follow the path that's opened, the same path Peter is on. You said yourself you think you may love him. Well give it a chance. And...' Sarah paused for a moment before continuing. 'Rachel. Remember earlier I told you about the circle I imagine, to block out unwanted negativity?'

Rachel nodded.

'Well the object that helps is called a Circle of Friends. You've seen them. You can buy them almost anywhere these days. Four or five characters standing around a candleholder, their hands linked? Well my shield is like that. Imagine a circle of friends with yourself at the centre. The circle makes up the perimeter of your shield. The people who make up the circle are your friends or family. All the love they each have for you, strengthens and is multiplied by that bonding, by their link... strengthened and multiplied Rachel, wrapping you safe and secure within the circle. Nothing bad can come through as long as you believe in your circle. The bigger the circle the greater the strength but even two can form a ring if they hold hands.'

Sarah kissed the top of Rachel's head again.

'Sweetheart, you are in the middle of your own circle. You are the candle that glows there. Though you may not realise it, those making up your circle love you so much. There's me, John and Claire, and of course your aunt. Even though she may not remember you, you can include her as part of your circle because you love her and she loves you. But it doesn't stop there. Waiting to join your circle, if you let them, are Peter and Sophie. They each need you in their own circles and you need them. If you let them join, your circle will protect you, Rachel, it will make you safer.'

Sarah fell silent, letting her words sink in, hoping the notion would take root. Then, in her mind's eye, she saw once more the tiny pinpoint of white light emanating from within Rachel and spoke again, 'And you'll never be alone now you have your own baby to consider. It will be in your circle and you in its.'

Rachel had been still and quiet whilst Sarah shared her idea but at her last words she shifted in Sarah's embrace.

'How could you possibly know that? I've not told a soul. Is this you being witchy again?'

Sarah smiled, and the smile came through into her words, 'Yes. It's me being witchy again. You could say it's in the family. And I saw it inside you... with my mind.'

'But how am I supposed to look after a baby on my own? I don't even have a mother to help me.'

'How do you think?' Sarah said. 'I can think of one person who would love to help you. He is the father after all. He's experienced and I'm sure he'd be more than willing to have more. In fact...' Sarah checked her watch. 'He should be downstairs about now, waiting in his car for me to send him a text.'

Rachel twitched and sat up to face Sarah again.

'Downstairs. But... how? Have you been planning this?'

Sarah smiled and taking hold of Rachel's hands, lifted her to her feet.

'In a manner of words. Rachel, I've known you haven't been yourself for some time. I didn't know the reasons... the terrible truth. I never knew you were pregnant until today. I love you as a sister and Peter loves you too but as a lover. Rachel, Peter losing his wife was tragic and at an early stage in their lives. He lost her when he was still deeply in love with her, when they were just starting out. They didn't separate or divorce or grow apart. Illness ripped them apart. Can you imagine what that must have been like? It would take someone extra special to make a person in that situation feel as if they could move on. He's besotted, and he's worried he'll miss an opportunity for happiness again, and I'm sure he feels he can offer you the same. I asked him to be here around now and wait for me. If he gets a text, he's up here. If he doesn't, he knows the answer and he's gone. It's up to you but I think you've already made the decision.'

An abrupt change came over Rachel. She became animated and energised. Within her mind's eye Sarah watched Rachel rise from the dark and sticky mire, a bleak swamp that was the very essence of misery and despair. She perceived a vision of the future where Rachel stepped with purpose and determination onto the shore, onto a path shining with light and hope.

She spoke with sudden urgency, the old Rachel shining through her already brightening aura.

'But look at the state of me. I must look like a disaster. Make-up's a mess after all this crying!'

'I thought you said he'd made you cry before. Perhaps if you let him upstairs he could make you cry again.'

Sarah smiled at her friend and with delight saw a flush rise within Rachel's cheeks, but the colour of her face wasn't the only shade Sarah noticed. An aura of tranquillity appeared around Rachel's head and shoulders, a mixture of blue's and purples, the colours of love and peace.

'Sarah. Will you text him for me?' pleaded Rachel. 'I doubt if my fingers would work.'

'Of course, and Rachel?' for a moment concern clouded Sarah's eyes. 'If you ever need to talk, call me and I'll come running. I can't make anything go away but I can listen to you, hold you and now… I'll sense you from afar. This isn't something that goes away in five minutes and I'm here to help.'

Rachel flung her arms around Sarah and held her close.

'Why am I so hot?' Rachel asked. 'What have you done to me? And… I'm so exhausted.' Then urgent once more, she pleaded. 'Quick… the text message.'

Sarah smiled again, did as her friend asked and walked to the front door to wait for Peter.

The downstairs call button buzzed and Sarah pressed it without speaking. As she waited to let Peter in, she became aware Rachel hadn't moved, hadn't shot into the bathroom to fix her make-up or wash her face. It seemed she wanted Peter to see her as she was. She gazed over at Sarah who stood in the hallway.

'So all I need to do is to imagine all the people who care about me holding hands, keeping me safe inside their thoughts… inside their hearts.'

Sarah nodded her head and with tears in her eyes, smiled.

'Yes. That's all you need do. No ifs or buts, just think of the circle. I think yours got bigger.'

Hearing a light tap at the front door Sarah turned and opened the way for Peter to enter. She whispered to him.

'Peter. She's very raw at the moment, but she needs you. I think at last she understands how much.'

Peter took Sarah's hands and squeezed them. He found no words to say but drew a deep breath, turned and carried his tall frame into Rachel's living room. For a few seconds Sarah waited by the door listening. She listened to Rachel's voice, once more thick with emotion.

'Peter,' she said. 'I'm sorry I've been an idiot. I'm sorry if I've hurt you but if you'll give me a chance I've got so much to tell you... no please listen. The first thing is... I think... no, I *know* I'm in love with you.'

Sarah smiled and sighed as she glimpsed the two lovers meeting in the middle of the living room in a close, warm and loving embrace, Rachel's head held against Peter's chest.

She turned and left the apartment, letting the door close gently.

Forty-three

'So,' said John as he walked into the kitchen. 'Seems Pete is looking forward to being a dad again. He called and the twenty-week scan went well. How's Rachel getting on?'

A few weeks had passed since Sarah visited Rachel and released her from her madness. Rachel had buried her secret deep for almost twenty years, limiting any hope for lasting happiness, poisoning her life. Sarah was still unsure how it happened, but she understood several events helped open the doors to the guilt and anger her friend had hidden away. First there was the time Sarah spent in hospital which left Rachel exposed and vulnerable... her only friend locked away inside a coma with the possibility she may never wake. Then Rachel met Peter who reached into her soul triggering something unexpected, something that left her wanting, though she feared it. And in the end Sarah helped Rachel see the truth of what she needed, that she was worthy of love and Peter was the one who could give it to her. Over the weeks however Sarah realised she hadn't actually done anything, not in any practical sense. All she had done was to comfort her friend, say a few words and act as a spiritual conduit... a channel that drained the pent up negative energy marring Rachel's life and threatened to ruin it forever. *Perhaps that's it*, she mused, *all I'm doing is opening a passageway, a path that allows the traveller to see and choose a different journey.*

But now life was taking a new course. John, Sarah and Claire were altering their own journey, readying themselves for a change that would take them north, back to John's homeland and to the place that, after meeting Beryl, Sarah realised was also her own native country.

She answered John's query concerning Rachel. 'How's she doing? A lot like the old Rachel, I'm glad to say, but changed too. She has a purpose which has given her extra energy.' Sarah fell quiet for a moment, reflecting on her relationship with her friend. 'Y'know… you get to know a person, get used to how they are but never really know what's going on under the surface… how much of a shield people maintain, what secrets lie hidden. How they hurt and never show it.'

John nodded his agreement but stayed silent.

They sat at the table making a list of what to pack, what to discard and what to put into storage. It was a few days before the spring half-term holiday and they were in the last stages of packing ready for the move to Ayr. Their own house was still unsold, but they had no need for the finances to fund a house in Scotland. Thanks to Hamish, they already had a ready-made home.

'I'll maybe tell you the full tale one day,' continued Sarah, 'but Rachel had a horrific experience that made her distrust men… and distrust herself I suppose. She needed a helping hand to realise the truth. Realise how beautiful she is and worthy. I may have helped a bit.'

'A bit? I think you helped a lot from what Pete has told me. He's like a kid in a sweet shop, like all his Christmases have come at once.'

Sarah smiled at her husband. His delight for Peter and Rachel was genuine, but he was hardly overflowing with joy. His eyes still spoke of a grief unleashed.

John had everything arranged for their move, leaving

nothing to chance, taking the tiniest detail into consideration. He was almost obsessive and Sarah figured it was his way of being in control. And yet she knew he wasn't. At odd times she'd seen a flicker of release in his eyes but each time a barrier slipped back into place. One day soon she knew the barrier would fail and his healing would begin, but she also knew she couldn't force it.

Later that week, early on Saturday morning and at the start of the school holiday, they left behind their old life and headed north. Neither John nor Sarah were too concerned about Claire missing the last half-term at school.

With mixed feelings they drove the three hundred miles and John was quiet for most of the way. But during the journey, as they crossed the border, Claire voiced their thoughts.

'I'm going to miss Papa when we get there. The house was always nice and cosy and his whiskers always tickled.'

Sarah gazed through the window and wept silent tears, but when John reached over with a comforting touch, she gripped his hand.

Despite Claire's words and their tiredness from the long journey they were surprised at how welcoming the house was when they opened the front door. They unloaded their bags and carried them into the hallway, and as if driven by unspoken word wandered into the living room. It was mid-afternoon and a bright sun lit up the garden. The grass needed a trim but everything was bright and alive.

John broke the silence.

'I can feel...' he paused and swallowed hard. 'I can feel him... all around... in this room... clattering about in the kitchen. And I can see him down in the greenhouse.'

He turned towards Sarah and Claire and found they were both smiling and realised he was smiling too. Sarah watched with interest as he reached up to brush a hand across his forehead and the purple glow around his head and shoulders spread a little wider. She had to fight the urge to grin as she understood a change was close. Something was going to happen soon though she was unsure what that something may be.

'C'mon you two,' she said. 'Let's get unpacked and we need to go shopping otherwise it'll be cheese and crackers for dinner!'

The following day dawned bright and breezy and, after a walk on the beach to give Mags a well-deserved run, Sarah sent John into the garden while she and Claire carried on unpacking boxes and arranging the kitchen. After a while they settled into the living room while John pottered about outside mowing the lawn and checking on the greenhouse.

As she'd entered the last three months of her pregnancy Sarah often became tired during the afternoons, so she settled into a chair while Claire watched a film. Apart from the murmur from the television everything was quiet and Sarah reflected on the last six months of their lives. How could everything change so fast? Talk about a roller coaster ride. How can a person, let alone a family, cope with such dramatic and tragic events? And yet, despite turmoil and anger or rejection along the way, she felt more at peace than at any other time in her life. The only concern left was for her husband. She ached to hear him laugh again, but she feared to push, heeding Beryl's warning. He needed to ask for help unless help came from elsewhere.

But for now though she looked forward to tomorrow. She'd agreed with Beryl's solicitor to view the cottage and lands at around midday. After the viewing she would decide what to do. She expected, as John said, that due to Beryl's age the property may have lain empty and unused for a while and be in a state of disrepair. If so she could always sell.

As the minutes ticked by sleep crept up from her toes, but something disturbed her thoughts and pulled her awake again. The room lay silent, and she realised Claire had stopped the film. The young girl was on her feet, staring across the room at her mother. Sarah stared back and for several minutes they extended their thoughts towards John. Driven by a familiar but half-forgotten influence detected by her percipience, Sarah shifted her head and peered through the patio doors. Claire moved across to Sarah's armchair where she too peered into the garden.

Halfway along the garden path and holding something in his hands John stood immobile, head up, transfixed by something. Sarah followed his line of sight searching for what had caught his attention. After a few moments both Sarah and Claire located the source of his interest. Perched atop the bird table only a few feet away from where John waited stood a robin. On tiny feet it stood unmoving, as still as if it were made of stone, communing, it seemed, in thought. For many moments they remained motionless, joined in spirit until with a single twitter of farewell the little bird lifted its wings and disappeared over John's head and out towards the west, towards the sea.

Moments later John entered the house and made his way through into the living room. On the surface, and to an outsider, he appeared much the same as over the past weeks, but with her growing spiritual senses Sarah saw that his face shone with a light she had not seen for a long time, a light that made her eyes widen and her heart beat a little faster.

'Look!' he said holding out his hands, and there was excitement in his voice.

John was holding a seed tray. Vivid green shoots covered its surface, many dozens and each at least three inches long. Sarah smiled up at him.

'Oh wow. That's wonderful. But when did you plant them?' she asked in puzzlement.

'I didn't. Papa must have planted them before Easter… before we came to visit that last time. They're sweet pea seeds he took from his allotment last year. You know how Nana used to love their smell, how he always grew some for her? He must have planted them just before… just before…'

John's voice faltered and an involuntary hitch shuddered

through his chest.

'But how have they survived?' asked Sarah, and John continued, measuring his breathing to get his words out.

'Papa used a self-watering system in his greenhouse... in case he was away or couldn't get down there every day.' A single tear spilled out and ran down John's cheek... dripped from his chin. 'Sarah, don't you see? It's a cycle, a never ending cycle. He grew the flowers for Nana and kept growing them every year from seeds he picked from the previous year even after she was gone. He picked these seeds from those he grew last year and planted them this year. It just goes on and on. Oh God.'

John's chest hitched again.

'Sarah, he left a note in the greenhouse with them as if he knew they'd survive... that they would grow. And there's something else. Remember on the beach the day you asked me how I felt when I sensed him? I think... I think whole... greater than before, as if something had joined me... or someone.'

With trembling hands, John handed the note to Sarah and with a lump in her throat, seeing how big this revelation was for her husband, she read what must have been Hamish's last written words.

> *Here we go son. These are for you, to continue growing on and on for Sarah as I did for your nana. It's just a little thing really but a ritual we always kept. See if you can beat my record, which is 44 years without having to buy new seed.*
>
> *I know you'll have a hard time to start with after I've gone, but like these seedlings, everything in this world continues, especially the love we have*

between us.

Take care of your family, and remember, this isn't goodbye it's just goodnight, for dawn will come again.

Deeply moved, Sarah regarded the tears in John's eyes, blessed tears. She opened her mouth to speak, but a sudden gasp escaped her mouth and after a few seconds and through a smile she said, 'John, sweetheart, put your hand here. I think your son is calling.'

John reached towards his wife, and she took hold of his hand and placed it on her tummy. As in an act of reverence John sank to his knees. For quiet seconds nothing happened but then a light but strong kick pushed against his hand as his new child stretched out a limb. Watching John's face Sarah saw the wall which had imprisoned him for weeks break apart and collapse, the wall that caged his soul and spirit and threatened to destroy what joy he had in life. His lips quivered and his chest heaved once more and then with full force his grief escaped, scouring his soul with its cleansing release. For many minutes John knelt before her with his head on her lap, his ragged and violent tears soaking into her clothing as his grief for the loss of both David and his grandfather made its escape and found a new place to live.

With utmost relief Sarah sat with a hand resting on his head, and as she did so a cold and dreadful energy surged through her fingers and she took it to mean something had left John, something lifeless and unneeded. But then she perceived another puzzling sensation she struggled to understand. Her eyes unfocussed and her inner sight drifted off out of the room. Moved by curiosity she tried to lift her hand from John's head, but found it difficult to do so as if some physical attraction, some elemental glue held it in place. Only with extreme effort was she able to move her hand, and as her focus returned to the room she felt as if she had joined with John in a way metaphysical or supernatural. Whatever it meant the moment left her confused, but also left her with an inexplicable and all-consuming joy.

Forty-four

It was at half past eleven on Monday morning when Sarah, John and Claire headed off, armed with a map and instructions describing how to get to the cottage. It was a simple enough route and one that took them past the layby where they had parked and taken a stroll into a hidden cave on Christmas day of the previous year. Sarah felt a lifetime had passed since she and John found the cave and shared a passion so intense she doubted if she'd ever forget it. Since that day Sarah believed an unseen influence had driven their desire, an outside force so irresistible and urgent that they were powerless within its grasp. The result was the life growing inside Sarah, one that grew stronger and larger day by day. The coincidental conception of their new baby and the death of Beryl mystified Sarah, making her question the very fundamental beliefs about life and what may lay beyond, the hidden mysteries. But on a different level, and as her belief system shifted, she accepted the mystery, accepted every aspect of it... as Beryl suggested, with faith.

They'd not been back to the cave since circumstance or timeliness had prevented it. Or perhaps, Sarah pondered, because they had no need to visit. But as they drove past the layby the moment wasn't lost on John and he reached over and held her hand.

Sarah checked the written instructions and spoke to John. 'Ok. It's the next turning on the left, only a short way now,' and as she spoke they spotted a roadway to the left heading upwards and onto the hillside.

Sarah's heart speeded up as John turned and drove uphill along a well maintained track for half a mile, a track that looped back almost parallel to the road they had just left. Whatever lay ahead was more or less above the cave, upon the hills that marched eastwards. A group of trees appeared as they rounded a bend and the road sloped downward a little before ramping up again. Ahead, a dry stone wall ran from left to right with a large opening allowing entry to the property. Moments later Sarah spotted several farm buildings clustered around a central yard. A car stood on an area of neat gravel at the front of a large cottage and John headed through the gateway towards it.

Sarah noticed on either side of the driveway opening and adjoining the stone wall a fence encircled the property, either to keep out roaming deer or to contain farm animals. The stand of trees they'd seen before they entered the grounds stood over to the left side of the yard and John recognised them as indigenous species… rowan, birch, alder and the tall Scots pine. They appeared to have stood for many a year and John knew landowners often planted wind breaks to protect buildings from the worst of prevailing gales.

The cottage at the centre of the yard was of a design typical to Scotland. A two up two down crofting cottage, but large with modern dormer windows jutting out from the roof and a stone built porch on the front. To the right-hand side lay a large barn and as John drove closer he glimpsed a sizable greenhouse beyond it. To the left of the main cottage lay a garden backed by tall shrubs, a typical cottage garden full of colourful flowers and herbs.

Painted white and spotless, the cottage itself and indeed every other building appeared to be well maintained and in a good state of repair... every building except one.

Further to the left, on the other side of the garden opposite the main property, and sheltered by the tall trees, stood the remains of a second cottage, smaller than the main house. At each end stood a chimney while between them half tumbled stone walls remained with openings that at one time would have housed window frames and doors.

John parked up alongside the car in front of the main house and Sarah climbed out, her attention on the ruined cottage.

'I think you were right,' Sarah said. 'I guess this is the one. We've seen a lot of places like this up here. An old steading sold off one building at a time and this is the last one. Beryl must have kept ownership of it for some reason. It must have been this way for over a hundred years. Wonder why she didn't sell it herself?'

John and Claire joined her as she walked over to the derelict cottage but they halted and stood together in mute surprise as the inside came into view.

John spoke first. 'This is weird.'

Sarah was silent, or at least she spoke no words. Inside though her soul was full of chatter as she received a virtual bombardment of spiritual conversation. There was so much energy coming from this place she had to close her circle to dim its psychic assault. However, the energy she detected brought no discomfort, no nausea. Instead it conveyed to her an insight into the celebration of life... uplifting and joyful. She did detect the occasional discord within the song, a melody that spoke of tragedy, but these subtle tones only confirmed what she now believed... all life was one huge harmonious symphony... made up of themes of light and dark, joy and heartache. The experience was mildly uncomfortable because of its intensity, but Sarah noticed John appeared fidgety as if he too felt restless.

'Come on, we can look at this later,' he said, glancing over his shoulder. 'The agent is here.'

Sarah had to exert an enormous effort to pull herself

away from the ruins of the cottage. But it was Claire who voiced the question that had gone unasked.

'Mommy, why's there a garden in here?'

Sarah answered in a quiet voice, her thoughts elsewhere. 'I'm not sure sweetie but perhaps we can find out.'

She lingered a moment longer but not before taking in the whole scene.

Within the walls of the ruined cottage the ground was well-tended. So many ruined crofting cottages across Scotland simply filled up with weeds, heather or shrubs as the years had their way with them. Not so with this one. The building appeared well maintained and the fabric of the chimneys secured with capped pots to keep rain out of the stonework. A path led inside from the main entrance and turned both right and left to allow a gardener to tend to the flowers and shrubs. At the farthest end of each path lay a wooden bench so the carer could relax within this walled place of solace. A myriad of flowering plants and herbs filled the space, many of them perennials mingled with other annual self-setters that would return each year. There were cottage garden varieties such as foxglove and phlox, geranium and marguerite. There was campanula and marigold, with the more cultivated varieties of delphinium and aster, and dotted amongst the flowering herbaceous plants stood rose and holly and the Scottish thistle, interspersed with lavender, sage and other perennial herbs. The object however which caught Sarah's attention more than the lush garden stood not to left or right, but directly opposite the entrance. Close to the back wall, and rising out of a carpet of forget-me-nots now run to seed, a head stone stood tall… a marker in the shape of a Celtic cross. The stone was weathered and ravaged from years of facing the harsh Scottish winters, and Sarah could see no sign of letters carved into its pitted surface. Laying at is feet sat a slab of granite with what seemed to be a plaque fixed at its centre. Sarah spotted sweet peas tumbling over the stone and it took a moment before the sight of them triggered a recent memory, and she lifted a hand to her mouth and gasped in surprise.

'Sweetie, are you coming?' called John, as he walked over to the waiting man.

'On my way,' Sarah called, but found she had walked inside the cottage and over to where the plaque lay. All around every sound had ceased. The trees that stood tall above her head stilled their rustling harmony as the light breeze fell. No birdsong reached her ears... none for several moments until a single familiar sound interrupted the silence.

Raising her eyes she smiled at a pair of robins that had alighted on the stone walls above the cross. She sensed rather than saw Claire walk up and halt beside her, and on a deep ethereal plane felt her daughter join with her.

'Hello,' they said to the birds, and in answer a chatter of melodious song greeted them. With a soul full of joy and excitement Sarah turned her attention back to the plaque and read the inscription.

For Rose.
For ever.
Mama, the search will never end.

Amber, 1701 to 1802

'Amber?... Rose?' Sarah muttered to Claire, and frowned as if the names held a hidden meaning.

Forty-five

Sarah stood at the kitchen sink gazing through the window into the garden. Near to the derelict cottage Claire was having a hard time filling up bird feeders in a gale which blew half of the seed to the ground. The tall stand of trees that sheltered the cottage swayed back and forth, playing out their own natural rhythm while the sound of rustling leaves carried a sense of tranquillity into the house. The autumn solstice was upon them, and the pale sun rode in a sky washed out by a thin blanket of high cloud. Each day the shadows lengthened and Sarah felt in her heart the approaching autumn.

As she watched her daughter struggle with her task Sarah smiled because Claire was not alone. A familiar scene played out. Around Claire's feet were a dozen or more small birds, pecking with eagerness at the scattered seed, or waiting nearby to feast from the hanging feeders. Sarah shook her head and wondered again how they had come to this. Many months ago she had spoken to Rachel about the before and after… her life before the attack and her life afterwards. Thinking back she never would have imagined the after could be so different. It was hard to imagine a year ago she, Sarah, was content with her life and all it had taken was an attack by a lost or damaged soul to alter it, an event that awakened a gift and changed Sarah's life and those of her loved ones.

While viewing the cottage for the first time in early summer, the solicitor's representative surprised and delighted Sarah by confirming she owned the whole estate... the cottages, outbuildings and ten acres of land. In amazement Sarah discovered Beryl had managed a business from the cottage for many years, a small but successful cottage industry selling herbaceous plants and herbs. This wouldn't have been enough to make a living, enough for the upkeep of the place if not for the fact that she owned the estate outright since it had been in her family for generations. To boost her income Beryl used her other gifts, offering an assortment of therapeutic treatments for those in need, or offering weekend healing retreats in a perfect setting.

The cottage had five bedrooms and three reception rooms besides the kitchen and dining room. The large barn had six rooms set out as treatment or relaxation rooms with a central lounge and communal dining. Everything within the estate was perfect, but the icing on the cake for John was the ten acres of land he could use and develop to follow in Hamish's footsteps.

The house in Penkridge sold a few weeks after they had moved to Scotland and they had a comfortable life to begin with, though it wasn't long before Sarah said to John, 'We can't live off the scenery. I need to make my way in the world and I think I know how. I'll carry on with Beryl's work, though I need to become qualified so I can practice legitimately... and I know just the person to help with the business promotion... the Internet stuff.'

'Oh you mean your geeky brother! I doubt if he'd refuse.'

'He wouldn't dare,' laughed Sarah, 'because if he did I'd put a spell on him!'

But despite the fairy tale ending, the life changing events

which brought them to their future via joy and tragedy, discovery and loss, Sarah still felt unsettled. When she discussed her thoughts with John though, unsettled wasn't the word she used. Unfinished was nearer the mark.

The ruined cottage, the verdant garden laid out within its walls, and the words on the plaque puzzled her, but it wasn't until they had been living at the cottage for almost a month and August was running towards September she learned something of the truth.

John didn't want to sell Hamish's house, wanted to keep it in the family, but they moved out and into the cottage. Not long after they settled in Sarah found an assortment of sealed boxes in a room in the converted barn. Each box carried a label, and she realised the boxes contained the possessions, books and a few pictures Beryl had kept with her in the nursing home. She assumed Beryl's solicitor had made arrangements to deliver them. Inside one box was an assortment of papers and journals. With time on her hands she'd read through them and discovered legal papers concerning the property... communication between Beryl and her legal representative. The letters prompted Sarah to speak to the solicitor. She'd found out the ten acre estate had been in the family since the middle 1700s, signed over to the family by an ancestor of the current firm of solicitors. Written into the agreement was a binding covenant stating that should the property be unoccupied for over ninety days, arrangements were in place to ensure it was maintained until such times as agreed by both parties. This meant the house wouldn't fall prey to the ravages of time if it were unoccupied. For example, and in Beryl's case, a family member becoming too old to be independent with no known heir.

'Seventeen hundreds?' Sarah said to John with surprise. 'That fits in with the dates on the plaque outside. So whoever Amber and Rose were, they may have been the first owners.'

'Makes sense. So if the land has been in your family

since, Amber and Rose must be your ancestors. Beryl was one hundred and seven, and this Amber lived for, what, one hundred and one years? Pretty impressive for the era.'

'But I'm wondering why the firm of solicitors handed over the land and why the memorial?' replied Sarah.

'Well, sweetie, keep digging. You never know what you might find if you keep at it.'

But now as she gazed into the garden, watching Claire and her avian menagerie, her thoughts flew away to John, her partner in all things, her friend and husband. As soon as her thoughts settled on his image she sensed a presence and turned away from the window. John stood in the doorway, his hands behind his back and a smile upon his face.

'Oh, hello my husband! And what are you smiling at?'

'You. I was just thinking you shine like the brightest of stars.'

'Why thank you, kind sir. That's very poetic. What brought that on?' Sarah smiled back but a frown creased her brow as she realised something was different, something had changed. In an instant within her mind's eye and with her gifted sight it became obvious. Ever since she'd returned home from hospital nine months ago and first perceived the aura surrounding her husband, the violet hue that spoke to her of peace and intuition, tranquillity and understanding, had been present. Only the tragic event of David's death had robbed him of it… until he rediscovered the joy in life. But to her surprise the colour now encircling John's head and shoulders was a very pure white. The change was so dramatic her mouth opened and a gasp escaped her lips.

'John. What is it? What's happened.'

'Well sweetheart. You shine like a star. In fact I'm sure if I saw that brightness with my eyes, it would blind me.'

Sarah frowned still further.

'With your eyes? What do you mean…?' She stopped in mid-sentence as the obvious occurred to her. She moved away from the sink and closed the gap between herself and John, standing in front of him, eyes burning with questions.

'With your eyes?' she repeated. 'Do you mean you can see my aura?'

'Yes,' he said. 'Yes I can.'

'But… but how, when, for how long?'

John's smile faded but with contemplation written across his face he answered. 'A while now, a few months. Is this what it's like for you, these different colours.'

'Yes but… months? John, why didn't you say something?'

'I didn't want it… tried to deny it. I'd seen the effect it had on you and I tried to ignore it. The thought of sensing everyone's pain was terrifying. I suppose I tried to blot it out.'

'But when did it start?' Sarah was eager for the truth, full of excitement.

'Start?' John paused, and a shadow crossed his face, momentarily dimming the light.

'The day Dave died.'

Sarah reached out and held John's hands.

He continued, 'You never told me about the wine glass did you?'

Sarah frowned. 'The wine glass?'

'Yes. The one you dropped on the kitchen floor.'

'Oh *that* one. Well no. It was only a glass but after what happened it wasn't important. But how…?'

'I saw it happen.'

Sarah's puzzlement deepened as John related his story.

'When Raoul pointed the gun at me I saw a tiny white light. It seemed to grow and right in the middle of it I saw you at the kitchen sink back in Penkridge. I saw you stop and look up, as if you could see me. The glass fell, and you covered your mouth. I spoke to you and I heard you reply.'

With mixed emotions, tears started in Sarah's eyes. 'Yes,' she replied. 'I saw you too.'

John continued. 'The next time was the day Papa passed on. When I turned and looked back at Claire I saw a bright light next to her, a light that faded as I watched. Of course it seemed to be Papa because that's what I expected to see. But there was this white glow around him… until it disappeared. Sarah, I tried to deny all of it but as the weeks rolled on it kept happening. I kept seeing colour after colour. Some bright and peaceful, just like you described. Others dirty or weak. Those were the ones I tried to blot out.'

'You need a shield of some sort, something you can call up to block out the bad energy.'

'Yes I know,' John said, and a smile returned to his lips, brightening his face once more. 'Because you told me.'

'Ok clever clogs. I'm glad you were listening. So what is your shield?'

'I'm looking at it.'

'What?'

'It's you, sweetheart.'

'Me?' Sarah frowned again but her heart ached with the intensity of her love.

'Yes, you. I said you're shining like a star. All I need to do is to think of you and your energy drowns anything out, leaving me safe and sound.'

Sarah melted into John's arms and hugged him with every fibre of her soul. Sealed within the joy of the moment Sarah came to a decision and took a deep breath. The time was right, she thought… the time to confess. With eyes full of chagrin she spoke.

'Sweetheart… I knew Papa was ill… that he was dying. He told me at Christmas… let me decide whether to tell you or not. But I didn't know what to do. I thought I ought to tell you, but I didn't want to affect the way the two of you were with each other… didn't want to spoil anything… didn't want you both to be awkward. I'm sorry.'

'Hush,' John replied with a soothing smile and kissed Sarah's forehead. 'Do you think I hadn't guessed?'

Sarah's puzzled expression only broadened John's smile. 'Guessed?' she asked.

'That you knew.'

'But how... when?'

John's smile faded once more, but he showed no hint of sadness. 'It would have been the day he died... or rather that night, when we'd gone back to the house after being at the hospital. Do you remember? We got home late, and we went on autopilot... the strange half-world we've been in before... not knowing what to do when there isn't really anything to do. Trying to find a place to be in... when the truth hasn't quite hit home and nothing seems real. You and I tucked Claire up in bed and we both had a wee dram. In fact we had several. I remember how strong you'd been down on the beach and all evening, and I figured to start with you were just being strong for my sake. But I puzzled as to how calm you were and I realised you were expecting it.'

'But you never said.'

'No... I wasn't in a good place. I needed to work it all out in my head, and afterwards I realised if my guess was correct you'd have had your reasons to stay quiet.' John paused long enough to kiss Sarah again. 'And, it wouldn't have made any difference if I *had* asked you about knowing. By then I'd begun to see inside you, feel what you were feeling, sensing your mood or your intentions. Whatever your reasoning, I respected and accepted it.'

They were silent for a while until John asked a question.

'How has this happened? How is all of this possible? It's just... well... incredible.'

With John's arms around her, Sarah muttered soft words. 'Remember what Beryl said? It all began with a major trauma or disaster, a tragedy of some sort. The same must have happened to you. With what happened to Dave and losing Papa and worrying about me. It must have triggered in you too.'

'But why a tragedy and why me?'

Sarah leaned back and smiled again at the bright glow radiating outwards from John's head. 'I think because that's the time when everyone needs a hand. We all have moments when things happen to us that are so overwhelming we're in danger of drowning, of losing ourselves. That's the point at which we most need help. People say the same about God. He's with you when you most need him. Well neither of us believes in God but we believe godliness is within us all and within our loved ones, living or otherwise. So when we need most support, it comes both from within and outside of us. It… awakens.'

John sighed. 'Makes sense.'

'On the other hand,' Sarah continued, 'we don't need to understand it do we?'

'No,' and a smile touched his lips. 'We don't. It just works. Why should it need explaining?'

'Yes. Something else I learned from Beryl. There is no why or how or what. There just is.' A question occurred to Sarah, and she spoke again. 'Hang on though. You said you tried to deny it… the gift, didn't want it. So what made you change your mind?'

John smiled again. 'A while back I suppose but this morning confirmed it, after I went rummaging around in Papa's stuff.'

'Papa's stuff?'

'Yes. I'd been up in his loft back at the house. Amongst the clutter up there I found two sealed boxes that seemed important so I brought them back here for safekeeping. I've been going through them. I found the usual legal stuff like deeds to the house, original marriage certificate, certificates of birth and baptism for both Papa and Nana.'

'Oh wow. Did you find anything else interesting?'

'You could say that… or at least Claire did.'

'And?'

John and Sarah stood in silence for a moment staring at each other, peering deep into each other's souls. Claire's familiar and care free giggling drifted in through the open door from out in the garden, but everything else was quiet. Even the wind seemed to have dropped, with only the faintest of rustling from behind the old cottage.

John continued. 'Sweetheart, Claire was reading Beryl's papers, y'know, browsing through those boxes you opened. She found this and told me to give it to you when we were together. That kid frightens me sometimes how adult she is. I figured that if she has accepted the truth of everything we have so should I. Anyway, I promised so here it is. I've not looked at it.'

John held up a long tube made of thick card, the kind used to send delicate papers through the post. He handed the tube to Sarah. With sudden excitement and a sense of expectation, Sarah flipped off the lid and teased out the contents... a roll of thick paper that felt more like parchment than modern paper. Laying it on the kitchen table she unfurled it with delicate care. John handed her heavy mugs to weigh down the corners and between them they peered at the spidery writing scattered across its surface. At first glance it appeared ancient, and in various handwritten styles displayed a family tree.

Near the bottom of the page she found Rose, her mother, and Jade, her grandmother. Tracing her finger up the page she saw Beryl and Beryl's sister Amber side by side, with a dotted line between Jade and Beryl, perhaps to show the true bloodline. Sarah now knew that Beryl was her real great grandmother and not Amber as her own mother told her.

Above Beryl and Amber was Celeste, their mother, with their father's name Ewan next to it. Tiny script noted Ewan's line of work as a crofter, though Sarah knew from Beryl's story he'd tried to move up the social ladder.

Above Celeste the line continued from daughter to mother with dates of birth and death recorded, along with the husband's name and chosen line of work. Every husband, Sarah noted, worked the land either in woodcraft, stonemasonry or animal husbandry.

The dates went farther and farther back in time until Sarah's eyes rested on the first entries. Here she found the name Amber and her mother, Rose. Amber's dates matched those etched onto the plaque inside the old cottage, recorded as 1701–1802, but her mother Rose appeared to have lived a short life. Rose's dates were 1684–1710.

Underneath Rose's name and alongside Amber's was another name. A boy's name. Hamish, with a single date of 1704 that Sarah guessed was his date of birth. It appeared Rose died when Amber was only nine years old, but there was no record of Hamish other than his birthdate.

'Wow!' Sarah exclaimed. 'This is incredible. A whole history of my family. I never imagined anything like this. Now I think I understand how the plaque in the cottage came to be. Why, is a different matter though? It looks as if there was a brother, but Rose died at a young age, younger than me. She was only around twenty-six. How sad. According to these dates all my other ancestors lived a long time. I wonder what happened to her?'

'That's something we may never know unless there's more stuff hidden away amongst Beryl's papers.'

'Maybe. I'll have to take a proper look. I'll have plenty of time when our new baby arrives. But this all started because you said you'd been going through papers from Papa's house. Did you find anything there?'

'Well not me, but again Claire did, and she gave me the same instruction… to open this when we were together,' John held up a leather bound folder. 'Again I've no idea what's inside but I guess it's something similar.'

John handed the folder to Sarah. Inside she found a similar paper to the one that lay on the table, though this one was folded flat.

She took the document and opened it with trembling fingers. John leaned in close, and starting near the bottom with Craig, his father, and his mother Muireall, he worked his way up through the generations. There was Hamish and Kathryn, John's nana, but the only date for Hamish was his birth date. It would be up to John to fill in the year of his death.

John's great grandfather Robert was next above Hamish,

with his great grandmother Morag alongside. Once again, a note recorded each spouse's line of work with dates of births and deaths. As John worked his way up the tree Sarah's sense of expectation increased, and she found she was holding her breath. She could no longer hear Claire's laughter outside but sensed her daughter was standing in the kitchen doorway, waiting in silence.

When John reached the top he found the name Hamish, with the dates 1704–1794 written next to it. The first entry, in large lettering, showed the name Rose, 1684–1710, and underneath it alongside Hamish's name was Amber, 1701. There was no recorded date of Amber's death.

'But… oh my God,' John whispered. 'I don't believe it.'

With the hairs on her neck tingling with astonishment, Sarah felt the floor tilting beneath her and she swayed to one side. In an instant, John grabbed her and with a firm but gentle grip held her upright. She turned towards him, seeing the shock in his eyes that surely mimicked her own. But there was something else. A reflection, perhaps, of herself, or maybe not a reflection but another part of her, a part which had lain hidden or buried until now. A picture of wholeness formed in her mind and in that moment she understood that two parts long since separated had become one again, completing the whole, bringing together as one entity spirits who had been searching in desperation for generations to be reunited.

As Claire stood in the doorway, a smile curling her lips, Sarah and John gazed into each other's eyes while something passed between them that formed a picture in both their minds. They saw a cottage in a clearing, a cottage engulfed in flames, clouds of black smoke rising. The image shifted to show two small children huddled together in a cave, hiding in the growing darkness. Then a small girl standing alone in a clearing, haunted eyes raised to the heavens, silent tears on her cheeks while in front of her the ruins of the small cottage still smouldered. And a small boy, taken without a sound in the early morning. And an endless search, a search that continued from generation to generation, to the end of life and beyond, but one at long last complete.

Sarah whispered, fearing to hear herself speak.

'Amber and Hamish... sister and brother. John... everything makes perfect sense.'

'Yes it does,' he breathed. 'We were meant to find each other, meant to be together.'

With utter bewilderment on her face Sarah wasn't sure what to do or how she should feel, but then she recalled the thoughts she'd had months ago while seated in a comfortable armchair talking with a new found relative.

What was family, she had thought, *if not a place to belong? Family was everything. It was a warm blanket... an embrace... a safe place to hide when the world threatened. A refuge where the door was always open and a friendly face welcomed.*

The impression of home she'd had when she'd entered the nursing home, she recalled, was less about the carpeted entrance hall and the heavy curtains and fresh flowers. It was the presence she'd sensed, the warmth calling to her from a quiet room overlooking the sea. Family!

With a sudden overwhelming need Sarah fell against her husband and despite the unborn child within her that had swollen her tummy, wrapped herself around him. Filled with amazement, John held Sarah close with one hand and placed his other onto her head, and as he did so he sensed a surge of warmth emanating from her very soul.

'John,' Sarah whispered. 'They were separated, Amber and Hamish. All those years ago. Why else would our family trees have no date of death for either of them? They never knew what happened. They must have searched all of their lives and never found each other.'

'Yes... until now. And if Rose died young when our ancestors lived into their nineties, I can only think she was murdered. She must have faced persecution daily until the end. The two children would have been damn lucky to escape.'

Sarah gazed up at John.

'Beryl told me about the cave. She said it was a hiding place and without it I wouldn't be here... or you.'

'But the children?' John continued. 'Someone must have taken Hamish for his own safety. Otherwise either one or both of them would have died too. Who and why?'

Still safe in John's embrace, Sarah thought for a moment before speaking again.

'I don't know. Must have been someone who cared what happened to them.'

'It's just occurred to me,' said John. 'Remember the deeds to this land, what we found out? You were wondering why this land was signed over to your family all those generations ago?'

'Our family,' she said with a smile. 'Our family.'

'Yes of course... our family. Well the only reason I can think of is guilt, an attempt to make amends for a wrong doing. Someone must have tried to ease their guilt by handing over the land.' John paused a second before another realisation occurred to him. 'Oh God... Sarah. The ruined cottage? It must have been where Rose died. I saw an image... in my mind... a dream.'

'Me too,' Sarah replied. 'I saw it too, but it wasn't a dream. It was a memory... of what happened. John, there's so much energy here. So much. Do you remember sensing it in the cave when we left it last Christmas? So much presence.'

'Yes I remember. I also remember the power of that place... how it affected me,' and he placed a hand on Sarah's tummy.

They both fell silent, recalling the power of their lovemaking, the passion that had received a helping hand. But as if in response to the memory Sarah doubled over and collapsed onto one of the kitchen chairs, leaning forward.

'Oh my. Ow!' and she hissed though her teeth. After a few seconds she glanced across at Claire, at the child who had discovered their shared past and thus ended a spiritual search spanning almost three hundred years. *Did she know?*, she wondered. Staring back at John with moist eyes she whispered, 'Sweetie. I think Hamish and Amber's story is about to start a new chapter.'

Forty-six

'Stay in the house as long as you want, until you find somewhere of your own, or make me an offer. I'll be more than happy to lend you the keys.'

John and Peter were standing in the kitchen, sharing news and drinking beer.

'Well the consultancy position in Glasgow is less than an hour away so it would be really helpful if you don't mind, though I insist on paying rent,' Peter said.

'There's no need but it'll be interesting to find out how I feel about being a landlord. The house has been in the family since long before I was born. But tell me, how's the baby doing, and how is Sophie handling the competition?'

'Sophie's fantastic with him… sings to him at bedtime… keeps an eye on him. As for Rachel, I can't imagine what Sarah said to her all those months ago, but she's taken to motherhood as if she's an expert.'

Rachel gave birth to a healthy boy two days after Sarah and John became parents again and had called Sarah from the hospital to share more than news of the baby.

'I knew you'd find a way for us to be close,' said an excited Rachel. 'We're coming to live in Scotland.'

'What… when…?'

'Peter's landed a job in Glasgow and they want him as soon as possible, so we need somewhere to stay.'

Sarah had a hard time speaking. 'Oh Rachel, that's wonderful. I'm so happy… for you too,' she laughed.

Rachel couldn't hide the glee from her voice. 'I'm so excited. We'll be coming up to stay for a bit while Peter checks out the details but we could be up there in a month's time.'

'Well you can stay with us while you visit. I can't wait to see the baby but you will send pictures won't you.'

'Yes of course. As soon as I get off the phone.'

Rachel fell silent for a moment and Sarah could hear her friend crying.

'Are you ok, sweetie?' Sarah asked.

'Yes… yes. Just worn out. And I can't believe all this is happening. You did something. You must have used a spell to bring us together.'

'I don't think I had much to do with that,' Sarah laughed. 'I wished it with all my heart, but—'

'Don't say it…' Rachel replied with amusement. 'It was destiny.'

While John and Peter chatted in the kitchen, Sarah gave Rachel and her new born a tour of the grounds. Wrapped in a warm blanket, the little one dozed in her mother's arms as they stood at the end of the drive gazing into the west to where the sun dipped closer to the horizon. It was getting late in the afternoon and the early October day had been mild with a light breeze that brought an early autumn chill to the air.

'Oh Sarah, this is perfect,' Rachel said with a peaceful sigh. 'Now I understand why you love it around here. Have you decided what you're going to do?'

'Train to be a healer,' replied Sarah and linked her arm in Rachel's. 'It runs in the family and I seem to have a knack for it.'

'I'll vouch for that.'

There was no need for conversation and they stood for

a while in comfortable silence. But with a shiver, Rachel said, 'I should have put a jumper on. I guess I'll get used to what clothes to wear, but I'd better take little John inside. Are you coming?'

'In a minute,' said Sarah. 'I do this every evening… stand and watch the sunset. It was Beryl's favourite time of the day.'

'Ok. I'll leave you to it.'

Rachel kissed Sarah and headed indoors leaving her closest friend to take in the late air. A few minutes later Sarah felt an arm slipping around her waist and turned towards her husband. A touch on the other arm alerted her to Claire's presence. Little Robert nestled within John's embrace.

They turned and gazed into the west.

'Y'know,' said John, 'the one thing puzzling me is why Hamish and Amber never found each other. Back in those days I doubt people travelled very far so surely they wouldn't have been miles apart.'

'Well think of his age. He was only five or six. Someone may have taken him to safety, but at that age he probably didn't know where he was taken from… no idea of where to look. I suspect danger still waited for them for many years, being so different. One thing I'm certain of though.'

'What's that mommy?' asked Claire.

'They're reunited now, but I guess we'll never know exactly what happened.'

'Yes, they are,' answered John, and huddled closer to his wife.

For a while longer they stood in silence, hearing nothing but the sighing of the wind as a late breeze caressed the hillside. Then Sarah lowered her shield, extending her thought out into the evening. As if in unspoken agreement John and Claire joined her, and together they listened with every sense not of this world. Hearing the chatter of psychic energies, Sarah knew she had much to offer, all she needed was for those in need to ask. But as the spiritual chatter became louder, they closed their doors and focussed on each other.

'Mommy?' asked Claire.

'Yes, angel?'

'I wish everyone could have a white aura.'

'Yes it would, sweetie, and I guess most people start off that way. It's life that dims the light. But I think we can help… each of us.'

Sarah glanced at her watch.

'That pie is just about ready. Claire, sweetheart, would you pop inside and take dinner out of the oven please. We'll be right behind,' she said.

Claire gave her mother a knowing smile, turned and skipped back to the cottage.

Sarah turned to John. 'So how are you feeling now?' she prompted. 'Are you comfortable with what you have?'

John gazed into his wife's eyes, but it was clear his focus was elsewhere.

'Dunno,' he eventually responded.

'Go on.'

'Well I'm still not sure if I want it.'

'Not much choice really.' Sarah was blunt.

John nodded and turned, gazing across the hillside into the fading light.

'I guess you're right,' he said. 'But I don't feel comfortable when I sense things I'm not ready for. It feels like an invasion… of my own soul. Probably sounds selfish because it cuts both ways… invasion that is.'

'You have a way to block don't you?' Sarah was trying to be supportive.

John smiled.

'Yes… I do, my shining star. But I've not the control yet to… to activate it in a split second. So if I'm near some poor soul who's screaming inside, I feel violated for an instant if I'm caught off guard. I guess it's early days. But you seem to have it under control,' he added.

'Yes, it's early days, and I'm not sure I can help much,

though I'm not in complete control yet, if I ever will be. I may be a little stronger than you, but that's only because I accepted it way before you did. I didn't really resist it… tried to understand it months ago. But I still have moments like you just described. But if you really don't want to use the gift as I do, that's ok. I think your gifts lie elsewhere. Don't you?'

John didn't answer at first, his thoughts drifting backwards through time into the years spent with his grandfather after his mother passed away. Hours in the garden, or at the allotment.

'Yes I do,' he muttered. 'Papa was a wizard at growing things, always had dirt under his finger nails, always a seed catalogue on the kitchen table. Funny how my dad didn't seem to inherit his interest or skills.'

'I think the gift was with him,' Sarah chipped in. 'It just hadn't awakened.'

John became present once more as he shrugged off his reminiscing.

'As usual, you're probably right,' he said. 'But… thinking about the future, I have the back field all planned, and sorted out how I'm going to continue with Beryl's herb planting, so as you say, I'm going to use my gifts in other ways.'

Sarah reached up and kissed John on the cheek.

'Good… and I think you'll be a wizard at growing things too.'

'Wizards and witches,' laughed John. 'What have we come to?'

'The start of a new life,' Sarah answered, but she laughed with her husband. 'Come on, we have dinner and guests.'

As they turned towards the house, Robert still secure and asleep in John's arms, a momentary shadow slipped across Sarah's inner sight, a dark cloud that dimmed her percipience. It took only a moment to pinpoint the source and she grabbed at John's arm.

'John, I just felt something.'

'Sorry? You what?'

'Coming off you, or from within you.'

John stopped and turned to face Sarah.

'You felt something? What did you feel,' he asked, a concerned frown furrowing his brow.

Sarah gazed into her husband's soul, seeking a reason for the disturbance, but found nothing to disrupt his spiritual well-being. The shadow had gone.

'I don't know,' she replied. 'It was just a moment… just a thought.'

A sudden memory returned, a memory she would rather forget. She was taken back to the day before Dave was killed, the evening she'd experienced a premonition and how she'd all but begged John not to go to work. *Oh God, I hope this isn't happening again.* But she realised the power of that previous feeling was colossal. The effects of it were overpowering. This time the moment arrived and passed in an instant, leaving her with only a mild discomfort.

She drew a deep breath, held it for a moment before blowing away the anxiety.

'You ok?' asked John.

'Yes. It was odd… caught me by surprise. Could have been anything I suppose. Perhaps an after-effect of my poking around in your head. Come on, let's see to dinner.'

She linked her arm through John's just as a gust of wind found its way around the shelter of the trees. With it came a few spots of rain. Then ahead, from the distant cottage, the cry of a small baby reminded them that within the warm comfort of their home close friends and cosy firelight beckoned.

Epilogue

As unmoving as a statue, and with a heart of stone, Amber stared at the prostrate form of the man as he lay asleep in his cot, oblivious to her presence. She had entered through an open window and crept through the house on feet that made no sound. Reaching forward, she pressed the sharp edge of her dirk to his throat and waited. The response to the cold metal was immediate. The man opened his eyes and in an instant understood his predicament. He lay still and did not move knowing his life hung in the balance and that his next words may be his last.

'Amber. I knew you'd come… one day. But you'll regret this for the rest of your life if you take this course of action.'

'How so? I will have final justice at last, justice against all of you, justice for my mother and my brother.'

'You've achieved justice already. I've seen the results of your punishment meted out over the years. But this is a mistake. I wasn't involved.'

'Why should I believe you? You are as guilty as the rest for my mother's murder. You may not have been there but you could have done something. You were too much of a coward.'

'Amber. All those responsible are now dead by your

hand and with no trace of blame leading to you. But I am not one of them. Don't make a mistake.'

Amber remembered the promise she made when she was nine, how she swore an oath to bring those responsible for her mother's death and her brothers disappearance to justice. No court of law would ever listen to her, a woman and a witch, and so she planned her own form of punishment. One by one she'd killed them, without arousing suspicion. A poisoning, a fall, an accident. She even lured one to his death using ways in which only a woman knew how, and even the violent death that ensued came as no surprise to the local sheriff. The victim was known for his evil ways and his early death was inevitable. Now there was only one left. The man before her.

Here lay the local magistrate and landowner, a man of power who controlled the land and exercised law around her. A man responsible for the actions of those he governed. And yet he allowed this murder to take place when the rulers of the land had outlawed persecution of witches.

'Why should I be making a mistake? It will end with your death, I can poison you and people will think you died in your sleep. I can cut your throat. I'm sure you have many enemies. Why will I be making a mistake?' she repeated.

'Amber, listen to what I have to say. Grant me that. I'll not move. I'll not shout for help. Over there against the wall, in the top drawer of my desk you will find papers. I drafted them years ago, waiting for you to come, certain that one day you would. You have my word I'll not move. Open the drawer and read them.'

Amber stared into the man's eyes and detected no fear. With her inner sight she sensed an honesty within his soul and maybe something else. A deep sadness perhaps. Moving the knife away from his throat she turned, walked over to the desk and withdrew the papers. With one eye on the man, she read through them. Two signatures lay upon the last page. One belonged to the man before her and the other, though she did not recognise the handwriting, belonged to the Duke of Argyll.

The papers outlined a proposal to transfer ownership of land to Amber and her future family. The land included an area where her mother's cottage once lay, on the hills above the village of Straiton. An additional ten acres were included within the proposal.

Amber stared at the man in disbelief.

'Is this a trick?' she demanded. 'A ploy to absolve yourself of guilt?'

'No,' the man replied as he sat upright on the edge of the bed.

'Amber look at me. Look into my heart.'

Filled with distrust and maintaining a tight grip on her knife Amber took a step towards the man and opened her inner sight. Peering deep into his soul she detected a connection which shocked her. She sensed once more a deep rooted grief, and it struck unbidden at her heart, awakening her own sorrow as it penetrated her spiritual being. *No*. She thought. *This cannot be*.

'Yes Amber. It is true. I can see in your eyes and I can feel in your soul that you see the truth. I am your father. I gave my love to your mother when she was sixteen but our love had to remain hidden. You must understand it was what your mother wanted. She believed it would make my life difficult and hers more so. She hoped I'd be able to control the people, change their fear and prejudice, so your mother and her kind could be accepted… our kind.' The man paused before speaking again.

'Yes Amber. I am also like you. I have the sight and the gift. That is how Rose and I found each other. Our love had no bounds, and we had two children. Which is why you would regret killing me. You would be killing your own father.'

Amber gazed into the man's soul and extended her percipience. She sensed no lie and felt again the connection. Her next words came as a whisper.

'But my mother's death… why… how?'

'Drunken. Violent. Ignorant cowards. They feared what they did not understand and that night I was too late to stop what they'd begun… too late. My only regret is I hadn't killed them myself. They robbed me of my love and my family. I lost everything and only my anger exceeded my grief. But I cannot change anything or do anything to right those wrongs except give you a place to call your home, a place close to your mother.'

'I have no father,' Amber shouted. 'I have never had a father and I have no need of one. Where is Hamish? Where did he go? Why was he taken?'

'I do not know where he is,' the man said with regret. 'I knew where the cave was. Rose took me there often when we were together. You and your brother were conceived in that place. I was also aware of the danger that threatened Rose, you and your brother every day, and I took Hamish from the cave the day after your mother died. I took him far away and gave him to tenants south of here in Dumfries and told them they must raise him as their own. But I heard when he was twelve he ran away. Not from misuse but from a need to find you. I heard he always talked about you. But he was so young, so young and I lost him.'

Amber felt sudden exhaustion, overwhelmed from years of searching, of the need for justice, of loss and pain. She thought of Hamish and wondered how he would be now, if he were safe and well. As she had done so many times over the years she put forth her inner sight in search of him, and for the first time sensed a tiny thrill of energy, a tenuous connection as if she had received an answer. Perhaps, she wondered, being near to her father lent an added power to her searching, allowing her spiritual strength to send forth its energies further than before. But moments later the sensation had gone, and she understood that somewhere out there Hamish was alive and searching.

Amber turned back to the papers and reached for a quill. She signed her name, blotted the ink and turned back to the man.

'You are my father, I see that, but you are unknown to me and we will not meet again. But I will take these papers, and I accept the benevolence with which they are given. I see compassion in your eyes.'

Without waiting for an answer, Amber left the room and padded back to the window she had used to enter the house. The man followed as she climbed through the opening and lowered herself to the ground. Before disappearing into the night she glared back and spoke to her father one last time.

'Yes. I will take the land and rebuild a home… and a family. And when Hamish returns, he will need somewhere to stay.'

The End

ABOUT THE AUTHOR

R V Biggs lives with his wife Julie in a small ex-mining community near Wolverhampton in the West Midlands, England. He and his wife have four grown-up children and a growing number of grandchildren.

Robert spent 35 years working for a large international Communications company, but now works for Birmingham Children's Hospital helping to support the mental health of young people.

This novel is book two of the Sarah Macintyre series.

Printed in Poland
by Amazon Fulfillment
Poland Sp. z o.o., Wrocław